Praise for the Novels of Jillian Cantor

Half Life

"Thought-provoking, skillfully written, and hard to put down."

—*Kirkus Reviews* (starred review)

"Cantor has created an absorbing biographical novel and performed an engaging riff on the 'what if' ponderings we all experience."

—*Booklist*

"In a time when many of us are more tuned in to scientific advances than we've ever been before, this reimagining of what might happen if pioneering scientist Marie Curie had taken a different path is just what the doctor ordered."

—*Good Housekeeping*

In Another Time

"*In Another Time* is a beautifully written, utterly romantic story about a love that transcends time. [It's] the sort of book you wish could never end."

—*PopSugar*

"Cantor elevates love as a powerful force . . . and shows how music speaks to even the cruelest hearts. [*In Another Time* is] a powerful story that exalts the strength of the human spirit."

—*Kirkus Reviews*

The Lost Letter

"A total page-turner."

—*New York Magazine*

"At the center of the novel are two beautiful love stories involving two seemingly star-crossed couples, whose love overcomes all obstacles. . . . Getting it right is an art, and Cantor is an artist. She got me from that first page, and I stayed hooked throughout. It's not just that Cantor kept me interested—she got me involved emotionally with the story."

—*Jerusalem Post*

The Hours Count

"[A] down-to-the-wire thriller."

—*New York Times Book Review*

"We kind of love historical novels, and Cantor's is quickly climbing to the top of our all-time faves list. . . . You won't be able to put it down."

—*Glamour*

"Cantor mixes fact with fiction to create a moving portrait of two of the most vilified figures in modern history."

—*Cosmopolitan*

Margot

"Inventive. . . . Cantor's what-if story combines historical fiction with mounting suspense and romance, but above all, it is an ode to the adoration and competition between sisters."

—*O, The Oprah Magazine*

"A convincing, engaging might-have-been. Francophiles will want to dig in."

—*People*

BEAUTIFUL
LITTLE FOOLS

ALSO BY JILLIAN CANTOR

Half Life

The Code for Love and Heartbreak

In Another Time

The Lost Letter

The Hours Count

Margot

Searching for Sky

The Transformation of Things

The Life of Glass

The September Sisters

BEAUTIFUL
LITTLE FOOLS

A NOVEL

Jillian Cantor

HARPER

An Imprint of HarperCollinsPublishers

BEAUTIFUL LITTLE FOOLS. Copyright © 2022 by Jillian Cantor. All rights reserved. Printed in the United States of America. No part of this book may be used or reproduced in any manner whatsoever without written permission except in the case of brief quotations embodied in critical articles and reviews. For information, address HarperCollins Publishers, 195 Broadway, New York, NY 10007.

HarperCollins books may be purchased for educational, business, or sales promotional use. For information, please email the Special Markets Department at SPsales@harpercollins.com.

P.S.™ is a trademark of HarperCollins Publishers.

FIRST EDITION

Designed by Jamie Lynn Kerner

Library of Congress Cataloging-in-Publication Data has been applied for.

ISBN 978-0-06-305126-3 (pbk.)
ISBN 978-0-06-305125-6 (Library edition)

22 23 24 25 26 LSC 10 9 8 7 6 5 4 3 2 1

Once again
to
Gregg

I hope she'll be a fool—that's the best thing a girl can be in this world, a beautiful little fool.

—DAISY BUCHANAN IN *THE GREAT GATSBY*

❧

SHE HELD THE GUN THE WAY A CERTAIN KIND OF CARELESS MAN held his glass of whiskey. It was illegal, illicit. But, nonetheless, it was hers. She would do with it as she pleased, consequences be damned.

The gun made her hot, restless, wanting. Her heart pounded in her chest, a Nora Bayes song. The one playing that sweltering, innocent night when she saw him, years ago. *Get your gun. Get your gun.* She had her gun now.

He didn't see her at first, as he walked out of his house, toward the pool. Tall and slender, his naked flesh so pale it was as if he'd made it through the entire summer without letting even the smallest bit of sunlight touch him. *Nothing touched him.* Wasn't that what made Jay Gatsby so great?

He stepped toward the pool, that arrogant walk, that look on his face. That *knowing.* He had it all; he had everything. He'd *taken* everything. But then, just before his toe touched the water, he stopped suddenly, looked up, as if sensing her presence. He noticed her standing there, half behind the shrubbery, and he smiled.

"You've come," he said, his voice thick with surprise. His eyes were on her face, not on her hand, not on the gun.

She raised her hand up higher, pointed the gun straight at his chest. And then somehow, from across the pool, he could suddenly feel it, her heat and her anger and her madness. It had been simmering for so long, and now it was boiling over. His face contorted. "What are you doing?" he spoke softly, slowly. He was working it out in his own mind. *Why? What? How?*

The distance between her gun and his heart was an easy shot. The trigger burned in the heat of the midday sun, as she closed one eye, aimed, squeezed. In an instant, the world exploded, the gun smoked. Her fingers shook and burned.

And then, all at once, his greatness flickered. He fell unevenly into the pool, water cascading into the sky like a choreographed dance of swans. Beautiful, unexpected. The cascade died off into limp waves, and she took a few steps closer. His pale flesh was sinking underwater now, ripped apart.

In front of her, the pool oozed red. And it was only then that she truly understood what she had done. *Who she had become.* She swallowed back a scream, the taste of bile rising up in her throat.

And then she turned away from the pool, and she ran.

Daisy

1917

LOUISVILLE, KENTUCKY

SOMETIMES I THINK IF I'D MET JAY GATSBY LATER, SAY, AFTER Daddy's and Rose's accident, I wouldn't have even noticed him at all. I think how everything, how the whole entire course of my life, and his, might have turned out differently.

Jay came into my life at a moment when I still believed that anything was possible. The war—and death—were somewhere so far away, out of my reach, that they might as well have not existed at all. I had everything and it never occurred to me that I could lose it all. Just like that.

It sounds silly to say it now, to remember how I was. To remember that careless, carefree girl. It sounds silly to say that Jay and I lived and died by chance, haphazard timing. That our paths crossed at the right time, in the right place.

Or maybe it was the wrong time, the wrong place.

"DAISY FAY!" MOTHER called for me up the stairs.

She had only one way of calling for me, whether she was angry, or excited, or simply calling me to supper. No matter the reason, she called for me with my *full* name, her voice trilling like a snow goose.

This afternoon I knew she was calling because of Rose. I'd promised my younger sister I would go with her to take food to the poor. But it was the hottest hour of the hottest day of August, and after I'd eaten lunch, I'd come up to my room to lie down. It was hard to move off my bed now, much less think about walking ten blocks to the almshouse with Rose's heavy basket of food.

Unlike me, Rose was thinking about the war, and she'd started growing vegetables in a victory garden in our backyard. Every time she harvested something, she was immediately ready to give it away to help people less fortunate than us. At lunch she'd been going on about her peas.

"Daisy Fay!" Mother's voice again. The snow goose was louder.

"Coming," I called back, weakly.

I sighed, got out of bed, and swiped my hairbrush through my hair, setting each side behind my ears and in front of my shoulders. I grabbed my fan, and walked carefully down the steps, trying not to break into a sweat from the exertion.

Just as I'd expected, Rose and Mother sat at the dining table together, co-conspirators, Rose's heavy wicker basket sitting in front of them. When I entered the room, they both offered me a frown.

"Daise, what took you so long?" Rose exhaled.

"It's too hot, Rosie," I protested, fanning myself, causing a swirl of hot air to press against my face, making me flush.

"You promised," Rose said. She wasn't pouting exactly. Rose never pouted. Instead she turned her heart-shaped face in such a way that it was clear I'd disappointed her. She expected better from me. Why, I didn't know, because I was acting the same way I always did. Petulant.

"Mother," I tried. "Don't you think it would be better if we go when the weather breaks instead? Next week, perhaps?"

Mother wasn't a bleeding heart like Rose, and God knows where Rose got it from, because Daddy certainly wasn't either. But Mother and Daddy *adored* Rose. Everyone adored Rose. I was the beautiful one, and she was the good one. That's not to say that Rose wasn't pretty in her own quiet way, too. But her beauty *was* her goodness. And the fact was, I loved her for that reason too. But not when it meant I had to suffer in the heat.

"Daisy Fay," Mother said. "Help your sister with that basket and stop complaining. You're not going to melt."

"Aren't I, though?" But it was too hot to argue. I sighed and picked up the heavy basket, then held my other hand out for my sister. "Come on," I said, wearily. "There's a party tonight at the Wrights' house, and we're not going to miss it. We'll have to be back in time to freshen up."

Rose laughed weakly. She hadn't attended half the parties I had this summer. She liked to blame it on the polio that had nearly killed her last summer and left her with a slight limp, but we both knew it wasn't that at all. Rose was well now, thank god. But Rose no more liked parties than I liked going to feed the poor. We balanced each other out that way. The good one and the pretty one. That's how all of Louisville knew the Fay sisters back then.

IT REALLY WAS too hot to walk, and as Rose and I stepped out on the street I wished I could take Daddy's Roadster. The problem was, Mother didn't know I knew how to operate it.

If there's two things I want you to know before you get married, Daddy told me, *it's how to drive an automobile and how to shoot a gun.* He'd taught me to do both by the time I was Rose's age. But it was with the understanding that Mother should never know about either one.

Now Daddy was off in Chicago on business, and his Roadster was sitting idle, parked out front. Rose and I walked past it and made it only two blocks before she looked like she truly was melting. Her limp grew more noticeable when she was tired, and I hated seeing her have so much trouble. Hated remembering the way we worried about her so last summer. What would the pretty one be like without the good one? Vapid and useless. Vain and sour. I hated even the very idea of myself without her.

"Rose, we really could take this food when the heat breaks," I said gently.

Rose shook her head and kept walking, taking all her effort to go faster, push ahead of me. I had to skip to catch up to her.

"Would you ladies like a ride?" I'd been so focused on Rose and her trouble that I hadn't noticed a shiny black car had pulled up next to us, that a soldier sat behind the wheel calling out to us.

Camp Taylor had opened in Louisville in June and this summer there'd been soldiers all over town: men in uniforms walking across the Big Four Bridge, driving down Main Street and through our very fashionable neighborhood in the Southern Extension. They'd show up in groups to our Saturday night parties and sometimes they'd ask me to dance. I did not yet see these men as warriors. I did not picture them traveling across the great wide ocean sometime soon to fight, and to die. They were simply handsome men, flirting with me. I had no qualms with that.

"Well? Can I help you out?" the soldier asked again.

My hair was limp against my forehead, and I put Rose's basket down for a second and made a futile attempt to fluff it with my fingers, before picking the basket back up, turning, and offering the soldier a smile. I knew some of the ladies who had tea with Mother on Thursday afternoons hated that our little Louisville was now being *overrun* by *common men in uniform*. But truly, I had yet to find one downfall to it.

"No, thank you," Rose said just as I said, "Yes, that would be grand." Rose turned to me and frowned.

"Come on," I said to her. "It's hot, and this nice soldier is offering."

That was enough for him to get out of the car, walk around, and take the basket from my hand. Our fingertips touched, and I looked up at him. He was tall with short blond hair and a pale, clean-shaven face. I had the strangest urge to touch him, to reach up and run my fingers across his silken cheek. But I restrained myself.

"I'm Daisy Fay," I said, clasping my twitchy fingers together. "And this is my sister, Rose."

"Jay Gatsby," he said, holding my gaze for a second before turning to smile at Rose. He had bright green eyes. The kind of eyes that would catch you, even across the room in a crowded party.

"Thank you for stopping, Jay Gatsby," I said. My voice caught just the slightest bit on his full name, my tongue feeling out the sound of it. It wasn't a familiar name. It definitely wasn't a Louisville name. I wondered where he was from, what his daddy did.

"You think I see the prettiest girls in all of Louisville needing a ride and I'm not going to stop?" he was saying now, as he opened the passenger door and motioned for us to get in. Rose didn't move, so I got in first. She sighed and finally slid in next to me.

"Don't go kissing him, just because he's giving us a ride," Rose whispered, as Jay walked back around to the driver's seat. She sounded like more of a snow goose than Mother.

"I won't kiss him *because* of the ride," I whispered back. "I'll do it because he's handsome. Did you notice his eyes?" Rose shook her head, not because she didn't notice, but because she found me incorrigible. In an adorable way, of course.

Jay got back in the car, put his hands on the steering wheel, and suddenly I was close enough to him that I felt the length of his leg against my own. I didn't move away, toward Rose. Instead I touched his arm gently and thanked him again for the ride. "We were so lucky to run into you," I said.

"Daisy Fay," he said softly. "I think I was the lucky one."

"MR. GATSBY, ARE you following me?" I'd spotted him across the crowded room at Marcy Hillet's party—he was walking toward the door, and I'd run to catch up with him before he disappeared from me again. Now, I stood before him, out of breath.

Exactly one week had passed since he'd driven me and Rose to the almshouse, then insisted on waiting and driving us back home. And tonight I saw those bright green eyes across the dance floor, stunning and hypnotic from afar, as I knew they'd be. I'd been looking for them, for him, ever since I got out of his car a week ago. I had not been able to stop thinking about him, the easy sound of his voice, the solid weight of his body, and the green pools of his eyes. The truth was, if I'd known exactly where to find him, I might've been the one following him.

"Daisy Fay," he said now. A smile erupted across his face, and he leaned down and kissed my hand. His lips lingered for a thrilling moment. And then he clasped my fingers. "I've been hoping to run into you again." *Hoping?* Not exactly following me, or, even making an effort to find me.

"Funny," I said. "I've been hoping you'd stop by all week to say hello." When he'd dropped me and Rose off at our house last week, that was how he'd left things. *Maybe I'll stop by and say hello sometime.* But then days had passed, he hadn't stopped by, and I'd wondered if I'd imagined that moment of connection I'd felt between the two of us in his car.

"I did stop by!" he said now, shouting to be heard above the din of the crowd and the loud swell of the dance music. "I asked your father to let you know. Didn't he tell you?"

I shook my head. Daddy had just returned on Tuesday from Chicago, and leave it to him to wreak havoc on my social life the moment he got back. Daddy didn't much care for me hanging around with soldiers; as Daddy said, they were unrefined men, hiding behind their uniforms. If I was going to hang around with a man, let it be a Louisville society man, from a good family, at least. Daddy didn't care that I found those men dreadfully boring. I had no interest in hearing about their hunting trips or their whiskey, which seemed to be all the *finest young men* in Louisville had to talk about.

"Would you like to take a walk?" Jay asked, interrupting my thoughts. It was nearly September and the air had finally cooled tonight. But the sounds of gaiety and laughter from the party had been interspersed with distant claps of thunder all night.

"Now?" I laughed. "But it's going to storm."

He pulled me toward the front door anyway, and I let him lead me outside. It was loud and stifling hot inside the party and my best friend, Jordan, had gotten a headache and had already gone home early. I was happy to get out of there, with Jay. The night air was damp, thick with the impending storm, and I shivered, imagining being caught in the rain, holding on to him for warmth. That thought was tempered only briefly by the thought of the look on Daddy's face if I were to come home a soaking wet mess. But right now, it was still dry and cool, and Jay took my arm, and we walked.

"Can I tell you a secret?" Jay said, breaking our silence after a little while. I nodded. "I actually was following you." I leaned in closer to him, held tighter to his arm, waiting for him to explain. "I asked around at camp about you, asked if anyone knew where you might be tonight."

"My social schedule is that transparent, I suppose," I said. "All of Camp Taylor knows my comings and goings, hmm?"

"This was the best party in town tonight, I heard," he said. "And where else would Daisy Fay be?" He spoke matter-of-factly, not teasing.

"Where else indeed?" I murmured. "The best party in town, and yet we've left it, you and I."

"I like it out here alone with you better." He squeezed my hand lightly. A warmth coursed my entire arm, and I squeezed his hand back.

We crossed the street, holding hands as we walked, heading in the opposite direction of my house, toward the river. Thunder rumbled closer; it shook the ground, but neither of us made a move to turn back.

There had been other soldiers this summer, ones I'd danced with, flirted with, two I'd even kissed whose full names escaped me now. But there was something about Jay Gatsby that felt different. It might have been the way he'd looked at me at the crowded party, the way he had looked at me the other day in his car. As if he could see past my blue silk dress and perfectly coiffed hair, see beyond all that. *See me.*

Deep down, the truth was I wanted to be more than a pretty girl. I wanted to be someone who mattered, but I hadn't quite figured out how yet. I wanted to be someone who didn't have to go to the best party in town, because maybe there were other, more interesting things I wanted to do. But how could Jay see this in me, when no one else ever had?

"Tell me about yourself, Jay Gatsby. I want to know you," I said now.

"There's not much to tell," he said, shrugging.

"I doubt that," I said.

We were almost at the river, and we stopped walking and turned to face each other at that spot right by the banks where Rose and I used to chase fireflies at dusk when we were little girls. A flash of lightning illuminated the sky now, and for a second, I could see Jay's face brightly, clearly. There was an intensity in his eyes, his expression, that told a different story: he'd seen and experienced things I couldn't even begin to fathom. It wasn't only that he was older than me, but also that he had already lived a whole entire lifetime outside of Louisville.

"Come on," I said. "Tell me something. One thing."

"I love the water," he finally said. "I had a friend who used to take me sailing on Lake Superior. Being out there, it makes you realize how great the whole wide world is. And I'd feel like I could do anything when I was out there. Be anyone. I'm always searching for that feeling on land . . . But I can never quite get back there."

I thought about Jay, lying out on a boat in a great big expanse of blue, in a place where the water meets the sky, and I smiled at him.

The first slow drop of rain hit my cheek, and Jay rested his hand on my face. I leaned closer to him. The rain came harder, but I didn't move.

"The thing is," he said, softly. "The way I feel out on the water? I'm feeling that right now. Here with you."

"Oh, Jay." My voice broke a little on his name. "That might be the nicest thing anyone's ever said to me."

"I don't have anything to offer you, Daisy," he said, his lips inches from my own, the rain falling harder, pounding in my ears.

So he didn't have money, or a family name we recognized. But I wasn't Daddy. That didn't mean anything to me. I was eighteen, and I wanted for nothing. "I don't care about that," I said.

"You should turn and walk away from me," he murmured. "Don't look back."

I stood so close to him that when I spoke again, my words tumbled into his mouth: "Stop talking, Jay Gatsby, and kiss me."

Jordan

IT WAS A BONA FIDE FACT THAT DAISY FAY HAD THE SHINIEST hair on this side of the Ohio River. I asked her once how she managed it. How, even on the hottest day of summer her acorn hair shone so bright I swear to god it shimmered like starlight. "Oh, Jordie." She'd laughed and waved me away with a faux modest flick of her wrist. Then she'd leaned in, conspiratorially, and whispered, "Egg yolks."

"*Egg yolks?*"

"Once a week," she'd whispered. "I soak my hair in six egg yolks, for a full hour."

And that was why at the tender age of thirteen, I'd snuck into Mr. Barnaby's chicken coop next door one morning, when Daddy was in court. I was in desperate want of extra egg yolks to make my hair as shiny as Daisy's. And I knew Daddy, who couldn't stand to waste food, would never approve.

But Mr. Barnaby was blind as a bat and dumber than a wild turkey, and he mistakenly thought I was an intruder. He shot first, and figured out it was me, later. He killed six of his chickens, but luckily, I was unscathed. That is, until Daddy found out. Once he got the whole story out of me about why I wanted the eggs in the first place, he cut my hair off with a pair of pruning shears. "Vanity is for the weak, Jordan," he told me.

I lay in my bed and cried for my hair that whole night. Not only would it never be shiny, but now it would be ugly, too. *I would be ugly.*

But then the next morning, I got up, and I saw my reflection for the first time. I ran my fingers through the short streaks of chestnut hair around my ears. I was a different Jordan with short hair, a better Jordan. A tougher Jordan. And maybe, tough *was* pretty.

Daddy's punishment wasn't really a punishment at all, I decided. But a blessing. I'd worn my hair short ever since.

IN THE FALL of 1917, I was sixteen years old, and Daisy Fay was still my best friend and, as Daddy always said ever since the chicken incident, my worst influence. Her younger sister, Rose, was my age, and Daddy always wondered why she wasn't the one I spent time with instead. Rose was fine; I had nothing against Rose. But she wasn't Daisy.

"I don't like the way Daisy runs around with all those soldiers," he said to me over breakfast one morning that fall. Daddy and I had taken a walk through Belgravia Court last night after supper, and on the way home, we'd seen Daisy driving by in a car with a soldier. It wasn't the first time, and it wouldn't be the last, either. Daisy loved to play, to flirt. Daisy loved to be admired. "You know better than that, Jordan," Daddy was saying now. "I hope you're not off doing that with her."

"Oh, Daddy, she's just having a little fun," I told him. "And I have no interest in those soldiers. They're all so . . . old." It was true. Most of them were in their late twenties or early thirties, and I, at sixteen, did not find them appealing whatsoever.

Daddy nodded approvingly, turned his attention back to his newspaper, and told me to go to the club to work on my swing. I finished the last bite of my breakfast, stood, and kissed him on the top of his round, bald head.

Daddy started teaching me golf when I was five, just after Mama died. He said he couldn't bear to leave me, so he would take me with him to the club on Saturdays. To his surprise, I picked up how to swing. And now, what would you know? Eleven years later, and I was a better shot than him, a better player than any other man in Louisville for that matter. Which was something he would remark on with pride to whomever he could, whenever he got the chance. Now Daddy was always after me to practice.

Most well-to-do fathers of daughters in Louisville worried about marrying her off to a man from a good family. Daddy imagined me on the professional golf circuit, winning championships. Never mind that the circuit only included men. Daddy believed that would change soon, that I would be a part of it. I loved him more for it. Because that was truly what I wanted for my future too. Not a man, not a marriage. Golf.

And the truth was, I agreed with Daddy about Daisy and the soldiers. What good would come of it? Eventually they'd all leave, ship out to this war so far away it almost felt imaginary. And what would Daisy be left with then?

When we were little girls, Daisy, Rose, and I used to play with Daisy and Rose's porcelain dolls, giving them pretend lives and hopes and dreams. And that was sort of how I felt about Daisy, hanging around with the soldiers. None of it was real. It was all playacting.

Until it wasn't.

⚜

"JORDIE," DAISY WHISPERED my name one lazy afternoon in October, not even a week later. "I have to tell you something."

We were lying across her giant four-poster bed, talking about what we should wear to Adelaide Cummings's engagement party that weekend. We both despised Adelaide, who was an incurable ninny. (Once, I'd overheard her poking fun at Rose's limp.) I couldn't have been more delighted that she was marrying a multimillionaire from Chicago and would move there with him directly after the wedding. *Good riddance*, Daisy had said with a giggle when Adelaide had first announced the engagement. Good riddance indeed. But the question we were hashing out, before Daisy announced her need to tell me something—should we wear our finest dresses to Adelaide's engagement party or something awfully ugly just to spite her and throw off the photographs?

I rolled over and turned my attention to Daisy, and whatever it was she wanted to tell me. Her face looked serious, her milky-white skin paler than usual. Her hair, though, was shiny as ever and splayed across her pillow. I reached my hand over and absently twirled a lock of it around my finger. "What is it, Daise?"

"I think I'm in love," she said, her silken voice suddenly huskier than usual.

I stared at her for another moment, not saying anything. Her pale blue eyes matched the opal she wore on a chain around her neck, a sixteenth birthday gift from her parents. "In love?" I repeated her words, my own voice breaking in disbelief. Sure, I'd seen her around, laughing with the soldiers, but that was just flirting, nothing serious. *Love?*

She sat up suddenly, and I let go of her hair.

"I met him at the end of August, Jordie. His name is Jay. *Jay Gatsby*. He's at Camp Taylor. I didn't mean to love him. I don't want to love him . . ." She held her hands up dramatically, then flopped back on her pillow.

"So don't," I said softly. As if it could be just that easy. Was there a way to change your feelings, to stop yourself from loving someone? I wish I knew.

"I want you to meet him," she said. "That's why I'm telling you. You're the only one, Jordie. The only one I can trust."

"Me? Not even Rose?" I asked.

"Especially not Rose." She shook her head. "Rose is too good. She wants me to be good, too. But I don't want to be good. I want to be happy." Daisy sounded petulant, but oddly, it was the first time it had ever occurred to me that there might be a difference between the two, that it might be impossible to be both *good* and *happy*. "I want you to tell me the truth about him." Daisy was still talking. "You're the most honest person I've ever known, Jordie."

"The truth?" I asked, meekly. Deep down, I wasn't sure I'd ever fully told Daisy the truth about anything.

"The truth about whether he's worth it." Daisy got out of her bed and gestured around her beautifully furnished room. "Whether he's worth giving up all this."

"Daise," I said, and this was maybe the most truthful thing I'd ever tell her, "no one is worth giving up all this."

"But Jordie," she said, "I think Jay is."

AS IF ADELAIDE Cummings's engagement party weren't bad enough, now I had to worry about meeting this soldier Daisy was infatuated with. No, *in love* with. Jay. What kind of a name was that? It didn't sound like a real name, a man's name, a soldier's name. It sounded like a bird and not even a full bird, half a bird at that. *Blue Jay. Magpie Jay. Ground Jay.*

"Jordie." Daisy grabbed my arm and motioned with her head across the dance floor. The music was so loud that I couldn't hear the rest of what Daisy was trying to tell me. Or maybe it was that I wasn't listening. I watched him instead. He was tall with cropped blond hair. His green uniform fit him well and matched his eyes. He had a serious face, until he saw Daisy, and then all at once, his face changed. He looked younger, a little boy playing dress-up in his army uniform, not a man.

"Isn't he a dream?" Daisy murmured. Then he reached her, grabbed her fiercely, kissed her too brazenly on the mouth. He pulled her away from me, onto the dance floor.

I watched them for a little while as they danced. I imagined him whisking Daisy away from Louisville, and from me, the same way he'd just whisked her onto the dance floor, and the thought of that made me queasy. He clung to Daisy in a possessive way, like he was claiming her, controlling her, taking her all for himself. And I couldn't understand it; what made him so great in Daisy's eyes. What made Daisy think he was worth giving up everything?

They danced for so long and then I lost them in the crowd. Daisy had forgotten I was even here. I left the party early and went home and got into bed. But I tossed and turned all night, caught up in half dreams where Daisy faded into an apparition, disappearing right in front of my very eyes no matter how hard I tried to hold on to her.

The next day I avoided Daisy for a while. I got to the club early and drove golf balls, one after another, out onto the range. Farther, harder, faster.

Daisy

1917

LOUISVILLE

I AWOKE TO THE FEEL OF HIM.

Jay's hand rested gently across my stomach. Claiming me. I tucked my body closer into his and smiled.

He'd climbed up the trellis last night and tapped on the glass of my second-story bedroom window. "What are you doing?" I'd whispered as I'd opened the window for him and he'd climbed in. I'd pulled him to me even as I'd chastised him, breathing in the warm feel of him.

I'd left him only ten minutes earlier in his car, down the street. We'd kissed hungrily. Then, said good-bye. Kissed again. *One last time.*

Jay would be leaving any day now. First to New York, then Europe to fight in the war. It was hard to let him go, wondering each time, each night, if this would be the last. The last kiss. The last embrace. The last time he sat before me, perfect and alive.

When I'd heard his finger tapping the glass, I'd almost cried with relief. I'd opened the window, and then there he was, in my bedroom. There we were, together.

"I feel like we're already married," he'd whispered into my hair, and I'd kissed him in response, tugging at the buttons of his uniform. I'd never done more than kiss a man before, never thought I would until I was married. But I'd agreed with Jay—we *would* be married. What difference did it make if we waited or not? My fingers kept undoing his buttons, until he'd stood before me, perfect, naked flesh. I'd put my hands on his bare chest and he'd sighed.

I buried my face in my pillow now, heat rising up my neck thinking about what we'd done last night. The linens smelled like him. Like summer and salt water and birch trees. I might never let Fredda wash them again.

"Good morning," he said into my neck now. I could feel the words more than I could hear them. His breath traced my skin.

"You'd better go before someone finds us out," I whispered.

He pulled me tighter to him in response. "Just five more minutes," he whispered into my hair. "Just five minutes more, Daisy."

AN HOUR LATER, at the breakfast table, I was worried Mother and Rose would be able to see what I'd done, that it would be noticeable in the new rosy hue of my cheeks. Or that they would be able to catch the slightest scent of him on my skin, the way I still could.

But Rose was getting ready to leave for Chicago with Daddy, and neither one of them were paying much attention to me. Rose was fretting about getting her suitcase packed, and Mother was fretting about whether her coat would be warm enough. Since Rose's illness Daddy had taken her back to Chicago every four months to be seen by a pulmonary specialist there. *The best money can buy,* Daddy said. Rose seemed all but recovered to me except for her limp, but Daddy wasn't ready to declare her completely well yet. I'd been so caught up with Jay this past month, I'd barely even noticed their preparations.

"Daise," Rose said now, interrupting my thoughts. "Are you sure you don't want to come with us? Daddy says you can, if you want to." She stared at me, her bright blue eyes wide, hopeful.

I smiled at her and patted her hand gently. "You know how I feel about doctors, Rosie." It was true. I'd feared doctors since I'd had mumps as a little girl and one had sat on me to force medicine down my throat. But what I didn't say, the real truth, was that I couldn't leave Louisville now. Not when Jay was still here, not when his time left here was fleeting.

Rose nodded, but cast her eyes down, disappointed. I reached across the table and tucked a stray blond hair behind her ear. "When you get back, it'll be Christmas," I reminded her.

I wondered if Jay would still be here at Christmas, and how, if he wasn't, I would ever be able to keep breathing at that joyous time of year without him.

"You'll wait for me to decorate the tree," Rose was saying now. Rose loved everything organized, all the red ornaments together, all the green, and so on. Beauty, to her, was order. Whereas I rejoiced in the beauty of chaos.

"Of course I'll wait for you," I said. "I wouldn't dream of doing it without you."

"And you'll look after my victory garden, make sure my lettuce doesn't die?" she asked.

I nodded. Rose's victory garden was supposedly helping with the war. But I wasn't exactly sure how her lettuce patch in our backyard was supposed to do anything. If only I could trade Rosie's lettuce for Jay's deployment overseas.

"Don't overwater or you'll kill them," she was saying now. "Just a little water, every morning, Daise."

"I know," I told her, kissing her gently on the forehead.

"And Daise—" She grabbed my hand and I thought she was going to tell me more about the lettuce.

"I promise you, Rosie, your lettuce will still be alive when you get back," I said.

She nodded. She was no longer worried about the lettuce. "Be good," she said softly, instead.

I inhaled, wondering if she really could see what Jay and I had done last night from the expression on my face, or, hear it, in the huskier tone of my voice. But then she smiled at me, that beautiful, pure Rosie smile. She didn't know. She was always telling me to be good. Always wanting me to see the world more like she did.

AFTER ROSE AND Daddy left for the train, I bundled up and headed to the club. I'd spent so much time with Jay these past weeks, I'd barely seen Jordan. And I knew if I wanted to talk to her now, it would have to be out on the course with her, walking beside her and her caddie.

It was chilly and windy outside; the December air felt almost crisp enough for that rare Louisville snow. But Jordan would still be out on the golf course. She was so obsessed with that silly little sport; she practiced in the heat of the summer and chill of winter.

The club course was a men's course, and truth be told, I wasn't exactly sure why they let Jordan use it at all, much less in any weather she pleased. But I suspected all the men in Louisville were a little afraid of Judge Baker, Jordan's daddy. And maybe, they were also just a little in awe of Jordan's game, which was supposedly very good. Not that I knew anything at all about golf.

Jordan was easy enough to spot on the course now, as no one else was out playing in this cold today. I found her preparing to take a shot on the ninth hole. I stood back, watched her for a moment. Her brow furrowed in concentration before she lifted the club, swung, and the tiny white ball flew through the air. Her power was impressive. And maybe a little terrifying, too.

"Daise, what are you doing out here?" she called out, noticing me watching. I waved and walked toward her. "Meet me at the next tee box," she said to the caddie, then took her bag of clubs from him and handed them to me. They were heavy, and I sunk for a moment before righting myself. I hoisted them over my shoulder and walked with her to find her ball.

"Jay snuck into my room last night," I told her, keeping my voice low. Though no one else was around to hear me now. "We were . . . *together*. All night."

Jordan paused, put her hands on her hips, and frowned. Then she exclaimed, "Oh! There it is." She walked around me to stand behind her ball. "Daise, nine iron." She held out her hand.

I shook my head and thrust the bag of clubs toward her so she could take what she wanted. "Did you hear what I said?" I asked her. She took a club and positioned herself behind her ball, rocking her hips.

She swung and the ball flew through the air again, until it dropped, then rolled ever so slowly into the hole up ahead. Jordan smiled at her success, walked ahead, and picked up her ball. I walked after her. "Jordie?" I was practically shouting her name. She was my best friend. I wanted her to reassure me, to help me. The way she always did.

"What do you want me to say?" she finally asked.

Jordan had told me a few days after Adelaide's party that she thought Jay seemed all right to have fun with, but not the kind of man I should fall in love with. *You're not going to marry him!* she'd said, laughing. And I'd been turning her words over in my head ever since.

"I think I am going to marry him," I said now, finally responding, weeks later. It felt as if Jay and I had taken that vow with each other last night. Not legally, perhaps. But we'd said it to each other, felt it with each other, and that meant something. That had to mean something.

Jordan put her club back into the bag, took it from me, and walked briskly toward the next hole, waving for her caddie to come back. I had to run to catch up with her. "Are you mad at me?" I called after her.

She stopped, turned around, and gave me a hard look. "Oh, Daise. We both know he's not the kind of man you'll marry. You're young and beautiful and why would you give yourself away, just like that, to a soldier?"

Her words felt like a slap. "I thought you were my best friend," I huffed angrily. "I thought you'd want me to be happy."

"Daise," she said somberly. "I do. That's why I'm being honest with you."

LATER THAT NIGHT, Jay tapped on my window again. I turned Jordan's words over in my head, that Jay was not the kind of man I'd marry. *Why would you give yourself away, just like that, to a soldier?* I swallowed back a bitter taste rising in my throat. Now instead of anger, I felt doubt curling up inside of me, wondering if she was right.

Be good, Rosie had told me this morning. But wasn't it good, to love a man for who he was, not what he was worth?

Jay tapped again, and I remembered how cold it was outside and ran to open the window.

"I missed you today," Jay said, his voice husky. He climbed into my bedroom. A cold blast of air entered my room with him, and I shivered. He quickly shut the window, and then he clung to me, kissed my hair. I turned warm again. The heat of his lips radiated across my head, and my face turned hot. Jordan's words faded away.

"I can't stand being apart from you," I said, standing up on my toes to kiss his mouth. He hesitated, then pulled back from me a little. "Jay . . . ? What is it?" My heart thrummed with what I suddenly knew he was about to say.

He pulled me toward him again, kissed my forehead gently. "Daisy, Daisy," he said my name softly, stringing out the letters like he was singing me a song. "I'm leaving in the morning."

I'd known it was coming. Known since I'd met him. But still, hearing him say it out loud now felt like a punch, and I could barely breathe. He could not leave me. And so soon. How could he leave me so soon?

"Come to New York," he said, his words tumbling out in a rush. "We can see the city together and get married there before I ship out at the end of January. You know I can't offer you much now. But after the war, I'll work hard, make a good life for us."

I closed my eyes and tried to imagine myself there, walking the streets with Jay. I'd been to Chicago before but never to New York. Even Chicago was so big, it made me feel small, anonymous. In Louisville everyone knew Daisy Fay, but in a big city, I could be anyone. I could be no one at all.

"I don't know," I said softly. What would Daddy say if I just left, like this? Worse, what would Daddy do? Jay didn't have money, or a family name. As he said once, he only had himself to offer me. I loved him, I did. But Jordan's words echoed in my head again: *he's not the kind of man you'll marry.* "I want to. I really do, but . . ."

"I'm not good enough for you," Jay said softly.

"No!" I put my hand to his cheek and stroked his face gently. "Don't say that, Jay. You must never say that." But I felt an ache in my chest, an unfamiliar feeling of worry about my future. "It's not that at all. It's that . . . Rose is gone. I can't just leave without saying good-bye." That much was true. If I were going to follow Jay, marry Jay, I would not just abandon my sister without even an explanation. I'd promised her we would decorate the Christmas tree and I'd water her lettuce while she was away. "I'll come to New York," I promised him. "I'll marry you. But after Christmas. I need to stay here to have Christmas with Rose."

In response Jay held my cheeks in his hands, pulled my face in closer to his, and kissed me. It was a hard kiss, a hungry kiss. A kiss that seemed to make a promise I wasn't sure that Jay could keep—that he alone would take care of me. That he loved me enough that anything was possible.

I HAD NEVER known what it was like to *need* someone, to feel a physical sensation of emptiness without someone. But once Jay was gone, I felt this hollow, this relentless pain in my stomach. It was hard to breathe and it was hard to eat, and I picked at my food during enough meals that Mother threatened to call Dr. Simms.

A week after Jay left, Jordan came over. Mother must've summoned her because she'd spent the whole evening before worrying I truly was ill when I refused to attend the Hillets' winter ball, which I always loved. The following day, Mother announced she was going to have lunch across the river in Jeffersonville with her old aunt. And then, Jordan was here. She lay across my bed with me, stroking back my hair as I cried. She truly was the best friend I'd ever had, and I felt guilty now that I'd ever been cross with her.

"It'll be okay, Daise," Jordie said softly. She twirled a strand of my hair around her delicate finger the way she always did, leaned back against my pillow, and sighed. "Everything will work out the way it's supposed to. You'll see."

"You'll look after Rose when I'm in New York, won't you, Jordie?" It occurred to me now I was asking Jordan to care for Rose the way Rose had asked me to care for her lettuce. Oh! Her lettuce. Had I even remembered to water it once since Jay had left? Rose had asked me for one simple thing. One *good* thing. And I couldn't even manage that.

There was a knock on my bedroom door, and Fredda called my name. She sounded frantic, which wasn't that unusual for her. Our longtime housekeeper had a flair for the dramatic. "Daisy!" she yelled again. I rolled my eyes at Jordan, got off my bed, and went and opened the door.

Fredda stood there in the hallway, her face ashen.

"Did you see another rat in the kitchen? I can go get Daddy's gun." I was only half joking.

She held out her shaking hands—she was holding a telegram. "Daisy," she said, tears running down her cheeks. "Oh, Daisy. There's been a train accident."

Catherine

"I HAD TERRIBLE TROUBLE WITH THE TRAIN," I SAID TO MY SISTER, Myrtle, first thing, before I hugged her even, at Grand Central. "There was an accident with another line heading out of Chicago, and they closed the tracks for four days. I must look a mess." I tried to fluff my bangs with my fingers, but it was no use. My hair was a limp, rotting strawberry. The station in Chicago, where I'd been waiting for the tracks to reopen, had been freezing, but the train had been hot. I felt covered in dried sweat and grime.

"Well, you made it, at least," Myrtle said, smiling wanly. "George read me the paper—sixty deaths in that crash. It was so bad, half the bodies weren't even recognizable. Imagine. Those poor souls. Torn apart, just like that." Myrtle grabbed me in a hug and held on tightly, fiercely. She smelled of an odd mix of flowers and diesel, nothing at all the way I remembered her smelling when she still lived in Rockvale, on the farm with me and Mother and Father. But Myrtle had left Rockvale to marry George, six years ago. Mother died a year later. Myrtle had been begging me to follow her to New York ever since, and finally I'd saved up enough money—and gumption—to join her.

But the rocky start to the trip made me wonder if I'd made a mistake, if I shouldn't have come here, after all. The trouble with the train had caused me to well up with dread, and here I was now in New York City, days later than I should've been. I already felt a pit of homesickness in my chest. Rockvale was quiet, snow covered and serene. Father longed for me to stay there and marry Harold Bloom, who owned a respectable dairy farm and who had been sweet on me for years. But I didn't want to marry anyone . . . yet. Much less a dairy farmer. New York was so much more modern— that's what had gotten me to finally step on the train in the first place. As of last month, women could even vote here. I could be someone in New York. Not someone's wife. *Someone.*

"Come on," Myrtle was saying now. She'd picked up my suitcase with one hand and she took my arm with her other. "Let's get out of the mess, Cath."

Grand Central *was* a mess. It was so crowded, we could hardly make it through the giant lobby out onto the street. All around us there were hordes of soldiers getting off trains. I looked at them for a moment before allowing Myrtle to drag me along. It was almost Christmas, and here all these men were, away from their families, getting ready to go halfway around the world to fight.

"It makes me so sad," I said to Myrtle, as we stepped out onto Forty-Second Street. The street was even more crowded than the station, and as we pushed through a wall of people to move forward, it was hard to breathe.

"What makes you sad?" Myrtle asked, once we'd reached a clearing, and stopped to wait to cross the street.

"All those men, those soldiers. They're off to war, aren't they? How many of them do you think will make it back here alive?"

"Come on, let's not think bad thoughts," Myrtle said, as we

walked across the street. "You're here now. We're finally together again. I'm going to stay in the city with you for a few days, help you get settled. Let's go get freshened up at your hotel now and enjoy a night out on the town." Her normally steady voice crackled with excitement.

"What about George?" I asked. George and Myrtle had fallen in love in a whirlwind in Chicago in 1911. Myrtle had gone for a week to visit our aunt, and George had been in town for an auto show; they'd bumped into each other on the street, literally. Myrtle fell—he'd helped her up. Myrtle liked to say he'd swept her off her feet, and as she'd always dreamed of a divine, rich life in the big city she was more than happy to marry him, leave Rockvale, and move to New York.

I'd met Myrtle's husband only once, the weekend of their wedding. But in the six years since, I felt I knew him from the stories about him and his garage in Myrtle's letters. From what I could tell, he was a hardworking man, a decent man, even if not the most romantic, and even if his garage in Queens wasn't exactly what Myrtle had dreamed of when she'd longed for the big city. He'd bought Myrtle a yard chicken for her birthday last summer. But Myrtle did like eggs, so I told her I thought it was sweet, even though, at the time, she was livid. *What kind of husband buys a birthday chicken?!*

I always had a feeling that Myrtle was a little bored, a little restless, that she was waiting for something else, someone else. I hoped that someone would be me. That both of us would be happier now that I was finally here in New York.

"WHAT DO I have to do to get a drink around here?" Myrtle cried out. A few hours later, I'd changed, and washed my face, and now we were at an underground saloon in Midtown that Myrtle said was frequented by all the people I'd want to meet. *Young, fashionable people,* she'd said, lowering her voice, as if the clientele were famous.

But inside, the small saloon was packed, and the floor pulsed with loud music. Despite the chilly December air up on the street, it was too hot in here. And looking around, all I saw were soldiers. More soldiers. Soldiers *everywhere.* The city felt overrun with them. In Rockvale, there weren't any soldiers. The war was only something distant we read about in the paper. Here it was palpable. The city seemed to pulse with green-clad men awaiting grim futures.

There weren't any saloons like this in Rockvale either. It was getting harder and harder to get a drink anywhere these days, and since the Eighteenth Amendment had passed in Congress just this month, I suspected it was about to get harder still. But Myrtle was more persistent than me, and she'd finally gotten a bartender's attention. She pushed her way to the front so she could get us drinks, while I found an empty stool and sat down.

A soldier was sitting next to me, and I couldn't help but stare at him. He was handsome, with broad shoulders and clipped blond hair, but that wasn't what made me stare. It was the expression on his face as he read a piece of paper he was holding in his hands, like someone had punched him. The words he read took away his air, and he grew pale.

"Are you all right?" I asked him, shouting above the music.

He lowered the paper, startled. He hadn't realized there'd been anyone else in the crowded room, much less sitting next to him.

"Sorry," I said. "I couldn't help but notice you looked upset."

He nodded slowly, picked up the glass in front of him, whiskey I presumed, and swallowed it all down in one fast gulp. Then he grimaced. "You ever loved anyone, Miss— Sorry, I didn't even ask your name."

"Miss McCoy," I said. "But please, call me Catherine."

"Jay Gatsby." He held out a hand to shake. His grip was firm, his fingers both strong and decisive. "So have you, Catherine? Have you ever loved anyone?"

I shook my head. I'd dated a few boys in Rockvale, but kissing them had made me feel nothing. And unlike Myrtle, I hadn't come to New York for a man. I was not here for love. I did not want an apartment over a garage in Queens and a backyard chicken for my birthday. I wanted a job in Manhattan, maybe a roommate. I wanted music and dancing and excitement and . . . autonomy. I wanted to be keeper of my own life, ruler of my own destiny.

"Then you wouldn't understand," Jay Gatsby said now. But then he kept on talking, as if perhaps changing his mind midsentence about what I might understand. "She isn't coming. She promised me she'd come and we'd get married here before I left. But . . ." He held the paper up in the air. "She's not coming." He sighed and folded up the telegram. And I wondered about the girl who'd decided to rip his heart out, just before he shipped overseas. What a careless shrew.

"Well then, she's not worth it, is she?"

Jay shook his head. "You're wrong, Catherine. She is. She's everything."

"I'm sorry, Jay," I told him. "But I say you deserve better than a girl who'd treat you that way."

He grimaced again just as Myrtle made her way through the crowd carrying what looked like two gin rickeys. She appeared in front of me, breathless, sweating, and she handed one of the drinks to me. Her brown eyes lit up a little, as if here, inside this crowded and loud saloon, she remembered how it felt to be truly alive.

Jay Gatsby stood, offering Myrtle his seat. She thanked him and took it, sipping on her gin with a little half smile, as Jay went to move toward the exit.

"Jay," I called after him, hopping off my stool to catch up. "Don't go dying in this war, all right?"

He grimaced again. "I'll try not to."

"And when you get back to New York after . . . look me up."

Detective Frank Charles

DETECTIVE FRANK CHARLES: Please state your full name for the record.

CATHERINE: Catherine Margaret McCoy.

DETECTIVE FRANK CHARLES: And exactly how did you know the deceased?

CATHERINE: Myrtle Wilson was my sister.

DETECTIVE FRANK CHARLES: Not Mrs. Wilson. Mr. Gatsby. Mr. Jay Gatsby.

CATHERINE: I don't know him. I never met him.

DETECTIVE FRANK CHARLES: Are you sure, Miss McCoy?

CATHERINE: I've heard of his parties, of course. Everyone's heard of his parties. I'm sure you've heard of his parties, Detective?

DETECTIVE FRANK CHARLES: But you never met him, personally?

CATHERINE: Never.

DETECTIVE FRANK CHARLES: And what about your sister, Myrtle? Did they have any kind of . . . relationship?

CATHERINE: My sister was a respectable married lady. I don't like that question.

DETECTIVE FRANK CHARLES: I didn't mean her any disrespect, Miss McCoy.

CATHERINE: Didn't you?

DETECTIVE FRANK CHARLES: Have you ever shot a gun, Miss McCoy?

CATHERINE: Yes.

DETECTIVE FRANK CHARLES: Unusual for a lady, isn't it?

CATHERINE: I . . . grew up on a farm in Illinois. I promise you every farm girl in Illinois has shot a gun.

DETECTIVE FRANK CHARLES: Please state your full name for the record.

JORDAN: Jordan Baker.

DETECTIVE FRANK CHARLES: And how did you know Mr. Gatsby?

JORDAN: I didn't, really. I went to a few of his parties this summer. Me and half of New York. (*laughs*)

DETECTIVE FRANK CHARLES: But you conversed with him at these parties. One night you even spent a few hours with him alone . . . in his study.

JORDAN: No. That never happened.

DETECTIVE FRANK CHARLES: Nick Carraway says it did.

JORDAN: Nick is an incurable liar.

DETECTIVE FRANK CHARLES: Nick said the same about you.

JORDAN: Have you ever loved a woman you couldn't have, Detective? (*long pause*) Well . . . have you?

DETECTIVE FRANK CHARLES: This isn't about me.

JORDAN: Isn't it?

DETECTIVE FRANK CHARLES: So you weren't with Mr. Gatsby, Mr. Carraway, and the Buchanans the night of Mrs. Wilson's accident?

JORDAN: I never said I wasn't.

DETECTIVE FRANK CHARLES: You just said you didn't know Mr. Gatsby.

JORDAN: I promise you, Detective. No one really knew Jay Gatsby.

DETECTIVE FRANK CHARLES: Do you know how to shoot a gun, Miss Baker?

JORDAN: I know how to shoot a golf ball.

DETECTIVE FRANK CHARLES: Please state your full name for the record.

DAISY: Daisy Fay Buchanan.

DETECTIVE FRANK CHARLES: And how did you know Mr. Gatsby?

DAISY: He was my . . . my . . . cousin Nick's friend. His neighbor.

DETECTIVE FRANK CHARLES: Where were you yesterday afternoon, Mrs. Buchanan?

DAISY: I was at home, with my husband and my daughter in East Egg. We have a lovely estate there on the water. I'm sure you know it? We were packing. We're moving to Minnesota imminently.

DETECTIVE FRANK CHARLES: This is a move you've been planning for a while?

DAISY: Of course. These things take time, Detective.

DETECTIVE FRANK CHARLES: Do you know how to shoot a gun, Mrs. Buchanan?

DAISY: (*laughs*) Now, what kind of a question is that to ask a lady?

✦

"FRANK, COME TO bed. If you're reading those interviews again, I'm gonna think you're stepping out on me with one of those women."

Frank sighed and shut his notebook. How did Dolores always have a sixth sense about what he was doing, even from the other room? Probably because he'd been talking about this case—these women—all through supper with her. And after nineteen years of marriage, she knew what was both his best and worst trait—he didn't know how to leave well enough alone.

"I'll be there in a minute," he called out now, tapping his cigarette in the ashtray. His notebook was no longer in his hands, but he'd reread his interviews enough times he had them memorized. He closed his eyes and he could still hear their voices, too: Mrs. Buchanan's sultry tones, Miss Baker's brash and husky denials, and Miss McCoy, whose voice had trembled throughout their whole interview. They were all lying to him. But how—and why—he couldn't put his finger on that yet.

Frank, why are you obsessing? Dolores had asked him over dinner. *I read it in the papers—they already said that Mr. Wilson killed him after Gatsby ran over his wife. They found Wilson on the property dead, killed himself right after with the same gun. The New York Times said the case was closed.*

I just have a feeling, he'd told her, vaguely.

But she'd nodded, understanding, by now, that was enough to take him seriously.

Dee was right, though—officially, the case was considered closed. Jay Gatsby had hit Myrtle Wilson with his car in front of Wilson's garage on the ashiest street in Corona, killing her. The next day, her grief-stricken husband, George, had gone out to West

Egg and shot Gatsby dead in his pool. Then he went out into the woods behind the house and shot himself.

But there was something else, something more among the ash heaps and millionaires that Frank couldn't quite let go. Something didn't smell quite right. For one thing, why didn't Gatsby just stop the car? Witness accounts said Myrtle Wilson ran right out into the road, didn't even look. The neighbor said George Wilson had kept her locked up and maybe she'd run in front of the car on purpose, trying to escape. So why didn't Gatsby stop? If that had happened to Frank—if that had happened to most men—he would've stopped the car, stayed at the scene of the crash. No one would've blamed the driver.

But then he supposed Gatsby hadn't been most men, living in that big mansion of his out in West Egg, throwing all the lavish parties. He was rumored to have been a war hero, or a bootlegger. Or both. Frank tended to lean toward the bootlegger theory himself, confirmed in his mind when Meyer Wolfsheim had come to the precinct yesterday morning and sought Frank out. Wolfsheim offered to pay Frank fifteen grand if he could find out the truth of what really happened.

Why me? Frank had asked Wolfsheim.

You're the one who solved the Calibrisi murder, Wolfsheim had said, matter-of-factly. It had been in all the headlines last year, a schoolteacher found shot dead by Flushing Creek. They'd arrested her husband, but Frank had thought something hadn't smelled right then, either, and six months later, he'd been the one to figure out she'd had a boyfriend on the side who was responsible.

Frank had nodded. *But what makes you think we don't already know the truth?*

George Wilson didn't have the guts to do it, Wolfsheim said, sounding so certain.

Frank briefly wondered how Wolfsheim and Wilson knew each other and also why Wolfsheim cared so much about Gatsby's death. But Frank had been fixating on something else—and this was the other thing he couldn't let go of, something Wolfsheim couldn't possibly know about. The diamond hairpin. Frank turned it over in his palm now.

Myrtle Wilson had died in a hit-and-run in his jurisdiction, and he'd tied her death to Gatsby's car the following morning. He'd driven out to West Egg, only to find Gatsby himself had just been shot. He'd decided to look around, and that's when he'd found this hairpin, on the ground in the shrubs behind Gatsby's pool. His Long Island colleagues had dismissed it—surely Gatsby had had lots of women out at his pool this summer. Any one of them could've lost the hairpin at any time. And anyway, they thought they already had the case all sewn up: *Mrs. Wilson, Mr. Gatsby, Mr. Wilson*, all dead by one another's hands. Open and shut.

But Frank wasn't so sure. The grounds were immaculate, and he didn't think the hairpin could've been there for long without a caretaker noticing it. He himself had picked it up as the six tiny diamonds had glinted with sunlight, catching his eye.

What Wolfsheim didn't know was that Frank wasn't ready to let this go yet, money or no money. He'd already started poking around on his own time, talking to the women. Might as well try and make this money too. Dee could be skeptical all she wanted, but with a payday of fifteen grand, he could make her happy next summer. She'd always dreamed of renting a house up in East Egg for the season, and houses there, even just to rent for a few months, were not something Frank would ever be able to afford on his detective's salary. She deserved it after all she'd been through these past few years. They both did.

"Frank!" Dolores called him again now.

"Coming, Dee," he called back. He put his notebook and the hairpin back in his desk drawer. He extinguished his cigarette in the ashtray and turned out the light.

But as he stood and walked down the hallway to go to bed, something Nick Carraway said about his cousin Daisy, which had struck him funny at the time, struck him again: *She's dead inside,* Nick had said. *I don't know what she's capable of.*

What exactly had Nick meant by that?

Daisy

1918

LOUISVILLE

A FULL MONTH AFTER CHRISTMAS DAY, OUR TREE STILL SAT NA-
ked in the parlor. Its branches, our house, devoid of any holiday
cheer. Rose's perfect ornaments sat packed away in the box on the
hard pine floor by the fireplace, untouched. I didn't think I could
ever touch them again. Ever have Christmas again. The tree was
dying, withering, but no one made a move to remove it, either. It
looked exactly how I felt inside.

The train crash had been so bad that Daddy and Rose had come
home in one single box, delivered with a letter from the railroad
company saying they could not guarantee that all parts of their
bodies had made it back to us. I read those words, pictured my dear
sweet Rosie torn up into pieces, and I vomited right there on the
spot, in the middle of the parlor. Then I tore the letter to pieces and
threw it in the fire, so Mother could never read it.

Mother spent nearly a whole month in the dark in her bedroom, crying. "How will we survive?" she murmured to me, when I
went in to check on her each morning. She knelt by her bed, praying through her tears. "Daisy Fay, pray with me," she'd whisper, the
snow goose hoarse, faltering.

It seemed a cruel joke, that God had cured Rosie of polio only to put her on a train that was going to run off the tracks a year later. And that he would be so spiteful to take Daddy with her. I did not believe that a god that hateful would exist, and then what was the use of praying to him any longer?

"I'm here," I said to Mother, kneeling beside her. Instead of clasping my hands in front of me, I put my arm around her shoulders. I pulled her close to me. "You have me," I promised her.

THE SECOND I read the telegram about the accident, everything changed.

Any sadness I'd thought I'd felt over Jay leaving was nothing compared to this. And I knew I could not follow Jay to New York as I'd promised him. I could not leave Mother, not after Christmas, not any time after that either. I sent Jay a telegram and told him what had happened, that I couldn't come to New York to marry him now.

But you'll wait for me? Jay wrote me a letter back. *After the war we'll be together, get married. I'll love you forever, Daisy. I'll wait for you forever . . .*

I'd folded his letter up and tucked it away in my jewelry box on my bureau. It had sat there ever since, a secret, a faraway promise. But I could not bring myself to write Jay back, to answer his question.

Sometimes in the weeks after the accident, I'd lie in bed at night and close my eyes, trying to remember the feel of Jay's hands upon my bare skin, trying to remember how I felt so much that I'd cared so little about my family.

Every time I tried to conjure Jay, all I could think about instead was my dear sweet Rosie, forcing me to walk with her to the almshouse in the depths of August. Me complaining about the heat. Why had I always complained so much? Why couldn't I have just happily done what she wanted?

Night after night I tried to conjure Jay, but instead, I heard her voice again and again: *Don't go kissing him, just because he's giving us a ride.*

I'd thought Jay was my heart, but maybe Rose was my heart. Without my sister, I was pale skin and marrowless bones, walking around Louisville like a ghost.

Be good, Rose had implored me, more than once. *I know you have it in you, Daise.*

But what if she was wrong?

By January, all her lettuce was dead. Her victory garden now a useless patch of dirt in the backyard. I'd done that. I'd forgotten to keep on watering it.

"WE'RE GOING TO have to sell the house," Mother announced out of nowhere one morning in March. She'd finally left her room, come down to the dining room for breakfast at the table, rather than having Fredda bring her up a tray, as she had for months. Since I'd just gotten over the shock of seeing her sitting here, dressed and real and breathing beside me, I could not immediately completely absorb her words.

Our house was a two-story brick Victorian in the most fashionable section of Louisville, the Southern Extension. Daddy had bought the house for Mother as a wedding present, and I'd lived here my whole entire life. "Why would we ever sell it?" I said. "And where would we live?"

"Daisy Fay, your daddy had some debts I didn't know about." Mother's voice was matter-of-fact, her affect strangely flat. She pushed her plate of eggs away, as if suddenly the food turned her stomach. "A lot of debts," she added.

"Debts?" I repeated the word now, still not understanding.

A lawyer I'd never seen before had come to speak with Mother last night, and they'd gone on for over an hour in hushed tones in Daddy's study. But I'd assumed it was in regard to Daddy's will or some legal paperwork from the railroad company that didn't involve me. Daddy had been a businessman, from a long line of Fay businessmen. Grandaddy had lived comfortably before he died, but to hear Daddy tell it, Grandaddy hadn't made half the money he had. "But Daddy said business was so good," I said to Mother now, sure she was confused. Her haze of grief made everything obscure and cloudy, and maybe I should be the one talking to the lawyers when they came back.

"Business *was* good," Mother clarified, her voice hardening. She spoke words but they were devoid of meaning. "But your father had formed . . . quite a habit with the horses apparently."

"Horses?" Daddy always loved the Kentucky Derby, but who in Louisville didn't? "What do horses have to do with anything?"

"He lost everything," Mother said quietly. "Betting on horses. You and I have almost nothing but this house, Daisy Fay. We're penniless."

I LAY IN bed later that night, holding Jay's letter in my hand, tracing over his neat script with my forefinger. *Wait for me, Daisy . . . I love you, Daisy.*

It was chilly tonight, and Fredda had lit a fire in my bedroom. I walked over there now, held Jay's letter out, and dropped it into the flames. I watched the edges of the paper turn yellow and blue, Jay's words hot with fire. Then they were gone.

I could not let Mother sell the house. I tried to imagine where we might go and what might become of us, penniless, homeless. To Mother's old aunt in Jeffersonville? Her house was abysmal, small, ugly, and run-down. Though she was just across the river from us—she was a world away from Louisville society, our tree-lined streets and Victorian mansions, my parties and Mother's afternoon teas.

I was the pretty Fay, and who was I without the good Fay? Rose had told me so many times I should be good, but what if all I needed was to be pretty? I could use my looks to help Mother, to help myself. If Adelaide Cummings had married a multimillionaire from Chicago—why couldn't I?

I knew what I had to do. I knew how I would fix everything.

Jordan

1918

THE TRAIN RIDE TO CHARLESTON FELT LONG, AND I CHEWED MY fingernails down to the quick. Daisy would chastise me, if she could see my stubby, nearly nail-less fingers now. But she wouldn't see them for at least a week. In fact, maybe they'd grow back enough that she'd never even know.

The whole entire train ride, I kept on thinking about what had happened to Rose and Mr. Fay on a train, and maybe that's why the ride felt so long. My stomach turned, considering how Daddy would feel if I returned to him a mangle of body parts in a box, not a golf champion.

And then that was the other thing that kept me biting—*golf*.

Daddy had paid to get me this spot in a women's golf tournament in Charleston. If I played well, then I might be invited to join the newly established women's amateur tour. But what if I really wasn't good enough? Daddy swore I was, that this money (how much money, he wouldn't tell me) was the best money he'd ever spent. I was just seventeen, but golf was the only thing I truly loved. The only thing I wanted. What if it didn't want me in return?

It was hard to think all these thoughts on the long lonely ride, and as I chewed on my thumbnail I wished Daddy were sitting next to me to ease my nerves, or give me a stern warning to calm myself down. He was supposed to be here. But his sciatica started acting up this past week and I'd left him back in Louisville, in bed.

I can't go without you, Daddy! I'd insisted yesterday.

To which Daddy had said, "Jordan Baker, I am ordering you, as your father, get on that train." Then he added. "And bring home a trophy."

Well, that shouldn't be hard at all, should it?

"Try not to worry," Daisy had said to me earlier this morning, as we walked toward the station together. She'd helped me carry my bags. "I'll look after your daddy while you're gone, Jordie."

I didn't tell Daisy but I was less worried about Daddy and his sciatica and more worried about the tournament itself. What if I didn't do well and I didn't even make it to the tour? This was it, my one real shot to play golf. The only genuine opportunity I'd have as a woman. If I didn't make it, then I'd return home to Louisville and do . . . what? I had no desire to spend the spring going to parties, looking for a rich husband the way Daisy planned to. I had no desire for any kind of husband. Wealthy or otherwise.

"I don't know, Daise," I'd said, as we waited at the station earlier. "I've never played outside Louisville before. I might not even be any good."

The train pulled in, and I'd taken my suitcase from Daisy, shifting it to manage with my clubs. Daisy gave me a fierce hug, crushing me against her. "I'm proud of you, Jordie," she'd said into my hair. "I really am, you know."

I'd offered her a wan smile and stepped on board, but even as the train had started moving, my entire body had still felt warm from her compliment.

⚜

I ALWAYS FELT different on the golf course. The sky was bluer and the grass was (quite literally) greener. I could breathe deeper, and when I swung a club, watched my ball slice the air, I felt a heady sensation of lightness. It was like floating on the river on the warmest of summer days. I couldn't imagine anything feeling more right than the moment when my club connected with the ball and made it soar.

"Nice shot," a woman's voice said as my ball rolled into the ninth hole, the last one of the afternoon. I'd finished the day three below par.

I turned, and one of the other competitors stood behind me. She was tall, taller than my five foot six, and dressed in a white sweater and skirt, like mine. She had pale brown hair, similar in color to Daisy's (but not as shiny, of course), and she wore it back in a tight, high braid.

"Mary Margaret Smith," she said with an easy drawl, walking closer to me. "Sorry to stare, but your swing is to die for."

"Oh." I let out a nervous giggle. I'd been so focused on my own game for the past nine holes that I hadn't paid attention to any of the other competitors up until now. I had no idea what Mary Margaret's swing was like or why she thought mine was *to die for*. "I'm Jordan Baker." I moved toward her, held out my hand to shake. She took it—her hand was small, her fingers delicate, but her grip was strong. "I'm from Louisville."

"Nashville," she said. She smiled, revealing perfect pearl-white teeth. "Well, Jordan Baker from Louisville, I hope I'll see you on the tour in May."

I nodded and felt a surge of confidence that I would be on that tour, after all. Maybe it was that someone else besides Daddy had been impressed by my golf game for the first time, or maybe it was that Mary Margaret seemed so kind and easygoing, I knew immediately we would be friends.

"Hope to see you, too, Mary Margaret from Nashville," I called after her. She stopped walking away to turn back and give me another smile.

I CAME IN second in the tournament, and two weeks later, back in Louisville, I received a letter from Mr. Hennessey, head of the Women's National Amateur Golf Tour, inviting me to join the tour in May. As soon as I opened the letter up, read it, I wondered if Mary Margaret had gotten one, too, and I wished I'd asked for her address or phone number in Nashville. Or that her last name wasn't Smith, so it would be easier to track her down.

Daddy was so excited when I showed him the letter, he jumped out of bed and howled, forgetting all about the sciatica. It took him a full minute to remember, that's how excited he was. Then, suddenly, he winced in pain.

I reached for him, to help him back to bed. "Now, Daddy, don't kill yourself over this. It's only a golf tour for ladies. Who knows how long it will go on, and if they'll decide to keep me once I'm there."

"Don't be a half-wit, Jordan," Daddy said, almost breathless from the pain. "Of course they'll decide to keep you. You're going to be the star of the whole league."

"YOU'RE LEAVING ME?" Daisy said later that day, when I showed her the letter. "I can't believe you're really leaving me, Jordie."

Daisy's face had taken a different shape since Rose had died.

Maybe it was because she hardly ever smiled anymore. It was hard to remember the way she was just six months ago, early last fall, when she was going on about love and marriage and running away with Jay Gatsby. Now Daisy looked pale, and too thin. She'd told me about all the money troubles her daddy had left behind, and lately all she could talk about was finding a wealthy man to marry, someone who could pay off her daddy's debts and keep her mama in their house. I'd told Daisy that maybe money and happiness weren't one and the same. But when I'd said that, she laughed at me.

"I wish I could take you with me," I said now. And I really did wish that too. Even if all the other women were as nice as Mary Margaret, and even if Mary Margaret were there, well, she wouldn't be Daisy. No one could ever be Daisy.

"Sometimes it feels like everyone has just gone and left me all at once," Daisy said. Her voice was wistful, and I couldn't tell if she was talking about me going on tour, Rose and her daddy dying, or Jay going off to war. There was a new crop of soldiers at Camp Taylor this spring, but I hadn't seen Daisy talking to a single one of them.

"I'll come back to visit, Daise," I promised her. "And you know we'll always be best friends. We'll always find a way to see each other, no matter what."

Daisy offered me a half smile. "I just never thought it would be so hard, Jordie," she said softly.

"What's that?"

She shook her head, and I reached up and smoothed back her hair. It looked a mess today—she had it back in a bun, but wayward wisps flew all around her face. I wondered if she'd given up on the egg yolks. "What's so hard, Daise?" I tucked her flyaway hairs back behind her ears.

"Life," she finally said. She sounded sad, and she sounded tired. "Growing up. Being an adult."

I pulled her to me in a hug. I wished I could help her. If I won out on the tour, I'd eventually get some money. Not a lot, but something. "I'll save up whatever winnings I can and send them to you," I told her now, clinging to her fiercely. "Don't do anything foolish while I'm gone," I added.

But not even a month after I left, I received a letter from Daisy telling me she'd done it. She'd met the wealthy man who was going to save her.

Jordie, she wrote, *I'm going to get Tom Buchanan to marry me, and then everything will be good again.*

Daisy

"YOU *HAVE* TO MEET TOM BUCHANAN," ANABELLE SAID, GRABBING onto my arm and pulling me out onto her moonlit balcony.

It was the end of April, and the air was thick with the smell of azaleas. With Jordan away, I'd forced myself into a sudden and quite vapid friendship with Anabelle this past month. Everyone knew her daddy came from the wealthiest family in Louisville, and she threw the most decadent parties. But Anabelle also had a persistent and silly laugh that reminded me of air escaping too fast from a balloon, and it was hard to force myself to laugh along with her rather than roll my eyes. Even when she said Tom's name now, she let out a hollow giggle. I sighed, missing Jordan again. But I allowed Anabelle to pull me out onto the balcony. It's why I'd befriended her in the first place, why I was here at her party tonight.

The Marlins' large balcony was crowded with handsomely dressed partygoers, but I instantly knew who Tom was, even before Anabelle stopped giggling and pointed to him. Anabelle had been telling me all week that Tom would be coming tonight from Chicago, that he was worth dressing for in my finest gown. *He's so rich he smells like diamonds*, she'd said, with another giggle, and I'd thought that was a silly way to describe a man, right up until the moment that I first saw him. All at once I understood, there was Louisville society money, and then there was Tom Buchanan money.

Though he stood alone, quietly sipping his drink, he was strikingly tall with a large, muscular frame and was dressed in a white suit that caught the shimmer of moonlight and almost seemed to glow. His face was all at once serious and perfect, like his features had been chiseled by an artist creating the exact man who was supposed to swoop into Louisville and save me from everything. And his eyes were an arresting blue gray, the color of dusk. "He played football with Benny at Yale, and now he's a horse man." Anabelle was still talking.

A horse man? Daddy's fixation on horses had gotten us into debt. Could Tom Buchanan's possibly get me and Mother out?

Tom looked at us, suddenly, and I wasn't sure what it was that made him understand Anabelle was talking about him. The mention of her brother, Benny, football at Yale, or the horses.

"I didn't just play football, I was the star," Tom said, approaching us. His voice was deep and easy, free of even the smallest trace of worry. "And, Anabelle, you know I prefer the term *ponies*."

"Horses, ponies, is there really a difference?" Anabelle rolled her eyes, and Tom shot her a look that made her erupt into another fit of airless giggles.

Tom turned to look past her then, right at me. His eyes met mine for a second, before trailing slowly down the length of my body, then slowly back up. His roaming gaze was so intense that it made my face turn hot.

"Tell me, though," I said, my voice escaping hoarsely, when his eyes reached mine again. "What is the difference between a horse and a pony, Mr. Buchanan?" In my head I thought, *Horses will bankrupt you; ponies are for the divinely wealthy.*

"In polo," Tom said, "we call them ponies. I collect polo ponies." I briefly wondered what a man *did* with such a collection. I supposed Tom played polo, but the amount of money he must have to own a whole slew of ponies specifically for that purpose? "It's why I'm here, in Louisville," Tom went on. "I've come down to the Derby the past few years to talk to the breeders and look for ponies worth buying."

"And to visit us," Anabelle added, finally recovered from her fit of giggles.

"Sure, if you say so," Tom said, flippantly. He turned back to look at me. "Why is it that I've never seen you around here before . . . what's your name?" he asked. "Anabelle, you didn't even introduce me to your friend you were so busy going on about *horses.*"

"I'm Daisy," I said quickly, before Anabelle could laugh again. "Daisy Fay. And I've always been here. Born and raised and spent my whole entire life in Louisville." I tried to keep my voice as light and easy as his. "Maybe you just didn't notice me before."

The truth was, of course, I hadn't made it to many parties last spring. Rose had still been recovering. And now it felt impossible that only a year later, Rose was gone, Jordan was away. I was trying desperately not to lose everything, and here I was, clinging to annoying Anabelle for dear life.

"No," Tom said, finishing off his drink and resting the empty glass on the rail of the balcony, "I definitely would have noticed you. And your name . . . Daisy. I would've remembered your name. Daisies are the most beautiful flowers."

"I quite agree," I said.

"Those pure white snow petals . . ." Tom's voice was husky, and his eyes dropped again, tracing my body greedily as he spoke in a way that made my skin feel hot. I had the sudden memory of Jay's hands on my skin, and I worried Tom could tell. That he could see it there, written across my body. I'd been with a man, and there was nothing *pure* about me anymore. But his eyes kept going and he kept talking. ". . . with a vibrant beating yellow heart center," Tom finished. His eyes traveled back up, met mine again, and we stared at each other, neither of us blinking.

"Daisy," Anabelle piped up, interrupting the moment. I'd almost forgotten she was here, but then there she went again, giggling. "You're blushing."

I'D BEEN TO the Derby several times before, but never on the arm of a man like Tom Buchanan, who was so tall and handsome and well-dressed in his tailored pearl-colored suit that he commanded attention. We walked into Churchill Downs a week after Anabelle's party, and it felt, impossibly, that all eyes went from the horses straight to Tom, this strikingly wealthy collector of ponies. *A man like Tom*, I wrote in a letter to Jordan last night, *that's exactly the kind of man who will always keep me safe. I'll never want for anything.*

Before I'd left Anabelle's party, Tom had invited me to lunch, and after a long and lavish meal at the Seelbach hotel, Tom had invited me to accompany him to the Derby. He had his eye on a pony, and he said he could use my advice. I'd laughed and told him I knew nothing at all about ponies, but his mouth had simply twitched into an easy smile. *You can be my good luck charm, Daisy.*

Is that what I wanted to be, someone's good luck charm? Did it matter anymore, what I wanted?

The last time I'd gone to the Derby was two years ago, the month before Rose had gotten sick. She and I had gone with Daddy, over Mother's protests that the horse track was no place for two nearly full-grown proper ladies. The memory of that afternoon sat in a golden ephemeral bubble in my mind. Rose and I had dressed in our fanciest pink dresses and matching pink hats and clung to Daddy's arms. The day was warm, the sun so bright it was almost blinding. Daddy had bought us caramel corn that we struggled to eat without making a mess. And as Tom and I walked into the viewing area now, the smell of that same corn was so strong, so overwhelming, it invaded my senses. It was Daddy and it was Rose. It was a past I could never have again.

"Daisy," Tom said. "Are you all right?"

I closed my eyes for a moment, blinking away tears. I could hear Rose's voice, telling me to *be good*. And Mother's voice, telling me we had *lost everything*. Had Daddy been losing money on the horses, even then? I inhaled, remembering the way Rose and I had both been so carefree here once, laughing at the stickiness of the corn on our fingers. There was no worrying about illness or death or money.

"Daisy?" Tom's voice cut through my memory.

I opened my eyes again, and there was Tom. In the bright afternoon sun, his beige suit glowed yellow. He was just a man, a collector of ponies, but in this light he looked positively ethereal. I smiled at him. "I'm sorry. I just got caught up in a . . ." I thought about telling Tom about Rose, about Daddy, but then I changed my mind. I didn't want to ruin the moment, or whatever glorious image he had of me in his head. A girl who'd lost her sister and her daddy in such a horrific way was no kind of good luck charm at all, was she? "I'm fine, really," I said firmly. "Should we sit and watch? Or should we go find your pony?"

LATER, AFTER THE sun set, after we had found Tom's pony and he had bought her, Tom walked me home. A wind came across the river, making the air turn crisp and cool, and as we approached my street, I shivered a little. Tom stopped walking, stood underneath a streetlamp, and took off his suit jacket.

"She really is beautiful, you know," I told him, as he gently draped his jacket across my shoulders.

"Yes," he said softly. He pulled the jacket tighter around my shoulders, then reached his hand up to touch my cheek. He stroked it softly with his thumb. "She really is, isn't she."

"I was talking about the pony," I said. Lillibelle was a striking mare, the color of night. And as soon as we laid eyes on her, I'd told Tom he should buy her. He'd gone and done it, without even inquiring about the cost. It was thrilling, the way I could say it, the way I could command him to buy something, and it was done. Just like that.

"So was I," Tom said now, his mouth falling into a teasing smile. His thumb caressed my cheek and then traced my bottom lip slowly.

That aching worry that had settled in my chest ever since Mother had said the word *debts* finally eased. And standing there on the street with Tom, I felt lighter again. His suit jacket was warm, and my face tingled at his touch. I put my hand up to catch his hand. And I held on to him for a moment.

He leaned in closer, and I thought he was going to say something, that he was going to ask me if he might kiss me. But then he just went ahead and put his mouth on mine so fiercely that for a second I couldn't catch my breath. My heart expanded in my chest, and my body shook. And Tom pulled me closer, held me tighter, and kissed me harder.

It was a kiss that took control of me, and I leaned into him, my body fading into his, relieved. For the first time in a long time, I suddenly felt that everything was going to be all right.

Catherine

MYRTLE SHOWED UP AT MY DOOR UNANNOUNCED, IN THE MOST sweltering moment of August, her neck wrapped tightly in a red knit scarf, her cheeks flaming red to match.

"Are you ill?" I asked her, ushering her inside. I lived in a tiny apartment in lower Manhattan with my roommate, Helen Dupont, who also worked with me as a wireless operator at the National Women's League. By day we patched calls and helped women find work, and by night we went to suffrage meetings and plotted protests to picket the Senate's inaction.

"No, I'm not ill," Myrtle said, stepping inside, gently unwrapping her scarf and placing it down on my sofa. She turned and I instantly saw purple marks cascading from the side of her neck.

"Oh my goodness, Myrtle." My hand instinctively went to her neck and she flinched before my fingertips even grazed her skin. "What happened?"

"Oh, it was nothing." A laugh gurgled in her throat and then died before it completely escaped her lips.

"It doesn't look like nothing."

It had been weeks since I'd seen my sister last, or, had it been months? I tried to remember now. We spoke on the telephone a few times a week, but the last time she'd come to the city to see me . . . it was before the summer. April, maybe. Had it really been that long?

I loved seeing Myrtle, spending time with her, but she had a drastically different life than I did. She had her husband and his business to worry about out in Queens. I had my job in Manhattan, my volunteer work with the suffrage movement, and on the weekends, Helen and I had gone to parties in the city all summer long. We were young and untethered here. We drank and we flirted with strange, beautiful men, and on some Saturdays we stayed out until dawn, just because we could. I never went out to visit my sister and brother-in-law. I didn't like it much out there, where it was always gray and dirty, with the smell of ash from the incinerator heavy in the sky. Anyway, Myrtle never invited me or wanted me to come to them. Instead, she came into the city to see me when she had the time and could get away.

I glanced at her neck again, guiltily. I should've been going out to see her, checking on her, invited or not. I'd moved to New York to be near her, after all. But I'd become wrapped up in my own life here, and Myrtle's life was consumed with George. I hadn't realized before now that maybe that should've worried me.

I reached my hand up to touch her again, and this time she let me. The bruises made an arched line on her neck. "Did George do this?" I asked. I imagined my brother-in-law's thick hands clinging so tightly to her neck that his fingers left marks, and it made me queasy.

"No, of course not," she said quickly, pulling away. "It was just . . . an accident. It was so silly really, I'm tired of explaining it. It's why I'm wearing a scarf in August, for heaven's sake."

"What kind of *accident?*" I raised my eyebrows and looked her directly in the eyes. She blinked and looked away.

"Oh, you know . . . What was it Mother always used to call me because I was never watching where I was going?"

"Turtle?" I said.

"Yes, right. Myrtle the turtle." Myrtle's voice came out thick with annoyance, but when Mother said it, it had always been in a completely endearing way, her voice brimming with affection. At home on the farm, Myrtle never watched where she was going—and there were so many times she had stepped in cow dung or had tripped and broken an egg. And Mother used to tell her to stop hiding that beautiful head of hers inside her shell. *Myrtle the turtle.*

What kind of accident could Myrtle possibly have had that made fingerprint-shaped bruises across the side of her neck? "But what did you do exactly?" I pressed her now.

"I don't want to talk about anything unpleasant," Myrtle said, ignoring my question, her tone brightening. "I got away for the whole weekend to visit with you. Take me to the nearest saloon and let's go dance and get smashed."

I bit my lip. Helen and I and a few other girls had planned to take the train to Washington, D.C., in the morning to picket in Lafayette Park with other suffragette groups. Helen was out now, buying supplies so we could make signs. What a disappointment it had been for all of us when the Nineteenth Amendment lost ratification by only two votes in the Senate last January. And months later, it still hadn't gotten passed. We'd discussed at our meeting last night that there was power in our numbers. That if only we could be loud enough, make our voices heard, the Senate would have no choice but to listen. And that's exactly what I'd intended to do this weekend in D.C.

But Myrtle was staring at me, her large brown eyes wide, hopeful, a little glassy. I couldn't just go ahead with my plans and leave her here now.

I sighed a little, picturing Helen and the others on the train, at the protest, without me. "Let me just leave my roommate a note," I said.

I hastily scribbled Helen an apology. *My sister needs me desperately*, I wrote. And, really, what good was it to help women, to fight to give women a voice, if I could not help my own sister?

"TELL ME," MYRTLE said, an hour and one and a half gin rickeys later. Her voice was softer, her words slightly slurred. I'd drunk only a few sips of my own drink, wanting to keep control, keep a close watch on her. "Is there a special man in your life, Cath?"

I shook my head. "Who says I even want a man?" I would never tell Myrtle, but I'd been known to kiss a man when I got drunk enough, sometimes even more than kiss. But that wasn't about having a special man in my life or finding a husband. And she would never understand.

She laughed now. "Don't be silly. Every woman *wants* a man. But the trick is to find a good one to marry. A refined one. A wealthy one. What about that one, over there." She pointed, and my gaze followed her finger to a man with a receding hairline who looked to be at least twice my age.

I grimaced and allowed myself another sip of my drink. "Do you know what I really want?" She shook her head. "I want the Nineteenth Amendment to pass the Senate. I want us to have a voice, a real voice in this country. Imagine that, Myrtle. Imagine not needing any man. Imagine if being a woman were enough."

Myrtle made a funny sound, a high-pitched drunken sort of

laugh. "Sometimes I forget how young and naïve you are," she said. I couldn't tell if she was complimenting or berating me now. She finished off her second gin rickey and sighed. "That's why I love coming into the city to be with you, Cath." She rested her head on my shoulder and leaned into me, sleepily, and I decided she'd been paying me a compliment. I reached up and smoothed back her hair.

"Are you going to tell me what really happened to your neck now?" I said.

She didn't say anything for a moment, just leaned her head into me. I wrapped my arm around her, pulled her close enough to me that I nearly lost my balance on the barstool. When she finally spoke, her words came out so softly, I could barely hear her. "You don't have to worry, Cath," she said. "It's never going to happen again."

"It better not," I said. "You tell George if he does it again, I'll kill him."

Jordan

EVERY DAY ON THE GOLF TOUR, THERE WAS A RHYTHM. WAKE UP at seven, breakfast, practice, lunch, practice some more, dinner, a little time to socialize, and lights-out. Once a month or so, we'd travel together to compete at a practice tournament, which broke into the rhythm but only just the smallest bit. Sometimes I thought about our days, parceled out and repetitive, and I felt like a factory machine, going again and again and again, every movement the same. By the summer, it was hard to remember why I'd ever loved golf in the first place.

There were eight of us women golfers in the Charleston league, and we did everything together. Much to my disappointment, Mary Margaret hadn't made the tour, and the other women here weren't even half as agreeable as she'd been. And then there was our chaperone, Mrs. Pearce, a stout older widow who always seemed annoyed she was being paid to watch us. I found her highly detestable, as I didn't need *watching*, and she was practically being paid to sit around and do nothing all day. I couldn't imagine too many easier jobs—why did she have to look so sour?

By the summer, I was miserable. My loneliness settled as a

continual ache in my stomach, a homesickness. I missed Daddy and Daisy and Louisville desperately, and I lay in bed at night plotting my escape back to them. I worried for Daisy, whose letters were drowning in infatuated stories of Tom Buchanan. Without me there, who would make sure she didn't rush into anything? And Daddy reported he was feeling well but admitted he was mostly confined to his bed. I was worried sick about his health, living in that big house all alone. That would be reason enough to leave the tour, wouldn't it?

But when I finally got up the gumption to suggest to Daddy in a letter that I may quit, return to Louisville to help him, he ordered me not to, under any circumstance. When would I ever get this chance again?

Jordan, don't squander this! he commanded me. In his exclamation point I could hear the rattle of his yell emanating from his chest, and I missed that sound so much even the very thought of it made me cry.

Deep down, though, I also knew he was right. Miserable as I was in Charleston, if I left now Daddy would see me as a failure. I would see myself as a failure. And I had no idea what I'd even do for the rest of my life if I didn't have golf.

MY DORMITORY ROOMMATE, Lena, was a tall gangly girl with long brown curls, and though her face was strikingly beautiful, she was also, fretfully, a bore. All she wanted to talk about was her fellow back in Tallahassee. Every night we got into our beds, and she'd want to talk endlessly about him, often just repeating what she had already told me the night before. *Danny this* and *Danny that*, and I yawned and closed my eyes and tried to tune her out.

In August, he made it home from the war, and he wrote her,

begging her to leave the tour, come home, and marry him. "Do you think I should, Jordan?" she asked me one night, as we lay in the dark in our bunk beds. I slept on the bottom, she was above me, and her question came to me as I was halfway to sleep, a disembodied voice.

"Leave the tour?" I repeated. I was surprised by her question, because in the past few months we hadn't really become friends. We didn't give each other advice or ask each other personal questions. I'd never mentioned to her my own ache of homesickness, my own thoughts about leaving. I thought about what Daddy had written me. *It would be a shame to squander this opportunity.* And I knew I should tell her that, but instead my voice caught in my throat and I didn't say anything for a moment. "Are you happy here, Lena?" I finally asked instead.

"Not really," Lena admitted. "Are you, Jordan?" Her voice was soft and ethereal, floating above me.

"No," I whispered into the darkness. It was the most honest thing I'd said to her in three whole months.

I heard her sigh a little, and I thought she was about to say something else, but then, a few moments passed, and I heard the soft whistle of her snore. It was a strangely familiar sound now, so much so that it almost brought me comfort. Part of the predictable rhythm of my life here in Charleston.

THE NEXT MORNING, I woke up and Lena was gone.

Maybe I shouldn't have been surprised. But I was. I wandered around our tiny room out of sorts, in a daze, looking for her. But her half of the closet was empty and her suitcase was missing too. She'd made her bed and left me a note on top that simply said: *Jordan, Danny makes me happy. Birdie for me. Kisses, Lena.*

I brought her note with me to breakfast, and though I supposed it was meant to be private, after I finished eating half a grapefruit, I handed it off to Mrs. Pearce like a slip of evidence. Better to let her read the note than to have to try and explain any part I might have had in this by daring to ask Lena if she was happy. "Lena's gone," I simply told Mrs. Pearce matter-of-factly, as I pressed the paper into her hand.

"Gone?" Mrs. Pearce pulled her glasses down the bridge of her nose, read the note herself. "Danny?" she said, frowning.

"Her fellow. Just got back from the war." It occurred to me as I spoke that I no longer had a roommate. But now I wasn't sure whether it was reassuring that I would be without Lena's nightly snores, or not.

Mrs. Pearce's face turned red, and she frowned deeply. "I'll need to speak to Mr. Hennessey about this. Not a word to the other girls, Jordan." I nodded. But for some reason she decided I wasn't taking her seriously. "I mean it."

What was she so afraid of? Most of the girls had fellows back home. Did she think they—we—were all so tired and sore and unhappy here that we'd follow Lena's lead and run back home, too? That the whole women's tour might fall apart, just like that, if they knew how and why Lena had left us? "Jordan," she said my name again, sharply.

"I know," I said. "I won't say anything. I promise."

She narrowed her eyes and stared at me for another minute before she said, "Go get your clubs and join the others on the driving range. You don't want to be late to practice."

I HIT THE balls, harder, faster. My arms ached as they sliced balls through the air one after another, after another. I thought about

Lena, halfway to Tallahassee on the train right now, and I imagined the weightlessness she must feel watching the sky roll by, Danny waiting for her on the other side of the line. I sliced the balls. Harder and harder. I was so used to my arms being sore by now that I barely even registered the pain. But today I hit hard enough that I did. My arms groaned, but I kept on hitting balls.

"Jordan, where's Lena?" Jerralyn Westport piped up with the question, interrupting my driving. She was a tiny raven-haired wisp of a thing who looked like she wouldn't have an ounce of power, but really, she had a mighty swing that seemed to come out of nowhere. I stopped hitting balls, and I was breathing hard, sweating. I wiped my brow with my forearm and hesitated for a moment, thinking about Mrs. Pearce commanding me to stay quiet. But what if I did tell Jerralyn the truth? What if all the women left and ran back home to their fellows and the tour was over due to lack of participants? That pit of longing, of homesickness, that grew and grew in my stomach each day could shrink again. No one could blame me for going back to Louisville if there was no tour at all.

I rested my club back in my bag and turned to face Jerralyn. She had her arms crossed in front of her chest and she frowned at me, like whatever had happened was all my fault. Like I'd done something to Lena. "She left to go home and be with Danny," I said. Then I quickly added, "But you didn't hear it from me. Mrs. Pearce made me promise I wouldn't tell anyone."

Jerralyn rolled her eyes, and I wasn't sure whether she was reacting to Mrs. Pearce or what Lena had done. Jerralyn was from Santa Barbara and she always acted like being from California made her better than the rest of us, more worldly or something like that. "Lena wasn't even that good," Jerralyn finally said, surprising me.

"That's not fair," I said. Because actually Lena was very good.

She'd come in second in our practice round robin in Savannah last month. And now that she was gone, and I'd probably never see her again, I felt oddly protective of this girl I didn't like all that much simply because she'd snored above me for three whole months.

"Women don't always get a chance like this, Jordan. You know that. You'd have to be a simp to give it up. Lena is an honest-to-god simp."

I nodded finally, so Jerralyn would leave me alone and I could go back to driving balls. But it made me wonder what she'd say about me, what they'd all say about me, if I ever just up and left one morning too.

THREE DAYS LATER, I woke up before the breakfast bell to the sound of someone knocking on my door. The rhythm of the day had been broken before it had even begun, and I got out of my bed, disoriented. Maybe Jerralyn had told Mrs. Pearce what I'd said, and now she was here to yell at me, away from the others. Or maybe Lena had changed her mind, come back. I swallowed hard, before I opened the door.

"Oh my! They didn't tell me I was rooming with *the* Jordan Baker from Louisville." I blinked for a moment before I realized who was standing there speaking to me: Mary Margaret. She appeared bright eyed and wide awake, even though it was not quite light outside yet. Her acorn hair cascaded down in front of her shoulders, and she reached up and tossed it behind her before stretching out her arms to grab me in a fierce hug.

"What are you doing here?" I asked. I barely knew Mary Margaret, but I felt this flood of relief course through my body at the sight of her, almost as good as if I'd opened the door and Daddy or Daisy had been standing there. Almost.

She stepped back, picked up her suitcase, and walked inside the room. "Some business about a girl having to leave the tour and apparently, lucky me, I was the alternate." She put her suitcase down, held up her hands, and shrugged.

She sat down on my bed, bouncing a little to test its firmness. "So tell me, Jordan, is everything as fabulous here as we thought it would be?" She looked up and stared at me expectantly. And all I knew was, now that she was here, everything would be better. The rhythm of the day would rise and fall. My arms would ache and ache. And Mary Margaret would laugh and we would whisper to each other at night in the darkness. And I would have a friend here and I might feel something close to happiness again.

"It is," I told her, smiling widely to hide my lie. "In fact, it's even more fabulous than we'd dreamed. You are going to love it here," I promised her.

Detective Frank Charles

THEY WERE LIARS, EVERY ONE OF THEM. THE MORE FRANK DUG into their stories, the more he could pull them apart, thread by thread. It reminded him of the way Dolores would undo a sewing stitch, and suddenly, an entire hem unraveled.

It was Nick Carraway whose version of the truth he trusted the most. And not, as Dolores had chided him, because *Nick is a man.* But because Nick was the only one he'd talked to who'd genuinely seemed broken up about Jay Gatsby's death. They'd been neighbors, friends. It was fair to say Nick had even idolized Mr. Gatsby and that his murder had left Nick a little . . . flattened. Then there was that thing that Nick had said, about Daisy being *dead inside.* Frank couldn't stop turning that over and over in his head. It sent him down to lower Manhattan at lunchtime last week, waiting for Nick to walk out of his office so he could chat with him again.

"What do you want?" Nick had asked abruptly when he'd spied Frank standing out on the sidewalk in front of Probity Trust smoking a cigarette. Nick gave Frank a wary look, shivered, and pulled his overcoat tighter around him. The air had turned, suddenly, and that sweltering heat of August, a month ago, when Jay Gatsby was bloodless and floating in a pool, almost felt like nothing more than a dream.

"I have a few more questions for you," Frank said.

Nick pulled up the collar of his overcoat and started walking.

Frank dropped his cigarette and squashed it with his shoe, grinding it into the sidewalk. "Hold on," he'd called, running after Nick. "I'll buy you lunch."

"I can buy my own lunch," Nick had said, frowning.

Now, a week later, Frank got off the train in Minneapolis, still turning Nick's final words to him over again in his head. *Why don't you talk to Daisy?* Nick had said. *She knew Jay so much longer than I did.*

Longer? Frank had questioned then. According to Daisy, Nick was the one who'd introduced her to Mr. Gatsby, earlier in the summer.

"Talk to her," Nick had said brusquely, before walking off, disappearing into the lunch crowd.

Later that night, Frank had combed through the files again. And then something had caught his eye that he'd missed before: Jay Gatsby had been stationed at Camp Taylor before the war.

Camp Taylor.

Frank's younger cousin, Barney, had been there, too, and Frank and Dolores had even gone down to Louisville to visit him one spring, before Dolores got sick. It was a memory Frank had discarded somewhere in the back of his mind after Barney was killed in the war. But it came back to him again suddenly: Barney's thin childlike grin, the great blue cascade of the Ohio River, the quaint brick storefronts of a city caught between the South and the Midwest. Daisy was born and raised in Louisville. Jordan too. And if he were a betting man, he'd bet the two of them had met Jay Gatsby there, once, years ago. Is that what Nick meant? And if so, why had they lied to him about that, of all things?

It was that question that got him to call Meyer Wolfsheim to let him know he needed some travel funds to go out of state to interview a witness. And that brought him on the long train ride from New York to here: Minnesota, where the Buchanans had been packing to move to long before Jay Gatsby had been murdered. Or so Daisy had claimed. What was it she'd told him? *These things take time.*

But whether she'd been talking about her move or whatever it was that had happened between her and Jay Gatsby . . . well, now he wasn't quite so sure.

PERHAPS UNSURPRISINGLY, THE Buchanans' new home outside of Minneapolis was a mansion so large, so massively sprawling, that it made their East Egg house seem somewhat ordinary in comparison. It sat four stories high and was propped up with marble columns that looked like something out of Ancient Greece. The house was next to wooded acres on one side, a sprawling bright blue lake on the other. Frank wondered if the Buchanans owned both the woods and the lake, too. And maybe that was the difference between being wealthy in Minnesota and in New York—even the mansions in New York were smaller and closer together than out here.

A housekeeper let Frank in and led him to a lavishly decorated, tidy parlor. It was well furnished with paintings on the walls, and there was no sign of boxes, or the kind of disarray you might expect from a move halfway across the country that had happened very recently. Maybe Daisy had been telling the truth about the planning for this being long in the works. Or maybe people as rich as the Buchanans never had disarray.

"Detective Charles," Daisy gushed, walking into the parlor, greeting him as if they were old friends. Her lips were poised in a smile, but her face was pale, and her eyes betrayed her. They were dim, tired. *Angry?* "Good heavens"—she was still talking, her voice an elevator rising so fast it could give you vertigo—"I could hardly believe it when Marie said you were here. Sit down. Can I get you a whiskey? Or maybe a bourbon? You look like a bourbon man, Detective."

He felt slightly unnerved. He *was* a bourbon man. Or he had been, back when it was legal. And truth be told, he still was in the privacy of his own apartment. But not when he was on the job. And at the moment, with the amount of money Wolfsheim had offered him, he was taking this job even more seriously than his real job. He cleared his throat. "No, thank you, Mrs. Buchanan. But I could take some water, if it wouldn't trouble you too much."

"Oh." She laughed. "You're one of those men, are you? *Water?*" She rang a bell and then the poor house servant ran in looking anxious and was tasked with bringing him water. He shot the servant an apologetic smile, but she didn't seem to notice before scurrying out.

He turned his attention back to Daisy. Her smile had momentarily faded and now she just looked tired. "So, Minneapolis, huh?" He forced a smile, trying to be friendly, hoping she'd let her guard down.

"Tom wanted more room for his ponies. There's more land out here. So much land." She frowned and leaned in closer, lowering her voice to an almost conspiratorial whisper. "I hear it's dreadful in the winter, though."

"I'm sure," he said. Even today, mid-September, it was cool enough to feel like a winter's day in New York. His hands had been cold since he'd stepped off the train, and now he held them in his pockets, running his fingers across the cool diamond hairpin, again and again. "Anyway, Mrs. Buchanan, thanks for seeing me. I had a few more questions for you."

She laughed and refused to meet his eyes, brushing her hair behind her shoulders with one well-practiced swoop of her hand. "You came all the way out here for a few more questions, Detective? I don't know whether I should be flattered or alarmed."

"I like to get out of the city for a few days this time of year anyway. Figured I might as well come in person." It was a bald-faced lie that he covered up with what he hoped was a reassuring smile. It pained him to leave Dolores alone overnight any time of the year, even though she'd insisted she could manage just fine without him. And her sister, Josephine, was two blocks away if she needed anything. Josephine already disliked him and Frank didn't need to give her more reasons for it. But he was here for Dolores, he reminded himself. Once he got Wolfsheim's paycheck, he'd be able to afford a nice rental house near the water next summer. They could celebrate their twentieth wedding anniversary in style.

"Still," Daisy was saying now, "you could've telephoned, Detective."

He could've. But he wanted to show her the hairpin in his pocket, wanted to observe her face when he sprang it on her. He wanted to watch the threads of her lies unravel right in front of his eyes, and maybe then he could figure out what they all meant. "I prefer face-to-face meetings, rather than the telephone," he said, nonchalantly.

"The telephone is a dreadful device, isn't it?" She clucked her tongue. And it was hard to tell whether she was humoring him now or being sincere.

The poor house servant rushed in with his water, and he took it from her. He took a small sip before resting it on the coffee table in front of him. "Anyway, I saw your cousin Nick last week."

"Oh, how is he? We grew so close over the summer and I'm afraid we've lost touch already since I've moved. That dreadful telephone again." She let out a muted laugh. He was pretty sure she was mocking him.

Nick had seemed agitated, angry, but Frank wasn't about to tell Daisy that now. "He said something that I wanted to ask you about, actually. He said that you knew Jay Gatsby much longer than he did."

Daisy opened her mouth, but then closed it again without saying anything. She frowned.

"But you told me you only knew Mr. Gatsby because he was"—he flipped through his notebook, making a show of rereading his transcript; really, he had the words, their entire interview, memorized from going through it so many times—"*my . . . cousin Nick's friend. His neighbor,*" he repeated now.

Daisy chewed on her lip, not saying anything at first. "That's all true," she finally said, her voice softer. Her eyes darted from her fingers, which she was twisting in her lap, to the wall somewhere just behind him. "He was Nick's friend. His neighbor in West Egg."

"But you knew him before that?"

She turned her fingers round and round. "I met him years ago, once, in Louisville, before the war." She stared at her fingers and spoke softly. "He probably didn't even remember me. I . . . I . . . didn't think it was worth mentioning to you, Detective."

Daisy looked up again and met his eyes. Her expression was so earnest, he might almost believe she was telling the truth now. Almost.

He pulled the diamond hairpin out of his pocket and laid it flat in the palm of his hand, holding it out for her to see. Her eyes widened and her cheeks flushed. "Where did you get this?" she demanded.

"It's yours?" he asked, hopeful. He was on the brink of something with her. What, he wasn't exactly sure. But . . . something.

She took the hairpin from him, ran her finger across the diamonds, and then handed it back to him. "No," she said. "I've never seen it before."

He sighed. So close, and now she was slipping back into her lies. "But you just reacted like maybe you had."

She laughed. Her face was pale, glass. Her eyes, stone. "Oh, Detective, you just surprised me, that's all. That looks mighty expensive for you to be carrying around in your pocket."

She was right. It did look expensive. It looked exactly like something a woman who owned a sprawling estate in Minneapolis, complete with her own forest and lake and goddamned Greek columns, might wear.

"You're sure it's not yours?" Frank prodded. Daisy pressed her lips tightly together and shook her head. "You have any idea whose it might be?" he asked her.

"Like I told you," she said more curtly now. "I've never seen it before in my life."

Daisy

"I COME BEARING GIFTS!" JORDAN EXCLAIMED, BURSTING THROUGH my bedroom door, without even knocking. I stood in front of my full-length mirror, examining my wedding gown, which was on but not buttoned yet. But I turned at the sound of her voice.

She was carrying two gold-foil-wrapped boxes with a letter sitting on top, and her cheeks were pink, matching her fuchsia maid of honor dress almost exactly. Was her flush an indication of happiness or was it this awful mid-June heat that had come over Louisville like a sweltering humid blanket these past few days? I'd taken a long cool bath before I'd put my gown on, but I was just waiting for the heat to hit me again, any minute.

"Gifts!" Jordan held them out to me.

"You know I love gifts," I said, ignoring her flushed face and this dreadful weather. There was nothing to be done about that. And I was getting married today. The doubts I'd drowned in gin two days ago were behind me now, and today I felt nothing but joy. Sweaty joy. But joy, nonetheless. "Can you button me first, Jordie?"

Jordan nodded and put the gifts down on my bed before

walking over to me and reaching up to the back of my dress. I felt her fingers looping up the pearl buttons slowly, one by one.

I watched in the mirror as she deftly worked her way up my back. "My goodness, Daise. Who knew a dress could have so many buttons?"

"It's *couture*," I told her, repeating the word Tom's mother had used to describe it, when she'd insisted on taking me to Paris to get it fitted.

"In other words, exorbitantly expensive?" Jordan laughed a little, causing her hands to shake against my shoulder blades.

I nodded. "It was made at a very fashionable atelier in Paris."

"Of course it was," Jordan said, her tone a little bit mocking. But then she quickly added, "It is beautiful, Daise. All this lace." She stopped buttoning and ran her fingers gently across my lacy back. "What a dream."

The dress was a dream: formfitting lace with a heart-shaped neckline and an excessive amount of pearl buttons—they wound all the way up from my backside to the nape of my neck. I wasn't sure exactly how much the dress cost, and I would've been afraid to even ask Mrs. Buchanan that question. When I'd fretted about it to Tom, insisting that really, it was all too much, this dress, the trip to Paris, the wedding reception with four hundred guests at the Seelbach—half of whom I was pretty sure neither one of us had ever met—he said I shouldn't even think about those things. As his wife I'd have everything. Too much was not enough. Money meant nothing any longer. And that thought washed over me now, making me feel light and happy, the way a bride should.

Truth be told, I was relieved to hear Jordan complimenting my dress. Relieved she'd taken a little time off from her tour to come home and stand up at the altar with me. I hadn't been sure how she would react to the news of me marrying Tom when we got engaged last fall. When I first wrote her about dating him, a year ago, she made it clear in her response that she didn't love the idea of me dating someone on the basis of his enormous wealth, and from Chicago no less. But Jordan was different when she'd come back to visit last Christmas, softer somehow. The golf tour seemed to be agreeing with her. And when I'd asked her then about coming back home for the wedding in the middle of June, being my maid of honor, she'd answered me with a squeal and a hug and an *of course*. And in that moment, neither one of us had even stopped to be sad about Rose, about the fact that she certainly would've been my maid of honor, if she'd still been here.

I thought about it later, though, after Jordan went back to her tour, after New Year's. When I traveled to Paris with Mother and Mrs. Buchanan and sat inside the small, warm atelier, looking over designs, allowing the old Frenchwoman to stretch her tape measure around my body, over my bosom and across my hips, I'd looked up, and Mother had had a cautious smile on her face and Mrs. Buchanan was looking, well, like Mrs. Buchanan. (Tom said when she wasn't deeply frowning that actually meant she was quite happy.) But I'd looked at them then, and in that moment, I could almost see Rose sitting there in between them, her bright eyes, shimmering with excitement, at me, her older sister, *in France*, getting her wedding dress.

Or would she have been sitting there shaking her head, reminding me to *be good*? Telling me how many poor people she could help with all the money going to pay for this too-extravagant trip across the Atlantic, for a too-extravagant dress that I would only wear once. Then I'd had another thought: in a world with Rose, I might have never even gone to Paris for my wedding dress, never even met Tom Buchanan at all.

"There you go, all buttoned," Jordan said, interrupting my thoughts. I examined my figure in the mirror, smoothing the lace down around my hips and pushing all negative thoughts away, too. It was my wedding day. I was here with my Jordie, and I was about to become Mrs. Tom Buchanan. "We still have to fasten your veil," Jordan was saying now. "But open your gifts first."

Gifts! From Tom. I'd almost forgotten about them. I clapped my hands together, gleefully. They were sure to be expensive gifts, beautiful gifts. I picked up the larger of the two boxes first and unwrapped the gold foil. Inside was the most gorgeous pink pearl necklace I'd ever seen. Jordan, who was glancing over my shoulder, let out a little gasp. "So that's what three hundred and fifty thousand dollars looks like on a necklace." She put her hand to her mouth. "Oh, I wasn't supposed to tell you that part. But Tom accidentally let it slip."

I smiled and shook my head. Tom didn't do anything by accident. He was calm and careful, everything calculated. He'd wanted me to know how much he loved me, how much I was worth. And he knew Jordan would be terrible at keeping such a secret from me. "Help me fasten it, would you, Jordie?" I wrapped the necklace around my neck and she did the clasp.

"God, Daise, that's stunning," Jordan said, stepping back to admire the pearls.

"It is, isn't it?" I murmured. In the mirror my neck was shimmering. But the weight of the pearls was unexpected, overwhelming. The necklace was so heavy it felt uncomfortable, almost like hands tightening around my throat. And I had to breathe slowly with purpose. In and out. In and out.

"Here—open the other one." Jordan reached for the smaller box on the bed and handed it to me. I unwrapped the gold foil, and when I opened the box, inside were two delicate gold hairpins, covered with diamonds. "To hold your veil in place," Jordan said, her voice rising with excitement. "I helped him pick these out."

"Oh, Jordie. I love them." I really did. They were beautiful and certainly expensive but small, tasteful. They'd sparkle just the right amount in my hair and hold my veil in place perfectly.

Jordan smiled and lifted my veil from the hat stand. She placed it gently on my hair. Then she took the pins from the box and fastened it to my head. When she was finished, she trailed her fingers down from my hair to my cheek, resting them there for a moment. "Oh, Daise," she finally said. "You're a bride."

I laughed a little, took a step back, and examined myself in the mirror. This woman staring back at me was indeed *a bride*, lacy, shimmery, pearlescent—I barely even recognized her. In my reflection, I suddenly caught sight of the third thing Jordan had brought to my room—a letter—sitting on my bed behind me now. "Is that a note from Tom?" I asked her, turning to go pick it up.

She shook her head. "No, I don't think so. Fredda handed it to me on the way up, said it had come in the post for you."

I examined the envelope, and there was no return address. But it bore a postmark, from Oxford. It had come for me, all the way across the Atlantic? I didn't even know anyone in England. I ripped the envelope open, wondering if it still might be another gift from Tom, after all. But as soon as I caught a glimpse of the handwriting on the paper inside, I inhaled sharply.

"What is it, Daise?"

I pulled the letter out and ran my fingers over Jay's neat script, the words swimming together as my eyes watered. Why today again, of all days?

Jay's letters had still come for a little while after he went to war, but then I met Tom, and I'd stopped opening them. I'd burned them in my fireplace, unread, feeling it was somehow disloyal to read them. Or maybe, I worried deep down, they might break my heart. But suddenly, about a year ago, they'd stopped coming altogether. I'd hoped it meant he had given up on me, not that he had died.

And now my heart rose and fell, holding this piece of paper, with his handwriting on it. *He was alive.* He had not been killed in the war. He was alive. And in England?

"Daise?" Jordan's voice shook me out of my reverie.

"Jay," I finally said, his name sticking in my throat, making me sound hoarse. "I just . . . I haven't heard from him in so long, Jordie. I didn't even know if he was alive."

Jordan gave me a careful, quick hug, not pulling me too close, to keep my dress perfect. "I'll give you some privacy," she said. "I'll wait for you downstairs. Car should be leaving for the church in twenty minutes?" Her voice sounded like a question, and I nodded in response.

She blew me a kiss and walked out. As she shut my bedroom door behind her, I looked at the letter again, blinked, and then focused on the words.

> *My Dearest Daisy,*
>
> *It has been a while since I've been able to write, but know that you have never been far from my thoughts. Every night in the trenches, I'd close my eyes, and you would be there. I love you. I have always loved you.*
>
> *But I've just heard your news, all the way across the ocean.*
>
> *In Oxford, everyone knows the Buchanan name. He has money, and I suppose he can give you everything. He has promised you everything. But he will never love you the way I love you. And you will never love him the way*

you love me. Remember, Daisy, that night in the rain?
When our lips met that first time, I knew. I just knew.
We're meant for each other.

I still dream about the feel of your warm flesh against my
hand, about the way I touched you and you made that little
sound, like a bird, a desperate lovesick sparrow. Can you close
your eyes and remember that moment, Daisy? He doesn't
make you feel the way I made you feel. I know he doesn't.

And still, you might think, the money. Yes, the
Buchanans have so much of it. But I will soon, too. I
promise you. The war is over, and I'm studying at Oxford
now. I'm going to figure out a way to make a fortune, so
I can take care of you the way you deserve to be taken
care of. I'll buy you a big house, and all the diamonds you
want, and we can live by the water and love each other
forever. But I just need a little more time.

Please, Daisy. Don't marry him. Give me another
year or two. I promise you. Wait for me?

Love always,

Jay

I reached the end of his letter and held the paper against my
chest, closing my eyes, the way he'd asked. I did remember. That
night in my bed, his fingers had trailed slowly up my thigh. The
sensation of pleasure at his touch had felt so intense, that a sound
had inadvertently escaped from my lips that I'd never made before,
or since. A *lovesick sparrow.*

But that was so long ago. When Daddy and Rose were alive.
When I was a different girl, an entirely different Daisy.

Mrs. Buchanan had said something to me in Paris that I

thought of again now. It was just after the seamstress had wrapped her tape measure all around me, clucking over the imperfections in my body, commenting in a French I supposed she thought I didn't know: *bosom too small, hips too narrow, legs too short. Corps de canard.* Did I really have the *body of a duck?* I'd held my breath and thought how I would've been much happier shopping at Marlene's shop in downtown Louisville, trying on the dresses she kept in stock.

"Daisy," Mrs. Buchanan had said, as we'd walked out of the atelier, and my body had felt ugly, somehow foreign, displaced from myself. "You're going to be a Buchanan soon. Go back in there and tell her to apologize to you. *Demand* she apologize. Or we will go to another atelier."

Mother bit her lip, clearly dying to be her snow goose self, but not wanting to step on Mrs. Buchanan's toes either.

"My French is rusty," I said, excusing the things the seamstress had said about my body with a wave of my hand.

"Well," Mrs. Buchanan said sharply. "Mine is not, and she cannot speak to you that way. Go." She put her hand on my shoulder and pushed me gently back inside the atelier. It felt like a test, and certainly, I was about to fail.

I glanced at Mother, who stood red-faced with her arms crossed in front of her chest, and I imagined what she would say, if she got up the nerve to talk: *Daisy Fay, mind your manners. You're a lady!* But she said nothing at all and Mrs. Buchanan frowned. What choice did I have but to walk back inside?

"You have forgotten something?" the seamstress said to me, in jagged English.

I took a deep breath and stared directly at her. "I do not have the body of a duck. I would like an apology."

Her face flamed, and she stammered out a quick apology, half

English/half French. And I'd felt something then, rising up inside of me. Money would give me a couture dress, and diamonds, and Tom. But it would give me this, this red-hot *power*, too.

I put my hand up to touch my necklace now. My neck had adjusted to its weight and the pearls no longer felt stifling. Instead, when I turned my head, even just the slightest, I could feel them there, formidable and stunning against my collarbone. What kind of a woman could wear three hundred and fifty thousand dollars around her neck like it was nothing? *Mrs. Tom Buchanan.*

I folded Jay's letter back up, put it in the envelope, and ripped it in half. Then I tore it again, and again, until it was no longer words with any meaning at all, but shreds of paper on my bedroom floor that Fredda would come in and sweep up later.

Jay was right. I'd felt something once. We'd felt something together. But I clutched the pink pearls in my fingers, now. Whatever I had felt then, two years ago, was nothing compared to what I had now. And being married to Tom, I'd never have to worry about Mother's or my comfort again.

I took one last glance in the mirror, straightening the diamond hairpins just a bit. And then I turned and walked downstairs. Mother and Jordan stood in the parlor, waiting for me, and Jordan sighed with what appeared to be relief when she saw me.

Mother stared at me, held her hands to her mouth. "Oh, Daisy Fay," she trilled when she found her voice. "I've never seen such a beautiful sight in my whole entire life. Your daddy would be so proud of you."

"Are you ready, Daise?" Jordan asked.

"Yes," I said, and I meant it. I really did. More than I'd ever meant anything in my life. "I'm ready to go become the happiest wife in the whole entire world."

Jordan

IT WAS SO HOT AT DAISY'S WEDDING THAT A MAN OUT AND fainted in the middle of the church, just after the ceremony ended. I saw the look on Daisy's face—that abject horror as she watched him go down—and then I could see all the worry turning around in her head that this one moment would define her entire wedding, ruin everything.

As the maid of honor, it was my duty to assist the bride in every way. And since Daisy and I had been best friends for so very long, I took this duty quite seriously.

"Don't worry," I whispered in her ear. "I'll take care of this." I dashed from my spot at the altar to the middle of the aisle where the man had gone down. "Move back, y'all," I shouted, waving my arms. "Give him some air."

The crowd stepped back, seeming collectively relieved that someone else had taken charge. The string quartet began to play as if to distract everyone, and it appeared to work. I moved my fan in front of the man's face; he was younger than I'd thought from farther back, maybe even just a little bit older than me, and that filled me with relief. No one would be dying at Daisy's wedding. Not on my watch. And indeed, after only a minute of fanning, he opened his eyes, blinked, and murmured something incoherent.

By that time, Mrs. Fay had made it over to us with a glass of water. "Here." I held the water out to him. "See if you can sit up and drink some of this."

He sat up, took a few sips, and wiped at his brow with the back of his hand. Then he gazed at me and smiled. "Are you an angel? Have I died and gone to heaven?"

Oh, for goodness' sake. He couldn't be serious.

"You're perfectly alive," I retorted. "But you're blocking the aisle and Daisy will lose her mind if people can't leave the church to get over to the Seelbach for the reception."

He chuckled a little, as if he knew Daisy (though I wasn't sure how—I'd never seen this man before in my life), and he might relish the thought of seeing her lose her mind.

I held out my hand. "Come on, see if you can stand. My house is only two doors down from here. You can cool yourself off there before the party. I'm Jordan Baker, by the way."

He grabbed my hand, and then he was on his feet again. "Blockwood Biloxi." He wobbled a little and I put out a hand to steady him.

"Blockwood?" I tried not to laugh at his ridiculous name because the poor man was already having quite the embarrassing afternoon.

He shrugged. He was probably used to it. "It's an old family name. But you can call me Blocks. Everyone does."

Blocks truly wasn't any better than Blockwood, now was it? But I bit my lip. "All right then, *Blocks*. Let's go."

He leaned his weight on me and the two of us made it out from the aisle. Daisy cast me a grateful smile. I winked at her, but she had already looked away, turned her attention back to Tom, who was talking to his parents in the front pew. She reached her hand up to fiddle with her *three-hundred-fifty-thousand-dollar* necklace. Was that a nervous fiddle? Daisy and I had grown up well-to-do, for Louisville. But girls we knew coveted a strand of pearls worth a few hundred dollars. I tried to imagine what it must feel like to wear something so expensive around your neck. To be given a necklace that expensive, by your *husband.* What a person could buy with that money instead! A mansion or maybe even a small town somewhere in the Midwest.

"I don't know if I can walk much more," Blocks said. We'd just made it outside the church, and he slowed down, started slumping.

"Come on," I said, pulling him upright again. "My house is just right up there." I pointed to the white Victorian two houses down—you could see the red front door from here. "Daddy already got tired and went home to rest before the party so just a few more steps and then he'll fix you up with some of his famous sweet tea."

"Jordan." He turned and stared at me, his eyes open wide. They were a pale, watery shade of brown, the color of hot cocoa. "I owe you. You saved my life."

"Oh, hush. Come on now. You're being ridiculous. Just a little June Louisville heat, that's all. I bet you're from up north, and you're not used to our weather."

He shook his head but didn't tell me where he was from. Instead he said, "Jordan, do you have a beau? I bet you do. Someone as beautiful as you must have a beau."

I sighed. As Daddy always liked to say, no good deed goes unpunished. I'd gotten Blocks up and out of there, and I was taking him to my house, and now I was subject to his annoying questioning. "I'm not looking for a beau," I said sharply.

"So then there isn't a special man in your life?" Blocks smirked as we walked up to my front door.

"Like I told you, I'm not looking. But no, Blocks. No special man in my life."

And really, that was only half a lie.

I COULDN'T IMAGINE myself ever getting married. Not to a man like Tom Buchanan who'd be arrogant enough to wrap pearls around my neck worth the price of a small city. And certainly not to a man who called himself Blocks and fainted from heat in the middle of a church aisle.

Blocks, as it turned out, sold boxes. He was a traveling salesman, he told me and Daddy the following morning over breakfast, and he'd been in Tom's class at Yale. He'd been *president* of Tom's class at Yale, which made Daddy smile and compliment him on how important it was to be *a good leader.*

"Who do you sell boxes to?" Daddy asked him. The answer was everyone. Lots of people needed boxes now that the war was over and shipping had picked up all around the country. I personally could not imagine a business more dull.

But Daddy was so enamored that he invited Blocks to stay with us for a few weeks while he "recovered from his fainting spell."

"Get to know Louisville," Daddy said. "Jordan'll show you around."

Blocks eagerly agreed, and I pushed away my grits, suddenly not very hungry for breakfast at all. I'd taken a month away from the golf tour, planning to rejoin them again mid-July. I hadn't imagined the time away would hurt me too much since all our matches this past year had been postponed till next year due to the influenza scares. My time off now was partly for Daisy's wedding but mostly to spend some time with Daddy, whose breath rattled heavy in his chest every time he took the stairs, and whose face had turned a worrisome shade of gray. The month away had seemed like more than a good idea when I'd left Charleston, but now that I was about to be stuck with Blocks, it felt like a mistake.

I spent the next few days taking Blocks around the city, and the man wouldn't shut up the whole damn time. Worse, he kept trying to hold my hand, and I kept on having to gently push him away and remind him I wasn't looking for a beau. *Yet*, he'd said several times, with a wink.

When I finally couldn't stand acting polite one moment longer, I took him to the golf club, told him I needed some practice and he could watch or hit balls, too, if he was so inclined. He said he'd watch and also insisted he wanted to buy me a gift there, as a *thank-you* for my hospitality. I didn't want him to be buying me gifts, but I'd been wanting a nice new aluminum putter, so I didn't say no.

"Your swing is mighty impressive, Jordan," he said after he'd watched me drive the balls, one after another, for almost an hour. My shoulders were sore. How quickly I'd fallen out of shape being back in Louisville.

I walked over to the putting green without responding to his compliment, and Blocks trailed along after me. I gave the new aluminum putter a whirl, relishing the cold weight of it in my hands.

"But you'll give this all up soon." Blocks was still talking. "Get married, have a family, won't you?" he asked.

"Oh, for heaven's sake, no. Why would I give this up?" I swung around so quickly, I narrowly missed hitting him with the putter.

He jumped back and laughed a little. "You might scare off a lot of men, Jordan Baker. But personally, I like a powerful woman."

"Oh, Blocks." I sighed. And I wasn't sure what else I could possibly say to the man and still maintain politeness. So I said nothing else at all. I shook my head, laughed him off, and turned my attention back to the golf ball.

"GOODNESS, THIS MAN is so annoying," I whispered one evening on the telephone to Mary Margaret, exactly three weeks after Daisy's wedding. "Blocks Biloxi who sells boxes, and to hear Daddy tell it you would've thought he knows how to spin straw into gold."

She laughed in response, that deep-throated, husky laugh. It made me miss her desperately. And I felt a sudden surge of homesickness for my life in Charleston, for our little dorm room where we'd spent hours whispering after lights-out. It was funny how I'd longed for Louisville for so long, but now that Mary Margaret was in Charleston and I was here, Louisville didn't really feel much like home to me any longer. Hearing her laughter now filled me with a simultaneous rush of happiness and sadness. I imagined her sitting in the hallway of our dorm, at the telephone, twirling a lock of her brown hair around her finger, pursing her pretty pink lips together as she talked. And I longed to be there right next to her.

At least I'd made Daddy install a telephone when I left for the tour last year, even though he'd complained it was really too expensive and he didn't need one. It had allowed me to keep closer contact with him this past year, and now it was connecting me to Mary Margaret.

"Jordan, it's so boring here without you," she complained. "How about you cut your trip short and come back tomorrow?"

I sighed. "It's only one more week, Ems." She made a little bird noise on the other end of the line when I called her *Ems*. The nickname only I had for her. "And Daddy really doesn't look well. He worries me."

"But Daddy has Blocks to keep him company, doesn't he?" I

could tell from her tone she was teasing but I grimaced in response. "And I hear he's just *absolutely delightful.*" She laughed again.

At the sound of her laughter, resonating all these miles across the line, I felt the tension ease in my shoulders a little and then I laughed too. What a ridiculous predicament I'd gotten myself into, all by being a good maid of honor.

We hung up a few minutes later, but I was still smiling as I walked downstairs for supper.

LATER THAT NIGHT, I was half asleep when I heard a knock on my bedroom door. I sat up, worried Daddy was having a bad spell. "Daddy?" I called out. "Is everything all right?"

The door opened, but it wasn't Daddy at all. Blocks walked into my room, shutting the door behind him, and dare I say, the man was almost completely naked, save his underlinen. "Blocks!" I whisper-yelled at him and turned my head away, covering my eyes loosely with my fingers. "What are you doing? Get out of here."

"Jordan," he said, ignoring me, walking closer to my bed. "You've been flirting with me for weeks. Playing hard to get."

Laughter erupted from deep inside of me. I couldn't stop it. It took me a moment to catch my breath, to realize he was being completely serious. "Oh, Blocks, I'm not *playing hard to get.*" I'd told him honestly from the get-go I wasn't looking for a beau, and all my conversation confirmed that. I'd been polite, nothing flirtatious about it in the least. Was this about the putter?

He was next to my bed now, and he reached for my hand, pulling it roughly to his nether region, forcing my fingertips to graze the bulge beneath his underlinen. I tried to yank it away, but he held tight. "Jordan, come on," he pleaded. "Don't be shy."

I was sure as hell not shy. And I was also fast, with better hand-eye coordination than almost any man, and certainly better than a goddamned box salesman. I slithered out of his grasp. He tried to grab for my hand again, but I dodged him.

I scrambled out of my bed and grabbed the first thing that caught my eye: the aluminum putter he'd given me. I wielded it above my head like a weapon now. "Get out," I said. He stood there frozen, but he didn't move. "Get out!" I shouted now, raising my voice so loud I probably woke my dear dead mama across town in the cemetery.

He stared at the putter, and then his face turned, like only in this exact moment did he understand I truly hadn't been interested in him all along. He scrunched up his big blocky cheeks, and I almost felt bad for a second. But then without another word, he turned and scurried out of my room like a rat. As my door opened again, I caught the shadow of Daddy, lurking in the hallway.

I threw the putter aside, got back into bed, and buried my head in my pillows, mortified at what Daddy had heard. What he must think seeing Blocks run out of my room half naked. I couldn't hear what Daddy said to Blocks, but he said something—both their voices were muffled through my pillows. Then footsteps on the stairs, and not even a few minutes later, the front door slamming shut.

"Jordan?" Daddy's voice came softly from the hallway, and I reluctantly took my face from the pillows. He walked slowly into my room. His gait was uneven, and I could hear his breath rattling in his chest as he sat down on the edge of my bed.

"I'm sorry I woke you, Daddy." I burned hot with a sudden rush of embarrassment, worried that Daddy might actually think I'd invited Blocks into my bedroom. "I didn't ask him to come in here like that," I added.

He nodded. "No . . . I'm sorry." His words escaped slowly, breathlessly. "I should never have invited that man to stay with us."

I sat up and gave Daddy a tight hug. "You were just being the kindhearted man you've always been," I told him.

"I just thought . . . I just thought . . ." Daddy's voice trailed off for a second. "He seemed like a nice enough young man at first. Daisy just got married. Maybe it's your turn soon, too, Jordan? Otherwise, who'll take care of you when I'm gone?"

For so many years Daddy had told me to focus on golf, and I had. But it seemed like there was something in him now that knew he might not be around much longer, that was driving him to act a little desperate. "Daddy, I don't need a man to take care of me," I reminded him. "That's why you and I worked so hard to make sure I could make my own living with golf."

"But," Daddy pushed further, "wouldn't it be nice to find a good man who would make you happy?"

"Oh, Daddy," I said, and now I felt a little breathless. My heart pounded so hard and so fast in my chest that I swore Daddy could feel and hear it too. I remembered what Daisy had said once, you could be *good* or you could be *happy*, but maybe you couldn't be both. "I don't think that will ever make me happy," I finally said, my voice coming out husky, the words catching on the way out. I inhaled sharply, wanting to say more but stopping myself just short.

Daddy's face was so close to mine now, and we stared at each other. Something honest but still-unspoken passed between our eyes in a quick flash, before Daddy looked away first. He patted my hand gently. "It's late," he said. "Get some rest. Everything will look different in the morning."

AND DADDY WAS right about that. The next morning, Blocks was gone; his things had completely disappeared. Daddy didn't come downstairs for breakfast either. The dining room was so quiet you could've heard a golf ball slice the air. And I ate my grits in peace.

But when Daddy still hadn't come downstairs by ten o'clock, I walked up to check on him. The door to his room was closed, and I knocked and called out for him. He didn't answer, and I closed my eyes for a second, remembering that moment between us last night. The way he had looked at me, like he knew what I was trying to say, that maybe he'd always known. And maybe that was why he'd been so keen on Blocks in the first place.

"Daddy," I tried again. Still nothing.

Finally, I opened his bedroom door, walked inside. Daddy lay in his bed perfectly still. I stared at him, but his chest didn't appear to be rising and falling. His eyes were closed, and his face was a preternatural shade of gray.

Oh, Daddy. *No.*

I ran to his bed, fell to my knees, and grabbed his hand. But it was limp, cold. Lifeless.

Daisy

THERE WAS A RADIANT SORT OF BLISS THAT SETTLED OVER ME IN the weeks after my wedding. It came on immediately in Tahiti, a place with the bluest shade of water and whitest pearls of beach I'd ever seen. Every day, it was me, and it was Tom, and it was sun, and the sand and the water. We languished in a straw hut with sheer curtains for walls, lying naked in our giant round bed, listening to the sounds of the sea. My face glowed pink from the heat and from the happiness, and from the feel of Tom's hands strumming lazily across my bare skin.

I thought about what Jay had written. That Tom would never make me feel the way that he had. But he was wrong. Every single nerve in my body felt alive on my honeymoon. Tom and I were together every day, every night. His skin felt like my skin; his body was my body, too. I woke up in the morning and there was no such thing as worry. Or sadness. There was nothing in the world at all but my dear, sweet, delicious Tom.

By the time we got to Oahu, six weeks after the wedding, we remembered how to put our clothes on, and one early morning we left our suite at dawn and took a walk through Kapiolani Park.

We clung to each other, strolling along the long grassy slope in between towering palm trees. I could still feel the breeze of the ocean, even though I'd lost sight of it for a moment, and my skin felt damp, my hair stuck to my cheeks. Had I checked a mirror I might have been horrified by what I saw, and yet, I felt the prettiest I'd ever felt in my entire life.

"They used to play cricket in this park," Tom said as we walked through the grass barefoot. "Father had a friend from Yale who moved to San Fran after college. Used to invite him here every May for a rousing cricket match."

"Cricket? That's like polo without the horses?" I asked.

"Oh, no. Not at all. I have so much to teach you still." Tom laughed, and pulled me to him, kissing the top of my head fiercely.

Tom had offered to let me ride his ponies when we were dating, but the one time I actually mounted a horse, I'd been much too high off the ground and had immediately panicked and begged Tom to help me down. Never mind the idea of actually batting around a ball, or, whatever it was Tom did when he played polo. *It's not a sport for a lady*, as Mother would say. Not that I'd let that stop me if I truly wanted to learn.

"Ahh, well. Cricket. Polo. What does it matter? The park is empty now." I pulled out of Tom's grasp, held my arms out to my sides, and twirled around in the grass enough times I started to get dizzy.

Tom ran to catch up with me, grabbed me, and kissed me hard, openmouthed in that intense way he always did that made my face burn instantly hot. "You're right," he said, pulling back a little. "The park *is* empty. Whatever could we do here?" His dusky eyes caught the sunlight and practically seemed to sparkle with mischief.

"Tom." I swatted his arm lightly. "You're positively wicked."

He pressed his body against my body, and I could feel every inch of his torso through the thin linen of his clothes. He had sinewy thighs, strong from riding, and when he pressed them against me now, I gasped a little. "Daisy," he whispered my name, like it was sinful, and moved my hand to the waistband of his pants, pushing my fingers down.

"Tom, really." I laughed and inched my hand up, resting it across the hard muscles of his stomach.

"You think I'm joking?" he whispered, catching the bottom of my earlobe gently with his tongue, then his teeth. "Look around, we're the only ones here. And I can't wait until we get back to the hotel."

I looked around again, and he was right. Kapiolani Park was still empty, except for us. It was very early in the morning. Everyone else in Oahu was just waking up, eating breakfast, or heading to the beach. Tom moved my fingers back to his waistband.

Mother's snow goose voice popped into my head. *Daisy Fay! Behave like a lady!* But then I heard Mrs. Buchanan, too, at the atelier. I felt a giggle of embarrassment rising in my throat at that thought; certainly she didn't mean anything like this. But I felt that red-hot power all the same. I was Tom's wife. I was no longer Daisy Fay of the Louisville, Kentucky, Fays. I was Daisy Buchanan, in the midst of an extended and lavish honeymoon in the South Seas. I could do as I pleased, when and where I pleased.

"Not here. Not so out in the open," I whispered, feeling illicit, even though there was no one around to hear me but Tom.

I took his hand and ran across the grass pulling him behind me. And then behind the shade of a towering palm tree I was warm and breathless. Tom swooped down and kissed me hard on the mouth again. I pulled back a little, moved my hands to his waistband, tugged his pants down. I smiled at him. And then, I held his gaze as I fell to my knees in front of him.

"Daisy." He closed his eyes and whispered my name, grasping a fistful of my hair in his hand. "Daisy, Daisy, Daisy."

Jordan

DADDY HAUNTED ME.

Back on the golf tour, I awoke in the middle of the night, and Daddy was my ghost. That image of his face came to me in my dreams, again and again and again. Not his gray face. Not that terrible dead gray face. *No.* That other face. The one I'd seen in my room the night before he died, when our eyes had met for one honest moment right after I'd told Daddy something I never should've said out loud. What *was* that face? Shame? Disappointment? Regret?

"Jordan." Mary Margaret's voice came for me through the darkness now. I heard her climb down from her bed and felt my mattress sink as she sat at the edge of mine. She reached her hand to my hair and smoothed it back a little, her fingers tracing a line behind my ear. "You were crying in your sleep, sweetie."

I reached up to touch my face, and she was right, my cheeks were wet. "Oh, Ems. I'm so sorry. Did I wake you again?" It was the third night this week Daddy had come to me and driven me to tears loud enough to get Mary Margaret up too. I was officially the world's most terrible roommate.

"It's almost time to get up anyway," Mary Margaret said. She lay down next to me, yawning, stretching out her legs. She rolled onto her side and wrapped her arm around my waist. "Almost," she repeated, sleepily.

I'd only been back on the tour for two weeks, and the adjustment had been hard. I'd thought the routine would be good after losing Daddy. And, besides, I didn't know what else to do with myself in Louisville after his funeral. Daddy's older sister, Aunt Sigourney, had come to town and would handle all the remaining details of selling the house and wrapping up Daddy's financial affairs. She insisted that Daddy wouldn't want me to let the golf tour down, that I had to return to my life. I knew she was right. But still, being back here, it had felt day by day like an uphill battle. I was exhausted and breathlessly overwhelmed. Not playing very good golf at the moment either. Mr. Hennessey was coming to watch next week and choose who would get to compete in the California practice tournaments in August, our first in over a year. And only four of us would be chosen. If I wanted to be one of the four, I had to get my act together.

Mary Margaret's breathing evened now; she'd fallen back asleep. Her body was warm against mine, and I curled into her, feeling comfort in having her so close. I had to get my focus back, my golf game back. Lying with her, feeling the rhythm of her breath against my back, I exhaled for a moment, and I closed my eyes. Daddy's face was gone, his ghost disappeared. I fell into a warm and dreamless sleep.

"ALL RIGHT," MARY Margaret said to me later that day, over lunch. "We need a plan." The two of us had taken our ham sandwiches to eat outside under the big chestnut tree in front of our dormitory. It was too warm and muggy, and even the shade of the tree didn't help cool us off much. But in spite of the thick July heat, I preferred sitting out here with her alone over sitting at the table inside the cafeteria with the rest of the girls. Besides, at least the air moved a little out here. Inside it was stifling. And here we could talk in peace.

"What kind of plan do we need, Ems?" I asked now, taking a bite of my ham. I was sweaty and famished after a long morning at the driving range. My shoulders ached, even from a motion as simple as lifting my sandwich to my mouth.

"You and I both need to get picked to go to California. Jerralyn thinks she has this in the bag since she's from there." Mary Margaret rolled her eyes, and I laughed a little. "I know I was just the team alternate. But I want to beat her. I've never seen the Pacific Ocean, and wouldn't you and I have a grand time together?"

I finished off my sandwich in one large bite, wiped my hands with the linen napkin I'd stolen from the cafeteria, and smiled at her. "At this point, you're gonna get picked to go over me. My game hasn't been, shall I say, up to par, since I got back."

Mary Margaret laughed at my pun; then her face grew completely serious. "Extra practice!" Mary Margaret exclaimed. "That's what we need, Jordan."

"Extra? How exactly will we do that?" We already practiced most of the day and had such a strict schedule there was barely time to brush our teeth in the common bathroom at night before lights-out. And Mrs. Pearce hardly let us walk out here to eat our lunch alone, much less go off on our own to do, well, anything.

Mary Margaret looked at me, her normally green eyes a crisp, almost cerulean color in this bright midday sun. "We'll sneak out tonight after lights-out. And play ourselves a round of night golf."

"Night golf?" I shook my head. It barely made sense. How would we see?

"It's how Charlie taught me to play back home. Girls weren't allowed on the course near us in Nashville, you know. So he'd sneak me on at night. I learned to play in the dark, with only a lantern and the moon. Charlie used to say that distance on the course was a thing you *felt*, not saw."

Mary Margaret's older brother, Charlie, hadn't come back from the war alive, and every once in a while she'd have a funny story about him that she'd tell me seemingly out of nowhere.

Grief, she told me once when she was talking about Charlie, *was forever. An endless, winding river.*

But I never really understood what she meant until now.

LATER THAT NIGHT I tried to suppress a nervous giggle as we ran out behind the dormitory toward the course. We waited an hour after lights-out, hoping Mrs. Pearce would already be fast asleep, and we'd tiptoed down the stairs, not daring to make a sound. Once we got outside, the sky was clear, the moon full and bright, illuminating the first tee box up ahead. But the ground was dark, and it was hard to see where we were stepping.

"Are there snakes in South Carolina?" I whispered, suddenly remembering a time as a little girl when Daddy had taken me camping and I'd nearly stepped on a rattler walking back to our tent at night. Rattlers were prone to sneak up on you like that in the summer in Kentucky, Daddy told me.

"Sure," Mary Margaret said. "I suppose there are . . . rattlers and cottonmouths and . . ." She gently swiped my ankle with the toe of her shoe, and I nearly jumped ten feet in the air and had to stifle a scream. She covered her mouth to keep her giggles from erupting too loudly.

"You . . . you . . . harlot," I whisper-yelled at her.

"That's not very nice. You hurt my feelings." But she laughed, not at all serious. "And, besides, you're with me every second of every day. You know I am most certainly not a *harlot.*"

We'd reached the course by then, far enough away from the dormitory for anyone to see or hear us, and we stood at the first tee box and both erupted into a wild fit of giggles. I was laughing so hard I could barely breathe, and then almost inexplicably my laugher turned into big gulping sobs.

"Oh, sweetie." Mary Margaret rubbed my back gently. "Just let it all out now."

Maybe she was right, that I had to let it out. I hadn't been able to cry at the funeral because nothing around me had felt quite real then. The casket had been closed, and in my mind it hadn't felt like Daddy inside at all. The only tears I'd had since Daddy's death were the ones that came to me in the middle of the night in fits of dreams. But now, here, in the dark, out on the golf course with Mary Margaret, I just couldn't stop the tears.

It hit me. It really hit me. Daddy was gone forever, and Daisy was married now. I only vaguely knew Aunt Sigourney from a few visits to see her in New York City when I was younger, back when Daddy was still in prime health. "I have no one," I choked out through my tears. "I'm all alone."

"Stop it." Mary Margaret's voice was soft, but stern. She stood in front of me and held my shoulders in her hands. "Stop it right now, Jordan Baker. You are not all alone. I'm right here. You have me."

I looked up at her, and my tears stopped as suddenly as they'd come on, like a late July thunderstorm. Mary Margaret's face was close to mine now. The full moon illuminated all her features, her tiny button nose, and her sweet plump cheeks. She opened her mouth a little to say something more, then closed it again. Her lips were mere inches from mine. And I suddenly had the strangest thought. All I had to do was take one step closer. One more step, and our lips would touch.

My eyes met her eyes, and it was like she was thinking what I was, feeling what I was. She moved her hand from my shoulder, traced her thumb across my cheekbone, gently wiping away one last tear.

"We should play night golf," she whispered, her breath hitting my lips as she spoke. But neither one of us moved.

"I . . . I've never done this before," I said.

Her thumb moved from my cheek down slowly, until she touched my top lip softly. And I knew she understood I wasn't really talking about the night golf. Her touch made it feel like she was giving me permission.

A few inches more. One more tiny step.

I couldn't stop myself. I didn't want to stop myself.

I took that step. And I touched my lips to her lips, slowly, softly.

Daisy

"DAISE!" JORDAN PRACTICALLY SCREAMED MY NAME AND GRABBED me in a big fat hug when she saw me standing out in front of the restaurant.

It was the end of August, and Tom and I had extended our honeymoon by stopping in Santa Barbara for a stay at the Santa Barbara Hotel on our way back east from Hawaii. Jordan had written me a few weeks ago, said she'd be out here for a practice tournament. And Tom said he knew of a good polo game he could join. After two months away, he was aching to go back to his ponies. I was aching for Jordan.

I clung to Jordan now, breathing in the warm familiar lilac scent of her. They were apparently under very strict rules in the golf tournament, practice, practice, practice hitting balls, or whatever it was they did all day. But Jordan had managed to sneak away to meet me this afternoon for lunch.

"Where's Tom?" Jordan asked, pulling back a little, looking around.

Tom was supposed to come along for lunch, too, but then he'd gotten them to make him a mint julep at the hotel and had just settled into a chair with his drink and the papers as I was ready to leave. He claimed he was too comfortable to get up. *You girls should catch up without me anyway*, he'd said, and I'd laughed at the careless way he referred to me and Jordan as *girls*. But the truth was, Santa Barbara wasn't the South Seas, and Tom and I had begun to spend time apart here. He'd already been off with his ponies all morning, and I was a little disappointed that he'd chosen to stay behind for lunch, too.

"Oh, I thought it was better if it was just us," I lied to Jordan now. I wasn't sure why I lied, even as the words came out of my mouth. But I couldn't stop them.

"Oh, Daise." She enveloped me in another hug. "I've missed you so."

Jordan looked and felt and smelled as she always had—small and trim with her short fashionable hair. But when I took a step back and examined her face, she had new lines around her eyes. Worry? Sadness? Maybe Tom was right. It would be better for us to be alone so we could really catch up.

"I'm so sorry about your daddy," I said, taking her hand as we walked inside and were led by the maître d' to our lunch table. It was up a flight of stairs, and outside on the rooftop, overlooking the ocean. He pulled out our chairs and handed us menus—Tom had told me to order a feast and put it on his tab—but I wasn't even hungry for food, and I put my menu down on the table without looking as soon as the maître d' walked away. I was hungry for my Jordie, for her stories, and her laughter and companionship.

"Daddy hadn't been well for so long," Jordan was saying now, fiddling with her linen napkin in her lap. Then she turned, stared off at the ocean for a moment, and sighed. The wind blew, and I shivered. In front of me the water was bright blue but, I'd learned when I'd dipped my toes in yesterday, shockingly cold. It felt impossible it was the very same Pacific we'd waded through in Tahiti. "Of course that doesn't make things any easier, does it?" Jordan was saying now. "He's gone now forever. And it's really hard, Daise."

I reached across the table and patted her hand. "I'm sorry, Jordie. It is hard. I know."

"I know you do." She offered me a half smile, squeezed my hand. She cleared her throat. "Let's talk about happier things, all right? Tell me, Daise. How's married life? Divine? Your cheeks are so pink you're positively glowing."

I reached my hand up to touch my face and wondered if my cheeks really were glowing or still had residual sunburn from Hawaii. "It's so blissful, Jordie. I wake up in the morning and wonder if I'm in a dream. I'm not in a dream, am I?" I held out my arm. "Pinch me." Jordan obliged and reached across the table and pinched the flesh on my forearm. "Ow!" I exclaimed.

"Nope, not dreaming," she clucked, amused.

I rubbed my arm a little and reached across the table to swat her hand lightly, but I was happy to see her smiling again. Everything was different now than it once was when we were girls in Louisville, but no matter, she was still the same old Jordie and I was still the same old Daisy. And when we were together, all felt right with the world again. I let out a happy sigh. "And what about you?" I asked her. "How's the golf tour?" She smiled, and her own cheeks brightened up.

"Well, I've been winning this week," she said. "If that's what you're asking. And only four of us girls were chosen to come out and compete in this practice tournament and I was one of them."

"That's marvelous," I said, having no idea what went into being chosen, and not really interested in those details either. All that really mattered was that she was here, sitting across from me. I didn't care about *how* she'd gotten here. How many balls she'd gotten in the holes or whatever it was she did exactly playing golf. "So then you're happy on the tour?" I asked.

"Sure," she said rather brusquely. "I mean, I suppose I am? My roommate, Mary Margaret, is a doll. You'd love her, Daise. I really wanted her to get picked for this tournament, too, so you could meet her. But . . ." She frowned. "That didn't happen."

"Well, I'm glad you've made a friend." My words came out terser than I'd meant them to, and I felt a little pinch of jealousy in my chest. I was glad Jordan had a friend, of course. I wanted her to be happy. But we had always been best friends, and I didn't relish the idea of this *Mary Margaret* taking my place. "But clearly, she's not nearly as talented as you."

"Oh, stop, Daise." Jordan waved away my compliment.

"Well, I'm certain it's true," I said. "Jordan Baker, you are the most talented girl on that tour."

Jordan blushed. "The truth is, it's all so political. There's another girl, Jerralyn, who's from Santa Barbara, and she practically demanded that they take her, even though Mary Margaret scored better in our round robin. But Jerralyn's daddy's business sponsors this tournament." Jordan rolled her eyes. "It's really not fair to Mary Margaret." She sounded so pouty now, and I felt this untoward jealousy boiling up inside of me. It wasn't that I wanted Jordan to be lonely; I just didn't want her to have a friend she liked better than me.

"Well, political or not," I said, "they chose you, because your talent is just that overwhelming, Jordie. I'm proud of you and I know your daddy would be proud too."

"Thanks, Daise," she said, with a half smile.

Out of the corner of my eye I caught the waiter staring at us, and I waved him over.

"What can I get for you, Mrs. Buchanan?" he asked. I still loved the way that sounded. *Mrs. Buchanan.* Crisp and delicious and erupting with power.

"Bring us one of everything," I said casually, handing him back the menu I'd barely glanced at.

"Certainly, Mrs. Buchanan." He took our menus and walked away.

Jordan stared at me, her gray eyes wider than I'd ever seen them. "Daise, *one of everything?* That's much too much food. I couldn't possibly. I have to play a round this afternoon."

I had this sudden flash of Rose, her victory garden, her fretting about going out to feed the poor on the hottest day of summer. But the war was over.

One of everything. It was the way Tom had been ordering for us our whole honeymoon, and it was funny how quickly I'd forgotten that, in itself, was out of the ordinary. Two months later, here I was, a full-fledged Buchanan. I shrugged a little. But Jordan still had her eyebrows raised sky-high. "It's what Tom likes to do," I said apologetically, feeling my cheeks brighten further. "And he wanted me to bring him some food back anyway. We'll eat the rest for dinner."

Jordan laughed and shook her head. "*One of everything,*" she repeated, sounding more amused now than astounded. "Well, look at you, *Daisy Buchanan.*" She whistled lightly. "Look at you."

JORDAN AND I only ate a few bites, and the restaurant sent all the boxed-up food back to our suite. We made plans to meet again, later in the week, at the beach, with Tom, too. But I hated saying good-bye to her, and I took a long walk by the ocean on the way back to the hotel in an attempt to soothe my nerves.

A few hours later, I found Tom in our suite, and that brightened my spirits again. I gave him an eager kiss and told him about all the food I'd sent back for dinner. "We can eat in bed." I laughed, pulling him toward me.

"I can't, Daisy," Tom said brusquely. "I made plans to go meet some of the fellows for a drink and a bite to eat." *The fellows?* His polo friends.

"You're leaving me." I pouted. "But I haven't seen you all day. I miss you, darling." I reached for the waistband of his pants, hoping to change his mind.

He pushed my hands away. "You met a friend for lunch, Daisy," he said, rather petulantly. "I can go meet friends too."

I supposed he was right, but that didn't make me feel any less sulky. And I'd wanted him to have lunch with me and Jordan. "All right." I sighed. "If you must."

"I must," he said. He leaned down, gave me a quick peck on the lips. And then, just like that, he left.

I got into my nightgown and ate some of the leftovers myself and thought about Jordan. She was staying somewhere across the city with her golf tour, but we were going to meet at the beach on Sunday, her day off, before she went back to Charleston. I thought about calling her now, telling her to come over to the Santa Barbara Hotel and help me finish off these leftovers. But this wasn't Louisville, and no matter what Tom called us, we were no longer girls. Jordan had a whole entire life and golf career that didn't even include me. This made me feel even more sulky.

I got into bed and flipped through the issues of all the latest magazines I'd asked the concierge to drop off in our suite. Halfway through *Harper's Bazaar*, I glanced at the clock—it was almost ten. I started to worry. How many mint juleps was Tom planning on having? An hour passed, and then another. I flipped through the magazines enough times the pages started to wear, and the ink left stains on my fingers.

I finally heard his key in the door, just past midnight, and I pulled the lamp and lay in bed, silent, unmoving. I heard him stumble in, bumping into a chair, cursing softly. I could smell bourbon from across the room.

I felt his body hit the mattress next to me, and the bourbon smell was so strong, I swallowed back a swell of nausea. Then I heard the almost immediate soft sound of his snore.

But I couldn't sleep. I tossed and turned for hours.

A WEEK LATER, I'd almost forgotten all about that sleepless night. Tom and I had settled into a new routine in Santa Barbara—time apart and time together, too. I went to watch Jordie golf, and he went to play with his ponies. We both met Jordan at the beach on Sunday, and the afternoon sun had bathed me with an overwhelming feeling of bliss. I imagined this would be the way much of our real married lives would stretch on out from here.

We'd spent all yesterday afternoon much the way we'd spent our time in the South Seas, naked and restless and clinging to each other. I'd fallen into a deep and dreamless sleep last night, and then when I'd awoken this morning I felt that glow of happiness again, even though Tom had already left for polo practice and I was in our suite all alone.

I put on my robe and called down for breakfast. While I waited, I opened the shutters, and smiled at the blue glow of the water in the distance.

Breakfast arrived and I took the tray in bed and started with my coffee. The smell of it assaulted my nose as I picked up my cup, and when I took a sip it tasted absolutely vile. I nearly spit it back into the cup. But I swallowed, like a lady, feeling nausea rise up in my chest. I went to reach for the telephone to call down and complain. But just as my hand touched it, it began to ring. The sound surprised me, and I jumped.

"Mrs. Buchanan?" A slightly familiar man's voice on the line. "This is Mr. Hapford, the hotel manager."

"Yes," I said. "I was just about to call down, about the coffee—"

"Mrs. Buchanan," he cut me off. "I'm afraid there's been an accident."

"An accident?" I repeated his words, suddenly breathless. *An accident.* I thought of Rose and Daddy, and the train. Jordan had left on a train yesterday. My mouth felt dry, my tongue too thick. It felt impossibly hard to swallow.

"Everyone's all right. It's just . . . Mr. Buchanan and Miss Wilde had a small bang-up in the car. They were taken to the hospital and Mr. Buchanan has a little bump on the head, that's all. But Miss Wilde broke her arm."

"Miss Wilde?" I repeated back the unfamiliar name, confused. Why was Tom driving to polo when it was close enough to walk? And I was certain I would have heard of a woman polo player. "There must be some mistake."

Mr. Hapford didn't say anything for a moment, but I heard him still breathing on the line. Finally, he said, "Mrs. Buchanan, I'm very sorry, but there isn't any mistake. Miss Wilde is one of our chambermaids, and I saw them walk out to the car together myself." He paused. And I tried to comprehend all the words he was saying that still didn't make sense. *Chambermaid. Tom. Walking out*

together, to a car? "We were hoping to keep this out of the papers."
Mr. Hapford was still talking. "But a reporter from the *Dispatch*
has already called me asking for a quote. So I thought I'd better call
up and let you hear about it from me, first." His voice sounded more
timid now, apologetic even.

"I don't understand," I murmured, still trying to make sense
of it. "Why was Tom . . . with the chambermaid?" But even as
those words escaped my lips I suddenly understood their meaning
perfectly.

I inhaled sharply and hung up on Mr. Hapford without even a
good-bye. I wasn't trying to be rude, but bile rose in my throat so
fast and I knew I was going to vomit.

I ran to the toilet and made it just in time, retching into the
bowl. I sat on the cool tile floor and rested my head against the
porcelain, too listless to move for a long while.

Detective Frank Charles

THE MCCOYS' FARM IN ROCKVALE WAS A WHOLE DIFFERENT KIND of sprawling than the Buchanan estate in Minneapolis. Grazing pastures as far as Frank's eyes could see, expansive enough to swallow the tiny redbrick farmhouse that sat off to the side, down a long dirt road.

He'd checked in with Dolores before he'd left Minnesota three days ago, and she said she was getting along just fine in Brooklyn without him. He hated extending his trip, but it felt worse for him to have come all this way for nothing. Rockvale wasn't too far out of the way home, and interviewing Daisy in person had given him nothing but more questions and a pressure ache just above his eyes. He didn't know if he'd get much more from Catherine McCoy, either, but he'd come this far. He had to at least try.

He'd gotten a taxi at the train station and had it drop him off at the end of the dirt road, figuring the fresh farm air might clear his head. But as he walked down the road now, he realized it was longer than he'd thought. The air was warmer here than in Minnesota, the summer humidity hanging on, even though it was the middle of September. By the time he reached the farmhouse, he had to take his handkerchief out of his jacket pocket and dab the sweat from his forehead.

"You?" Catherine's voice came through the screen, before he even reached up his hand to knock. Behind her a small dog barked. "Duke, hush," she said, turning to the dog. But Duke kept at it.

He folded his handkerchief and put it away, wondering if she'd been watching him walk up the long winding dirt road, seething. She didn't sound very happy to see him. People often weren't. It was all part of the job, albeit a part he'd never quite gotten used to.

"What are you doing here?" Her voice trembled a little, breaking on the word *here*. Maybe she wasn't seething. Maybe she was afraid. The dog yapped still.

"I was in the area and wanted to pay my respects," he said, shouting to be heard over the dog. The coroner had approved the request for transport of her sister's body just before Frank had left the city, and he knew the family planned to bury Myrtle out here in the family plot.

Catherine sighed a little, picked up the dog, walked him away, presumably to another room, because his barking suddenly got muted. Then she came back and opened the door.

She looked different than she had in New York last month. Her red hair was pulled back tightly against the nape of her neck, her face was pale, the freckles across her nose somehow appeared more prominent. Instead of the fashionable dress and heels she'd been wearing the first time he'd met her at the morgue, now she was barefoot and whatever dress she was wearing was covered up by a stained, mustard-colored apron. She held a dish towel and wiped her hands. Then she stepped aside, gesturing for him to come into the house.

He walked inside, his eyes going over the small living spaces, the sparse wood furnishings, the framed photographs on a parlor table of two girls. Babies, kids, teenagers. He picked up one of what looked to be a young adult Myrtle and a teenage Catherine. They were standing in front of the farmhouse wearing matching gingham dresses, arms around each other.

"Our mother sewed those for us to wear to our cousin Lillian's wedding," Catherine said. "That photograph was taken the morning Myrtle left for New York. She said she wanted to go into her new life wearing her best dress. I put mine on to match. Father took that picture of us . . ." Her voice trailed off, caught up in the memory. She raised her finger to the glass, traced the outline of her sister.

"I really am very sorry for your loss," Frank said, and he meant it. He was.

She took the picture and set it back down on the table. Her eyes snapped up to him. "You didn't even know my sister, Detective. Why are you really here?"

He opened his mouth, considered telling her the truth, that he'd gone on a long and fruitless journey to talk to Daisy Buchanan in Minnesota, and when that had led him to nothing but more suspicion, he figured he might as well stop here, too, on the way back to New York. But instead he told her another truth. "I had a sister . . . once."

"Once?" Catherine asked softly, raising her eyebrows. "What happened to her?"

"She died. Nearly twenty-five years ago now."

"I'm very sorry," she murmured.

Nothing had shaped the course of his life more than that one single event, when he was just a boy of fourteen, and his older sister, Lizzie, was murdered. Lizzie had made him breakfast that January morning before they'd both left for school, and then he never saw her again. She turned up dead in a Brooklyn alley the next morning. Just like that. They never caught the guy who did it, and that thought still pained him so much, even to this day, that he barely ever let himself think about Lizzie now, except at Christmas and when he went to church to light a candle on her birthday every May. But Lizzie was why he'd devoted his entire adult life to investigating and solving murders.

Catherine's face softened and she motioned for him to come sit down in the small kitchen. He took a seat at the round oak table, and he hated himself a little for using Lizzie in this way, for invoking her memory simply to get Catherine to open up to him.

"How'd it happen?" Catherine asked him now.

"She was strangled," he said quietly.

Catherine shook her head. "That's terrible."

He nodded. He was leaving out so much, but he wasn't here to talk to Catherine about Lizzie. He kind of wished he hadn't brought her up at all. He started to sweat again, and Catherine stood to get him a glass of water. He thanked her and took a sip. "I was just a kid still, and her murder was never solved," he said, trying to bring the conversation back around. "But if I'd had someone to blame . . . say, if a rich guy had run her over . . . even at the age of fourteen, I would've killed the son of a bitch myself." It was a shocking thing to say out loud. Even more shocking to understand it was the God's honest truth.

Catherine sat across the table from him, closed her eyes for a moment, and exhaled. "So that's why you're here. I should've known you didn't really want to pay your respects." She shook her head. "Even if I was the murderer you think I am . . . aren't you out of your jurisdiction for arrests?"

"I'm not trying to make any arrests here. I just want to know the truth, that's all. Someone shot a man, point-blank, and from what I hear about your brother-in-law, I don't know if he was capable."

"Oh, George was very capable. He loved pistols, don't you know? Pistols and cars." Catherine's voice was caustic, dripping in bitterness. She balled her hands into fists and shook her head. "Myrtle deserved better," she said. "She deserved so much better."

He wasn't clear now whether she meant better than George, or better than what happened to her—her body being crushed out in the road, in the end. But all that was beside the point, and he didn't ask. He suddenly hated himself for coming here, for picking at her raw wound with more questions. Even if she had shot Gatsby, he might have deserved it.

Catherine stared at him. Her eyes were defiant, a piercing shade of green, the color of the grass in Central Park at the height of summer. "You're wasting your time coming all the way out here, Detective," she said. "I didn't kill Mr. Gatsby." But her voice shook a little, betraying her.

Frank pulled the diamond hairpin out of his pocket and laid it in front of them on the oak table, following her eyes, watching for her reaction. Her mouth formed into the shape of an O. She put her hand to her lips.

"You recognize this, don't you?" He kept his voice gentle, non-accusatory.

"I . . . I . . ." She picked it up, traced the diamonds with her fingers, and he couldn't help but notice how different her fingers looked than Daisy's—her nails were short, her fingers stained and calloused from farm work. She was the kind of woman, rough enough around the edges, that maybe, just maybe, she had it in her to pick up a gun, kill a fellow point-blank. Especially if she knew that fellow had killed her sister. But then, she wasn't the kind of woman who would own an expensive hairpin, was she? So why was she floundering now, looking at it like she was about to cry? "I don't recognize it," she finally said. She refused to meet his eyes again, and her fingers trembled as she held the pin.

She was lying. But he'd been sure Daisy was lying, too. He didn't understand why they both would be lying.

"What about Daisy Buchanan?" he tried. "You ever see her wear this hairpin?"

She shook her head. "I . . . I wouldn't know. I've never met Daisy Buchanan." Her voice faltered a little, her eyes still on the hairpin.

"But you know of her?" he asked.

Catherine didn't answer, and instead she trailed her fingers again slowly across the diamonds. "This looks like something a person with money would wear," she finally said. "Look around you, Detective. Do you think I own any diamonds?" Her voice had turned cool, almost smug.

He couldn't argue with her logic, so he shook his head and chose his words carefully. "Maybe it was a gift?" he said. He watched her as he spoke; her face turned instantly bloodless, making the freckles on her nose appear bolder, almost black. Like poppy seeds on a bagel. He was onto something.

He still didn't know exactly how or what had happened, but there must be more to Mr. Gatsby running over Myrtle and leaving her there, in the street. What if Catherine understood more than she was letting on? What if her grief was compounded in some way now by her own connection to the man? "Maybe . . . and I'm just spitballing here," he said, "but maybe Mr. Gatsby bought that for you?"

She laughed, but the laugh caught in her throat, coming out sounding more like a strangled cry. "That would be impossible." Her voice verged on defiance now, too, and the color slowly returned to her cheeks. She handed him back the hairpin. "Like I told you, Detective, I never even met Jay Gatsby."

Catherine

IT WAS FUNNY THE WAY A PLACE COULD LOOK EXACTLY THE SAME and be nothing at all like it once was. Though I supposed that same thing was true for people, too. When I looked in the mirror, I still appeared almost unerringly like that girl who'd stepped off the train from Rockvale into Grand Central three years ago: same cute strawberry hair, pink lips, powdered nose to hide those ridiculous, errant freckles.

But inside, I was nothing at all like her any longer. In Rockvale, I'd been a girl, wide-eyed at the possibility of the great big city and being a part of my sister's—what I once wrongly assumed to be—glamorous life. In New York, I'd become a fighter. A woman. I had a bona fide office job. I made my own money and paid my own rent, and I even saved a little to give to Myrtle so she could buy herself some small nice new things once in a while. And most importantly, I'd had a cause. For nearly three years my roommate, Helen, and I had spent our weekends gathering with the other suffragettes, plotting and protesting and pushing . . . and at long last, *winning*. Now the Nineteenth Amendment had been ratified. And Helen and I had been spending our weekends more recently fighting for a new kind of freedom. The freedom to just . . . be. Not someone's wife or someone's mother. But just two women, enjoying our lives out in the city. Of late, we'd been exploring speakeasies and drinking all the forbidden gin.

I was thinking about all this as I sat in the very same underground saloon where Myrtle and I had come right after I first arrived in New York, three years ago. I hadn't been back since. But even though the bar looked very much the same now as it had then—dark and crowded, and with the same tacky red stools off to the side—there were no soldiers all around me (at least not in uniform). And now the gin I held in my hand was most certainly illegal.

"My goodness, Catherine, you haven't changed a bit in these years, have you?" I turned at the sound of his voice, and I tried to recall what he'd looked like exactly when I'd met him here, once, briefly, three years ago. I remembered only the pale green soldier's uniform he wore, the Dear John letter in his hands that had devastated him. But I could not recall his face.

When he'd called me out of the blue, last week, I'd barely even remembered those details, until he'd reminded me of our brief encounter. *This is Jay Gatsby*, he'd said over the telephone. *You told me to look you up after the war.* I didn't say anything at first, and his voice sounded somewhat sheepish. *I thought maybe . . . you'd like to get a drink?*

His name rang a bell, and I did remember our meeting, a little. I had said that, hadn't I? That he should look me up, after the war. *Should we meet at the same saloon?* I'd finally asked him, breaking my silence on the other end of the line. *Do you remember it?*

He said a fellow never forgot the exact place his heart broke in two, and only then did I remember that telegram that he'd held in his hands that night.

I looked at him now. He was handsome, I would give him that. Tall with broad shoulders and clipped blond hair. His skin was sun-kissed, golden; the summer sun had been kind to him. "You look exactly the same too," I lied now, because I still didn't truly remember. So much had happened since then, and my goodness, he'd fought in a war and had returned right here, miraculously unscathed. "Exactly the same," I repeated, as if saying the words twice would make them truer.

He smiled. He had nice straight white teeth. "Let me get a drink," he said. "And I'll join you."

I nodded, sipped my gin rickey, and watched him walk away to order something. My throat burned a little and my face grew hot. Not from the gin but from this overwhelming sensation that maybe I'd made a mistake, that I shouldn't have come here. Shouldn't have accepted his invitation at all. When I went out, it was always with Helen, or the other women I knew from the office or from the cause. I didn't want a beau—I enjoyed my life, living it exactly as I saw fit. And now I grew worried that by accepting his invitation to meet tonight, I'd given him the wrong idea.

He was back in a few moments with what looked like a whiskey, and I bit my lip, held up my gin to clink glasses. We both took a sip and swiveled on our stools to face each other. "I have to be honest with you, Mr. Gatsby," I said firmly now.

He touched my arm gently. "Please, call me Jay." His voice was soft and kind, and I faltered for a second, took another sip of gin.

"Anyway, Jay," I continued, "it was nice of you to telephone me. I'm glad to see you're alive and well. But I'm not looking for any kind of relationship. Not dating. Certainly not marriage."

He laughed, a deep, hearty laugh, shook his head, and downed his whiskey in an impressively large gulp. "Well, that makes two of us," he said, placing his empty glass on the counter. "I should've made myself clear over the telephone. I'm just back in New York from a stint in Oxford after the war, and I don't know too many people here yet. I thought it might be nice to have someone to talk to while I had a drink. That's all."

"Oh." I let out a nervous laugh, not sure whether to feel embarrassed I'd said anything at all or annoyed that the thought of dating me hadn't crossed his mind. Mostly, I just felt relief, and a little warm and relaxed from the gin. I smoothed my hair behind my ears. "Well, all right," I said, smiling. "So shall we talk about something else now?"

"And have another drink?" he suggested, raising his arm to signal to the bartender we'd like two more.

"Talking and drinking," I said, finishing off my own glass.

Perfectly harmless.

I WOKE UP the next morning, sunlight streaming in through the tear in the middle of my blinds, assaulting my eyes. My head throbbed, and I groaned, remembering, slowly: the gin. How many gin rickeys had I had? One, two, three . . . had I had more than three? I couldn't remember after three. And . . . Jay Gatsby. He'd poured out all his heartache about his girl marrying some rich fellow while he was away. He'd drunk enough so his words were thick, slurry: *Daisybuchanan* coming out as one long drawn-out, sad word. I drank until I told him about Myrtle's bruises, my worries for her living out by the Corona ash dump with George, which was something I hadn't even told Helen up until now. What time had we stopped drinking and said good-bye? I couldn't quite remember that, either . . .

I suddenly felt a hand on the small of my back, and I startled.

Oh no. We hadn't said good-bye last night at all, had we?

His hand slid up my naked back now, tracing my spine. "Good morning," Jay whispered in my ear, his mouth close enough that I could feel his breath on my cheek, his thumb caressing my neck.

I sat up quickly and wrapped the sheet around my chest. I faced away from him, toward that annoying too-bright tear in the blind. *What had I done last night?*

I closed my eyes for a moment, breathed slowly in and out, tried to imagine the path we would've walked to stumble back to my apartment from the speakeasy, but I couldn't remember actually walking that path. In a flash I remembered warm, wet lips pressed hard against my neck. I reached my hand up now and the skin felt tender.

"Catherine," Jay said my name softly and sat up. He reached for my shoulders, rubbing them gently.

"Just drinking and talking, hmmm?" I said. I most certainly remembered that's what we'd agreed to, before we'd downed too much liquor and somehow ended up . . . here.

"Drinking and talking," Jay repeated. His hand traced back down my spine slowly and I shivered a little. He leaned his face in close to my hair, kissed the nape of my neck. "And this, too," he whispered. "It doesn't have to mean anything," he repeated. "We could just . . . get together from time to time."

"*Get together?*" I laughed a little. "Is that what people are calling it these days?"

"I enjoyed your company last night," he said, ignoring my sarcasm. "I've been alone for months now, and it's hard to be alone all the time."

His hand felt kind of nice on my back, and I almost understood what he was saying. What it was he wanted. That finding pleasure with another person was fine and even good, and maybe I wanted it too?

"All right," I finally said softly, which somehow felt like saying too much, and not enough, all at the same time. But then I added, "Do you mind leaving through the fire escape? I don't want to have to explain you to my roommate."

MYRTLE LIKED TO call me *Saint Catherine*, due to my very *dull* (her word) love life.

Oh to be young and single in the city, she would say, her voice exuding the kind of longing that came with being married to a man you didn't quite love for so many years. That came with wondering how other men might treat her better or believing that, at the very least, I should be able to find one of those so-called *good* men and she could live vicariously through me. She looked at me and saw so much wasted possibility. I looked at her and saw what I never wanted to become: a woman who was trapped.

But Myrtle was wrong. I was no *saint*. I was never a saint. There had been men since I'd moved to New York that I'd never dream of telling her about. Not men I'd ever marry. But other men I'd snuck out through the fire escape. Three of them, in fact, in the past three years. One named Jack my first year living here who I'd even dated for a little while until we both lost interest and stopped telephoning each other. Two others I'd met, brought back here for only a night, and then had discarded, just like that. I could not imagine the look on Myrtle's face if she were to know about these men, these illicit and enjoyable things I'd done with them. But why was it wrong for a woman to want pleasure, with nothing else attached to it? Why did sex have to mean anything more for a woman than it did for a man?

"I'll call you," Jay said with an easy smile, as he disappeared out my bedroom window, down the three flights of steps to the alleyway below.

And I thought it was fifty-fifty whether he actually would telephone or not. Either way, I felt okay about it.

Daisy

MOTHER ALWAYS USED TO TELL ROSE AND ME THIS STORY WHEN we were little girls, about when I was a baby. I came into this world in December of 1899, just weeks before Governor Goebel was shot and the whole entire state of Kentucky went crazy. We were on the brink of a civil war. Violence erupted in the streets of Louisville, and there Mother was, with a newborn baby girl. Daddy was terrified and wouldn't let her leave the house, even to take me on a walk down the street in my carriage. Mother said she stayed at home, shut entirely inside the house for the first six months of my life. It wasn't until summer that she dared to let sunlight touch my skin.

I never knew what I was meant to do in this life, Mother would tell us, *until I had this tiny little baby. My tiny little Daisy Fay. And then my whole life was certain. My only job was to keep you safe. My only job was to protect you from this world.*

Rose loved this story. She would always say she couldn't wait to grow up to be a mother. She wanted five babies, preferably all girls, and whenever she said that, Mother would laugh and kiss her head and say, *Oh my Rosie, I hope they're all as sweet as you.*

But I would always stay quiet. I didn't dream of babies, of being a mother. I'd never much relished the idea of taking care of anyone else aside from myself. And I'd never quite thought past marrying a man, becoming a wife, to what might inevitably come next.

I'd never quite thought about it at all, until I found myself on that hard tile floor of the Santa Barbara Hotel, vomiting into the toilet.

In that exact moment, I'd tried to count back to the last time I'd seen my monthly visitor and I couldn't remember, precisely. But it had been . . . months, sometime before my wedding.

And then I'd leaned my cheek against the cool porcelain of the hotel toilet and I'd cried.

TOM AND I left Santa Barbara almost immediately after his *accident*. We went to Boston first, where his family owned an estate. He wanted to go on to Europe from there, but I wanted to return to Louisville instead, at least until the baby was born.

"I need my mother," I insisted, like I was still a pouty little girl, and not this grown-up married woman about to be a mother in her own right.

Tom finally, reluctantly agreed, and by the first of 1920, we were back in Louisville, staying in Mother's house. I retreated to my old bedroom and made Tom go down the hall to Rose's. I told him the baby and I needed our space in bed. But as my stomach swelled, my nausea grew. And even if I might have wanted Tom to touch me, my body wouldn't stand for it.

We never discussed *the accident*, about what had happened with the chambermaid in Santa Barbara or why Tom had been driving in the middle of the night in a car with her. Tom had come back to our suite later that afternoon, a goose egg on his forehead, and had simply said, "What would you like for supper tonight, Daisy?" As if my entire world hadn't just burst into spontaneous flames, with one telephone call and one realization stretched across the cool bathroom floor.

I'd answered him by saying: "I think I might be pregnant."

Tom had opened his mouth, then closed it. He didn't say anything at all for a few moments. When he finally spoke he said: "A baby?" It was more a question than a reaction, good or bad.

We'd stared at each other, the ocean breeze wafting in through the window I'd opened to try and ease my nausea earlier. It gave me a chill; I shivered a little, but neither one of us moved to shut the window.

There were so many things left unsaid in that moment, but neither one of us said them to the other, either.

IN LOUISVILLE, MY belly grew and grew, and I had never felt more unattractive, more ill, in my entire life. Mother couldn't stop crowing about what a blessing this baby was. I'd walk by her in the mornings, on my way to try and swallow down some breakfast, and she would put her hand on my belly and trill like a snow goose. *Blessings* and *grandbabies* and *new life*! It was like she forgot all other words but these.

But this was the first time in my life I truly despised being a woman. I no longer felt, in the slightest, pretty. When I looked in the mirror, I saw unfamiliar bloated and blotchy cheeks staring back at me. And I felt like I was suffocating from the inside out. Trapped by this baby swelling up inside of me, taking over my body, making me ugly. And trapped by Tom, too.

Mother would never understand it, and so when she cooed, I smiled politely, and kept all the awful feelings inside. I couldn't bear to tell her that Tom had been unfaithful to me. I couldn't bear to admit out loud what I now understood deep down: any power I'd thought I'd gained in becoming Mrs. Buchanan was all an illusion. Instead, by marrying Tom, I'd given up every last part of myself. Even now, my beauty.

And then I hoped to God this baby would at least be a boy. That it would come out of me already having choices.

I AWOKE ONE night in the middle of April, my stomach clenching. Mother called for the doctor, and he came and gave me ether for the pain, and then I truly was grateful she was close, her snow goose trilling and all. I was in and out for hours or days, sweating and screaming and pushing. Mother held my hand. Maybe Tom was down the hall in Rose's room, or, maybe he wasn't. I didn't know where Tom was.

Then, there came the ether again; a dark and dreamless sleep followed.

When I awoke again, there was Mother's face, hovering, and the doctor's voice. He placed a baby into my arms. "It's a girl," he said, brightly.

A girl.

I tried to squeeze back tears, but I didn't have the strength to stop them now. Mother cooed with delight, and I cried and cried until I had no more tears left. When I cried myself out, I felt the weight in my arms, this baby. This *girl.* I examined her soft pink skin with my fingers, and she was so beautiful, it felt like the greatest cruelty.

"All right," I said, more to myself than to Mother, who was still hovering. "I'm glad it's a girl. And I hope she'll be a fool—that's the best thing a girl can be in this world, a beautiful little fool."

"Oh, Daisy Fay!" Mother's snow goose voice. "Why would you

say that? We want her to be a lady, *a beautiful little lady.*" Mother cooed that last part in the baby's face in a baby snow goose voice.

"Daisy Buchanan," I corrected Mother now, softly.

Daisy Fay might've been a beautiful little lady, once. But Daisy Buchanan was nothing more than a fool. A goddamned fool.

I AWOKE SOMETIME later, the middle of that night, or, the next night. The baby cried and Mother brought her to me, and I slept in between. In and out. Time was nothing.

But now, my eyes fluttered open and my room was dark. Tom stood over me, a shadow. His hand reached for my shoulder. He lowered his lips to my forehead and kissed me gently, and I could smell that whiskey and cigarette smell of him. "I'm so sorry," he whispered. "I love you. Daisy, I love you so much."

I closed my eyes and exhaled. My body was tired, but the swelling in my ankles and face had already gone down, and when I'd looked in the mirror earlier, I'd had the slightest bit of hope I might be beautiful again, soon. I wondered if Tom saw it now too?

I moved my arm slowly, patted the space on the bed next to me. Tom got in and wrapped his arms around me, pulling me tightly to him. I relaxed against him, and he stroked my hair softly. We lay there for a little while, saying nothing at all.

"Let's go to France," Tom finally said. "You and me and the baby. We're a family now, and I'll never hurt you again. I promise you, Daisy."

I didn't say anything for a moment. I imagined Paris, walking down the Champs-Elysées, holding Tom's arm, pushing the baby in the carriage. It was spring, and the air would smell like flowers. And we would be so gay, laughing, stopping to kiss each other whenever the moment struck us.

"Please forgive me, Daisy," Tom whispered into my hair. "Please try to love me again. I miss you."

I curled in tighter to him. "Hush," I finally spoke. "You're my husband. I'll always love you, Tom Buchanan."

I felt like I could breathe deeply again for the first time in months. Tom had made a mistake, but he was here, holding me, apologizing. We could still be okay.

He loved me; he needed me. And that made me more than a fool, didn't it? That, in itself, gave me all the power.

Jordan

IT WAS HARD TO BELIEVE THAT DAISY HAD A BABY. A REAL BONA fide *person* that she'd grown inside of her and pushed out of her tiny body. She wrote me letters after I saw her in Santa Barbara, told me the news about her pregnancy and then the birth and, then, their move to France. I knew that they'd named the baby Pamela because that had been Rose's middle name. *We wanted to honor Rosie, but I couldn't call her Rose,* Daisy had written. *That would hurt too much . . .* I knew all this, and yet, none of it felt real to me until I stepped into the Buchanans' château in Cannes, and Daisy placed a plump, pink . . . baby into my outstretched arms.

I wasn't sure how to hold her—she was deceptively heavy, and she squirmed and squealed like a pig, then burst into tears. Daisy attempted to soothe her with kisses to her little forehead, then called for Yvette, the nurse, who ran in and whisked Pamela away from me, almost before I had time to register that she was a real, live, breathing girl. *Daisy's girl.*

Daisy grabbed my hand and led me into the sweeping parlor. Their château was a large three-story mansion, on the edge of the Mediterranean. And the parlor had an entire wall of windows looking out onto the bright blue water. My eyes widened as I looked around, taking in the view. "Isn't Pammy a doll?" Daisy murmured.

I turned back to look at her, and I nodded. Because that's exactly what she'd felt like, *a doll*. Something fake and porcelain, delicate and unreal, like the dolls we used to spend hours playing with as kids. "I still can't believe you're a mother, Daise," I said. It felt almost more impossible because Daisy stood across from me now, looking the same as she always had: same shiny, shiny hair, same trim waist. How exactly had she grown and borne this . . . *child?*

Daisy laughed, invited me to sit, and poured me a cup of tea from a tray already resting on the coffee table. "Well, I still can't believe you're finally here, in France." She handed me the tea and then clapped her hands together, letting out a little noise of glee.

"And I can't believe you actually live here." And I didn't just mean France, but this towering château perched on the edge of the Mediterranean.

We looked at each other then and both burst out laughing. That was life, wasn't it? Everything you could never believe happening to you, happening just like that, right before your very eyes.

"Oh Jordie." She leaned back against the sofa and smiled. She sounded and looked so very happy. And a happy Daisy was the best kind of Daisy. I loved seeing her this way. It almost made me forget that anxious feeling that had risen in my stomach up through my chest during the whole long journey to France. Now, I was just relieved to be with Daisy and also very tired. I couldn't help myself, I yawned. "Tomorrow, after you've had a chance to sleep away your travels, we'll go to the beach, all right? It's the most beautiful beach you've ever seen."

"More beautiful than Santa Barbara?" I asked her sleepily. I leaned my head back against the plush sofa and thought about that last afternoon I'd spent with her there. I'd met her and Tom at the beach, just before I'd gone back to Charleston. Daisy had not been able to keep her hands off Tom then, running her fingers intimately across his face. I'd felt like I was invading a very private moment between the two of them, and I'd looked away, stared off at the beautiful deep blue water. Santa Barbara's beach truly had been stunning.

Daisy's expression suddenly turned sour, and I noticed she had new creases around her eyes. But she shook her head a little and then, she was smiling again. "The water here is not just beautiful but warm. It's like the bath, Jordie. Better than anything back home. I promise."

I AWOKE MY first morning in Cannes following a restless night. In spite of my exhaustion from the long trip, I'd slept fitfully, tangled up in half dreams of Mary Margaret. She was here and then she was gone. And then when I opened my eyes and sunlight streamed in through the large French doors, I was relieved to see it was finally morning.

I wrapped myself in my robe and wandered outside, where I sat on the balcony—large enough for the whole women's golf team to fit and only one of six on this side of the house. I stared out at the blue, blue sea. What had Daisy said yesterday? Better than anything I'd ever known back home. Still, I could not ease that steady ache in my belly, that restlessness that had kept me tossing and turning all night long. Now it hit me: I was homesick.

It was hard to believe it had only been a few weeks since I'd last been in Charleston with Mary Margaret, Mrs. Pearce, and the other girls. We were to have the months of August and September off, and then when we returned, in October, we'd be preparing for our first real paying tournaments, which would start just after the first of next year. I'd been doing well enough in the practice tournaments that I imagined in only a few months' time I might be able to count on the money I could win golfing as bona fide *income.* That would be a huge relief, because right now Aunt Sigourney controlled everything Daddy had left for me in trust. And other than sending me a small monthly allowance for clothing and necessities, she wouldn't let me touch any of it. She hadn't even wanted me to come to France to see Daisy on my break—she'd wanted me to go to New York and stay with her instead. Daisy had generously paid my fare.

Still, I hadn't told Daisy that she and France were truly my second choice. My first had been to go home to Nashville with Mary Margaret.

She'd invited me a few weeks ago, in the middle of the night, after she'd crawled into my bed and was holding me in the dark. I'd entwined my leg with hers, in that careless way we had of doing now, as if my limbs were her limbs. And in the black of night, it sometimes felt uncertain where one of us ended and the other one began.

"How will I survive two whole months without you?" I'd whispered into the darkness that night.

Her arms had pulled me tighter, and I'd felt the weight of her body sigh against me. "Don't," she'd whispered directly into my ear. "Come home to Nashville with me."

Her whisper was a promise and a dare, and I told her that I would.

But the next morning, everything had been bright and different, the way it always was. "Do you really want me to come to Nashville for the break?" I'd pressed her, watching her eat a piece of rye toast for breakfast. She chewed daintily around the edges in that funny way she had of eating all the crusts before any of the center. Her eyes widened a little, but she didn't answer at first, she just kept on chewing. "Daisy wants me to come to France," I'd said, matter-of-factly. I didn't mention Aunt Sigourney in New York, a very distant, and unlikely, third.

She'd continued on with her toast, each bite agonizingly precise, until she finished the whole piece. "France, Jordan," she'd finally said, averting her eyes from mine. "Wouldn't that be marvelous."

I'd nodded but understood what she was really saying. Her whisper in the middle of the night had been a half dream. In the light of the morning, fully awake, she was consumed by fear. Afraid of what everyone would see, what her parents might think, watching us together for two whole months.

"France," I'd repeated then. I'd ripped my own piece of toast in half, eating the center and leaving the crusts behind on my plate. "And, boy, it'll be good to see Daisy again." That was certainly true—I'd missed Daisy. But I hadn't said it for that reason. I'd said it because I'd wanted to watch Mary Margaret's cheeks redden, wanted to watch her sweet plump lip curl just a bit, with what was almost certainly jealousy.

"France," she'd repeated, gulping down her grapefruit juice, refusing still to meet my eyes.

And now, here it was before me: *France*. And Daisy, too, of course. With her baby doll and her happy marriage. And the blue-green Mediterranean Sea out in front of me, almost close enough to touch from my balcony. I had everything here, everything money could buy. So why did I still feel so sad, and so restless, and so empty?

A FEW HOURS later, Daisy and I lay out on their private beach together, just steps down a path from their château. We sat on a blanket in the sand, under a large umbrella. For the first time since I'd gotten to France, I could breathe again. The warm salty air drifted in and out of my lungs, and I sighed.

Daisy lay back on the blanket. I did the same and reached out my hand for hers. She took it and squeezed my hand gently. We lay there like that, just holding hands and soaking in the view.

"Tell me, what's the best thing about living in France?" I asked her after a little while. My voice, my whole entire body, was hot and lazy.

"Easy," she said. "This." It was hard to tell whether she meant this moment, right here, the two of us holding hands on the beach, or just her proximity to the beach itself.

I squeezed her hand again. "Lucky girl," I said. "Your wealthy husband whisking you away to every beach in the world: Tahiti and Hawaii and Santa Barbara and now Cannes."

She didn't say anything for a moment, and then she rolled over on her side, faced me. Her eyes were darker, her expression more serious now. "Jordie," she said, "Tom did something awful in Santa Barbara."

Something awful? Her words hit me like a punch, and I reacted with a surprised, strangled cry. Daisy seemed so happy here. She'd been so happy when I last saw her then. There was money and a doll-baby, and the Mediterranean! "I don't understand, Daise."

She sighed and rolled back over on her back. "I'm not sure I do either."

"Well . . . what happened?" I asked carefully.

She was quiet for a moment, and I propped myself up on my elbow and twirled a lock of her hair around my finger. It was just as soft and silky as it had always been in Louisville. I assumed she still bathed it in six egg yolks, once a week. Well, why not? She certainly had the money now.

"There was an . . . *incident*. With Tom and a chambermaid," she finally spoke, her voice flat, her affect matter-of-fact. "They were off together doing god knows what, and all of Santa Barbara found out when they had a bang-up with their car." *All of Santa Barbara found out*, and yet, she hadn't told me. How was I just learning about this now? "We've put it all behind us," she said. "But sometimes I lie awake in the middle of the night, and I wonder . . . What did she have that I don't, Jordie?"

I tried to take in what she was saying, an incident with Tom and a chambermaid. Tom had cheated on Daisy? *On their honeymoon.*

"I shouldn't have even said anything now." Daisy was rambling, her voice taking on a higher pitch. "I don't even know why I told you. It's over. It's all in the past."

"Daise," I murmured softly. "Of course you should've said something. Why didn't you tell me sooner?"

"You weren't here," she said meekly. "I was too ashamed to write it in a letter. But then yesterday you brought up Santa Barbara, and I was up half the night thinking about it again."

Her eyes welled up with tears, and I stroked her hair back. "I'm sorry. I'll never mention Santa Barbara again, okay?"

"Don't be sorry." She sat up and wiped at her cheeks. "It's not your fault, Jordie."

"But what can I do?" I asked her. "You want me to murder Tom for you when I see him next?"

She laughed, and then I laughed a little too. We both knew I was joking. Sort of. "He promised me he'd never do it again. That everything would be different here in France."

"And is it?" I asked her.

She nodded. "But it's just hard to forget the past, you know?"

I nodded. I did know.

I lay back and took her hand again. We both stared off at the water for a while. I thought about telling her my own truth, and the words were poised right there on the very tip of my tongue. I could tell her about the way Mary Margaret's hand felt when it traced my hip as she got into my bed in the middle of the night. About the way my lips felt when I'd kissed her that one time in the dark on the golf course.

But then I thought about Daddy, and how his face had turned that night when Blocks had come into my room and I'd tried to tell him the truth afterward. And instead of letting my words escape now with Daisy, I bit my lip and said nothing at all.

WE SPENT THE next few days at the beach, intoxicated by the sun and the salt of the water drying on our skin. And everything else slowly and wonderfully melted away. There was the nurse to care for the baby—I don't think I ever even heard little Pamela cry after our first introduction. Tom played a lot of polo and only joined us in the evenings for supper, where I was happy to see him act overly devoted and loving with Daisy.

I tried to compose a letter to Mary Margaret but had only gotten as far as the first sentence, unable to put into words exactly what I wanted to write to her. I missed her desperately, and yet, I felt quite happy here in France with Daisy again. My arms longed to swing my clubs and reach for Mary Margaret in the middle of the night. But I couldn't bring myself to write any of that down, and so I wrote nothing at all.

Still, I woke up in the middle of the night, a week after I'd first gotten to France, hot and restless. I'd gotten overheated on the beach, and then I'd fallen into a fast, early sleep and had dreamed Mary Margaret here, in my bed. When I'd awoken, and remembered again where I was, I tossed and turned and couldn't fall back to sleep. I finally decided that drastic times called for drastic measures. I put on my robe and tiptoed downstairs with the intent to steal some of Tom's whiskey.

I got to the bottom of the stairs, and I heard movement in the parlor. I wrapped my robe tighter around my chest and began to retreat back up the stairs, but then I heard the unmistakable sound of a woman's giggle. *Daisy.*

The giggle came again, and I continued slowly on toward the parlor. But when I turned the corner, I realized it wasn't Daisy giggling at all, but little Pamela's nurse, Yvette. She was lying back against the sofa, her skirt hiked up above her knees, her eyes closed. A man knelt in front of her on the floor, his head buried in between her legs. I suddenly understood what was happening, and I gasped before I could stop myself. Yvette heard me, hurriedly pulled her skirt down and pushed Tom's head away. And he turned and saw me watching.

Everybody froze for a second, the three of us all so completely still that I could hear the ticking of the grandfather clock down the hall, the sound of my own breath escaping my chest.

Finally, Tom moved first. "Yvette, you should be checking on the baby before bed," he said. His voice was steady and calm, as it had been over supper when he'd been discussing the score of his latest polo match.

Yvette looked at him, hesitated for only another second before pulling her dress all the way down. She stood, quickly smoothed her appearance with her hands, and rushed off.

Then Tom turned to me and had the gall to give me a little half smile as if nothing untoward had just happened. A denial of what I'd just seen with my very own eyes. I imagined how he would explain it all away, in that smooth, moneyed voice of his if I pressed him. *There was nothing going on, Jordan,* he would say with an easy laugh. I felt an anger boiling up inside of me.

It was that same blinding rage I felt when Blocks came into my room. And lucky for Tom, I didn't have my aluminum putter in France. I rushed toward him now and slapped him hard across the face. It made a shockingly loud sound, and I worried for a moment it had echoed through the whole entire château, that somehow it had woken Daisy two stories above us. But the only sound that came in response was the ticking of that grandfather clock down the hall.

Tom reached his hand up to his face and rotated his jaw. "Have you lost your mind?" he said quietly. He rubbed his cheek gingerly. "That's going to leave a mark."

What he really meant sat between us in the air, unspoken. Daisy would see the mark. Daisy would ask about the mark. Everything that had transpired tonight up until then had been invisible, except for my hand slapping his cheek.

"Good," I said, defiantly. I walked over to the bar and grabbed what I'd come down here for, his whiskey decanter and a glass, and then I turned and faced him, as if daring him to try and stop me. He glanced at the whiskey, then at my face, and he frowned. "Tom," I said, managing to keep my voice steady, even though I could feel my fingers trembling a little, clutching too tight to the whiskey and the glass. "If you hurt Daisy again, I'll kill you."

Detective Frank Charles

October 1922
NEW JERSEY

THE DAY FRANK DROVE DOWN TO NEW JERSEY TO WATCH THE LA-
dy's golf tournament, it was exactly three years to the day that the
doctor had given Dolores a fifty-fifty chance of surviving.

He'd tried not to think about it in the weeks and months and
now *years* since, but sometimes his mind slipped back there anyway. He'd be working a case, poring over a file, conducting an interview. And then, almost abruptly, he'd remember again: that sterile
white hospital room in Presbyterian. The way joy had turned to
heartbreak in an instant and both had constricted his chest, made
it hard to breathe but in slightly different ways. Joy was breathless.
Heartbreak was suffocating.

For the three months before that morning in Presbyterian, he
and Dolores had thought that there would be a baby. After so many
years of trying, finally they would have the child they'd always
wanted. Then instead, there was blood on the linoleum floor, an
ambulance ride to Presbyterian. And there wasn't a baby at all but
a cancer burrowing deep inside of her. The doctor who'd done the
hysterectomy had an accent—German or Polish; it made everything he said sound even bleaker. Fifty-fifty chance of surviving

three years, he'd said. *It was a flip of a coin*, Frank had thought then. Heads Dolores lived three years. Tails she didn't.

Miraculously, it had come out heads and Dolores reassured him this morning before he left, exactly three years after that day in the hospital room, that she felt *just fine*.

"You look a little pale, Dee," he said, putting his hand to her forehead. He knew that wasn't a monitor of anything—it wasn't a fever that would kill her but a cancer that could regrow inside her that neither one of them would see before it was too late. And yet, it still made him feel he was checking on her, in some outward way, by putting his hand on her face. Her skin was cool. He leaned over and kissed her.

"Frank, really, I'm fine," she reassured him. She was knitting a hat for the neighbor's new baby, and her fingers kept tumbling the needles even as she spoke and he fussed around her forehead. She didn't stop; she never stopped. That was Dolores. "Don't you have that important interview in Jersey today?"

He kissed her softly on the lips now, and he felt her lips arch into a smile before he stepped back. "I might be home late," he told her. "You don't have to wait up."

FRANK HAD BEEN following the lady's golf tour in the papers, thinking about going to talk to Jordan Baker ever since he got back from Illinois last month. He was frustrated by the lack of answers he'd gotten from Catherine and Daisy and he knew, he just knew, that the diamond hairpin was the key. But he hadn't wanted to take another trip away from home, away from Dolores overnight. Not so close to the three-year anniversary, which, every time he thought about it still—*fifty-fifty*—made him gasp for air all over again. So he'd bided his time, knowing that the tour was meandering up

north, before heading out west for the winter. Today they were playing in South Jersey, a course close enough to the ocean that when
he got out of the car, he could immediately smell the salt in the air.

It was almost two by the time he arrived, and the golfers were
just breaking for a late lunch. He stood off to the side and watched
them walk off the course, one by one, in their matching white golf
dresses. Jordan stuck out—she was a little taller than the rest of
them and her dark hair was shorter, clipped close to her head. She
looked up, noticed him standing there, frowned, but kept walking
past him anyway.

"Hey there, Miss Baker," he called out, running after her. She
turned and glared at him. "Could I have a few minutes?"

She opened her mouth, then closed it. Her eyes narrowed, and
he suspected that inwardly, she was telling him to go to hell. But a
few other girls had stopped, noticed him, too. They were all staring,
wondering. And then she sighed; she didn't want to make a scene.
She told the girls to go on without her and walked over toward
him. But she pursed her lips together, waited to say anything until
the other girls had all moved on. Then she said, rather brusquely:
"What do you want?"

"Just a few minutes of your time," he repeated.

"I'm very busy," she said. "I'm in the middle of a tournament,
for heaven's sake."

"How's it going?" he asked her. "The tournament, I mean."

"I'm winning," she said huffily.

"Congratulations."

"That's premature. There're nine more holes after lunch." She
put her hands on her hips and glared at him, making it clear she
had no patience for him or his questions. No use for his congratulations, either.

He was in no capacity to force her to talk to him. So instead, he smiled. Dolores always said you catch more flies with honey than with vinegar. "I'm just following up on a few loose ends, that's all." He kept his voice light, easy. "I found something valuable, and I thought it might belong to you."

He pulled the hairpin out of his jacket pocket and held it out to her, in his palm.

"That's not mine," she said quickly. "I'm afraid you've driven all the way down here for nothing, Detective." Her tone was matter-of-fact, her eyes remained right squarely on his face. She appeared to be telling the truth.

"Are you sure?" His own voice faltered a little. He hadn't exactly expected that Jordan would claim the hairpin, but he'd expected to get a sense she was lying to him, the same way he had with Daisy and Catherine. That maybe Jordan's lie would reveal something about the other lies. But Jordan . . . appeared to be telling the truth? There was all that business in the past with her and the cheating scandal. Nick Carraway had told him she was *an incurable liar*. Out of all three of the women, Frank had been apt to trust Jordan the least, going in. "You've never seen this before?" he prodded.

She leaned in to examine it closely. "Well . . . it might be Daisy's."

"Daisy Buchanan's?" He repeated her name, while trying to make sense of everything in his head. If it was true, and the hairpin was Daisy's, wasn't Jordan supposed to be her closest friend? Why would she tell him the truth and potentially incriminate Daisy?

"I guess I couldn't tell you for sure," Jordan was saying now. "But it looks an awful lot like the hairpins I helped Tom pick out for her wedding present . . ." Her voice trailed off and she seemed to be remembering something, in another time.

"Well," he said now. "I appreciate your honesty." He did, even if it also confused the hell out of him.

"I don't know why you're fixating on it, though," Jordan said. "Daisy was at parties at Jay's house all summer. She could've dropped it anytime." She barely finished that thought when she turned, began to walk off toward the clubhouse to join her teammates for lunch.

"Miss Baker," he called after her. "One more question."

She whipped her head around and cast him an icy stare. Men had certainly withered from less. "Did you really move the ball?" he asked her.

Every paper said she had. Her first professional golf tournament, she'd been in the lead, but supposedly she'd moved the ball and had been thrown out of the tournament for cheating. At that point, she'd retreated to New York, and that's what had eventually put her there last summer with Daisy and Catherine, Nick Carraway and Jay Gatsby. Yet, here she was, back on the tour now. If she'd cheated, why had they let her back? And if she was *an incurable liar*, as Nick had told him, why was she the only one who seemed to be telling him the truth?

She chewed on her bottom lip a little, like she was considering whether or not to answer him or to simply walk away. But then she said, "What do you think, Detective?"

"I think . . ." What did he think? Jordan was tough and smart and here she was today, winning the tournament on her own. "I think maybe you didn't," he said.

She screwed her face into a funny half smile and she nodded. And then just like that, she turned and ran off toward the clubhouse.

Jordan

THE NIGHT BEFORE THE END OF EVERYTHING, I FELT LIKE FIRE.

My body was hot, emotion coursing through my veins, explosive. I could feel it in my skin and on my lips and in the pounding of my heart. It was the adrenaline rush of a real paying tournament the next morning. But it was more than that too. It was a confidence, a sheer, bright, stupid confidence that I could have it all. I could have everything I ever wanted. That I, too, could be happy.

The whole team was staying a few blocks away from the tournament. It was a quaint little southern inn, with only a few rooms, and we took up all of them. In spite of that, Mrs. Pearce warned us all upon arrival not to disturb any other guests. At which point Mary Margaret had turned to me, rolled her eyes. I suppressed a giggle, and Jerralyn shot me a dirty look. Mrs. Pearce didn't notice any of it, and she kept on talking. ". . . Breakfast downstairs, promptly at eight," she was saying. "The tournament will begin at ten . . ." We'd already received a schedule and I already knew all this, so I tuned her out. It was late, nearly eleven. The train ride had felt interminably long, and my body was already jittery with the fire in my veins. I shuffled my feet while she continued to drone on and on and on.

At last, she was finished with her diatribe, and we all carried our bags upstairs to our rooms. Mary Margaret and I were sharing, just like we always did back in Charleston. But instead of bunk beds, here we would share the room's one double bed. We stood in the doorway for a moment, both just staring at it. Then Mary Margaret put her bags down first, sat on the bed to test it, bounced a little. "Which side would you like?" she asked me, her voice sounding cool and polite. She refused to meet my eyes.

We'd kept a careful distance from each other since my return from France, her rescinded middle-of-the-night invitation to Nashville still an unspoken weight between us. She hadn't climbed down into my bunk bed even once back in Charleston, and now I eyed the double bed and my cheeks flushed. "I don't care," I told her. "It's up to you, Ems."

"I suppose I could sleep on the floor," she said. Her voice came out so husky now that I had to resist the urge to go to her, to run my hand across her throat, her chin, up to her lips, to trace the origin of that *voice*.

"Don't be silly," I said, my own voice raspy in my throat. "You won't ever get a good night's sleep on the hard wood. You stay on that side. I'll sleep on the other one."

I took my nightgown from my bag, turned my back, and changed quickly. When I turned around, she was staring at me, but when she noticed that I noticed, she quickly averted her eyes. And then, I felt it, coursing through me: heat and bravery and stupidity. It burned too hot, out of control.

I got into the bed, slipped under the covers, and pulled the lamp. Only then did Mary Margaret get up and change. I watched the shadow of her, then closed my eyes until I felt her slip back into bed. We both lay there silently, breathing heavily. From the sounds of her breath, I was certain she was still awake.

I slowly moved my arm across the bed and reached for her hand. I'd done the same with Daisy a thousand times lying in her bed in Louisville. There was nothing wrong with holding her hand. But Mary Margaret pulled her hand away so quickly when I touched her, it was like she knew she was touching fire, and she didn't want to get burned. "What are you afraid of, Ems?" I whispered into the darkness.

She didn't say anything for a few moments, and tears stung hot in my eyes. I felt hurt by her pulling away from me, her silence. The hurt turned a little angry. The fire started to simmer into rage.

But then she spoke, just one tiny, enormous word: "Everything," she said softly. And my fire turned from rage into something else, desire.

I rolled over on my side and stroked her arm. Her skin was soft, but her muscles were toned from golf. I ran my fingers slowly from her wrist to her shoulder and back.

And then she rolled on her side, too, and we were shoulder to shoulder, face to face. Her mouth was inches from mine. Her breath hit my lips. "I'm so afraid, Jordan. Afraid of people finding out what I feel," she whispered. "And I'm afraid of leaving this room and never feeling the way I feel right now, ever again in my whole entire life."

"Shh." I put my forefinger to her lips. She stopped talking, and I traced her lips lightly with my finger. We had kissed only once before, that one night on the golf course. It was so long ago now that sometimes I wondered if it had really happened at all or if it had been a dream. And aside from that, there were nights when Mary Margaret had crawled into my bunk bed, and we'd held each other in the middle of the night. But the next morning, in the light of day, we pretended it had never happened at all. And really, nothing *had* happened. We were roommates, friends. Every touch between us could be explained away as chaste.

Then I'd gone to France and lain out on the beach with Daisy and had caught Tom with the nurse in the middle of the night. And all I could think that whole time, that whole entire time, was that I felt sorry for Daisy. She loved a man, and men were animals. And maybe I would be lucky to never love a man in my whole entire life. Maybe I was the lucky one, after all. Maybe Mary Margaret and I both were.

"Ems," I whispered now. "I'm not afraid." I moved my finger from her lips to her cheek, and then I leaned in just another inch and put my lips on her lips. It was different this time than it had been that other time, on the golf course. There was nothing quick or soft or remotely chaste about this kiss. I was fire and she was fire, too—my bravery made her brave. We kissed each other hungrily, greedily. My tongue explored her mouth and met hers.

"Wait," she said, pulling back after a few minutes. Or a few hours. I'd lost track of time and place, and I was dizzy and breathless. She sat up and pulled her nightgown over her head, threw it on the floor. The only light was the light of the moon casting a glimmer in through the sheer-curtained window, but it was enough for me to see her body. I'd seen her before many times, of course, changing. But I'd tried not to stare then. This time, it was different. She wanted me to stare. She sat before me naked and beautiful and still. And I stared. Her breasts were larger than mine, perfect, round summer peaches, jutting out from her tiny rib cage, her narrow waist.

It was as if my eyes on her, my expression, made her newly brave. She sat up on her knees, crawled closer to me, and lifted my nightgown over my head slowly. I shivered a little as my bare skin felt the cool January air, but my blood ran hot; my cheeks flushed. She left her hand hovering in the air, just above my breasts. "Can I touch you?" she whispered. I nodded and reached up for her hand, pulling it to my chest. Her fingers were hot on my cool skin and I shivered again.

But bravery ran through my veins, hotter than blood, and I pulled her toward me, held her body against mine, and kissed her again.

THE NEXT MORNING I woke up to the sound of banging.

I opened my eyes, and sunlight streamed in through the window, too bright. My body felt hot and tired and hungover. I tried to move, and I realized Mary Margaret was lying half on top of me, naked, still asleep.

I closed my eyes again and remembered, like flashes of a silent film rolling through my mind: Mary Margaret's fingers in between my legs, my mouth all over her body. I reached my hand up to my lips and they felt swollen now.

"Jordan and Mary Margaret." Mrs. Pearce stormed in through the door, bellowing our names. That's what the banging was. *The door.* There was a lock on it, and I'd turned it when we'd come in last night, but of course, Mrs. Pearce also had a key. "Do you know what time . . ." She suddenly caught sight of us, there in the bed, naked and entwined, and she stopped talking midsentence.

Mary Margaret's eyes popped open at the sound of Mrs. Pearce's voice. They caught mine, and I saw in them everything she'd told me last night she was afraid of. Mrs. Pearce just stood there in the doorway, staring, her mouth agape.

I rolled out from under Mary Margaret and pulled the covers

up, over both of us. "Boy, it was too warm in here last night, wasn't it?" I made an awkward half attempt to explain away our nakedness. I heard the sound of my own voice, too high-pitched, nearly shrill. It rose up above me and hovered somewhere in the room like smoke.

Mrs. Pearce just pressed her lips together and stared, and it was probably only a few seconds, but time seemed to suspend and it felt like hours. My heart sprinted in my chest, and I could hear Mary Margaret breathing heavily, but she did not say a word. None of us did.

"You're both late," Mrs. Pearce finally said, turning her head away from the bed. "It's eight thirty. Get dressed and get downstairs. We're leaving for the course in twenty minutes, with or without you." She spun on her heel and walked out.

"She knows," Mary Margaret said, her voice breaking, as soon as Mrs. Pearce shut the door. "Oh my god, she knows."

"She doesn't *know* anything," I said quickly. Though my heart still pulsed furiously; fire still filled my veins. I stood and my body felt wonderfully sore. I began to get dressed, and the silent movie flashed on again in my head, Mary Margaret touching me. And I stopped moving, closed my eyes for a second, trying to make it stop. Wanting it to go on forever.

"How could she not know?" Mary Margaret was in tears now. She got out of bed and yanked her clothes out of her bag with more force than was necessary.

I walked over to her, only half dressed in just my skirt and my brassiere. I reached for her shoulder, pulled her toward me, and hugged her tightly. I smoothed back her hair with my hands. Here we were again, in the light of day, when everything was bright and different and . . . gone. And I didn't want it to be gone. I wanted to hold on to it, keep it close, keep *her* close. Forever. "No one knows what happened last night but us," I whispered into her hair. "It's just us, Ems. Mrs. Pearce can think what she wants but she'll never say anything. She can never prove anything, and, besides, any hint of scandal would doom the tour."

"Jordan." My name escaped her lips like a strangled half cry. "I already miss you."

"Shh, Ems. I'm right here," I said. "I'm not going anywhere."

GOLF HAD ALWAYS been my sanctuary and strength. After Mama died it made me into a tough little girl and then, after Daddy died, a fierce young woman.

I went out onto the course that day in Atlanta more determined than ever to focus on the ball, to play my best, to win the $1,000 tournament prize. If I won, it would be money to do with as I pleased. Not Daddy's money. Not Aunt Sigourney's money. Daisy had money, but Daisy's money meant her being with Tom. I wanted money all my own. A life all my own. And choices that only I was in control of. And besides, if I was the best today, if I won the tournament, Mrs. Pearce wouldn't dare say a word about what she thought she saw when she walked into our room this morning.

As I stood at the first tee box, I closed my eyes for a moment, remembering again the feel of Mary Margaret's hands on my skin. I took a deep breath, inhaled. Exhaled. I parted my feet and readied my club and stared at the ball.

But when I raised my arms to swing, everything else disappeared: Mary Margaret, Mrs. Pearce, Daisy. It was just me and the club. Then I swung, and all my power and my fire channeled into that one tiny little white golf ball that soared like a dove through the air.

✤

THE TOURNAMENT WAS to be played slowly: eighteen holes today and eighteen more tomorrow. At the end of the first eighteen, I was in first place, and all the girls came over and congratulated me, even Jerralyn. Mary Margaret gave me a long hug—she was currently in last place, and I felt, guiltily, that somehow I'd taken away her focus. Her failure today was my fault. But I consoled myself with the thought that I would buy her a present with my winnings, maybe something pretty she could wear in her hair.

"You did great, Jordan," she said to me, interrupting my thoughts. She let go and I pulled her back, held her to me for another second, close enough to feel the pounding of her heart. I thought about what she said this morning, half in tears, that she already missed me, and I wanted her to see that everything was okay, that I was still right here.

I hugged her for another moment, but when she pulled back again, I looked up. And there standing just off to the side of the green were Mr. Hennessey and Mrs. Pearce, their heads together, both staring at me. I offered them a cool nod, raised my club a little to acknowledge my success today. And the truth was, I still felt like fire. I still felt like I was untouchable.

I AWOKE THE next morning to an empty bed. Mary Margaret had said she needed some fresh air after dinner last night, and unable to contain my exhaustion from a full day of golf and hardly any sleep the night before, I'd sat down on the bed and fallen into a long and dreamless sleep.

Now it was morning, Mary Margaret had never come to bed, or she'd slept quietly and had woken up early and already left for breakfast without me. It felt strange to be here, all alone. But I barely had time to stretch and make sense of that thought when the door opened. I looked up expecting Ems. But instead, it was Jerralyn standing there in my room, frowning, a newspaper in her hand.

"You little bitch," she spat at me. Her words were so jarring, so unexpected, they felt like a slap.

Had Mrs. Pearce told her, told everyone what she thought she saw between me and Mary Margaret? I couldn't believe she would, no matter what she might have suspected. It wasn't the sort of thing a proper southern lady would ever speak of, and, if nothing else, Mrs. Pearce really fashioned herself a proper southern lady.

I stood and wrapped myself in my robe. "I don't appreciate you barging into my room this way," I huffed angrily, trying to hide my confusion wrapped in fear, with an outward sort of aggression. It was the same aggression I always channeled into the golf ball.

Jerralyn stared at me, unfazed. "We all thought you were so great at golf," she said. "But you've been cheating all this time, haven't you?" She crossed her arms in front of her chest, and I caught the headline on the newspaper she was holding: "Lady Golfer Thrown Out of Peachtree Tournament After Moving the Ball."

Did Jerralyn think that headline was referring to me? But that was impossible and blatantly untrue, and she was utterly mistaken. "I've never cheated at golf in my life," I said. "How dare you accuse me of such a thing."

She shoved the newspaper into my trembling hands. I skimmed the article beneath the headline and saw the words *Jordan Baker*. I suddenly felt cold all over, too light to stand, too heavy to sit back down. I grabbed the bureau for support. This article *was* about me. It said I, *Jordan Baker*, had moved the ball, and that was how I'd come in first place yesterday. "But . . . but . . . this isn't true," I stammered, clutching the side of the bureau for support and for breath, neither of which it gave me. "This . . . didn't happen. I never moved a ball."

"Oh Jordan." Jerralyn sighed and shook her head a little, like now instead of being angry, she felt sorry for me. "Mrs. Pearce told us how she saw you do it. Mrs. Pearce saw everything."

Catherine

JAY GATSBY.

His name sat on the tip of my tongue, cool and a little tart, like the illicit taste of gin with lime. And yet I didn't utter it. I just left it there, tasting it for a moment, feeling the bold, intoxicating texture of it. Instead I just looked at Myrtle and shook my head.

"Really?" she repeated. "No man in your life at all?" She rested her chin in her palms and sighed.

I'd taken a taxicab out to Queens for dinner tonight. I hadn't spoken to Myrtle in over two weeks, and she hadn't made it into the city for months. I was worried about her. For one thing, I knew my sister thrived on social interaction and the buzz and hum of the city, and for another, I never forgot those bruises on her neck. Every time she kept her distance from me, I wondered and worried about what it was she was hiding. Why it was exactly she didn't want to see me.

I'd called her earlier this morning to let her know I was coming today for a visit and I hadn't given her a chance to tell me not to. A few hours later, I'd entered her small home above George's garage and found it immaculately clean. Myrtle herself was in a pretty floral dress and had done up her hair. But there was something in her eyes, something a little flat or a little lost. It made me feel I was right to be worried after all. Right to have come out here practically unannounced.

"I've told you a thousand times, Myrtle," I said now, in response to her question about having a man in my life. "I'm never getting married." We'd eaten a quiet dinner, just the two of us, ham and potatoes. Both had been a little dry, but I'd choked them down and complimented them all the same. Now we sipped coffee and worked our way through a small lemon cake, which was also a little dry for my taste. "I don't need a man," I reiterated, working my fork through the cake, watching it fold easily into crumbles.

Myrtle put a forkful of cake in her mouth and chewed carefully. "Yes, but wouldn't it be nice to have one, Cath? You're young and pretty. You could find a rich man who would buy you anything. Give you everything." She sighed and finished off her piece of cake.

Looking around at her sparse, dimly lit kitchen, I knew my sister desired so much more than this life with George. I was living out some wayward fantasy in her eyes—young and living in the city. I just wished she understood that this fantasy, my life, didn't have to be about a man. Why couldn't supporting myself, earning my own money, and living my own life be what she wanted for me? What she wanted for herself, too? And that's exactly why I didn't let the name Jay Gatsby escape my lips. We'd been lovers now for months, but it was nothing more than that. It was never going to be anything more. I didn't want a relationship and neither did he. And that was something Myrtle would never understand. If I were to mention his name now, she would hang on to any tidbit I offered her about him, even just that: *Jay Gatsby*. And she would fixate on it. I certainly didn't want her doing that.

"Do you want more cake?" she asked me now. I shook my head, and she stood to cover the cake plate. The sleeve of her dress shifted a bit, and I caught a glimpse of purple encircling her wrist. The cake I'd just eaten rose in my throat, threatening to come back up, and I swallowed hard. I had been right to be worried, to come out here today.

"What's that?" I asked, pointing to her wrist, trying to keep my voice steady. She ignored me or pretended she hadn't heard. But clearly she had because she tugged her sleeve down a little before she finished covering the cake. "Myrtle," I said her name loudly, and she startled a little, jumped.

"Jeez, Cath. You'll wake George." It was early evening on a Saturday, but George was exhausted from a long day at the garage and Myrtle said he'd sent his apologies but had gotten into bed before I'd arrived. He'd taken an early supper and had conked out. I'd wondered how much whiskey he'd had to wash down the dry ham and potatoes.

"Sorry." I lowered my voice. I certainly didn't want to upset her, or wake George. "But what happened to your wrist?" I asked softer.

"My wrist?" She sounded distracted and focused all her energy on finding the perfect spot for the cake on her kitchen counter.

I stood and walked over to her, put my hand lightly on her wrist, and she flinched. I pushed up her sleeve a little, and there it was, a round purple bruise. "Dammit, Myrtle." I cursed softly before I could stop myself.

She yanked her arm away. "Mother would turn over in her grave hearing that mouth on you," she chastised. "That's all you've gotten from living in the city, Cath? No man and a mouth like that." She tsked softly.

I frowned, though it was true. Mother never could stand for

impropriety. And well, honestly, Mother would probably turn over in her grave for half the things I did with my life these days. The gin I drank, the nights I spent with Jay, and even all the protests I'd marched in with the other suffragettes. "Myrtle, that's beside the point." I picked up her wrist again, pushed up her sleeve, traced my hand around the shiny ring of purple.

She flinched, then forced a smile. "Cath, it's nothing. Really . . . it's nothing."

It didn't look like nothing. It looked like George had hurt her, again. I swallowed back this hard, hot hatred that rose in my throat for him, my brother-in-law I barely knew. The few interactions I'd had with him, he was always quiet, almost bordering on dim-witted. I tried to imagine him in a fit of rage, tearing at my sister, and tears burned my eyes. How dare he do this? How dare he?

"You should leave him," I said bluntly.

"Leave?" Myrtle laughed a little, but the sound caught in her throat and came out sounding like an odd quack. "And where would I go?" Her voice floundered as she sat back down at the table. "Look around you. I don't have much. But at least I have . . . something."

I thought about it for a moment. "You could come live with me and Helen in the city."

"In that small apartment? There's barely room for the two of you to move."

I shook my head and kept talking, undeterred by that one tiny, factually correct detail. "Maybe I could get you a job . . ." The Women's League wasn't hiring for any more wireless operators at the moment, but there must be something there I could find for Myrtle. Anything would be better than this.

"A job?" She laughed a little. "So I could have less than I have now?"

Sure, the apartment I shared with Helen was very small, a quarter of the size of Myrtle's tiny place, and I didn't make a lot of money working for the Women's League. But I always had food to eat and plenty of fun, and most of all, plenty of freedom. How could she believe she would have less?

"I'm worried about you," I said. "I want to help you. You deserve so much better, Myrtle."

"Oh, Cath"—she patted my hand—"marry a rich man and I'll come live with you in his mansion." She laughed a little; she was joking, but only half. The other part of her was dead serious.

LATER THAT NIGHT I lay in Jay's bed, my head on his bare chest. We were naked and both satisfied and he absently stroked my hair with his hand, twirling a strand in between his fingers.

I'd come to his apartment straight from Myrtle's, directing the cabbie last minute to take me here instead of to my place. For the past few months, I'd been coming here once a week or so, or Jay climbed up the fire escape to my bedroom if I knew Helen would be out. But one of us always telephoned the other first. There was a propriety to our affair, a sense of mutual agreement. We didn't barge in. We didn't cling or demand commitment. We scheduled ourselves into each other's lives whenever it was mutually convenient.

Tonight, though, was different. Driving away from the ashes of Queens I'd felt sad and helpless, and I'd suddenly *needed* Jay in a way I'd never wanted to need anyone. I'd directed the cabbie to change routes, take me here. And I'd shown up at his door without telephoning first.

"Cath?" His face had turned in surprise when he'd opened the door and saw me there. I'd pushed myself into his apartment and kissed him hard enough to make us both dizzy. And then, what had ensued, a rush to pull off clothes, to fall naked into his bed, to grope and tumble until we both were satisfied—it had nothing to do with love or commitment, but everything to do with *need*.

"Is everything all right?" he asked me now. "You seem . . ." He didn't finish his thought but instead kept absently twirling my hair.

I leaned into his chest, closed my eyes, but all I could see was that horrible purple bruise on Myrtle's wrist. Jay and I didn't normally talk about our lives, beyond small talk. I hadn't talked to him about Myrtle since our first drunken night together. But I couldn't keep it inside of me now, and I told him everything: about Myrtle's continued bruises and George and how she believed leaving him and being poor and alone was worse than being with him.

When I finished talking, I was crying, which I only realized when Jay's fingers moved from my hair to my cheeks. His thumb brushed away the wetness, then trailed down to my lips. "Poor Cath," he said softly. "Let me help."

"I don't know how you can," I said petulantly. In fact, now I wasn't even sure why I'd told him. Saying it all out loud hadn't made me feel better at all. I felt decidedly worse.

"I've been making a good amount of money working," Jay said. I knew that he'd gotten a new job a few months ago doing something with drugstores, and that he was making good enough money now that he insisted on buying me drinks on the rare occasion we left one of our beds and actually went out. But I didn't exactly know what he did or how much he made, and his apartment in the Village was a little roomier than mine but nothing special. "I'm growing a nest egg," he said now. "Maybe in a few months, I could help your sister. Give her enough money to make a fresh start."

I rolled over and propped myself up on my elbow. I stared at his face. His eyes were a startling green. His blond hair had grown longer since the end of the war, since he no longer had his soldier's cut, and now it was messy. Almost shaggy, falling across his forehead. I reached over and brushed a strand out of his eyes. "Why would you do that?" I asked him. "We're not . . ." I let my voice trail off, not exactly sure what we were or weren't any longer. We were lovers. But we had no obligations to each other; we made no promises. Myrtle would never be Jay's family, Jay's responsibility. "Why give your money to my sister?" I finally said.

Jay closed his eyes and sighed. "I thought . . . I thought . . ."

"What?" I whispered, feeling my heartbeat speed up.

"If I had money. If I made enough money, I thought I could make her love me again."

Her. Daisy. Something washed over me, but was it relief or . . . disappointment? Or annoyance? It was hard to tell the difference in that moment.

"But she's gone forever now, isn't she, Cath?" He was still talking. "He took her to France and now I hear they're the toast of Chicago." He frowned.

This girl. This stupid, vapid girl who'd broken his heart before the war and who still haunted him. Sometimes, when we were together, when we were naked and senseless and nearly numb with pleasure, he called out her name, *Daisy.* Whether he realized what he'd done or even remembered afterward, I wasn't sure, because I never said anything about it to him. Inwardly, I hated her. Not because he clearly still loved her, and he would never love me. I didn't even want him to love me! No, I hated her because Jay was a good man, a kind man, and years ago, she'd broken him. She left him broken still. I worried that one day she might ruin him.

"You deserve better," I said to him now, echoing the words I'd said to Myrtle just a few hours ago in her kitchen. Why was it so easy for me to see this and so hard for both of them to understand it?

Jay sighed and leaned back against his pillow, closed his eyes. He was picturing her now, behind his lidded eyes. I knew he was. Wishing Daisy were lying next to him, not me. I had this strange feeling, like I was outside myself, hovering, watching. Catherine but not Catherine at all. I was just a shell of a girl, who brought Jay this strange and twisted kind of comfort. I had the thought that I should get up. I should get dressed and leave and not see him anymore. There were other men in the great big city of New York. Plenty of them who weren't wishing I were another girl every time they were with me. But even as I thought all this, I didn't move a muscle. There was an odd comfort in being here, lying with a man I knew would never love me. Who would never expect too much from me.

Finally Jay opened his eyes, looked at me, gave me an apologetic half smile. His eyes were clear, compassionate. Daisy had left him once again, and he remembered me, Catherine, lying here next to him. "The point is," he said, "I've been saving up money for something—for someone—who will never come back. So let me use it to help your sister, Cath." He paused for a minute. Then he added, "Give me a few more months and I'll have enough money to help her."

Daisy

1921
CHICAGO

THERE WAS A STORM COMING.

The sky above our estate in Lake Forest grew dark and pearly gray, the wind cut through the oak trees, snapping branches, and I stood out on the veranda, watching lightning tear across the silver sky, feeling vastly unsettled. I'd been feeling this way for a few weeks now, since we'd moved here from France. Weary and restless at the same time. It was hard to breathe and even harder to remember to smile. I fell asleep each night just after supper, exhausted, then woke at midnight and roamed the grounds, jittery. Sometimes, when I awoke, Tom was lying in our bed, snoring. Sometimes, he was just . . . gone. I roamed and roamed and there was no sign of him, anywhere.

That's what unsettled me. Where was Tom exactly, in the middle of the night? But it was more than that too. Where was I? Or perhaps, more importantly, *who* was I?

I'd spent the first twenty years of my life in one city, one house. Every corner of every street in Louisville was familiar and had a memory attached. The woods where Daddy taught me to shoot a gun, and the abandoned road by the river where he'd taught me to drive the Roadster. The five blocks that led to Jordan's house from mine that I could practically skip in my sleep because my feet knew the way and the number of steps it took to get there. And even the sound of Mother's snow goose voice, trilling my full name up the long winding staircase. All that was *home*. Since my wedding, two years earlier, I'd become unmoored. The South Seas, Santa Barbara, Boston, Louisville, and France. Now, Chicago. All that moving around, it was enough to give any girl whiplash.

"We weren't going to stay in France forever," Tom had said, laughing a little at the absurdity of it, when I'd complained about us leaving there.

"Well, not forever," I'd huffed. "But I was finally starting to feel at home here, and now you want to move again?"

He'd kissed my head. "You'll love Chicago," he'd said, his voice taking on an annoyingly condescending tone. Our move hadn't been presented to me as a choice. That morning, he'd simply walked into breakfast in our château in Cannes and announced that he was ready to return to the States. That he'd found a place for us in Lake Forest, not too far from his parents. It didn't matter that Chicago was the last place Daddy and Rose had been before the train crash, that I could hardly bear to think about that city, much less *live* there. "And we can't change our plans now." He was still talking, while he poured himself a cup of coffee. His movements were easy. He hadn't a concern in the world. "I've already begun preparing the ponies," he'd added.

Heaven forbid we should change the ponies' plans. I'd bitten my lip to avoid saying that out loud.

And so in Lake Forest I felt myself constantly pining for Cannes. Or maybe not Cannes, exactly, but for something, somewhere. For the feeling of home, of being settled in one place long enough to get my bearings. Our house here was grand and lovely with views of Lake Michigan. And fully staffed, so I didn't have to lift a finger. We were just a train ride away from Upper Boul Mich and Lakeshore Drive, the pulsing shiny hearts of the city, where there were so many parties to be found, so many young, beautiful wild people just waiting for us to have a gay time with. But the air was desperately chilly in Lake Forest, even though it was still summer. And I had not been able to truly warm up since we'd left France.

Out on the veranda now, the oak branches crackled, and the thunder rumbled loudly. I stood there frozen, trying to remember how to breathe. Trying to settle my senses and my mind and my soul. The rain began, and the wind whipped so hard that water poured at me diagonally in sheets, washing over me, soaking right through my dress to my skin.

"OH MY GOODNESS, Daisy. You're positively scandalous," Tom said to me, his voice taking on a wicked edge. I'd walked up to our bedroom to change before dinner; the rain had soaked me through and through, and I shivered a little.

He walked over to me now, drew me to him, in spite of my sad, wet state. He brought his hand up to trace my breast, and I looked down and noticed it was completely visible through the wet fabric of my beige dress. "Tom, not now," I protested weakly. "We have company coming for dinner." It was true, much to my chagrin, Tom had invited a polo friend, his wife, and their teenage daughter for dinner tonight, mentioning it to me only this morning at breakfast. Not much time to prepare myself to put on a show for strangers. *Not strangers*, Tom had corrected at breakfast. *Maybe they'll become our friends?*

"Ahh, yes, the Buckleys," he said now, a tinge of annoyance in his voice, even though this dinner had been his idea. He let his hand linger on my breast still another moment, before dropping it back to his side. "Daisy . . ." He said my name, but then didn't finish his thought.

He looked at me, and we held each other's gaze for a moment, but neither one of us said a word. So much was unspoken between us now. Perhaps Tom wanted to ask me when we would ever *be together* again? If not now, *when?* I'd recoiled from his touch since we'd left France, and partly it was that feeling; I was so unsettled my skin crawled and my limbs twitched. I was so desperately homesick for something or someone or somewhere that didn't actually even exist. What was my *home* with Tom? Where was it?

But then there was the other thing, too. That question that lingered in my mind, when I awoke in the darkness and our bed was empty. And I roamed the grounds, listening for him, but hearing only the gentle rush of Lake Michigan in the distance. *Where did Tom go in the middle of the night?*

"Daisy . . . I . . ." he said again.

"What is it, Tom? What do you want to say?" I implored him now, nearly taunting him. Daring him to tell me where it was he went. Who it was he was with.

But instead he broke into a hesitant smile. "I miss you, Daisy. That's all." He leaned in and kissed my cheek tenderly in a way that evoked every warm memory I held inside of me from Tahiti, from Kapiolani. From the Punch Bowl, where he'd carried me to the car to keep my shoes from getting wet during another rainstorm, what felt like a million years from this one.

I softened a little. "I'm right here, Tom," I said.

"Are you?" he asked me. "Are you really?" His hand went back up, and I expected him to reach for my breast again. But instead, he reached around, unbuttoned the brass buttons on my dress carefully, one by one. He pulled the sleeves down over my arms and my dress dropped to the floor, leaving me before him naked, wet, and shivering. "Let me get you a towel," he said gently. "Before you catch your death."

He left and returned a moment later with a large white towel from the linen closet down the hall. He threw it around my shoulders, rubbed me gently dry. And I suddenly wondered if he was just restless too. If somehow even living here together, we were simply moving around each other in opposite directions, and all we had to do was walk toward each other once again.

I looked up and caught his eyes, and I smiled a little. A thank-you. An apology, too. "I suppose we do have a little time before supper." I breathed the words softly, like a whisper-song. "And Marion can always keep them waiting in the parlor . . ."

Tom made a little noise of surprise, or delight. A laugh or was it a groan? I dropped the towel—I was dry enough—and I stood before him totally naked. The restless twitch had finally stopped, and I felt warmer again. Right here, with Tom, was exactly where I belonged.

TWO HOURS LATER Josephina Buckley droned on about her azaleas, and I tried to catch Tom's eye across the length of our long dining table, while nodding and murmuring along with her. Tom was engrossed in his second glass of whiskey and his discussion about polo with Harold Buckley. For a short time before dinner, we'd connected again, but that moment was fleeting. And my legs twitched, restless again.

Josephina was at least ten years older than me, maybe fifteen. But she may as well have been Mother's age from the frumpy way she dressed and went on and on and on about her garden. Tom was wrong—we were never going to be friends. Just this dinner felt interminable, and I stifled a yawn.

Across the table from me Rebecca, the Buckleys' daughter, picked at her chicken with a fork, exhibiting the same boredom and annoyance I was feeling for this conversation. She was sixteen and beautiful with plump rosy cheeks and curls the color of churned butter. I considered that she was closer to my age than her mother was. And yet, I was a mother myself now, and Rebecca was still a girl.

I remembered being a girl so vividly. It wasn't all that long ago that Rose was still alive, and Jordan and I had giggled in my bed about that handsome soldier I'd snuck into my bedroom. That time felt so close, and also, like another lifetime. I could no longer remember the exact contours of Jay's face or the feel of his hands on my body. But I could very much remember the endless rush of joy, the happiness and warmth, the glow of my own teenage innocence. When she finally looked up from her chicken, I shot Rebecca a sympathetic smile.

She smiled back. "Could I see the ponies?" she asked me, surprising me with the clear blue sound of her voice. She looked like a young woman, but at sixteen, she was very much a child still, a little girl excited at the idea of seeing a pony.

The ponies. Tom's goddamned ponies. There was a stable where he kept them, back across the yard, halfway to the lake. I knew it was there, I'd seen it from a distance, and yet I'd refused to step foot inside since we'd moved here.

"Oh, Rebecca, mind your manners." Josephina let out a nervous titter, waving away the request in a way that reminded me a little of Mother, always telling me to *be a lady*. Rebecca cast her eyes down, back to her plate.

The rain had stopped and the air from the open door wafted in, heavy and humid and filled with the sounds of crickets preening in the distance. If Rebecca went to see the ponies, then this awful dinner could be over and I could go upstairs and still read Pammy a story before she fell asleep. Then I could get into bed myself. Exhaustion had settled over me, somewhere between the talk of Josephina's peonies and the azaleas. I was so very tired now, I wondered if I might sleep all through the night, for the first time since we'd come to Lake Forest.

"Tom," I said his name loudly enough that he stopped his conversation with Harold, midsentence. "Rebecca wants to see your ponies, darling."

Tom made a face; I couldn't quite tell if it was disdain or amusement from so far away down the table. He finished off his whiskey and stood, slapping his hands on the table. "All right then, let's all go see the ponies. Harold, Josephina, will you join us? Daisy?" Now he was smirking, like he was thrilled by the prospect of trapping me into finally going out to his stables, and even more thrilled that I'd brought it upon myself by interrupting his conversation.

Josephina glanced at me, as if for permission. "I'm going to excuse myself to go put the baby to bed," I said. "But you all go on ahead without me."

"The nurse will put the baby to bed," Tom said, quickly.

"Pammy likes it when I do it," I said. Josephina nodded, cast me a knowing smile. Tom frowned deeply—he hated it when I *chose Pammy* over him, always reminding me that we had staff to look after her, to care for her every need. He didn't understand the way that holding her, reading her a story, kissing her good night each night, feeling her soft skin and smelling her baby girl powder smell quieted the restlessness inside of me for the smallest of moments.

Sometimes it felt like I needed Pammy more than she needed me. "Anyway"—I stood—"it was so nice to meet you, Buckleys. I hope I'll see you again soon."

I could feel Tom's disapproving eyes on me as I stood and walked away. And later, when I awoke restless again, at midnight, he wasn't in bed.

WE WOULD NOT see the Buckleys again soon, thank goodness. Or at least, I wouldn't.

Tom played polo with Harold still, but in the months that ensued, we looked elsewhere for social engagements. We began going into the city for parties at least once a week, and there we found a younger crowd, a wealthy crowd—friends Tom had known from Yale or boarding school who'd moved back. But still, they were Tom's friends. They had wives, and they had girlfriends, but I wouldn't say I really became *friends* with anyone on my own right in Chicago. There were other women I talked to at parties—we compared diamonds and pearls, and stories about baby nurses. And one time in September we were at a soiree so gay, we ended up all taking our clothes off and diving into the cool waters of Lake Michigan sometime just before dawn. Tom lifted me up in the water, and I was laughing, and the world felt all at once bright and surreal. But he was so drunk that night that back at home, he slept for two days straight and still had a hangover and a frown on his face the following Sunday.

Still, I lived for those parties. Dressing up and going into the city on Tom's arm. Lake Forest was too quiet. We were far enough from the city that I only went in for a specific engagement. At least in Cannes, I had the beach to while away my days. Here it became almost too unbearably cold to spend much time outside, even by the end of September.

Tom played polo most days, and I was left behind at home with only the staff and Pammy. Sometimes I wondered if everything might be better if I took Pammy's care all onto myself. She would keep me endlessly busy, and being with Pammy always made me feel happy in a way nothing else did. But when I mentioned it to Tom, he said he wouldn't hear of his wife being a nursemaid.

I desperately missed Jordan, missed having a friend and a companion to brighten up the house and my days. I was hazy on the details, because she didn't share them with me. But I knew there had been some kind of scandal in the golf tournament a few months back, and that Jordan had left it for a little while, gone to New York City to stay with her aunt. But I also knew she barely knew her aunt and didn't like her much either. I wrote her letter after letter, imploring her to come to Lake Forest, to stay with us. She wrote back only once and simply said she wasn't feeling up for parties. *No parties*, I promised her. *We'll stay in the house and just talk and talk the way we used to back in Louisville.* But that letter got me no response.

I got so desperate for companionship that I wrote to Mother in late October, inviting her to come stay with us for a spell. She said she didn't relish the cold winters in Chicago, and that maybe we could come to Louisville in the spring. What neither one of us wrote, what sat there unwritten between us, was that it was almost December. Almost the four-year anniversary of the train crash that took Daddy and Rose from us. And we Fay women were just superstitious enough that neither one of us was willing to travel that same exact train route at the same exact time of year.

And then maybe it was being in Chicago. Maybe it was the bone-chilling cold that rolled in with November, the thick layer of ice that turned the lake white and inhospitable. Maybe it was that I was lonely and friendless and increasingly uncheered even by the parties I continued to go to with Tom. But I missed Rose more desperately than I had in years, since the months around when the accident first happened.

ROSE CAME BACK to me again in my sleep.

One night, she appeared in my dream. She was dressed in her white Communion dress, her pretty blond hair tied back with a pink ribbon. She was Rose before the polio had hit, no limp and no trace of illness in her lungs.

She ran fast across our Lake Forest yard, not even out of breath, laughing, imploring me to follow her. She ran and ran and I chased her, and then she ended up at Tom's stables, and she beckoned me to go inside with her.

She unlatched the door and walked in, and I followed after her, watching her pet the ponies on their heads, cooing to them. I was fully aware that it was my first time entering Tom's space since we'd moved to Chicago, but that didn't bother me in my dream. What bothered me was, I couldn't catch Rose. No matter how fast I walked, she was one step ahead of me. I longed to touch her, to hug her, to hold her, for just one more moment. But she was just out of my reach. Even when I started running, I couldn't quite catch her.

Rose, I cried out. *Wait!*

I opened my eyes and she was gone again. My bedroom was dark, empty. A pale blue and orange fire crackled in the fireplace across the room, and I was chilled but also sweating. I rolled over, and Tom was gone, too. His side of the bed was still unslept in. I checked the clock and it was just after midnight. And then I stood and went to the window. I could see his stables from here, and the building glowed a little, in the distance. *Rose?* I blinked back tears. No, of course it wasn't Rose at all. It was Tom. That's where Tom went, in the middle of the night, when he couldn't sleep? To visit with his goddamned ponies.

Daise, be good, Rose's voice whispered in my ear.

I walked downstairs and grabbed my coat and a lamp. We'd been in Chicago six months and I'd yet to go out to the stables. But now I was half asleep and I still felt Rose lingering on my skin, making me brave or senseless. *She was just here.* Just petting the ponies. And I knew she wasn't in the stables now. Truly, I knew she wasn't. But Tom was. And maybe if I showed an interest in his ponies, everything would feel better again. I could go to him there and bury my face in his neck and inhale that deep spicy smoke and whiskey scent of him. And I would stop feeling so desperately lonely.

I put on my boots and trudged across the lawn to the stables. The frosted grass crackled as I stepped, the sound so loud it seemed to reverberate against the cool quiet of the December night. But we were so far away from everyone and everything, there was no one else around to hear it but me.

When I reached the stables, I was breathing hard, sweating a little under the heavy wool of my coat. I put my lamp down to fiddle with the latch on the door. And then, once I got it open, I heard a sound. A strange, unexpected sound. It was a feral cry, but not the kind of cry a horse makes. It was a human sound. A woman's cry. She was in pain. In my head, I knew it couldn't be Rose, but my dream was still so close, so real, my heart didn't quite believe it.

I'm coming, Rose.

I picked up my lamp again and ran inside. The stable was dim, with a trail of lamps lining the floor, and it smelled so strongly of horses it turned my stomach. But still, I continued walking, toward the light, the row of lamps. Toward the desperate sound of the girl crying out.

I turned the corner, at the lamps, and there in an empty stall, I made out familiar shapes: my eyes roamed from the ground up, strong muscular bare legs, buttocks, back, hulking shoulders. *Tom.* He was standing, thrusting himself into a woman, who was pushed flat against the wall.

I stood there silently, suddenly weak with shock, frozen, unable to move. Why had Rose led me here? Why had she wanted me to see this truth with my very eyes? It was one thing to suspect, to wonder. But another altogether to watch him, this way. Naked and animalistic and powerful. His arrogance, his betrayal, they were nearly blinding. My head throbbed and I could barely see.

Tom thrust harder, finishing with his own stupid cry, and then suddenly, the woman's head turned toward mine and she gasped.

And there it was: the churned butter of her curls. The plump rosy hue of her cheeks. Rebecca Buckley. Sixteen-year-old Rebecca Buckley.

Jordan

AUNT SIGOURNEY LIVED IN A BROWNSTONE MANSION, IN A ONCE fashionable section of the Lower East Side. I showed up on her stoop, exactly one week after Jerralyn had shoved that newspaper at me. Aunt Sigourney had opened the door with a frown but had ushered me in all the same.

"You can stay as long as you like," she'd said. "As long as you don't make any noise. I don't enjoy noise."

I'd promised her, no noise, and into her guest room I went. Aunt Sigourney was in her late seventies and mostly deaf, and the irony was, she wouldn't hear me even if I did make noise. But even that thought brought me no cheer. Nothing brought me cheer any longer, certainly not old deaf Aunt Sigourney. But where else was I going to go?

Not even an hour after Jerralyn had come to my room that morning in Atlanta, Mr. Hennessey had dismissed me from the team for *cheating*. He'd handed me a train ticket and told me to pack my bags. No matter that I'd tried to plead my case, that I'd insisted it was all a lie . . . a mistake. Mrs. Pearce had just looked directly at me, told me to leave before things *got worse*. And Mr.

Hennessey had looked me straight in the eye and swore he and Mrs. Pearce both saw me move the ball. I'd never felt so flattened by the weight of another person's lie before. His words crushed me, so that the entire train ride from Atlanta to Grand Central station, I could hardly breathe.

Then there was Mary Margaret.

As I'd packed up my own things, I'd noticed that her bag was already gone. The other girls were whispering that she'd already left for Nashville, weighed down by *shame*. They whispered that it was the shame in knowing what I'd done, in hiding my secret. But their words took on a different meaning in my head. Were they right? Was she ashamed of what had happened between us?

My eyes had stung hot with tears, thinking that everything Mary Margaret was afraid of had happened. She'd been right to be scared. I'd been stupid and foolish, and I'd ruined everything.

Once I made it to Aunt Sigourney's, I telephoned Mary Margaret's home in Nashville. Her mama picked up, and when I told her who was calling, I heard her suck in her breath a little on the other end of the line. "She doesn't want to talk to you," her mama said sharply. "After what you did, Jordan Baker, you should be ashamed." There was that word again, that feeling. *Shame.*

"But . . . I . . . I didn't move the ball." My protests had begun to feel futile, my words hopeless. No one would ever believe them. Why even keep saying them aloud?

"Don't call here again."

"Just tell her that I don't regret it. I don't regret anything that happened," I cried out into the telephone.

Her mama slammed down the receiver in response.

I called back every evening for weeks, but after a few nights, they just stopped answering the telephone altogether.

And then by the summer, I stopped calling. I wrote Mary Margaret a letter, telling her where I was and how she could reach me.

But by the fall that made it back to me, entirely unopened, a big fat *Return to Sender* stamped across the front.

LOSING GOLF WAS one thing, but losing Mary Margaret was another.

Sometimes it felt like I'd left my life and my breath and my soul back in that inn in Atlanta. I was listless for months. I slept until noon and got into bed again at five P.M. I only ate a little, one meal a day at best, and my dresses started to hang loose around my frame. My muscles from golf disappeared, and I was just flesh and bones. A barely breathing apparition of my former self. *Grief*, Mary Margaret had told me once, *was forever. An endless, winding river.* And here I was drowning.

Each afternoon, I walked. I walked and I walked around the city, never stopping, never talking to anyone. One foot in front of the other. It was funny the way you could be in a place with so many people, and yet you could be so all alone. I both loved and hated that about New York City. I was in no mood to be with other people, anyway. Not even Daisy, especially not Daisy.

She'd written and invited me to come to Chicago, but I hadn't been truthful with her back in France. I hadn't told her about Mary Margaret or about that time I'd seen Tom in the middle of the night with their nurse. And were we really best friends if we no longer shared secrets? The idea of being with her now, of seeing her each day and having to talk to her and not tell her the truth about anything at all, or to confess and confide all my truths at once? It was too much. It was just too much.

I wrote her back that I was here, in New York, for Aunt Sigourney. That Aunt Sigourney needed me. It was entirely a lie. Aunt

Sigourney would've been overjoyed if I'd left her house to go stay with Daisy.

Daisy's letters kept on coming after that, but I left them sitting in an unopened stack on my bureau.

ONE DAY IN December, I was walking through the village. The air was chilly, but I hadn't thought to put on a heavy coat, and my cheeks stung from the wind. Still, I kept walking and walking, one foot in front of the other, counting city blocks in my head. I was up to seventeen when I heard an unfamiliar man's voice, calling for me. "Jordan," he shouted. "Jordan Baker?"

It had been so long since anyone had called my name. I thought about the last time, that last day in Atlanta when the announcer had said it at the tournament: *Jordan Baker in the lead after the first round*. Tears stung hot in my eyes and I sped up, walked even faster.

"Jordan Baker!" the man called again, and then I heard footsteps pounding behind me. Was he chasing me?

I stopped abruptly and spun around. He slid to a stop. I didn't recognize him at first, but, maybe there was something vaguely familiar about him. He was tall with blond hair that fell across his forehead, casting a shadow over his bright green eyes. He stared at me for a moment and then broke into a smile. "Jordan Baker, that *is* you."

"Excuse me?" I said quickly. "I don't know you."

"Jay," he said. "Jay Gatsby. We met in Louisville, before the war."

Jay Gatsby. That soldier Daisy had been ready to run away with. He looked different now. Older and broader shouldered, and better dressed. He wore what appeared to be an expensive gold suit, a red silk tie. I remembered my quiet disdain for him back in Louisville when I was still a naïve girl of sixteen who could never have understood how much her own life would crumble. And now it occurred to me that I disliked Tom so much more than I'd ever disliked Jay. That Tom had done exactly what I'd feared Jay would once—hurt Daisy.

"Let me buy you dinner," Jay said now. "We could catch up."

"I don't think so," I said. "I have plans." I had no plans, other than having a silent meal with Aunt Sigourney. But dinner with Daisy's old lover sounded like the most detestable kind of dinner.

"Maybe another night then?" he suggested.

"Maybe," I said, not really meaning it at all.

"Where are you staying?" he asked. He moved his stance, so he was blocking my way, and now it seemed he wasn't going to let me by until I told him. He was taller than I remembered, pushier too.

"With my aunt, Mrs. Sigourney Howard," I told him. "She's in the book." Then I pushed past him, walked briskly, until I turned the corner and he was completely out of sight.

WHEN I GOT back to Aunt Sigourney's, I thought about writing Daisy, telling her who I'd run into on the street. *Isn't it funny?* I might write. *That poor soldier I'd thought would ruin your life once— now he lives in New York and owns an expensive gold suit.*

But instead, I finally opened the stack of letters she'd sent me and read through them all. She went on and on, at first, about all the gay parties she was attending in Chicago. She loved Lake Forest! The baby was very happy in Lake Forest. Tom had a stable out back for his ponies and played polo nearly every day. But then, in her latest letter, her tone suddenly shifted. She wrote that they'd be leaving Chicago, soon after the first of the year. Tom had had an . . . *indiscretion.* I read that word and remembered in a flash that night in France, Tom's face buried in between the nurse's legs. It felt like a hundred years had passed since then, not just a year and a half. Guilt washed over me. I should've told Daisy what I saw. Why hadn't I?

My hands shook, holding her letter now, remembering the way it had felt to slap Tom across the face that night, the way I'd threatened him then. The next morning at breakfast, before Daisy came down, he'd promised me it would never happen again. It had been a terrible mistake. *Never again, Jordan, I swear.* Liar. Tom was a goddamned liar.

I continued reading Daisy's letter, rage hot behind my eyes. They would be moving to East Egg, Daisy wrote. And this would be a *permanent move. At last we'll live near each other again, Jordie!* East Egg was on Long Island, a short drive from the city, just across the sound. Daisy and I would practically be neighbors again.

I felt a strange mix of emotions at that thought. Happiness, sure. But it was tinged with dread. I longed to return to those carefree Louisville days, when Daisy and I would lie on her bed and laugh. But that was the past. I was twenty years old and ruined. I had nothing, no one. And Daisy had tethered herself to that wretched man.

But then I imagined just being with Daisy again, laughing. Would I even remember how to laugh? The thought of it now brought me the smallest bit of cheer. Just enough so that I finally responded to her letter. I told her to let me know as soon as they arrived. I'd come out to East Egg to visit.

THE DAY AFTER Christmas, Aunt Sigourney knocked on my door in the middle of the afternoon. I'd just gotten back from my walk and I sat on my bed, my fingertips still tingling, my cheeks ruddy from the cold. We'd spent Christmas together yesterday, cheerlessly, without either a tree or presents. Aunt Sigourney said she didn't care much for celebrating holidays. I desperately missed Daddy, who used to make such a big deal of Christmas every single year—I struggled to understand how Aunt Sigourney was truly his blood sister.

"Jordan," she called out now. "There's a man here to see you."

A man?

She opened up my bedroom door and slowly stepped inside, thumping about with her dreadful cane. "A suitor, perhaps? He says you have dinner plans." She cast me a toothy smile. There were so many things I was tempted to say to her in response, but instead I sighed and walked past her to see what the heck was going on.

Jay Gatsby stood there in Aunt Sigourney's living room, looking somehow both affable and arrogant. He wore a different suit today, a pale gray one, but the material didn't look any less fine. How many expensive suits did the man own now?

"What are you doing here?" I asked him, sharply.

"I've come to take you to dinner," he said. "You promised me a dinner and told me to look you up at your aunt's, remember?"

I didn't remember it exactly that way at all. I shook my head. "I've already eaten dinner."

"No, she has not," Aunt Sigourney piped up cheerfully from behind me. "And she would love to go to dinner with you." She gave my shoulder a little push. "Go ahead, Jordan. Go freshen up and get your coat. I'll entertain your young man."

Jay cast her a warm smile, and I realized he'd become just the kind of man that old ladies loved to fawn over. It didn't seem right and it didn't seem fair that Jay Gatsby had turned himself into *this* while I had gone and lost everything. But I supposed I was stuck going to dinner with him or I'd have to sit here and watch Aunt Sigourney drool over him all night.

I sighed and grabbed my coat. "All right, fine," I said. "Let's go to dinner."

AN HOUR LATER, Jay sat across from me at Le Chez, the most expensive restaurant in lower Manhattan. He'd reserved us a table in a private room and had them send out the meal prix fixe: caviar and escargot, a soup course and a salad course, a medium rare, buttery steak, and even an illicit and expensive bottle of French wine, the likes of which I hadn't tasted since I'd been at the Buchanans' château in Cannes. I wasn't sure how Jay had gotten possession of such a treat. I took a delightful sip and wondered whether it was worth telling Jay I had no interest in him before we finished the bottle. I kept my mouth shut. Might as well enjoy this dinner, if I was forced to be here.

"Jordan," he said, after I'd downed a glass of the Sancerre. "I need to ask you something."

My cheeks felt flushed as I looked at him. His eyes were earnest, and he must've gotten a haircut since the last time I'd seen him on the street, because now that his blond hair didn't fall in front of them, I could see the intensity of their greens.

"You and I . . ." I told him, my words feeling loose, slippery against my tongue. They escaped me, slurry. "Are never gonna happen."

He stared at me for a moment and then he began to laugh, a big hearty deep-down laugh that made his chest shake. "I'm sorry," he said, as my face reddened. "Forgive me." He shook his head and raised his arm. "Hey there, old sport"—he beckoned for our waiter, who quickly rushed over—"pour another glass for the lady, would you?"

Before I could protest, the waiter was pouring me more wine.

When he walked away, Jay had gotten control of himself again, and his features were stoic and calm. "I'm sorry for laughing. It's just . . . you've misread my intentions, Jordan. What I needed to ask you was . . . how's Daisy?" His eyes opened a little wider, his mouth parted a little, and he rested his chin in his hands, staring at me intently. Was it possible that after all this time, all these years, he was still *in love* with Daisy?

I bit my lip, then took another long sip of wine, and I thought about how to answer. I decided to tell him something true that wouldn't really tell him anything at all: "I haven't seen Daisy in over a year, since I visited her and Tom in France." He grimaced when I said Tom's name. It made me soften toward him a little, as I felt the way his face looked: angry and disappointed and a little bit sad. Tom was no good for Daisy; maybe we could both agree on that.

"But you've talked to her . . . written to her?" His voice floundered. He'd been expecting so much of me at this dinner, but only in terms of how it related to my knowledge of Daisy. He knew nothing of my scandal, or, if he did, he didn't care to bring it up. That, in itself, was refreshing. "Is she happy in Chicago?" he asked now.

I wondered how he knew she was in Chicago, how closely he'd been keeping track of her, and how he'd gotten any information about her at all. Not that the Tom Buchanans were the sort of couple who ever kept a low profile. Maybe it wouldn't be that hard to keep track. I supposed they were all over the society pages.

"Happy?" My voice faltered a little on the word, and I took another large sip of wine.

Later I would think, if I hadn't had almost two glasses of Sancerre, I wouldn't have said what I did next. And maybe, if I'd just kept my mouth shut, everything would've turned out differently.

But at the time, my head was foggy, and I was angry at Tom. I'd promised him I'd hurt him if he hurt Daisy again, and what better way to do it than this? "Actually," I said to Jay, "I don't think they are very happy in Chicago at all. In fact, they're moving, after the first of the year. Out here. They bought a house in East Egg."

Jay's eyes widened again, and they were such a bright shade of green, they reminded me of the glow of the Mediterranean outside my bedroom veranda first thing in the morning in Cannes. "East Egg," he said softly, turning the idea of it over in his mind as he spoke. "Daisy is moving, here. To East Egg."

"Yes," I said. "Just across the sound. She'll be practically close enough to touch."

And though it was the day after Christmas, I smiled a little to myself, and I thought, *Merry Christmas, Daisy.*

Merry Christmas, Tom.

Detective Frank Charles

CHRISTMAS WAS THE HARDEST TIME.

For one thing, every childhood memory he had of the holiday was wrapped up in Lizzie, in her sheer delight of all things holy, bright, and sparkly. Every year when Dolores started unpacking ornaments, hanging them on their tiny tree, he could picture Lizzie doing the same, could suddenly, clearly remember the sound of her laugh.

Christmas had gotten doubly hard for him these past three years, since Dolores had gotten sick. Now, it was a bona fide fact—they would never have a family of their own. Never have a little girl with a laugh like Lizzie's or a little boy with Dolores's sea glass green eyes to enjoy Christmas with them. It was just Frank and Dolores, and who knew how many years he'd even have Dolores here with him. *Fifty-fifty*. Three years had come and gone. But would four?

"Frank?" Dolores said now, as they sat on the couch together, listening to Christmas carols on the phonograph. "You look so far away. Are you thinking about the Gatsby case still? It's Christmas," she chided him.

He nodded, smiled sheepishly. Sure, better to let her think his mind was lost in the case than in imagining a bleak and terrible future without her. "Sorry," he apologized and wrapped his arm around her. He pulled her closer, kissed the top of her head. Her hair smelled vaguely like the turkey she'd roasted in the oven for dinner and the cinnamon from the cake she'd made for dessert. *Would this be their last year, their last Christmas?* he wondered for the fourth year in a row. It felt impossible and also strangely inevitable.

Dolores shivered a little, and he pulled her tighter to him. It was chilly outside, drafty inside their small apartment. The fire glowed across the room, but it wasn't enough to warm her. Dolores hated the cold.

He used his free arm to tap his cigarette in the ashtray on the end table, and then he thought about summer. About the vacation Dolores had always dreamed of, in East Egg. He'd love to give her one of those beautiful houses that backed straight up to the water, for just one summer. He'd been hoping this case would be wrapped up by Christmas, that he'd have collected his money from Wolfsheim by now and he could've given Dolores the *summer of 1923* as a gift, a photograph of their rental house wrapped neatly in a box with a giant bow. Something to look forward to. Something to keep on living for.

But the case was far from being wrapped up, the money from Wolfsheim far from certain. Frank still had more questions than answers. Summer was months away, and Christmas was making him melancholy. Instead of the promise of summer, his Christmas gift to Dolores was a small square serving dish he'd been able to get from the sale table at Macy's.

"Frank," she'd said when she'd opened it earlier, clutching it to her chest. "This is beautiful." And that was Dolores, always making the best of everything awful.

But instead, he wanted to give her the best. She deserved the best.

HE COULDN'T SLEEP that night, and after Dolores got into bed, he feverishly went through his notes again, lighting another cigarette. Then another. He poured himself a glass of the good bourbon that he'd been keeping for special occasions (there hadn't been any of late). It was Christmas. That was enough. He took a large swig, and the bourbon burned his throat. After another, Lizzie's laughter faded again; so did his worries about Dolores.

Here in front of him was the evidence, the interviews. The lies. If there was one thing he knew from his years as a detective it was that liars always made mistakes. He just had to figure that out in this case.

By 2 A.M., his thoughts had come down to this: If everyone had lied to him about the hairpin, except Jordan, why had Nick been so convinced that Jordan was *an incurable liar*? The two of them had been together for a time last summer, and he wasn't sure how it ended. Still, Nick must know something about her.

By 6 A.M. Frank was convinced that the answer to everything was just a train ride away: Nick Carraway's apartment on the Lower East Side. He walked into the bedroom, kissed Dolores on the forehead, and she rolled over and mumbled something incoherent.

"It's early," he whispered to her in response. "Go back to sleep, Dee. I have to go into work for a few hours, but I'll be home for lunch."

She mumbled something else, about Christmas, rolled over and fell back to sleep.

Now, he lit another cigarette as he got off the train a few blocks from Nick's apartment. It was early still, just about eight. Frank hadn't slept at all last night and had drunk too much bourbon. The early morning cold suddenly made him feel heavy with exhaustion. He really could use a cup of coffee.

What was he doing here? He felt like he was chasing a ghost, looking for answers that might not even exist. Chasing a goddamned paycheck that might not ever come.

But he was just two blocks from Nick's place. He blew on his hands to warm them, and soldiered on.

"MERRY CHRISTMAS," FRANK said when Nick opened the door. The cold and the walk had sobered him, and now he felt nearly lucid again.

"Christmas is over," Nick said abruptly, frowning.

Frank nodded, pushing his way into Nick's apartment without waiting for an invitation. It was small and dark inside, no Christmas tree. Just a bed and a desk and a tiny stove in the corner. It was quite a downgrade from his house out in West Egg. "Nice place," Frank said, not really meaning it.

"I like it better here," Nick said, somewhat defensively. "It's close to work. A ten-minute walk." He paused, and then he added, "And I already told you everything I know, Detective. Didn't I tell you to go talk to Daisy?"

Frank nodded. "I did talk to Daisy. Went all the way out to Minnesota. Quite a place your cousin's got there."

"I wouldn't know." Nick frowned again. "I haven't been."

"Then I stopped to talk to Catherine McCoy—Myrtle's sister—in Illinois." Nick frowned, knowing perfectly well who Myrtle was even if he might not know Catherine. "And then, in October, I went down to New Jersey to talk to Jordan Baker."

"You've been busy," Nick said drily.

"Sure," Frank said. "I suppose."

"What do you want from me?" Nick asked, sighing. He looked exhausted, as if life in the city had really weighed on him these last few months. New York had worn on him, the way it always seemed to do on young people who didn't have quite enough money to live the high life in the city.

"Jordan Baker," Frank said now. "You were seeing her last summer."

"Sure . . . But it wasn't anything serious. We had dinner a few times, and then it sort of petered out."

"You know, she's playing on the golf tour this fall," Frank said, watching Nick's face closely.

Nick nodded, stone-faced. "I'd heard that."

"But it doesn't make sense. Why would they let her back at all after they threw her out once for cheating?"

Nick shrugged. "Who knows how she managed it. Jordan is . . ." He let his voice trail off for a moment as if looking for the right adjective. "Resourceful, to say the least."

"But you told me the first time we spoke that Jordan is . . . What were your exact words, Nick?" Frank paused a moment for effect even though he already knew the words he was looking for. Nick frowned, deeper, maybe remembering them, too. *"An incurable liar."*

Nick nodded. "A good liar generally is quite resourceful, Detective."

Frank pulled the hairpin out of his jacket pocket and showed it to Nick. "But I asked all three of the women about this hairpin, Nick. And it seemed like the only one who told me the truth about it was Jordan. I need you to help me understand that."

"Jordan? Told you the truth?" Nick choked on the words, a laugh sputtering out of him. He took the hairpin from Frank and examined it closely. "Jordan told you about this hairpin? What'd she tell you exactly?"

"Daisy and Catherine both said they'd never seen it before. But Jordan told me flat out it looked like it could be Daisy's."

Nick laughed. "It probably *was* Daisy's. Jordan doesn't own anything. Daisy gives her everything. It isn't a give-and-take kind of friendship. It's a take-and-take-and-take kind of friendship, if you know what I mean?"

He nodded again. Sure . . . Maybe he did.

"So it might've belonged to Daisy," Nick said now, handing the hairpin back to him. "But Jordan wore it last summer. Every date I went on with her, she had a pin that looked just like this in her hair."

Frank thought back to his conversation with Jordan in South Jersey. He'd been so flabbergasted by her apparent *honesty* that it hadn't occurred to him until right this very moment listening to Nick what it was exactly Jordan had said: *Daisy was at parties at Jay's house all summer. She could've dropped it anytime,* Jordan had insisted.

But he'd never told her where he'd found the hairpin.

Myrtle

THE END OF EVERYTHING BEGAN WITH THE YELLOW CAR.

You didn't see so much color out here among the ashes. It was part of the reason why I lived for my weekends in the city with Cath—color. Everything there was just bursting with it—red and green awnings of storefronts, pinks of taxicabs, the purple blue of the lilacs that bloomed in Central Park this time of year. Staring out my apartment window, above George's garage, the entire world always looked dirty and gray.

So I watched the fancy yellow car drive into our lot with fascination. We rarely saw expensive cars like that around here, only once in a while, when a millionaire from East Egg might stop for gas on his way into the city. But I couldn't recall seeing any car so bright. It felt a little like that first daffodil bloom peeking up through the April snow back in Rockvale: hope.

Still, I stared at the yellow car, at first, only a moment, before dismissing its importance. Probably just a rich man who'd gotten lost or had car trouble on his way out to Long Island. Wouldn't be the first one, and certainly wouldn't be the last. I walked away from the window and carried on with my morning. I'd put away the breakfast dishes and was trying to scrub a large spot of grease out of George's brown overalls. I kept on scrubbing, scrubbing even though my knuckles were already raw from washing the dishes. There was a rhythm, a painful monotony to my housework. Depending on the day, I either let that put me at ease or drive me slowly mad.

"Myrtle, get down here!" George's voice called for me up the stairs, and I jumped at his unexpected call, dropped the overalls.

I wiped my hands on a dish towel. "Coming," I yelled back. George never wanted me down in the garage unless he was so busy he needed me to ring up customers. But as far as I could tell from looking out the window, only the yellow car was here. George wasn't busy at all.

I bounded down the stairs to the garage below, feeling a sickness swell in my stomach, rising to my chest, worried that George was angry with me. I tried to swallow it back. George had been in such a pleasant mood this morning, at breakfast. I hadn't even seen him since—what could he possibly be mad about? We were fine, George and I, except when I occasionally forgot myself, when I *acted ungrateful*, when I accidentally showed him how I despised this small life of ours. Day by day, it wasn't so hard really, to pretend to be happy, to force a smile.

I reached the bottom of the stairs, and George stood there, his arms across his chest. He looked more amused than angry, and I exhaled. Behind him, a man dressed in a pink suit leaned against the yellow car. When he saw me, he tipped his cream-colored hat, and his blond hair tumbled out across his forehead. I glanced nervously at George, not sure what was going on.

"George?" I said his name softly, a question, not daring to make eye contact with the man from the yellow car, but feeling his eyes on me all the same.

"This man says he's Catherine's friend," George said. "You didn't tell me your sister had a rich beau, Myrtle."

"I didn't . . ." My voice trailed off and I shook my head. Cath hadn't told me anything of the sort. No matter how many times I'd prodded, begged her, *pleaded* with her, she'd said there was no special man and she certainly hadn't mentioned anyone . . . rich. "I didn't quite believe it myself until . . . well, I saw him standing here," I corrected myself. Lying to George was second nature by now, and whoever this man was—Catherine's beau or not—I wanted the opportunity to speak with him myself. George would only let that happen if he believed this man was completely attached to my sister.

"He said he had a question for you," George said. "I told him your father's still alive back in Rockvale. If it's Catherine's hand in marriage he wants permission for, he'd better take a train out to Rockvale like I did."

"I told you, old sport," the man said gently. His voice was easy, calm. "There's no marriage on the horizon. Just a favor I want Myrtle's help with. Something to . . . surprise Catherine with. If I could just speak with Myrtle for a minute or two, and then I'll be on my way."

George glanced at the man again, then glanced at me. He hesitated, still not sure he wanted to leave me alone with this man, but not quite wanting to get himself caught up in anything concerning Cath, either. George barely tolerated her as it was—god forbid something might be asked of him, regarding her happiness. Luckily for both of us, another car drove into the lot and stopped by the gas pump. A black weathered sedan, part of our normal color palette. George shot me a warning look, then walked off to help his customer.

"Who are you?" I asked the man now. "And are you really seeing Cath? She's never mentioned you."

He smiled. He had a warm, bright smile and stunning green eyes. *Handsome and rich.* Why hadn't Cath mentioned him? "Catherine was a friend of mine in the city, yes," he said.

"Was?" I questioned, not liking the sound of that.

"I've just recently left the city. Bought a house in West Egg, right on the water."

I shook my head. None of that answered my questions. He kept on smiling, in a calm, easy way that was almost unsettling. "I don't understand," I said. "What do you want from me?"

"Catherine mentioned to me once or twice that you could . . . use some extra money." My face turned an instant red at the very idea that Cath had discussed me, and my life, with this wealthy man *friend* of hers.

"I'm doing just fine," I lied, huffily. He looked around, raised his eyebrows. It was abundantly clear that I was not doing just fine.

"Well, the thing is"—he kept speaking, undeterred—"I need a woman to do something for me, and I can pay you a hundred dollars to do it."

A hundred dollars? That was a lot of money, more than George made in an entire month. And if it was a hundred dollars George was none the wiser about, I could do with it as I pleased. George had two loves, cars and pistols, and any extra money he made he put toward those, not me and my happiness. But with my own money, I could treat myself to a nice dress, a new pair of shoes, the kind of things a girl needed to make herself pretty that I'd almost forgotten after so many years living in the blacks and whites and grays above George's garage . . . "Wait a minute," I said, stopping myself midway through the fantasy. "What does this have to do with Cath?"

Instead of answering, he took out a photograph from his jacket pocket—a picture of an unfamiliar but well-dressed man. The photograph was torn—you could still see a woman's disembodied arm clinging to the man in the picture, a diamond bracelet snaked around her wrist—and I wondered who it was he'd ripped out from the other half of the photograph. "I need you to find this man," he said. "He takes the nine o'clock train from East Egg into the city every Friday. I want you to find him on that train, sit with him, and talk to him."

I frowned, confused. Why was he willing to pay me $100 to find a man on a train and sit and talk to him? "I don't understand," I said again.

"It's very simple, really. I need a beautiful woman to do me this favor." I blushed at his implication that I was *beautiful* and reached a hand up to smooth my hair. "So? Will you help me out?" he said easily.

I wasn't stupid. Something illicit was most likely going on here. Certainly, at the very least, something . . . strange. But one hundred dollars? And all I had to do was ride the train into the city, find and talk to one particular handsome stranger. "All right," I said. "I'll do it."

CALL CATH.

That's what my head told me to do later that night as I stared at the crisp $100 bill in front of me, John J. Knox's spectacled eyes staring back at me, taunting me. It was after supper, after George had gone to bed. After I'd lied to him and told him the man in the yellow car had only wanted to know Cath's favorite gemstone so he could pick her out some new jewelry. *Diamonds, of course,* I'd said with a forced laugh, picturing the snaking bracelet on the disembodied arm. *What man doesn't know every girl prefers diamonds?* George had rolled his eyes, already tiring of the subject.

I knew I should pick up the telephone, call Cath, and ask her what was going on. I should ask her who this man was and why had he come out here, to me, of all people. And besides all that, if she really had dated him, a man wealthy enough to drive such a bright, extravagant car, why hadn't she ever told me that? And why in heaven's name had she let him get away from her? A house in West Egg, on the water, was probably a very nice house indeed.

I had so many questions, but, as I put my hand on the telephone, I pictured Cath on the other end of the line, getting quickly frustrated, worried, fretting over me that way she was so inclined to do. I could already hear her raspy voice, imploring me not to go, not to get on that train. Maybe this man I was supposed to talk to on the train was dangerous . . . a murderer? But I looked around my small, dark kitchen, and I wondered if there were, perhaps, worse fates than being murdered.

I walked away from the telephone. I'd tell Cath the next time I saw her in the city. We could laugh over gin rickeys that I could afford to buy her for once. And maybe we could even go shopping and I would buy her something pretty.

Catherine

"YOU'LL NEVER BELIEVE IT," MYRTLE SAID TO ME, AS WE BOTH sipped gin rickeys inside the Monte Carlo, my favorite and right now, on a Saturday afternoon, very crowded speakeasy. "I've met someone."

"Met someone?" I turned to look at her, and we sat so close together I could see every detail of her face. She smiled slyly, and her cheeks were pink, glowing, in a way I hadn't seen them in, my goodness, years? Since we were girls in Rockvale maybe.

"A man," she clarified, lowering her voice. "A wealthy, beautiful, delicious man, Cath."

I stopped drinking the gin, mid-sip, wanting clarity to understand this unexpected news. For years I'd been worrying about Myrtle, wanting her to leave George and come live, unfettered, in the city with me. I never considered she'd leave him, for another man. "You left George?" I asked, both stunned and a little proud that she'd finally been so brave.

"Not yet," she said, lowering her voice. "He still has a wife. But he's going to leave her soon, and then I'll leave George."

"Oh Myrtle." I sighed.

"Don't *Oh Myrtle* me, Saint Catherine. People get into unhappy marriages. It happens. I should know." She paused to take a sip of her drink, and I pushed my own away as a new worry bubbled up inside of me. "Anyway, he set me up with a real nice apartment in Manhattan, and I've told George you need me to spend more time with you, so I'll be coming into town, more and more. We can see each other when I come to see him! And he buys me such pretty things, Cath. Look at these." She turned her head to the side and pointed to the two sparkly hairpins, peeking out slyly from underneath her hat.

"Are those . . . diamonds?" I asked, not quite believing that they were even as I reached my finger up to touch them. The stones were cool and sharp, and too sparkly to be anything but diamonds.

"You'd better believe they're diamonds," she said. "Tom only buys me the best, Cath."

"Tom?" I repeated his name, and it felt unexpected on my tongue. Sharp and cold like the illicit diamonds in her hair.

"Why are you frowning?" Myrtle pouted. "I'm finally happy."

I forced a smile. "I'm glad you're happy. But . . . a married man?" My voice faltered a little. I felt this new fear for my sister rising up inside of me, creeping and spreading in circles in my chest like a spider methodically building a web. "And what if George finds out?" It frightened me to think of what he might do to her if he did.

"He won't," she said, vehemently. "He thinks I come to the city for you, Cath. How would he ever know?"

I bit my lip, trying to force myself not to speak again until I could think of something cheerier to say. "Those hairpins are real pretty, Myrtle," I finally said.

"They are." She sighed, happily. "Aren't they?" She ran her fingers across them, then paused for a moment. "You know, I'll give you a key for my apartment and you can come in and borrow them anytime you like. Borrow anything you want, Cath. I've got a whole collection of nice things now."

I thanked her, but I knew I'd never do it. What use did I have for diamond hairpins anyway? And nice things, bought for her by her married lover? They felt . . . tainted. "So fill me in, how'd you even meet Tom?" I asked her. Myrtle didn't get out of Queens much, except to visit me, and I certainly hadn't introduced them.

"It was the funniest thing, Cath. And really, I guess I owe it all to you."

"Me?" I shook my head, not understanding.

"Yes, your friend, in the fancy yellow car. He set us up."

IT HAD BEEN months since I'd seen Jay.

On a chilly evening at the end of last January, he'd climbed up the fire escape, knocked on my window. I'd gone to open it and noticed a creamy yellow convertible sitting in the alleyway below. "You bought a car?" I'd asked, laughing at the sheer impulsiveness of it, as I'd opened the window for him to climb in. He hadn't telephoned first, just showed up. And when I'd seen him last, at his place, he had not even owned a car. Certainly not an expensive yellow one.

"Rolls-Royce. I just bought her," he said, breathless from the cold. He climbed in through my window, his face ruddy with excitement. "She's beautiful, isn't she, Cath? Any girl would love her, wouldn't she?"

I nodded, though I couldn't care less about a car. But I was happy to see him. I'd had a long day, my feet ached, and I'd just taken off my shoes before he'd shown up. "Sure," I murmured. "Your car is lovely." I stood on my stockinged tiptoes to kiss him.

But he gently pushed my face away, and he offered me a cool smile instead. "What's wrong?" I asked.

"Nothing's wrong," he breathed out slowly, his voice still quivering with excitement. "Everything is right. Daisy is moving to East Egg."

Daisy. I fought the urge to roll my eyes. "Just Daisy?" I asked gently, instead. "Not . . . her husband, too?"

"No, no. Him, too. But I can deal with him." *Deal with him?* I let out a nervous laugh. "She's going to be so close, Cath," he said, still talking excitedly. "I can see her again. I can make her love me again. I have money now. I can make her happy now." His voice was higher than usual; he spoke faster than usual, and he reminded me suddenly of a desperate rat trying to claw its way up the sewer grate before it drowned.

"Oh, Jay." I put my hand on his cheek. His soft, familiar cheek. Daisy had married another man several years ago; Jay hadn't seen her since before the war. There was no way she still pined after him the way he pined after her. Or else why would she have gotten married at all? But poor Jay would never believe me if I told him that. He was going to have to find that out for himself. Still, my heart ached for him, for the pain he was about to feel when she rejected him. Again.

"I know I promised you I was going to help your sister," he was saying now. "And I'll still try to find some way, Cath. But I just used almost all my savings to purchase a house in West Egg. It's beautiful and grand and quite impressive. And right across the water from where Daisy will be in East Egg."

It was stunning, the amount of calculation that had gone into this, and in such little time, too. A few weeks earlier, just before

Christmas, Jay and I had lain in my bed, naked and restless and hungry for each other. And now, suddenly, he'd used all his money to buy a house and a Rolls-Royce and god knows what else, to impress *Daisy*. I could hardly believe or understand it. "So you're leaving the city then?" I asked, still trying to make sense of it. He nodded. "Is this good-bye?"

He leaned in and gently kissed my cheek. Tears stung my eyes, but they annoyed me and I tried to will them away. We'd both known this wasn't forever. I just hadn't expected it to end quite like this, with Jay Gatsby fleeing the city, choosing a ghost of a woman—a married woman at that—over me, all in the blink of an eye. "Good-bye, Cath," he whispered.

And then just like that he was back down the fire escape, gone from my life forever.

AFTER I GOT drinks with Myrtle, I walked uptown with her to see her new apartment. It was the end of May. Jay was far away and hazy and back inside my chilly January bedroom. Now the air was redolent with flowers and trash seething out on the sidewalk for pickup. And I was sweating straight through my sundress as we walked arm in sticky arm uptown.

I'd had two gin rickeys as Myrtle had told me her story about Jay, and maybe it was the alcohol, or the way I'd just found myself caught up in my own memory of the last night I saw him, but none of it made sense. Even now as we walked, I still couldn't understand it. Her man in the yellow car had to be Jay. But why had he paid her $100 to sit with Tom on a train? Had he felt some sort of wayward loyalty toward me after all, remembering the promise he'd made to help Myrtle? Had he known, somehow, that Tom and Myrtle would fall in love? That Tom would make her *happy?* Did he believe that Tom could do what Jay had promised once, pull Myrtle from her small, impoverished life in Queens? But how could he possibly have known that? It made no sense.

To hear Myrtle tell it, there'd been an instant attraction between her and Tom on the train. She'd sat across from him, touched the beautiful white silk of his shirt. Then she hadn't been able to stop herself—she'd gotten off with him in the city and followed him into a taxicab, into a hotel, her body barely even realizing she'd left the train. *We couldn't keep our hands off each other, Cath. It was like he was my destiny.*

A destiny orchestrated by Jay. But why?

"Did I tell you he's a polo player?" Myrtle was saying as we walked into her new building now. It was one of those nice apartment buildings with a doorman and everything. My sister's demeanor changed as she walked inside; she stood up straighter, held her head higher, and got a sly, entitled smile on her face I'd never quite seen before. It was almost an arrogant smile. "Did I, Cath?"

I shook my head and didn't admit I wasn't even exactly sure what polo was. Something with horses, a game rich people played, and I had never concerned myself with any more detail than that.

"Yes, in fact, Tom Buchanan is one of the best polo players on the whole Eastern Seaboard," Myrtle bragged with pride now, like she'd invented both the man and the game herself. It was the first time she mentioned his full name and it rang a little funny in my ears.

Buchanan. Buchanan. Where had I heard that name before?

"Myrtle," I interrupted her, as she was still going on about polo. "What did you say his wife's name was?"

"I didn't," she huffed. "And why do you have to bring her up, Cath? He doesn't even love her." She pouted.

But suddenly it all made sense, and the reality of it swelled in my chest, the gin threatening to come back up right there in the beautiful marble lobby of Myrtle's new building.

"Daisy," I said softly. "Daisy Buchanan."

Daisy

OUR HOUSE IN EAST EGG WAS LAVISHLY GRAND, A FOUR-STORY redbrick Georgian colonial. It felt excessively large, the same way the château in Cannes and the mansion in Lake Forest had. And I supposed wherever it was we Buchanans moved, an embarrassingly opulent house awaited us.

Like Cannes, in East Egg our yard backed straight up to the water. Only here, instead of the Mediterranean, it was the Long Island Sound. And instead of warm blue water and blue horizon as far as my eye could see, it was cool, gray-blue water that stretched only as far as the tip of West Egg on the other side. There, across the sound, I could see the small speck of dock, meandering out from a West Egg mansion. Sometimes, when we first moved in at the end of March, before I knew who lived there, I would sit out underneath the green light on our own dock and wonder. Was there a family in that house, just across the sound? It was always lit up and bustling and alive.

West Egg, Tom droned on over supper one night, was for the nouveau riche. The *real wealth,* he told me, arrogantly, was in East Egg.

And still, I wondered who lived there. If there was a family across the sound from me, were they happy? Did they love each other? Perhaps new money felt a little less like a weight upon the woman's chest than old money. Of course, this was a silly line of thinking. The weight in my chest wasn't from money at all, new or old. The weight was Tom. After that little spree of his in Chicago, I could barely even look him in the eyes without remembering the plump childlike glow of Rebecca Buckley's face that night in his stables.

He'd brought his goddamned ponies to East Egg, too. We, of course, had a stable on our property, about a quarter of a mile down the road from the main house. But I never walked far enough in that direction myself to visit it.

You promised, I reminded him, the week after we moved in, when he first put on his riding gear, to go out to the stable and unload the ponies or whatever it was he did with them upon each one of our moves. *You promised. This is a permanent move, Tom. I need a real home. Pammy needs a real home!*

He kissed me on the top of my head. His kiss was chaste, his lips cool. It was already clear to both of us, perhaps, that his impropriety would find a new way to rear its ugly head no matter where we went, no matter what city we lived in. No matter how grand our house was. It was only a matter of time.

And yet, still somewhere deep inside of me, I believed, however foolish it was, if I demanded that this would be our permanent home, and not just for me but for *our daughter,* Tom might actually have it in him to behave himself.

TWO AND A half months after we moved in, a car sputtered in wildly through our gates before spinning to a stop at the top of the drive. It was midafternoon, two weeks before the longest day of the year, and I watched through the parlor window, feeling a sudden rush of joy at the sight of that swerving, reckless car. My Jordie was here! No one else we knew would dare drive that haphazardly.

I told her as much when she walked in the door, carrying a suitcase.

"Oh, Daise," she admonished, before putting her suitcase down and kissing me on both cheeks. "It takes two to make an accident. And I was the only one driving up the drive."

It was so good to see her again, I laughed, grabbed her tightly, held on to her. She felt skinnier than she used to, too thin. And when I pulled back and took a good look at her, I noticed the lines of her face looked a little different too. Her cheeks were hollower; there was a sadness about her now that she hadn't had as a girl in Louisville or even when I'd seen her last in Cannes. But she still looked beautiful nonetheless, draped in a white gauzy dress nearly identical to mine. Just this morning the *Times* had proclaimed white the "smartest summer color," and here Jordie and I were, still fashionable, even after everything life had thrown at us.

I pointed to the suitcase resting on the white marble floor. "I hope this means you're staying for a while, Jordie?"

I'd telephoned her at her aunt Sigourney's upon our arrival in East Egg and had invited her to come stay with us for the whole summer. For as long she liked, really. She said she'd think about it. But after she'd spent most of the last year ignoring my letters, I hadn't been sure what to expect, or whether she would show up in East Egg at all. Now that she was here, I didn't know if I could stand to lose her again.

"We'll see," she murmured after a few moments, considering it. Then she added, her words tumbling out in rush, "I've just come from a match and I lost and I'm famished. What do you have to eat?"

"Whatever you want," I said. And wasn't that the truth about my life as a Buchanan? All the excess. Whatever I wanted, whenever I wanted it, more than I could ever want or need. And as a young girl back in Louisville I couldn't have ever dreamed that I would have all this and still somehow feel vastly empty.

"Oh, Daise," Jordan interrupted my thoughts and gave me another quick hug. "It's so good to see you again."

I felt the same, and I suddenly wondered if Jordie was that *something else*. East Egg would be our permanent home, and if I could get Jordie to stay, too, maybe I would remember how to feel happy again. I hugged her again. "Come on into the dining room. I'll have the chef fix you something."

AN HOUR, AND two ham sandwiches later, Jordan and I stretched out on the parlor couch together. Jordan sipped a gin and tonic and put one hand across her stomach and sighed. I reached for her other hand and squeezed it and leaned back and closed my eyes. The French doors were open, and the wind blew in off the sound, bringing in a warm, sticky, restless breeze, swirling the white gauzy bottoms of our dresses up, like fans.

It was a moment, just one simple moment when I suddenly felt at peace. Jordan and I, we could lie like this, forever and forever, holding hands and feeling the warm breeze on our faces.

Then I heard the telephone ringing in the distance, interrupting my fantasy. I sighed and let go of Jordan. "Can't your butler answer that?" she intoned sleepily.

I shook my head. "It's probably Mother." It had been a few days since she'd called and the snow goose loved to check in at the most inopportune times.

I rose and answered the telephone still feeling warm: "Buchanan residence," my voice tumbled out lazily.

I heard breathing on the other end of the line.

"Hello," I said more sharply. "Anyone there?" I heard the abrupt click, but I still said *hello* one more time into the dead space. Then I pulled the phone away from my ear, held it in my hand for a second, and just stared at it. "Dammit," I said softly.

"Daise, my goodness. You sound like a sailor." Jordan laughed. She'd drunk down her gin, and her eyes were still closed. "Who was on the line?"

"Wrong number," I said, and I went back and sat down next to her.

She picked up my hand again and squeezed it. "Damn all those wrong numbers to hell." She giggled a little.

I opened my mouth, poised to tell her the truth, but then I couldn't make the words come out. It was as if saying it out loud would make it undeniably true. And I wanted so badly to believe still that everything would be different here than it was in Lake Forest. That East Egg truly could be our permanent home.

A LITTLE WHILE later, Tom walked back into the house from the stables, and Jordan and I still hadn't moved a muscle from the couch. The breathing on the other end of the line had magnified in my head, become something bellowing in the hour or two since it had happened. Tom leaned down and kissed my cheek. He reeked of sweat and whiskey, and I flinched. He acknowledged Jordan by patting her on the head, like a dog.

"There was a telephone call for you," I said, sitting up to glare at him, not able to keep the anger from burning up my voice.

"A wrong number," Jordan slurred, tracing her finger around her sweaty glass.

"Yes, very, very wrong." I shot Tom a withering look.

He shrugged, pretending he didn't understand the implication, that the breather on the other end of the line was a woman, calling for him. Two and a half months. We had only been here *two and a half months*!

"Daisy," he said, changing the subject altogether. "Your cousin's coming for dinner in an hour. Shouldn't you get ready?"

"Ready?" I laughed. "I'm ready enough right here." Sure, I was in a day dress, not an evening dress, and I was lying on the couch holding on desperately to my dear, sweet, slightly drunken Jordie. But I wasn't going to let Tom decide what I did at the moment.

"All right." He frowned, then shrugged. It would be hard for him to care less about me if he tried.

"Dinner with your cousin?" Jordan's voice slurred a little. Her eyes were still closed and she'd missed the bitter dynamic between me and Tom altogether. "But we just ate lunch," she exclaimed.

"It's four o'clock in the afternoon," Tom said, sounding disgusted, and I didn't at all like his tone.

"You stink," I said to him. "Go wash yourself up. Or else Nick might think I've married a polo pony not a polo player."

Tom shot me another look. And then he clarified to Jordan that he'd known Nick in college, that Nick had stayed with us for two nights once in Lake Forest.

"I'd say this cousin, *Nick*, already knows you married a pony," Jordan said, snorting a little, amusing herself. And then Tom just shook his head and walked off upstairs.

Jordan opened her eyes, turned back to me. "Who is this cousin of yours, Daise?" she asked. "And how come I've never heard of him before?"

I told her: Nick Carraway was a second cousin, once removed, Daddy's cousin's son. He was a few years older than us, and I'd never known him very well. He'd been raised in Minnesota and we'd only met once as children, in Chicago. Later, he was at Yale with Tom and then in the war without him. He hadn't ever been to visit us in Louisville and hadn't been able to make it to my wedding, either. I couldn't even remember why now. Other than the two pleasant enough days he'd visited us in Lake Forest, I truly didn't know much of Nick at all.

It was Mother who'd told me Nick had moved to West Egg just after I'd moved to East Egg, and then I'd wondered to her if maybe it was his house, right across the sound from mine. What a coincidence that would be, east and west cousins, staring across the great wide sound at each other. But Mother had laughed and said Nick certainly didn't have the money to stay in a house like that, even just for the summer.

"I can't believe I never mentioned Nick," I said, glancing at Jordan now. Her face looked far away, a little sleepy. Really, I could believe it. Nick had been of little consequence in my life, and I'd forgotten all about this dinner I'd scheduled weeks ago, too, until Tom had just brought it up.

But Nick was unattached—Mother had told me this much, repeating Cousin Marianne's lament that her son was almost thirty and in *no great hurry to marry*. And Jordan was single, as far as I knew. If I could get Jordan interested in Nick, maybe that would keep her here for the entire summer, with me, too. I already felt so much better, so much happier, since she'd sped up the drive earlier this afternoon. This new plan hatched in my head, and excitement over it bubbled up in my chest, replacing the anger I'd just felt for Tom. "Actually, I think you might *really* like him, Jordie," I added, nudging her with my elbow.

"Hmmm." Jordan swallowed down the rest of her gin and rested the sweating glass on the end table. "I don't know, Daise."

Jordan had never had a beau. At least not one she'd told me about. Of course, she had her golf game to worry about, but she was twenty-one now! Her daddy was gone and her aunt Sigourney was, by all accounts, dreadful. It was time for her to start thinking about marriage. It was well past time. "Well, I know you have impossibly high standards, Jordie," I said now. "But just give him a chance at dinner. You might really feel sweet on him. Even though they were at Yale together, he's nothing at all like Tom, I swear it."

"Well, thank goodness for that," Jordan cackled. "The world couldn't handle two Tom Buchanans, now could it, Daise?" Her tone was light, but we both knew she was only half joking.

She squeezed my hand again, closed her eyes, and leaned back against the couch. I did the same, slinking down until I rested my head on her shoulder. She reached up and twirled a lock of my hair around her finger the way she always had when we were girls, but now her finger caught on one of my diamond hairpins.

"I'm surprised to see you wearing your hairpins still," she said softly. Though I hadn't explicitly told her the details of Tom's little spree in Lake Forest, it felt like she somehow knew, like she could sense it. Like she saw Rebecca Buckley's plump pink cheeks when she closed her eyes at night too.

"I only wear them knowing you picked them out," I told her, and that was the honest truth. The hairpins might have been paid for by Tom, but they were chosen by Jordan, and that made them more her gift than his.

"I always loved those pins," Jordan said, touching one again, rolling her finger across it. "Just a little row of diamonds in your hair. Elegant and simple all at the same time, just like you, Daise."

Elegant and simple. Inside I felt like neither one of those things. My life, instead, felt like one great big, complicated, devastating storm. I reached up and pulled one of the pins out of my hair. Then I gently leaned over and pushed it into Jordan's hair. "Actually, Jordie, I think it suits you much better, what with your cute little pixie cut."

She smiled at me, then reached up and ran her fingers across the pin in her own hair. "But Daise," she protested softly. "It's yours. It belongs to you."

"You wear one for the summer. For as long you like," I told her. What I really meant was, *Stay here, stay with me for the summer. Don't leave me again.*

"I've got a nice place here." I suddenly heard Tom's voice coming in through the front door, booming. Bragging.

Then my cousin Nick's softer, more even tones, replying that yes, the house was *very, very nice indeed.* I heard their footsteps as they walked into the room, and a breeze erupted, swirling all the curtains about. Tom slammed the French doors shut.

"Just give Nick a chance," I whispered in Jordan's hair, my breath landing just below the diamonds of the hairpin.

Jordan

IT FELT AS IF I HAD BEEN ASLEEP FOR A VERY, VERY LONG TIME. And then suddenly Daisy swept me up into a hug, handed me a ham sandwich and a G&T, and all at once I was awake again. I was alive again.

There had been a time before I'd been thrown off the golf tour. Before I'd even *joined* the golf tour. Before I'd met Mary Margaret. Before Daddy had died. There had been a time once, when I was sixteen years old and the entirety of my happiness had been wrapped up in spending lazy, hot, summer afternoons in Louisville lying around with Daisy, listening to the sound of her voice. There had been a time before Tom had taken her away from me, and now, somehow, years later, I'd driven up from the city, a little broken and a little dead inside, walked inside the Buchanans' sprawling East Egg mansion, and found that Daisy was still right here. She was still mine. And maybe I wasn't dead at all.

I felt that for a few hours, a breath of gin and the summer breeze coming in off the water. I felt that way lying on Daisy's couch, a little drunk, and a little warm, holding Daisy's hand.

My head tingled as she pushed her diamond hairpin in just

above my earlobe, pulling my hair back. "Jordie," she whispered, her breath hot against my face, "you're beautiful."

DAISY'S COUSIN NICK was a bland-looking midwestern man with an indistinguishable face. He wasn't disagreeable by any stretch of the imagination, but in spite of Daisy's machinations, I was never going to fall in love with him. It was my fault that Daisy didn't understand this, of course. But she didn't know about the golf tour, either. For whatever reason, I'd heard myself telling her I'd lost a match just before I'd driven up, and that I'd play again tomorrow in Westchester. And it occurred to me that I should tell Daisy the truth, that I should tell her *everything*. But Daddy's face still haunted me, and I couldn't bring myself to do it.

So there was Daisy, none the wiser about the way my life had crumbled this past year, fluttering around trying to set me up with her cousin. She arranged the supper table so I was directly next to Nick. Her cheeks glowed pink as she introduced us—she was enjoying this. I sipped another G&T slowly, liking the way it made me feel warm and hazy, like I was glowing from the inside out. I reached my hand up to touch the diamond hairpin Daisy had just placed in my hair. And I smiled wanly as she ordered Nick to tell me about the bond business.

Jordan Baker, Nick repeated my name, instead. *The golfer? I've heard of you.*

What he really meant was, he'd heard about my scandal. No one remembered a lady golfer's name otherwise. But to Nick's credit, he was kind enough not to mention that part out loud.

Dinner was served, and Tom droned on about some insufferable book he was reading. Then, the telephone jingled in the distance, and Tom stopped speaking midsentence. Daisy suddenly slapped her hands on the table, stood, and stormed out. Tom quickly followed after her.

Daisy's voice rose in the distance, and Nick started babbling on about something but I shushed him, trying to make out the angry words Daisy and Tom were saying to each other in the other room. I could only hear the tenor of their voices but not the words themselves.

"What's going on?" Nick asked, finally catching on that something was, indeed, going on.

I shook my head, but I was thinking it through.

The telephone hang-up earlier. Daisy's anger now. I thought of Tom, that night in France, his head inside the baby nurse's skirt. Daisy's mention of an indiscretion in Santa Barbara. Something in Lake Forest, too, that had brought them here.

And even through my drunken haze, I suddenly understood. "Tom has got another woman," I said, matter-of-factly. Maybe I shouldn't have said those words out loud to Daisy's milquetoast cousin. But that's what happened when I had too much liquor. I was prone to a new level of verbosity, even for me.

Nick frowned. "I didn't know," he said.

"But you're not surprised?"

Nick opened his mouth, hesitated for a moment, but then before he could answer, Tom and Daisy rushed back in and took their seats at the table. "Sorry," Daisy apologized, still frowning. "It couldn't be helped."

I glared at Tom, but he didn't notice my gaze, or he pretended not to. Nick tried to break the tension by talking about his neighbor in West Egg, a man named *Gatsby*. I heard his name, and my skin suddenly grew cold, remembering how I'd told Jay a few months ago about Daisy's move here. Had he moved out here, because of what I'd told him?

I turned to look at Daisy to see if she had heard what Nick said, but all at once, the telephone rang again in the distance. She stood quickly, her face flaming. But this time instead of running out of the room, she went straight for the gin, poured herself a tall glass, and topped it off with only a little bit of soda water. Daisy never drank. She didn't like the way it made her feel *out of control*.

"Daise?" I questioned.

She shot me a terse smile in response, raised her glass in the air as if to toast, and then took a large gulp.

I'D ONLY EVER seen Daisy drunk one time, just before her wedding to Tom, when she was suddenly filled with a wayward sort of doubt her mother assured her all new brides have. But in hindsight now, I had to wonder if she'd known. If she'd always known deep down that Tom would never be faithful to her. If I'd ever married a man like Tom, I think I would've been drunk every single day of my marriage. Daisy had, up until now, shown remarkable restraint.

That night, just before her wedding, though, Daisy was so drunk her mother had called on me for help. I'd only been back in Louisville for a minute, and I'd arrived at the Fay house, breathless and sweating, feeling out of my element in what had once been my most familiar surroundings. Mrs. Fay asked me to get Daisy sobered up for her bridal dinner, and I'd found Daisy in her room, blubbering uncontrollably on, waving her hands in the air nonsensically.

Daise, I'd finally said, taking her by the shoulders, shaking her a little. *Enough!* And then she'd lashed out at me, tried to punch me in the face. I'd ducked and she'd punched the air instead.

Drunk Daisy was the worst kind of Daisy, and a few hours after dinner, after Nick had gone home, I was lying in bed, still worrying about her. I'd excused myself not too long after supper, claiming I had to be up early in the morning to get to Westchester for a tournament. Now, the house was quiet, too still, and I was wide awake, suddenly sober and swimming in the weight of my own lies. I supposed I'd have to wake up early in the morning, pretend to drive off to the tournament, and then invent a story about how I'd done to regale them with over supper tomorrow night. If I kept this up all summer, it would be exhausting.

"Jordie." Daisy rapped softly on the door now. "Are you up?" Her tone was surprisingly light, not angry, despite her words being a little slurry.

I cleared my throat. "I'm awake," I called out. "Come on in."

The door opened and Daisy stumbled in. She was still dressed in the sheer white dress she'd been wearing all day but now it had slipped a little down her shoulder, showing a hint of her brassiere. Her hair looked disheveled, mussed, but only on the one side, where she'd removed the hairpin earlier to give to me. I imagined whatever mess she now looked on the outside could only be half as bad as she was feeling on the inside.

I pulled back the covers and patted the spot next to me in the bed. Daisy crawled in and lay down beside me. I rolled on my side and played with her hair, stroking it with my fingers, the way I always used to do when we were those carefree girls back in Louisville.

"Oh, Jordie." She sighed. "I thought everything was going to be different here. But Tom is never going to change, is he?" She paused, and I twirled a lock of her silk hair around my forefinger, before resting it gently against her ear. "Did you hear what Nick said, though, about his neighbor? *Gatsby*, he said. Do you think it could be him, Jordie? After all this time, could Jay Gatsby really be right here, just across the sound?"

"I don't know," I lied. My fancy dinner with Jay Gatsby six months earlier was hazy in my mind now. Escargot and illicit French wine. But I distinctly remembered telling him about Daisy's move to East Egg. I'd thought he might drive out here, visit her, upset Tom a little. I hadn't expected he would *move* just across the sound from her, ingratiate himself with her cousin. "Would you even care if it was him, Daise?" I asked her now. "You haven't seen him in so many years."

"No . . . yes . . . maybe. I don't know." She sighed again. "I do wonder sometimes if I made a big mistake marrying Tom, you know, Jordie?"

I closed my eyes, and I could suddenly envision the shape of Mary Margaret's naked shoulders shimming in the moonlight, just across the bed from me in Atlanta. My hand reaching for her, reassuring her that everything was going to be all right. She had no reason to be afraid. "Everyone makes mistakes," I said softly.

"But I have a daughter." Daisy said it breathlessly, as if she still could hardly believe it herself. "It's not only about me anymore, Jordie."

It suddenly occurred to me Pammy must be old enough to talk and walk by now, but I hadn't caught sight of her since I'd arrived in East Egg. In my mind she was still the little babe she'd been in Cannes. I hoped to god her nurse here in East Egg was old and horribly unattractive.

I opened my eyes, and Daisy had propped herself up on her elbow on her side, while she'd been talking. Her eyes, a little glassy from the gin, were wide, searching mine.

She reached up and stroked my cheek with her fingers. "My

dearest, sweetest Jordie. Thank heavens you're here," she said softly.

Her thumb made a soft circle around my cheekbone, and my face warmed. "Are you still drunk?" I asked her. This Daisy, though, was so different from the last drunk one I'd witnessed, years ago, just before her wedding. Her anger had been replaced with a still sort of melancholy, an unusually soft longing.

"Maybe a little," she admitted. Her thumb swirled across my cheekbone and then grazed my lips. She giggled. She was definitely drunk. More than a little.

"You should go to bed," I told her. "But drink a tall glass of water first. You'll have a killer headache in the morning." I should know. It had happened to me a few times, or maybe, a few hundred.

"Can't I just sleep here with you, Jordie?" She strung her words together like a pouty song. Then her thumb moved down my chin and traced the front contours of my neck. I heard myself moan softly, and I bit my lip to try and keep from making another sound.

Daisy giggled again, then moved across the bed and kissed me softly. She might've been going for my cheek, but her drunken aim put her lips somewhere just on the corner of my mouth, the side of my chin. Then she lowered herself down on the bed, put her cheek on my shoulder. "Oh Jordie." She gave another big exhale. "You're the only one who really loves me, the only one." She was murmuring now.

She turned her cheek a little, nuzzling it into my shoulder. And then I heard her breathing even, felt the weight of her body sigh against the bed. She was sound asleep.

Catherine

MY SISTER HAD BECOME A NEW WOMAN THIS SUMMER. *MYRTLE the turtle* cast off her shell, and she had suddenly, at the age of thirty-six, blossomed into someone else altogether, someone rosy-cheeked, well-dressed, and a little bold. Even the tone of her voice changed, became higher pitched, aggressively louder.

She came into the city with a new regularity. Nearly every weekend. And she would telephone me when she was finished with Tom, invite me up to her apartment, pour me a glass of whiskey from a seemingly endless stash Tom kept in a locked drawer.

We'd lie on her couch there and drink a little and tell stories about our weeks. It was the way I'd always imagined city life with my sister before I'd ever moved to New York, and I was glad to finally have it, and her, nearby. Even if it meant that she was being unfaithful to George.

I was no saint, of course, no matter what Myrtle thought. It didn't bother me about the cheating, as much as it did the excuses Myrtle made for Tom. I didn't relish her being anyone's mistress. *Daisy's Catholic,* she said, *so she won't give Tom a divorce without a fight. But it'll happen, in time.*

Catholic. So maybe Daisy was the one who was the saint then? Part of me wanted to telephone Jay up in West Egg and ask him what was really going on, but whenever I thought of Jay now, it was only with disgust. I wanted nothing to do with him. Maybe out in East Egg he was carrying on his own affair with Daisy, and part of me almost hoped he was. Because then, perhaps that would mean Tom truly would leave her, that he would do right by my sister.

I DIDN'T ACTUALLY meet Tom until one Sunday afternoon in early July. Myrtle telephoned me just after lunch, told me to get a taxi-cab up to 158th right away. "Tom's here and we're having a party," she exclaimed, her voice effusive with a lustful sort of joy. "Oh, and Cath," she said. "Tom just bought me a dog!"

She hung up before I could ask her anything practical about the dog. Where on earth would she keep it, and who would take care of it during the week, and what would George say if she dared bring it back home? I supposed she would expect me to take care of the dog. And who kept a dog in a small city apartment?

I pushed that thought away for the time being, put on a nice dress, drew in my eyebrows and my lips, and slipped on my dressiest pair of heels.

"Are you going to church?" Helen asked me from her spot on the couch when I walked out of my bedroom. She had her hair in rollers and was wearing her housedress and flipping through a copy of *Town Tattle*—Myrtle had stacks of them in her apartment, and I brought her read ones back for us each weekend. Helen lowered the magazine, caught my eyes, and laughed. We both knew she was joking, about church. Neither one of us was a practicing anything.

"The church of ill repute," I shot back easily.

"Your sister's back in town?" Helen raised her eyebrows. I hadn't told her everything, but she knew Myrtle had a sweetie who'd gotten her an apartment in the city. That I was worried about how the situation might end up for her.

"Yes," I said now. "They're having a party, and I'll finally get to meet *the* Tom Buchanan. Do you want to come?"

Helen shook her head and nodded to the stack of magazines on the coffee table. "I'm good here. I've already got a roaring headache from last night."

I nodded. I did too. Last night Helen and I had downed one too many gin rickeys at the Monte Carlo, and we'd stumbled home after midnight. I could feel the ache just above my brows now. But the idea of finally meeting this Tom Buchanan was something I just couldn't pass up, and I was going to Myrtle's purely for the company.

A LITTLE PARTY was already brewing inside Myrtle's apartment when I let myself in. I recognized the older couple who lived in the building and cast them a smile, and then, my eyes caught on two unfamiliar men. I assumed the one whose lap Myrtle was perched upon was Tom; the other introduced himself to me as Nick Carraway. Myrtle clarified he was Tom's friend, though Nick made a strange face, like he wasn't so sure.

Before I could ask him, Myrtle jumped off Tom's lap, threw her arms around me, and gave me a sloppy kiss on the cheek. I could smell the whiskey on her already. She offered me some, but I declined. "I'm already up without it," I said, massaging my aching temples a little with my fingers.

"Nick's cute," Myrtle whispered too loudly in my ear, so I was certain he'd heard every word. "Don't you think, Cath?"

My face reddened and I shushed her. I had not formed any opinion on Nick, who now sat quietly in a chair carefully sipping his whiskey. I supposed he was somewhat handsome, in a rather ordinary, quiet kind of way. "Was this a setup, Myrtle?" I sighed. Nick might be all right, but I had no interest in getting together with one of Tom's friends.

"No, of course not, no. Not at all. Come meet Tom, Cath."

Myrtle grabbed my hand and yanked me toward the couch, making quick introductions. Tom stood, and he was shockingly tall, a hulking, muscular man who seemed to almost seethe arrogance from his pores by the brutish way he held himself. So this was the kind of man who brazenly cheated on his wife, who bought his mistress diamond hairpins, an apartment in the city, and . . . a dog? *This was the kind of man who'd taken Daisy away from Jay, once, years ago.* I wouldn't dare say any of that out loud, of course. Instead I forced a smile and said: "I hear you play polo, Tom."

"You know a lot about it?" His voice took on an edge of excitement. His arrogance faded, and he leaned closer, remarkably eager, like a little boy. I wished I did know something about it. I had a feeling I might like him more if we discussed polo. But I shook my head, and he frowned and sat back down.

"The dog! Cath, you have to meet him. He's a little doll," Myrtle exclaimed and rushed back into the bedroom. She returned with a wiry-haired gray-and-black puppy with white paws. He might have made a good farm dog, except the bright red bow tied around his neck made him look small-headed, gauche, and ridiculous.

"What's his name?" I asked, because it seemed a more pleasant question than the obvious, *How will you possibly take care of him?*

"I don't know yet. Tom? What do you think a good name for him is? I like Duke, maybe. It sounds regal."

Tom shrugged, uncaring. Myrtle sighed happily, settled herself back onto Tom's lap, with *Duke, maybe* on her own lap. "Yes," Myrtle murmured, stroking the dog's head, softly scratching his chin. "Duke is a very nice name for you, isn't it, puppy?"

Tom suddenly reached around, grabbed her hard, and kissed her so boldly on the mouth that it occurred to me he was jealous of the dog. I tried to suppress a giggle at that thought. But then their kiss went on and on, and *on*. I began to feel like a voyeur, and I turned my head away.

"Are you sure you wouldn't like a drink?" Nick asked quietly. He'd moved closer and now sat just a few inches away from me. His face revealed the sort of bold distaste for Tom and Myrtle's display that I was feeling inwardly. I tried to put my finger on what bothered me about it exactly, because nothing would make me happier than if Myrtle left George. But Tom was holding her now too tightly, like a possession. And worse, one he may not ever admit to having, outside this room. "Whiskey?" Nick offered again.

I shook my head and took a chair next to him. "No thanks."

"Ah, you're a teetotaler."

"Not at all." I laughed. "My roommate and I had quite a time last night at the Monte Carlo. Do you know it?" He shook his head. It was our favorite little speakeasy, just two blocks from our apartment. But it was deliciously dark and maybe a little seedy and probably not the kind of establishment where Tom and his friends would gather. "Anyway"—I wanted to change the subject—"tell me where you're from, Nick. And how do you know Tom?"

"It's . . . a . . . Tom and I . . . Well, we were both at Yale at the same time. I'm living out in a little rental in West Egg this summer, and Tom is in East Egg and we reconnected. But I was born and raised in Minnesota."

"The Midwest." I smiled at him, feeling a little more at ease. "Myrtle and I grew up in Illinois. So how's West Egg treating you?"

"It's a strange little place, but I like it all right." He downed his whiskey, poured himself some more.

"I actually know a man out in West Egg." I kept my voice light, nonchalant. "Jay Gatsby, you know him?"

Nick's brown irises swam around, his pupils already glassy. "I do. He's my next-door neighbor," he slurred. Then he laughed a little and spit out a more sober sentence: "I mean, if anyone really knows Gatsby."

I did. There were so many things I could tell Nick right now about Jay: the way the skin on his stomach felt soft against my fingers, like a baby's, or the way he kissed me hungrily, like he was always searching for something I could never give him. Or perhaps, most notably, that he had an unhealthy fixation on Tom Buchanan's wife. But with that thought, I bit my lip.

"You've been out to one of his parties?" Nick was saying now.

Parties? That's what Jay was doing this summer now in West Egg, throwing parties?

"Sure," I lied, not wanting Nick to ask any other questions about how I knew Jay.

Myrtle had finished kissing Tom, and she suddenly stumbled across the room and plopped drunkenly on my lap. She told Nick the same story she'd told me, about meeting Tom on the train. But she left out the part about anyone sending her there. She had rewritten it all in her mind, a truly, lovely romance, bounded by fate and destiny.

"Daisy's Catholic, and she doesn't want to give him a divorce," Myrtle was saying to Nick now, her words stringing together in one drunken loop. "But she will and then we'll go out west for a while until everything settles down."

Out west? That was news to me, and it sank in my stomach, a cold, hard lump.

Myrtle and Nick were still talking, but I looked around the room. Voices rose and fell, drunken and strung together and tangled with laughter. I had the strangest, dizzying feeling that the entire room was upside down, swirling and drunk and smoky. I was the only one sitting still, right side up, the only one sober. The only one who would remember any of this tomorrow.

Myrtle kissed my cheek and then sashayed across the room to talk to Tom. She said something to him, and his face instantly reddened. "I don't want you to say her name," Tom yelled, his voice cutting above the din.

"I'll say it if I want to," Myrtle yelled back, drunkenly obstinate. "Daisy," she shouted loud enough now that the rest of the room stopped talking. It got so quiet I could practically hear the rage simmering up inside of Tom. It was red hot on his face, and he arched his hulking shoulders, standing like a linebacker. "Daisy, Daisy, Daisy!" Myrtle shouted in his face.

What happened next came so fast that the motions were blurry through the haze of smoke. Suddenly Myrtle's nose was gushing blood, and Tom stood there, his hand covered in it. And that's when I realized he'd punched her in the face. *He'd punched her in the face.* He'd broken her nose.

This arrogant, rich, swine of a man had just broken my sister's nose.

The room continued to be still, and the whiskey had made everyone slow, but me. I jumped up and ran to Myrtle, tilting her head back. "Jesus, what have you done?" I shouted at Tom.

"I didn't . . . I didn't . . . mean to . . ." Tom stuttered, staring at Myrtle's blood all over his fingers, seemingly in disbelief that he had made her bleed. "Myrtle." He reached out for her with his clean hand, but I slapped his hand away. She was sobbing now, and I pulled her to my chest, shushing her, rubbing her back, and trying to keep her head tilted back.

"Get me a towel," I said to Tom. He didn't move. No one did. "Get me a goddamned towel, Tom!"

That seemed to wake him up, finally, and he ran into the bathroom. I grabbed a copy of *Town Tattle* to catch the blood in the meanwhile, until Tom returned a few moments later with a small stack of towels. "Now get out," I said to him. He shook his head and didn't move. "Everyone out!" I shouted.

Nick and the neighbor couple listened and filed out, but Tom stood there, staring, as I lifted Myrtle's head back again, told her to squeeze the bridge of her nose to try and stop the bleeding, and held a towel against her lips to catch the blood. "Tom," I said, firmly. "You, too. Get out."

I placed the towel in Myrtle's hand, told her to hold it there. I glared at Tom, until he finally looked away, walked to the door. I followed behind him. "Tell her I'm sorry," he said, somewhat contritely. I shook my head. "You know I didn't mean to hurt you, Myrtle," he called out over me, but it was hard to hear much but the sound of Myrtle's continued cries now.

"I want you to leave my sister alone," I told him firmly. "You have a wife. Go home to East Egg to her." He shook his head. "I mean it," I said firmly. "Leave Myrtle alone."

"Or what?" He snickered a little, his voice thick with whiskey and condescension.

I leaned in closer, lowered my voice. "If you hurt my sister again,

I don't care who you are, Tom Buchanan. I'll kill you." I meant it. I really and truly did. But maybe it was hard to tell because my voice came out so shaky.

Tom's mouth bent into a half smile, like I amused him. My hands shook with anger. But then he finally spun on his heel and left.

The apartment was totally quiet now, except for the soft sound of Myrtle's continued sobs. I went back to the couch, and held her, rocking her back and forth.

"What'll I tell George?" she whispered to me, once the bleeding had finally stopped. Her nose was already a peculiar shade of purple, her upper lip crusted with blood. Her eyes were wide, frightened.

She was afraid to tell her husband, who had hurt her for so long, that another man had done the same. *Oh, Myrtle.* Tom wasn't ever going to save her from George. Tom *was* George, only with more money, more arrogance.

"You're going to tell George that you walked into a pole on Fifth Avenue. I'll come back with you. I'll tell him myself. We can say it was my fault. I was drunk and I wasn't watching, and I tripped, and . . . and . . . you saved me."

Myrtle nodded slowly, squeezed my hand. "Thanks, Cath," she whispered.

"You shouldn't see him anymore, Myrt," I said. "Tom's no good for you."

"But I love him," she cried out. "And he's going to leave Daisy and we'll go together out west and we'll be so happy." The fantasy cracked in her voice as she repeated it now, and maybe, no matter how much she claimed to believe it, deep down she, too, knew it was broken, haphazard, unlikely. "Everything will be different soon," she said, unconvincingly. "You'll see, Cath."

I stared at Myrtle's purple swollen nose, and I shook my head. All I could think was that Jay was to blame. He'd brought Tom into her life. He had done it for his own selfish, stupid reasons, and now Myrtle sat before me bruised and bleeding. Anger boiled up inside of me. A fast-brewing, uncontrollable sort of rage. This was all Jay's fault.

Daisy

THE RAIN CAME DOWN SO HARD THAT I COULD BARELY SEE THE scenery as we drove across to West Egg. East Egg, West Egg, old money, new money. It all looked the same: a blur of green, and the giant gray sound in between, and mansions obscured by a wash of raindrops.

Nick had telephoned yesterday, invited me for tea this afternoon. And he had told me, rather cryptically, to come alone. Or rather, his exact words were, *Don't bring Tom.*

Tom who? I'd joked over the telephone.

But there had been something in the sound of Nick's voice that had seemed so very serious, and I'd left the house this afternoon without telling anyone where I was going, not even Jordan. She and Nick, to my delight, had become quite friendly these past few weeks, and I wondered now if maybe he wanted to speak to me privately about her.

I'd been prepared to drive myself this afternoon, but then when I'd walked out to the garage, Ferdie, our chauffeur, said he wouldn't allow it. "Not in this weather, Mrs. Buchanan." He was a sweet, older man, and I took his chastising with the kindness in which I was sure it was intended.

I'd relented, given him Nick's address, and then had watched from the back seat as old money blurred into new money. When we finally arrived at Nick's adorable little house, the rain had slowed to a drizzle, and Nick walked outside to greet me.

I got out of the car and straightened my hat, gave Nick a quick kiss on the cheek. "So this is your home? It's absolutely charming," I exclaimed.

It *was* charming, in that I'd almost forgotten how adorable a normal-sized house could look. I thought about my beloved childhood home back in Louisville. It was a grand house, for Louisville, but still small enough so I'd known every room intimately. There was something nice about that, something refreshing about seeing Nick living somewhere so . . . ordinary.

"Tell your chauffeur to drive around for an hour," Nick whispered into my ear, so secretively.

I did what he asked. Then Nick took my hand, gripped it earnestly, and pulled me toward the porch. His expression was so serious, and his color turned a little pale. "Nick, now you're making me nervous."

"Just come into the house," he said, opening the door and pulling me inside.

I took off my hat, smoothing my dampened hair with my hands. And my nose was immediately assaulted with the smell of fresh flowers. Nick's parlor was small but the whole entire area of it was filled to the brim with flowers, vases and vases overflowing with what appeared to be the same bluebells and lilacs that grew wildly each spring in Louisville. "Nick?" I questioned again, but before he could answer, I suddenly heard footsteps, coming in from the other room.

I looked up, and Jay Gatsby stood there across Nick's parlor, through the rows of bluebells, as I might have seen him once years ago back in Kentucky. He looked older, his hair was a little longer, his skin more weathered. And now instead of a soldier's uniform he wore a tailored cream-colored suit with a silver shirt and gold tie. But it was unmistakably him. My heartbeat sped up; color rose in my cheeks.

Jordan had told me Nick's Gatsby was indeed one and the same, that Jay was here in West Egg just across the sound. She'd gone to a party at his house a few weeks ago and had confirmed it to me afterward. But I didn't quite believe it until right this moment. Besides, Jordan had said he was *otherwise involved*. That like me, he had moved on, and she suspected he barely remembered me at all.

Good, I'd said, waving my hand in the air. *I feel the same about him.*

But standing across the room from him again now, I wasn't quite sure what to feel. Seeing Jay felt like seeing a ghost, seeing my beautiful, precious dead past standing right here in front of me, suddenly beating and gold and silver and alive all over again. And I heard Rose's voice in my head: *Daise, be good.*

I closed my eyes, and she and I were walking to the poorhouse in Louisville, young and innocent and free and sweltering hot. And then the soldier's car pulled up alongside us: *You think I see the prettiest girls in all of Louisville needing a ride and I'm not going to stop?*

"Daisy," he said my name now, and his voice was still exactly the same. The déjà vu of it broke my heart. I opened my eyes, and he'd walked closer to me. His eyes held mine. I'd forgotten how shockingly green they were.

"Jay," I said his name, and it felt funny on my tongue. Familiar and unfamiliar all at once. "It's been a long time."

"Five years," he said softly.

Five years. It was hardly any time at all; it was a lifetime. I could barely remember that girl I was five years ago, that life I had and took for granted. That careless way I'd lain with Jay in my childhood bed and thought the hardest, worst thing I'd ever feel was him leaving for New York, then for war. I'd naïvely thought Rose would always be with me, forever and ever after she survived the polio. That I'd have my daddy well into my older years.

I suddenly felt a little faint, and I gripped the edge of Nick's couch. Jay caught my shoulders. "Sit down," he said gently. "I'll get you some water."

He disappeared into the kitchen, and then I realized Nick was gone too. It was just me and the pounding of my own heart in my chest, and a million little bluebells floating in glass around Nick's parlor. Until Jay swept back in, through the forest of flowers, a glass of water in his hand.

"Where's Nick?" I asked, longing for my cousin to sit in between us, to break this weird spell I was feeling in Jay's presence again.

"He stepped out for a bit," Jay said softly. *Stepped out?* Of his own tea party.

Don't bring Tom. Of course, there was no tea party. Nick had orchestrated this whole thing; it had been a setup all along to bring me and Jay together. I'd thought Nick was my friend. He was my cousin. But, no, his loyalties seemed to be with Jay. I might be upset with him if I weren't also so overwhelmed with nostalgia.

I sipped my water slowly, and my body calmed. I took a breath and looked up. Jay was staring at me, his gaze so intense that I felt strangely naked. Overexposed. "So, tell me, Jay, how have you been?" I asked, my voice teetering with awkwardness.

"Daisy." He touched my arm, and his fingers were warm. I had the sudden memory of them trailing down my bare stomach.

"I'm married," I said quickly. "I have a daughter." I was a different person five years ago. A girl. Not a wife. Not a mother. Not a Buchanan.

He nodded. He knew all this. Nick must've told him everything he thought there was to know about me. Jay stood and grabbed a folder from a satchel on the bench by the door. "Daisy, he's no good for you." He handed me the folder.

"What's this?" I asked, uncertain I wanted it, whatever it was.

"Proof that he doesn't love you," Jay said.

Proof? A laugh caught in my throat and rose up, turning into a strangled cry as I thought of Rebecca Buckley's pink cherubic cheeks catching the midnight lamplight in the Lake Forest stables. Wasn't that all the *proof* I'd ever need?

Jay opened up the folder, pulled out the photographs inside, and handed them to me. Unmistakably they showed Tom, on a train, huddled in close with an unfamiliar woman. She was stout and beautiful, with a maturity to her face that made me think she was older than me. God, at least she wasn't a child. Jay probably thought these photographs would be a bombshell, but instead they were just a drop of rain in one of the giant puddles out front. I pushed the pictures away, closed my eyes, and sighed.

"He doesn't love you," Jay repeated. "But I still love you."

I opened my eyes and focused in on the woman's face in one of the photographs: Tom's woman in the city. The one who called our house too many times during supper. She really was quite beautiful. I pictured Tom with her, holding her possessively, the way he once held on to me.

And then suddenly, I began to cry. I couldn't help myself. I'd understood all summer Tom would be . . . Tom, even after I'd insisted East Egg would be our permanent home. But now the indignity of it, the continued humiliation of it, and experiencing those feelings, in front of this man I might've married once . . . I felt the tears rolling down my cheeks. They made Jay's face blurry, almost ethereal. Maybe he truly was a ghost.

He reached his hand to my cheek, gently wiped away my tears with his thumb. His touch was familiar and unfamiliar, the past and the present colliding right here, in Nick's floral living room. The past had a softness to it, an innocence that I'd lost long ago. That thought only seemed to make my tears multiply. "Don't cry, Daisy," Jay said gently. "Please don't cry. I'm here now. We can be together again."

"Five years is a long time," I choked out through my tears. "I'm not the same girl I was, Jay."

"I'm not the same either." Excitement rose in his voice. "I have money now. A lot of money, Daisy. I can take care of you the way you deserve. And we can go back now to how we used to be. Just erase the last three years."

Jay put his hand on my cheek again, pulled my face in close, and I had a sudden flash of us standing there in the middle of another rainstorm, lightning tearing across the sky, that first night we ever kissed in Louisville. Was he right? Could I go back to being that careless, carefree girl I was at eighteen, just like that? I'd been happy then, hadn't I? And it had been so long since I'd felt such a lightness.

I could feel his breath against my lips, and I realized he was going to kiss me now, again, here, five years later. A lifetime away from that other night.

I knew I should stop him, push him away; I was a married woman, a mother. But my marriage vows had lost their meaning long ago, back in Santa Barbara before our honeymoon had even officially ended. They meant nothing to Tom. Why should they still mean anything to me? It thrilled me a little to think that I could be getting even. That Tom could run around with a woman in the city and I could be here, in West Egg, kissing another man. And if I were to recount this to Tom later, hint it to Tom even, he might turn red and scream and break apart at the seams. I smiled a little at that thought.

Jay thought my smile was about him, and he moved in a bit closer. Touched his lips to mine softly. He tasted of grapefruit and sunshine and money. Not at all like that salty, desperate, hungry soldier I once snuck into my bedroom.

I kissed him back. But I was thinking about Tom, about what I might tell Tom later about this moment, about the way Tom's face might look when he realized that I, too, could be unfaithful. When he realized that I could feel something for another man.

The only problem was, I felt absolutely nothing.

I pushed my mouth against Jay's harder, wanting so desperately to feel *something*. But I could not summon that thrill I'd had as a girl in Louisville. My blood ran through my veins icy cold; my heart ticked along slowly. Every bit of that girl I'd been once, she truly was gone. Life with Tom had ruined me, made me numb and unfeeling.

I pulled back. Jay's eyes were wide, his cheeks ruddy. "Jay . . ." I shook my head. I felt certain now. "We can't relive the past. It's gone."

"We can," he insisted. He tried to pull me closer, but I pulled back again. "Daisy." Jay's voice sounded higher, more desperate. He grabbed my shoulders roughly. "I'll give you everything you've ever wanted."

But what did I want, exactly? Not his life, parties all summer long. I longed for quiet. The monotony of a permanent and steady home for Pammy, a world that wasn't ever-changing, that felt sure and solid beneath my feet. I no longer dreamed of anything gay or romantic. I only wanted certainty.

Suddenly Nick walked back in, and Jay let go of me. I stumbled back a little and Nick stared at me; his eyes widened, almost frightened. Oh, I must look a mess. I grabbed my bag and got a handkerchief to wipe my face.

"I didn't mean to interrupt," Nick said quietly. What a thing for a man to say in his own house. Though I supposed it served him right for setting me up this way.

"I need to be getting home anyway." I kept my voice light and avoided Jay's eyes.

"Don't leave yet," Jay said, his words stretching out, desperately. "Walk next door and see my house first. Let me show you everything I have."

I glanced out the window. The sun was shining now, but Ferdie still hadn't returned. I really should've driven myself. I sighed. I supposed I had no escape.

Jay grabbed my hand. "I won't take no for an answer," he said.

"Only if Nick comes with us," I relented. Having my cousin there would at least keep the rest of this afternoon innocent enough. Old friends, catching up. Nothing more.

LATER THAT NIGHT, I lay in bed in the darkness all alone. Tom was god knows where. When I closed my eyes, I could see the woman's face from the photographs Jay had shown me earlier. Her round cheeks and her soft curls, the voluptuous curve of her bosom, and the hint of wrinkles at the corners of her eyes.

Jay had given me a tour of his giant house, top to bottom, from his voluminous library to his sweeping bedroom, to his houseguest playing piano. Then he had begged me to dance with him. *Just like in Louisville*, he'd exclaimed, grabbing my hand and pulling me toward him.

But he was wrong. Nothing now was what it once was in Louisville. Time hadn't stopped or stood still. It had moved forward and wrecked me. Until almost five years had passed and seeing Jay again had made me realize one thing and one thing only: I was merely a shell of that girl I once was.

Every single day living with Tom, living in this mansion or that one, had begun to feel like an eternity. Each betrayal stripped me again and again, peeling back another layer of my skin. I alternated between feeling raw and feeling numb. And then, here I was again, alone tonight and picturing her, that voluptuous woman in the photographs. On the telephone, she was a phantom. But now, she was a real, bona fide woman. What did she have that I didn't?

I threw the covers back and got out of bed. I walked down the hall and peeked into Pammy's room. She was sound asleep in her little bed, exactly where I'd left her a few hours earlier, her plump toddler cheeks puffing slowly in and out as she sucked on her thumb. She was so beautiful and so innocent, and my chest ached watching her sleep now.

I'd wanted East Egg to be our home, our permanent home. I'd wanted Pammy to grow up and run across the grass to the water, to ride a pony, and go to school, but what then? Attend parties? Meet a rich man who would treat her the way her father had treated me? No, I didn't want that for her at all.

I shut her door quietly so as not to wake her and wandered down the stairs. The entire first floor was dark and quiet, and I walked into Tom's study. There was a large window behind his desk that looked out onto the sound. I pulled back the curtains and stared at the green light that illuminated the end point of our dock.

It burned brightly, close enough that Tom's entire study glowed green. It was the same green light Jay had shown me earlier from his own window—only from here it was much closer, brighter, hotter. I looked past the light, across the sound. Jay was having yet another party, and his house was twinkling with a thousand lights, yellow and gold, swimming like the fireflies Rose and I used to chase by the river as girls. I remembered now how I'd capture them in glass jars, just to watch them glimmer for a little while, until Rose always made me let them go. *Oh, Rose.*

I turned away from the lights and sat down in Tom's tall chair behind his desk, closed my eyes, and inhaled the familiar scents of him ingrained in the leather, cigarettes and whiskey. I ran my hand across the smooth wood of the desk, and then, I opened up his top drawer and pulled out his pistol.

I laid his gun on the desk and ran my fingers across it. Tom had kept his gun here, in the same place, in the same desk in Lake Forest, in Cannes, too. I knew it was here; I'd seen him take it out to clean it. But I'd never before come into his study just to touch it, just to run my fingers across it and feel the wicked thrill of the metal. I never invaded Tom's space or touched his things, not his ponies, not his pistol. But touching the cool metal of the gun now, I felt a sheer wicked delight in holding something so dangerous that wasn't mine. It coursed through me like a fire in my blood.

Daddy had taught me to shoot a gun when I was twelve years old. *For protection,* he'd said, but really I always thought it was because he was sad he didn't have a boy, and there were just some things he couldn't stand not teaching a child of his. He'd made me swear I'd never tell the old snow goose, who didn't believe such a thing was ladylike.

I remembered now aiming at the bull's-eye he'd hung on the old oak tree, pulling the trigger, hearing the snap and feeling it pulse through my veins, giving me a heady feeling of power. Pulling that trigger at twelve would make me feel that same way I did pulling Jay into my bedroom at eighteen. And there was a power now in simply touching Tom's gun, too. In knowing I could pick it up, wait for Tom to return home from wherever he was, and just hold it up, aim, pull the trigger. His betrayals, his power over me, would end, just like that.

"Daise, what are you doing?" Jordan's voice cut through the darkness, and I jumped, wrapped my hand around the pistol, and quickly shoved it back into Tom's desk drawer, hoping Jordan hadn't seen it. I wasn't exactly sure how to explain to her what I was doing, what I was thinking, how the woman in the photographs had pulled me into this dark moment.

"I couldn't sleep," I finally said, which explained nothing.

She didn't press me, and instead stepped farther into Tom's study, walked to the window to look out. "That man has a party every night, doesn't he?" she said, commenting on the lights at Jay's, sounding quite churlish about it.

"I saw him today," I said softly. "He thinks he loves me still. He wants to be with me." I laughed a little, but it caught in my chest, and came out sounding more like a sob.

Jordan turned back to face me, put her hand on her hip. "And do you want to be with him, Daise?" The green light shone on outside the window behind her, and it illuminated the curves of her body, turning her white, gauzy nightdress sheer.

I didn't know what I wanted. I thought about Pammy sleeping so peacefully up in her bed. And I suddenly felt silly for coming down here, for pulling out Tom's gun. I briefly wondered what I would have done with it if Tom had come home first, if Jordan hadn't come down when she did, and the thought flickered inside of me, embarrassing me with its recklessness.

"Do you want him?" Jordan repeated her question.

"I don't know what I want," I said softly. And that might have been the truest thing I'd spoken out loud all summer.

Jordan

THE SUMMER STARTED OFF WITH ONE TINY LITTLE WHITE LIE TO Daisy about the golf tour. And then it spiraled out from there, on and on, until I began to realize more lies came out of my mouth than truths. I lied to Daisy about the things Jay Gatsby had said to me when I saw him one night at his party. I lied to Daisy about how I felt about Nick. I lied to Nick about myself. Sometimes, by the end of July, it was even hard for me to tell the difference any longer between what was true and what wasn't.

It was easier to lie when I drank, and drink I did. Somehow Tom had an endless supply, gin and whiskey flowing each night before supper, during supper, after supper. He and Daisy bickered, or, depending on the night, they stared at each other quietly, angrily. And either way, I sipped my G&Ts until their faces blurred and their voices dimmed. I loved Daisy and I hated Tom, and I drank to soften their edges. To soften my own edges. I drank to forget what was true and what wasn't.

Some nights Daisy would tiptoe into my room very late, lie down in my bed with me, and fall asleep. I'd still be a little drunk, even then, and I'd close my eyes and reach for her hand.

"It's all right," I'd whisper-lie to her. "Everything will be all right, Daise. You'll see."

And then I'd even start to believe that lie a little myself. I'd fall asleep remembering what it was like to be young and hopeful and free and have our whole entire futures ahead of us again.

IN LATE JULY, I went into the city one afternoon and stopped at Aunt Sigourney's. I was supposed to meet Nick at the Plaza later for dinner. A *date*—and one of several we'd had this month, much to Daisy's delight. A few weeks earlier, we'd been to the Plaza for tea, a party at Jay Gatsby's, and even another tea in West Egg at Nick's house.

I stopped at Aunt Sigourney's first to say hello to the old bird, which she insisted on as a condition of releasing my pitiful monthly allowance. When I walked in, she handed me a pile of mail, and there, right on the top, was a thick cream-colored envelope with a Nashville postmark.

"When did this come?" I asked Aunt Sigourney, feeling around the plump edges of the envelope with my thumb.

She shrugged. "The other day. No . . . last week."

It was thick, heavy. My name had been scripted in unfamiliar handwriting. And still my heart rose and fell in my chest. *Mary Margaret.* It had to be. I didn't know a single other living soul in Nashville.

I tore the envelope open quickly, pulled out the thick cream card from inside:

Dr. and Mrs. Harold T. Smith request the honor of
your presence
at the wedding of their daughter, Mary Margaret

to *Whitaker Witherspoon III*
on Saturday, *the twenty-sixth of August, nineteen hun-*
dred twenty-two . . .

I put the card down on Aunt Sigourney's parlor table, unable to read the rest. My hands shook, and I suddenly felt like I was about to throw up.

Mary Margaret was getting married? And to a man called *Whitaker Witherspoon, the third?* What sort of ridiculous name was that?

No more ridiculous than Jordan Baker *is for a lady*, I could hear Mary Margaret's response in my head, her voice rich with laughter. I closed my eyes.

"Jordan?" Aunt Sigourney questioned, bringing me back to her apartment. "You're pale as a ghost. Was it bad news, dear?"

"An old friend," I said slowly, trying to swallow back the bile that rose in my throat. "She's getting married. To a man she doesn't love."

Aunt Sigourney laughed a little. "Well, she wouldn't be the first, and she certainly won't be the last. A woman who marries for love is a foolish woman, Jordan."

"And what about a woman who never marries at all?" I shot back.

Aunt Sigourney grimaced. She'd been a widow since I was a baby, but at least she'd been in a respectable marriage once. I'd dared to speak aloud her greatest fear for me. "So you plan to spend the rest of your life sleeping at the Buchanans and *golfing*, do you, Jordan?" The way she said *golfing* she might as well have said robbing banks. And if only she knew the truth, that I wasn't even golfing at all anymore, only lying about it. I'd told her that little white lie that I'd rejoined the tour in the beginning of the summer, too. The truth, the desperate, terrible truth, was that I wasn't sure they'd ever have me back. But that truth was so terrifying, I barely ever allowed myself to think about it.

"I have a date tonight," I finally said to Aunt Sigourney, an attempt to mollify her a little. But even as I said those words, all I could think about still was Mary Margaret. The warm feel of her skin, the sweet and sour taste of her, the rich sound of her voice. *She was getting married.* Grief really was a river. And now I was drowning again. Aunt Sigourney's words were tugging me underwater and holding me there, making it nearly impossible to breathe.

"Well, try not to muck it up, Jordan." Aunt Sigourney emphasized that, her final point, by tapping her cane on the hardwood floor. Then she turned to shuffle off into the dining room to eat her own early supper.

A FEW HOURS later, sitting across the table from Nick at the Plaza, I was highly distracted. And I was most certainly about to muck it up.

I fiddled with the diamond pin in my hair and thought about Daisy, back in East Egg. After leaving Aunt Sigourney's I'd longed to skip this dinner with Nick, flee back there, tell her the truth about Mary Margaret, the whole entire truth. But what was the whole truth, exactly? That night in Atlanta with Mary Margaret felt like a fever dream now, all these many months later. *She was getting married.* Maybe it had never even happened at all.

"Jordan," Nick said now, interrupting my thoughts. "Did you hear what I said?"

"Hmm?" I murmured. I took a sip of my water, wishing it would sting my throat, numb my thoughts like gin. Nick wasn't Tom or Jay. All we had to drink with dinner was water and too-tart lemonade.

"Daisy and Gatsby. I was saying, I think she might leave Tom for him."

I laughed, nearly spitting water across the table. I wiped my mouth with the back of my hand, coughing, sputtering for air for a few seconds. Well, listen to Nick. In Daisy's life all of one summer and here he thought he was some kind of expert on her. But Nick wasn't there when Rose died, or when Daisy got so drunk before she married Tom she tried to punch me, or at Daisy's sweltering hot wedding when I saved her from Blocks Biloxi, or on her beach in Cannes. What did he know about Daisy?

"You should've seen them together at my house a few weeks ago," Nick insisted now. "They're in love." Nick looked practically doe-eyed when he got so emphatic. Another girl might have found it adorable, in a foolish sort of way. But it did nothing for me. And really Nick was no better than Tom or Jay, or any other man who believed that whatever he wanted, whomever he wanted, was simply his for the taking.

I thought of Daisy, the night after she'd been to Nick's little setup. I'd found her sitting in Tom's study, clutching his gun, staring out the window at Jay's bright obnoxious party. She certainly hadn't been acting like a woman *in love*. In fact, seeing her there, that fragile, it had terrified me.

"Anyway—" God, Nick was still going on. "Jay made me promise to bring you back to his house tonight after dinner, so you can help him. I'll take you there when we're done. I have my car."

"Really, Nick," I said curtly, "are you dating Jay Gatsby or are you dating me?"

"What kind of a question is that?" Nick's face turned bright red.

"I think it's a very logical question," I shot back. "Given that here we are on a date and you can't stop talking about Jay Gatsby."

His cheeks were positively beet-colored. "I thought you'd want to help Daisy. Since she's your best friend and all."

"Exactly." I guzzled my lemonade, wishing it were gin, puckering my lips at the tartness. Across the table Nick just stared at me, like he wasn't at all sure what to make of me. "That's exactly what I want to do."

AFTER DINNER WE drove toward West Egg in silence. Maybe Nick finally understood there wasn't really anything between us. Or he was just afraid to say anything more to me about Jay and Daisy. Or maybe he realized that, if we didn't talk about Daisy, we didn't have anything much to talk about at all.

"Jordan," he finally spoke, when he stopped the car in front of Jay's house. He reached his hand up to touch my hair, his fingers lingering on the diamonds on Daisy's pin. "I . . ."

"Please don't," I said, pulling away. I was tired and not in the mood. And I definitely couldn't muster up the will to kiss him back if he kissed me. "Why don't you go on home, Nick. I'll go in and talk to Jay and then I'll telephone you in the morning. I'll get a taxicab back to East Egg."

"But . . . I . . ." A mild protest sputtered out of him, but then he gave up and simply nodded. We stared at each other another moment, not speaking, but from the look in his eyes it seemed like he finally understood me. He knew there was no way in hell I was telephoning him in the morning.

"YOU LIED TO me," Jay said, the second I stepped foot in his study. He sat behind his desk, nursing a whiskey. From the way he strung his words together, I suspected it wasn't his first.

"Me? Lie? Never." It was warm in here and I let out a little laugh and fanned myself as I sat in the empty chair across from him. "Don't you know I'm a respectable southern lady, Mr. Gatsby?" He snorted a little, and I was annoyed I'd listened to Nick, come here at all. I leaned back into the leather of the chair and sighed. "What do you want, Jay?"

"You told me you'd help me get Daisy back."

I shook my head. That wasn't what I'd said at all. A few weeks earlier, I'd come to one of his parties with Nick. Jay had summoned me into his study that night and had begged me, drunkenly, to help him see Daisy again. I'd finally relented, told him I'd get Nick to set something up at his house, if only to get Jay to leave me alone that night. And I *had* done that much. I'd had Nick arrange a tea. I'd kept my promise. It wasn't my fault that Daisy wasn't interested.

"Look," I said quite firmly now. "You have to face the facts. She doesn't want you. She's moved on." I spoke the words to him, about him, but as I talked, tears rose up inside of me and I bit my lip to keep them at bay. *She didn't want me. She'd moved on.* Mary Margaret was getting married. How could she be getting married?

"I can't accept that, Jordan. I won't." He slammed his fist on his desk so hard, the noise startled me and I jumped. Then he paced his study, making circles around me.

"You can't make a woman love you," I said softly. If there was a magical way, I wished I would've found it myself.

Jay walked to his window, stared out. I knew he was looking at the green light in the distance, Daisy's light. He turned back to face me. "Look, Jordan. If you help me, I'll help you."

I laughed again. "I don't need your help. Nick and I are . . ." What were Nick and I exactly? A whole heap of nothing.

"Not Nick. Golf," he said. He turned to stare out the window another moment, then looked back at me, sneering a little. "I went up to Westchester a few weeks ago. Thought I'd watch you play, but imagine my surprise when you weren't there on the tour at all."

My heart suddenly pulsed too hard in my chest. "I was feeling ill that day." Another lie popped out of me. Plant one seed and then, it grew and bloomed and fluttered all over until there were a million, like a field of dandelions in the late spring in Louisville.

"Were you?" He was still talking. "Because my boss, Mr. Wolfsheim, actually knows Mr. Hennessey quite well. And Hennessey has some . . . very interesting things to say about you, Jordan."

Mr. Hennessey. I remembered the look on his portly face that last day in Atlanta when I'd hugged Mary Margaret on the course. Mrs. Pearce, whispering in his ear. His voice the next afternoon when he insisted that he saw me do it himself. He saw me *move the ball.* "He thinks I moved a ball," I said contritely.

Jay turned, looked me in the eyes. His eyes were a piercing shade of green, so bright, even in the darkness it felt as though they could see straight inside of me, into the very depths of my soul, which already felt emptied, hollowed with a Mary Margaret–sized chasm. "Sure . . ." Jay said slowly. "The ball. But there was another matter, too. With a girl, a teammate of yours. A Mary, from . . . Nashville."

I swallowed hard and looked away. "He doesn't know what he's talking about," I said.

Jay shook his head. "Look, I won't tell anyone your secret, Jordan," he said. "In fact, I think Mr. Hennessey could even be persuaded to overlook it too. To take you back on the tour, with a generous donation from me." He paused, finished off his whiskey. "But you have to help me get Daisy back. See . . . we can help each other, you and I."

It was a threat thinly veiled inside a shiny promise. Do what Jay wanted and I could have golf back. But if I didn't, he'd tell everyone about me and Mary Margaret. Ruin my entire life. And maybe hers, too.

"Jordan," he interrupted my thoughts now. He'd walked closer to me. "I love her so much," he whispered, his hot whiskey breath against my neck.

"You're drunk," I said. But his threats still shot around in my head like sparks.

"I want you to bring her here to me on Saturday afternoon," Jay said. I stared at him, shook my head a little. "Yes, Jordan. I need your help. And *you* need *my* help." And though he smiled, as he spoke, his green eyes were dark now, electric, and I didn't doubt for a second that he'd ruin me if he ever had the chance.

Catherine

I HELD MY ANGER FOR JAY QUIETLY INSIDE OF ME AND TRIED TO push it down, ignore it. It was too strange to feel such a hatred brewing for this man I'd held so intimately close to me for months. And better, I told myself, not to think about him at all any longer. Instead I thought a lot about my sister; I worried desperately for my sister.

Myrtle had telephoned me only once since that Sunday when Tom punched her, and it was just, she said, to check on her dog. As far as I'd known, she hadn't been back into the city at all. And Duke now seemed to live with me and Helen, which I swore to Helen was only temporary, though I couldn't explain to her exactly how that might be true or when Myrtle might come to take him back. I'd formed a strange attachment to the little mutt, even letting him sleep at the foot of my bed and looking forward to his happy tail wags after work.

Then, the first week of August, Myrtle telephoned me out of the blue and summoned me up to 158th Street. She was sobbing on the other end of the line, saying it was *an emergency*. And she made no mention of her dog.

"Myrtle, are you hurt?" I cried out into the telephone.

"Cath, come right away," she sobbed on the other end of the line.

I could still picture the bright red of her blood on my hands, on Tom's hands. Soaking through the battered copy of *Town Tattle* and the white linens from the bathroom. The last time I'd left her, later that same evening at her apartment in Queens, her nose had been purple and twisted. George's face turned bright red as I'd regaled him with my story of the light pole and Myrtle swooping in to save me, and I wasn't quite sure whether he'd believed me or not.

Tonight it was a seething hot Thursday, and I had barely gotten home from work when she called. But I'd already changed out of my work dress and into my housedress and slippers. Her call left me so distraught that I ran out without grabbing Duke or changing again, and I hopped in a pink cab uptown without even thinking what I looked like.

"Cath, what are you wearing?" Myrtle asked as soon as she opened the door. She eyed my housedress and slippers and frowned. Her face was tear-streaked, but I looked her over, head to toe, and she appeared unharmed.

I gave her a fierce hug, clinging a few seconds too long. "You scared me," I said, when she finally pulled out of my grasp. "I ran out of the apartment without changing." I followed her inside and sat down next to her on the couch. "What's going on, Myrtle? What's your emergency?"

"George," she said softly. She stretched out her fingers and nervously twisted the simple gold band she wore around her ring finger, round and round. "He found Duke's leash on my dresser."

I shook my head, not understanding why that rose to the level of an *emergency*. "So tell him Duke's my dog," I said. And anyway, wasn't that more than half the truth by now?

"I did, but the leash. . . . Tom bought it for me—it has diamonds on it. George didn't believe it was yours for a second. You know what he said to me, Cath?" I shook my head. It was warm inside the apartment, and I felt perspiration beading up on the back of my neck. "He said, *God knows what you've been doing; God sees everything.*"

"You don't even believe in God," I said. Well, I knew I didn't. I wasn't sure whether Myrtle did or not. But I didn't think so the way she'd been carrying on.

"That's not the point, Cath." Her voice rose. "He knows about Tom."

"How could he possibly?" George didn't seem to have it in him to understand and connect the minutiae, that this diamond dog leash meant his wife was cheating on him with the brutish and ultrarich Tom Buchanan.

"Well, he suspects, anyway." She sighed and her shoulders collapsed, and then she blew her nose in a handkerchief. I noticed it was embroidered with the initials *T.B.* and I grimaced. "I snuck out after he'd had enough whiskey to fall asleep, got the train straight out here. I've been telephoning Tom all night to tell him we have to go west, now. We can't wait any longer. But he's not answering."

"That's your emergency," I said softly, reaching up to rub her shoulders. Myrtle bit her lip and tears rolled down her round cheeks. It seemed unlikely that Tom would leave Daisy and go west with Myrtle. Not now. Not ever. I felt it, deep inside of me, no matter how many diamonds he bought her or dogs or anything else. And the truth was, I was relieved about that. She didn't need another man who hurt her whenever his fists got restless, not even a wealthy one. Especially not a wealthy one.

"Why don't you forget about Tom and leave George and come live in the city with me?" I said gently.

She let out a laugh that turned halfway into another sob. "And tell me, where would I stay inside that shoebox you call an apartment?"

"Well, Duke has a nice spot at the end of my bed. There's room for you there too." Myrtle frowned. "I'm kidding . . . about the foot of my bed. But . . . you can stay on our couch. Helen won't mind. We'll work something out." Helen likely would mind, but I'd worry about that later. She was already cross about the dog; she'd probably move out if I brought Myrtle into the apartment too.

"And what would I do for money and what about all my nice things?" She glanced around the room, her eyes catching on a crystal vase on the table.

I had barely enough money to get by myself, and I didn't have any answer, other than one I knew Myrtle wouldn't like. She could scrape by; I always did. She could find a job and we could pool our pennies. We'd be poor as dirt, but we'd have each other.

I remembered the promise Jay had made to me once, that he would help Myrtle. That he would get her away from George, give her some money to start on her own. And then, what had he gone and done instead? Gotten her mixed up with Tom, gotten her into this whole mess and made everything terribly worse. My anger for Jay burned up hot inside of me, boiling over. I couldn't push it down any longer; I was going to have to confront him.

"Listen, Myrtle. I want you to go back home and don't let George know you've been out here. I have a plan, but I need a few days to put it in motion. Can you just wait it out a little while longer?"

"What kind of plan?" She wiped her eyes and stared at me, wide-eyed with skepticism. "You'll go see Tom?"

I bit my lip. There was no way I was going to see Tom. But I was betting I could get Jay to help once I showed him how angry I was. "Just trust me, Myrtle, please?"

She hesitated for a moment but then she finally agreed. I knew she longed for Tom; I knew if Tom telephoned right now or swept in here and carried her off into the night, westward, she would leave me—and Duke—without even looking back.

But that didn't happen. Instead, she cleaned up her face in the bathroom. She gave me hug, and picked up her bag, and then I walked downstairs with her.

I helped her get a cab to take her back to Queens, and just before she got in the car she turned back to me, she hugged me fiercely. "Give Duke a kiss from me, will you, Cath?"

I didn't know it then, but those were the last words she'd ever say to me. The last moment I'd ever see my sister alive.

Daisy

August 1922
WEST EGG

ONE SATURDAY IN AUGUST, WHEN IT WAS ALMOST TOO HOT TO breathe, Jordan insisted in the middle of the afternoon that we were going out.

"Now?" I said, lying on the couch, fanning myself. "Must we really, Jordie?"

July had rolled lazily into August, almost every day a repeat of the one before. The monotony of summer broken up only by an occasional party or polo match. Tom swore to me a few weeks ago he wasn't seeing his woman in the city any longer, and yet, last night and the night before, the phone had rung on and on and on during supper. Jordan had looked at me, sipping her gin and tonic, with worry all over her face. I supposed that's why she was demanding something of me this afternoon. She was concerned.

"Yes," she insisted now. "You need to get out of this house, Daise. I'm not taking no for an answer."

I sighed and told her I'd go get ready. It was easier to go along than to argue with her, and besides, maybe she was right. Maybe getting out of here would do me some good.

I fixed my hair and my face, and then I found Pammy to say

good-bye. She was eating a late lunch with her nurse. In spite of her nurse's cries that she was a mess, I smothered Pammy's plump, sticky cheeks with kisses as she erupted into a fit of giggles, and I wondered, for a moment, if maybe this was all I truly needed to cheer me.

"Daise," Jordan interrupted, sounding impatient. "Let's go."

"Mama's going out for a bit with Aunt Jordan," I told Pammy. "But I won't be gone long, precious." She turned back to her nurse and her lunch, unperturbed. Still, I stared at her for another second. She was so beautiful and happy, blissfully unaware of her father's indiscretions or her mother's misery.

"Come on, Daise," Jordan said, grabbing my arm and leading me out front. "I'll drive."

I got in her car and Jordan quickly revved the engine and swerved down the drive. I remembered again why I didn't like to drive places with her. She was a terrible, reckless driver. And I wondered briefly as she spun out onto the main road if she might hit something, and if we might both die. Then Tom would be truly free to be with whomever he wanted, and what would happen to Pammy? That thought burned up angrily inside of me.

"Jordie, slow down," I insisted, my fingers tensely clutching the door of the car. "Where are we going in such a rush?" She didn't answer me, but she eased back on the gas a little and I exhaled. Then she made the turn toward West Egg. "Nick's?" I asked.

Jordan and Nick had been getting along swimmingly all summer, and I'd wondered if there might even be wedding bells in their future.

But she swerved the car now down the main throughway in West Egg Village, finally sputtering past the turn for Nick's driveway. And then it hit me, where she was taking me. Not Nick's. Jay's. She was taking me to Jay Gatsby's.

LAST WEEK, WE had all gone to a party at Jay's. He'd sent over a personal invitation for me and Tom, addressed quite formally to *The Buchanans*—and Tom, curiously, had insisted we go. Or maybe not so curiously at all as Jordan had let it slip upon viewing the invitation that we had both known Jay back in Louisville, once.

Knew him how? Tom had asked, blowing a ring of smoke from his cigarette.

Daisy knew him very, very *well,* Jordan said with a little giggle, and I had to kick her under the table. But it was delightful to see the deep crease of the frown on Tom's face at that moment. Tom's jealousy was somehow both his best and worst quality.

We went to that party, Tom and I. And I danced a foxtrot with Jay when he asked me to, all the while keeping my eyes on Tom, on the bright red spread across his cheeks, the fire burning up his gray-blue eyes. Jay was whispering to me while we were dancing, but I couldn't make sense of what he was saying. I was so busy reveling in Tom's beautiful, reckless jealousy.

On the drive back to East Egg that night, Tom had reached across the seat for my leg in the back of the limousine, ran his fingers up under my dress, high up my thigh, reaching up inside my undergarments. "Tom, stop." I'd pulled away, but my skin felt like fire, and the truth was, I wasn't sure I'd wanted him to stop at all.

"I'm done with her," he'd whispered in my ear then. "I promise you, Daisy. It's only you I want. Only you."

And for a minute, I'd believed him. His fingers crawled back up my thigh, under my undergarment, stroking me until I couldn't help myself, I let out a moan. Tom's face softened, and he looked like that man I married again.

JORDAN TURNED OFF the car in front of Jay's house now, and I pushed away the memory of that other night, the last time I was here. Tom's jealousy, his sudden craving for me. But all that was superseded by his need for this woman in the city, I supposed. Or else why had she called so many times last night during supper? He'd lied to me. He wasn't done with her at all.

"What are we doing here, Jordie?" I sighed as I stared at Jay's sprawling estate in front of us.

"It'll make Tom awfully jealous. And serves him right after all those telephone calls through supper last night."

"But Tom doesn't even know we're here," I said.

Her face twisted a little, somewhere between a frown and a smirk, an expression I couldn't quite place. "Well, I left a note on his desk to let him know exactly where I've taken you."

"You're positively wicked, Jordie." But it warmed me a little to picture the look on Tom's face when he walked into his study and read Jordan's words.

Seeing Jay again was the last thing I felt like doing, and I wished Jordan and I could've simply taken a drive and then lied about it. I was about to suggest such a thing when Jay walked outside, came right up to the car. "Daisy!" he exclaimed, opening up my car door and tugging gently on my arm to pull me upright. "Come on in."

"I'll drive around and come back in an hour," Jordan said. And then she sped off into the heat of the afternoon, abandoning me, before I could protest.

"I'm sorry to just drop in on you like this uninvited," I said to

Jay, suddenly feeling nervous to be here with just him. The last time we'd been all alone, at Nick's house, I'd felt so powerless that it had sent me spinning in Tom's study later that night. "I don't know what Jordan was thinking. I could walk next door to visit Nick."

"I won't hear of it." He grabbed my arm, as if to say that now that I was here, he would never let me go again. I shifted back, out of his grasp, uncomfortable. "I have your favorite tea," he spoke quickly. "The kind you used to like back in Louisville."

"Chamomile?" I asked. He nodded. It was really Rose's favorite tea, not mine; she used to make it all the time for both of us, and the truth was I hadn't drunk it in years. It tasted and smelled and reminded me entirely too much of her. "I'm really not . . . in the mood for tea," I said. I eyed the path to Nick's and fought the urge to break into a run. I wasn't at all wearing the shoes for it.

"Well, we can have lemonade instead. Come on, we'll sit out back. Reminisce about the good old times we had." He stared at me, his eyes refusing to move from my face. And I supposed it was either that or stand out in the hot drive for the next hour waiting for Jordan to come back while he stared.

I relented and followed him into his house and through it, out onto the back veranda, and down the steps to his large sparkling pool.

"The water is the perfect temperature, and I've barely gotten to use it all summer," he said. "We should go in!"

"I don't have my swimsuit," I said quickly. Though we were outside, surrounded by the woods on one side, the sound on the other, and a great big blue expanse of summer sky above us, I suddenly felt trapped. What had happened to the lemonade? The reminiscing?

Jay stared at me now, his eyes roaming my body, a little glassy like he was remembering the way every inch of my skin looked naked. I felt my face turning hot. Everything about Jay felt suffocating, all-consuming. He would push and push and wouldn't stop until he claimed me, would he?

But then he looked away, bent down, removed his shoes and socks, rolled up the bottoms of his pink trousers, and walked toward the water. "Come on, Daisy. We'll just put our feet in."

Sitting at the edge of the pool with his trousers rolled, he looked innocent, like a little boy. I slipped my own shoes off and dipped a toe in carefully—he was right, it was the perfect temperature. I let my feet sink in next to his, and I sat down next to him, swirling the water gently with my toes.

He moved his foot closer and tapped his toe gently against mine. "Do you remember when I climbed up into your bedroom in Louisville? The way we felt when we were together." Jay covered my foot with his foot, moved closer and trailed his fingers across my knee.

"Oh, Jay." I slithered away from him, splashing a little water. "I'm no longer the girl you knew in Louisville. And you're not that man, either. You have so much to offer now. I bet there are a thousand women in New York who'd want to be with you."

He moved closer to me, undeterred. He put his fingers on my thigh and gripped hard so now I couldn't slither farther. "But Daisy," he said, squeezing my thigh through my dress, "I only want you. All I've ever wanted was you. And you want me too. I know you still do."

It would be so easy to surrender to him, to kiss him, and let him pull off my dress and to dive headfirst into his pool. How easy it would be to betray Tom the way he had betrayed me, over and over and over again. How easy it would be to ruin him with the knowledge that I'd been with another man. When Jay leaned in all at once, kissed me hard, on the mouth, I was still thinking about

Tom's red-hot jealousy. And I let him kiss me for a minute without pulling back.

"I'm going to make you remember how to feel good, Daisy," he breathed heavily. "Erase the last three years." He slid his hand under my dress, ran his fingers roughly up my bare calf.

"Jay," I protested.

He ignored me, moved his hand up higher, my knee, my thigh.

"Jay, stop," I protested again, trying to move his hand, but he wouldn't budge.

He pushed his hand all the way up my thigh. His lips were on my ear, his voice a whisper, but also a command. "You love me. Say you love me."

In that moment I realized that I was going to betray Tom, here, now, whether I wanted to or not. And maybe it would be easier to just give up, to give in. To pretend to love it. To pretend to love him again. If I pretended hard enough, could I feel something again, for real?

"Tell me you love me, Daisy."

"I . . . I . . ." I felt hot tears running down my cheeks.

"Jay Gatsby!" A woman's voice screamed Jay's name from the veranda, and he froze. I pushed him off me and jumped out of the water shaking with relief. I wiped at my cheeks and fumbled with my shoes.

A gorgeous wisp of a girl flew down the veranda steps. She wore a bright red sleeveless dress that matched her beautiful strawberry bob. She looked at me, opened her mouth a little, shook her head.

"Jay Gatsby," she said his name again. Now her hands were on her hips as she moved toward the pool. "Why, I can't leave you alone for a second, can I?"

"Catherine," Jay finally spoke. "Daisy's here."

She glared at me, then frowned. "Daisy Buchanan." She said my name like it was something distasteful, dirty. I didn't relish the idea that she thought she knew me when I'd never seen the girl before in my life.

"I was just leaving," I said. I wasn't sure how much time had passed but I hoped to God Jordan had come back for me and was waiting out front. If she wasn't here, I'd escape to Nick's.

"Daisy, don't go." Jay stood and reached for my arm, but I yanked away, hard. "Daisy," he cried out my name again.

Catherine's eyes shot me daggers, and I didn't know why, but all of a sudden I started laughing. I laughed and laughed so hard that I almost couldn't breathe. Jay had spent the summer chasing after me, staring at my green light, inviting me to his parties, begging me to be with him, practically forcing me to be with him. And here he already had another girl. A goddamned Catherine.

I finally stopped laughing, and then I felt like I might cry again. "You men are all the same, aren't you?" I said.

"Oh, Daisy, no . . ." Jay protested.

But I spun on my heel and ran up the stairs to the veranda, too fast for Jay to get out of the pool and catch me. And besides, I didn't think Catherine would let him.

As I ran out front of his house, down the path to Nick's, I promised myself I would never come back here again.

Catherine

"YOU RUINED EVERYTHING," JAY YELLED IN MY FACE, GRABBING onto my shoulders too hard, after Daisy ran out. "Goddammit, Catherine."

It had thrilled me a little to make a show of things in front of Daisy. He deserved it, after all. But I hadn't expected such rage from him in return. I struggled to pull from his grasp now, but he held tighter, harder. I finally broke free and rubbed my shoulders a little.

The months I'd known Jay, the months I'd been with him, his touch had never been anything but gentle. But now his anger was red-hot, dangerous. I was pretty sure his fingers had left marks on my shoulders. Daisy was right about one thing. All men were the same.

"You're a fine one to talk," I finally shot back at him, regaining my composure and remembering why it was I'd gotten a taxicab all the way out here to West Egg in the first place. I rubbed my shoulders again. "And how about, *nice to see you, Cath.*"

"It's just . . . Daisy . . ." His voice trailed off and he stared behind me into the house, hoping maybe she might come back.

The truth was, Daisy wasn't half as beautiful as I'd expected her to be, and she hadn't appeared half as enamored with Jay as he was with her. And if it hadn't been for the way Jay had brought Myrtle into all this, I may have even felt a little sorry for the way I'd behaved, and for the forlorn way he looked now, like he was realizing he'd just lost her all over again. But then I thought about the crack of Tom's fist against Myrtle's face, her nose spurting blood, and I remembered my anger. "You ruined my sister's life."

"What?" Jay finally stopped spinning and pining after Daisy and he seemed to hear what I'd said to him. "What are you talking about?"

"You set Myrtle up with Tom Buchanan, Jay," I said. "And he's the last man Myrtle needs. He's worse than George."

"Set her up?" Jay shook his head, confused. "No, I just wanted to stage some photographs, that's all. I paid her simply to sit and talk to him on a train."

"You sent my sister to meet a wealthy, philandering man on a train," I yelled at him. "What did you think was going to happen next? Of course she'd fall in love with him."

"Love?" His voice rose in surprise, and then he let out a boisterous bellowing laugh. "Well, that's a very good development indeed."

I frowned; his excitement turned my stomach. *A good development?* "He punched her in the nose a few weeks ago. But she still believes he's going to take her out west. Her husband is getting suspicious now and god only knows what he'll do to her if he finds out she's been with Tom. I really need your help to get Myrtle away from both of them. You said once you'd help her. And now you've gone and made things worse. You owe me."

Jay opened his mouth, then closed it again. He broke into an almost diabolical grin. "Take her out west, you say? Well, I like the sound of that."

I took a step back, away from him, shook my head. "He's a horrible man. I'll never let him take my sister away." My voice trembled as I spoke, because I realized even as I said the words that they weren't true. I hadn't been able to stop George from hurting her in all these years, and I couldn't stop Tom from doing whatever he pleased either.

"Jay," I tried again. "If I ever meant anything to you . . . please. I'm begging you, you have to help Myrtle."

Jay cocked his head to the side, and I could see the green of his eyes catching a hint of summer sunlight. They sparkled, emeralds, like the grass of the lawn behind him. "The thing is, Cath," he said, matter-of-factly, coldly, "you never really did mean anything to me."

Jordan

AFTER I DROPPED DAISY AT JAY'S HOUSE, I DROVE AROUND WEST Egg for a while. There was a golf course a few miles down the road, and the car eventually took me there without me really thinking about it. It was a piping hot Saturday, but a summer Saturday nonetheless, and the course was swarming with men in pink pants and white golf polos. I parked my car and walked down as far as I could to the course without actually stepping on it. And then I just stared at those men, feeling something swell in my chest that I hadn't felt for so long: desire. Not for another person at all, but for a game. Oh, sweet, beautiful golf! I missed the way my arms felt when they were slicing balls through the air, the way my mind felt when I was calculating the distance to the hole, the precise amount of spin to add to my swing. I missed the smell of the green, the solid feel of the trim grass beneath my feet.

"Looking for your husband, miss?" A man's voice broke into my thoughts. I turned and an unfamiliar man stood behind me, his clubs strapped to his back. "Are you looking for your husband, out on the course?"

I frowned. Of course he would think the only thing I might be doing here, watching, would be looking for my husband. I had half a mind to take his nine iron from his bag and beat him silly with it. "I'm just a fan of the game," I huffed. "Just watching, that's all."

"Lady," he said, laughing at me as he shook his head, "this is a private club. Get out of here."

Before I could think of an appropriate insult to say back to him (and later, I would think of several), he walked off. He disappeared onto the course and blended in with all the others. They were terrible golfers—I could see from here. Money might've offered them access to the nouveau riche club of West Egg, but it certainly didn't buy them any talent. That thought raged endlessly in my head, sounding stupidly snobbish like Tom. Tom. *Daisy*. I'd forgotten about Daisy!

Nearly two hours had passed since I'd left her, and I sped the whole way back to Jay's. But when I hurtled down his drive, I caught no sight of her at all. Jay was standing outside on his porch, all alone, shoeless, looking downtrodden and forlorn.

"Where is she?" I asked, upon pulling the brake and hopping out.

He shrugged. And he looked so out of sorts that I had this terrible feeling that something had happened to her.

"What did you do to her, Jay?"

His eyes shot cool, green daggers at me before he sat down on the stoop, put his head in his hands, and sighed heavily. "She's fine, Jordan. She left a while ago. I suppose she went to Nick's."

I took a deep breath and I could still feel the sharp, cool smell of newly cut grass from the course lingering in my nose. "All right. Well, I did what you asked." I swallowed hard, pushing back the guilt I felt about having left Daisy here earlier and then forgotten her, too. "I brought Daisy here today. And you promised you'd help me, with golf."

He ran his hands through his hair, agitated, messing it up, making him look a little wild. I pictured him again as that soldier the first night I met him, sweeping into a summer party in Louisville and whisking Daisy away, holding her too desperately close, a possession. "No, no, you have to help me get Daisy back first," he said now, sounding petulant, like a child.

It occurred to me that we were playing this dangerous game, Jay and I, and neither one of us was likely to win in any way we found satisfying. Jay would never have Daisy. I could pretend to help him, set up more meetings, but I'd sabotage them all the same. Wasn't that what I'd done today by letting Tom know of this little endeavor? And the more we went round and round in this precarious circle, the more I'd want golf, and the further it would be from my reach. That thought made me so angry, I could barely breathe.

"Did you know Tom has another woman on the side?" Jay was saying now.

"Of course." I sighed, exhaling and letting the anger out. "Everyone knows that, Jay. Daisy even knows that."

"Yes, but did you know she wants to run away with him? Wants him to take her out west?"

A laugh bubbled up from deep inside my chest. But it came out sounding more like a dying bird. This woman who'd taunted Daisy all summer with her endless telephone calls thought she could get Tom to take her *out west* just like that. Then I had a more sobering thought: *Could she?*

"Tom needs to leave with Myrtle," Jay was saying. "That will fix everything."

Myrtle? It felt funny to know she had a name, that she was a real, living breathing woman who desired something unattainable too. Just like the rest of us. Golf. Daisy. Tom and the west.

"You'll convince Tom to take her far away, Jordan. California," he added.

"Me?" Now I did laugh. "How am *I* supposed to convince Tom?" Tom didn't even listen to me about the simplest things, like what we should eat for supper. Tom only tolerated my presence because Daisy made him. And even that, it always felt like I was some sort of penance for him.

"Easy. I want you to tell him Daisy is in love with me. Convince him Daisy wants him to go, that she wants to erase the last three years with him. That his only chance at happiness is going west with Myrtle."

"I can't do that," I said. For one thing, Tom wouldn't listen to me, and for another, it would break Daisy's heart. I stared at the tops of my white shoes. They'd gotten a bit muddy at the edge of the golf course, and I swiped at them with my hands now, crumbling brown streaks of dirt across Jay's beautiful, clean white porch.

"You can, and you will." His voice was dark, quiet, serious.

I shook my head.

"Jordan," Jay said my name softly now, as if to disguise the threat that simmered just beneath. "Jordan, Jordan. We have to help each other, you and I. It's the only way we'll both get what we want."

He sounded crazed, and I bit my lip and stared at the ground, afraid to say anything at all.

He walked over and put his hand on my arm, like he was about to give me hug. But then instead he looked me straight in the eye and smiled a little. "I really could destroy you."

❧

LATER THAT NIGHT, I was already three G&Ts deep by supper. The phone rang on in the distance, but it sounded muted to me now, far away. Daisy's and Tom's faces were fuzzy but somehow clear enough that I understood Tom was already drinking too much, too; his face was flushed. Maybe from too much sun playing polo today, or maybe from the whiskey, or maybe it was anger over finding my little note. It was hard to tell.

The telephone jangled again, and Daisy glared at Tom across the table. He scraped back his chair, then rushed off and answered the call. He spoke in the other room in hushed tones. Daisy buried her face in her hands. It was hard to believe he'd ever really leave Daisy. Go westward with *Myrtle*. But if I didn't try to do what Jay asked, would he really *destroy me*? He had money and power and Mr. Hennessey's talk about me, and maybe it wouldn't even be all that hard.

Tom suddenly slapped the table, and I jumped. He'd come back from the telephone, his face even redder than before. "You think it's all right for him to call you during supper, Daisy?" Tom sounded indignant.

Him?

"Who?" Daisy asked, but then the realization dawned on her, dawned on both of us. She opened her mouth, let out a sigh that sounded a little like a kitten mewing.

"Well, I've invited your lover to lunch here on Monday. We may as well all get to know each other better." Tom's voice was dripping with anger and sarcasm and maybe even a hint of sadistic delight.

Daisy frowned and her face turned pale, and Tom snickered and stood to pour more whiskey.

"Jordan, call Nick and invite him, too. We may as well make it a party," Tom slurred, making his way back to the table.

"It's too hot for a party," I said, downing the rest of my drink, then standing up to make another. And I had no desire to see any more of Nick.

"Never mind," Tom spoke roughly. "Daisy, you do it," he commanded. "He's your cousin."

Daisy

August 1922

NEW YORK

AND THEN THERE WE WERE: THE HOTTEST HOUR OF THE HOTTEST day of August.

I felt a strange sort of déjà vu, for that other too-hot August day in Louisville, five years earlier. That day Rose dragged me to the almshouse and Jay pulled up alongside us, offering us a ride. *I should've said no then*, I thought now. I should've listened to Rose and turned down Jay's ride. Nothing good came of the decisions I made when it was this hot. Nothing good would come from this lunch with Tom and Jay and Nick and Jordan. I knew it, and still, I let it happen. I'd even called up Nick like Tom had asked and invited him. Of course, Nick agreed. Nick agreed to everything that summer. If you looked up agreeable in *Merriam-Webster's* I was pretty sure you'd see Nick's photograph.

Jordan and I had put on our nicest white dresses for lunch, but even the effort of getting dressed had made us practically combustible. We'd landed on the couch, and we were fanning ourselves, when Nick and Jay arrived together. I heard the door, heard them walk down the hallway, then enter the parlor and say hello. And I immediately thought, *This is a mistake. This is a terrible, terrible mistake.* I thought of Jay and his awful creeping fingers at his pool the other day, and I had the urge to run out, to run upstairs, to hide away in my bedroom until everyone had gone home. But truly it was too hot to move, and so I didn't. I just lay there on the couch, letting Jordan hold my hand and fan me.

The telephone rang again in the distance, and I heard Tom answer it. "He should've invited his woman in the city, too," I said. "Then it really would be a party."

Nick denied that such a thing could be true in that sweet innocent overearnest midwestern way he had of looking at the world. Agreeable *and* earnest. It occurred to me in that very moment that things were never going to work out between him and Jordan. Jordan was much too cynical. She could never stand for such earnestness over the long haul.

Jay stood across the room, dressed in a pink suit, his arms crossed in front of his chest. Tom's voice elevated from the hall, but his words were still impossible to understand. Jay frowned and strode toward me. "He's no good for you," he said, his voice husky from the heat.

He leaned down toward me all of a sudden, grabbed me, and kissed me on the lips. He pressed hard, and it was so hot that I could barely breathe.

"Mama?" Pammy's voice suddenly cut through the heat, and I sat up quickly and pushed Jay away hard enough that he stumbled a little. I put the back of my hand to my lips, speechless for a moment. What had she seen and what did she think?

I was shaking, but I held out my arms. "Come here, my precious." Pammy ran in to hug me. Her nurse had dressed her in white, arranged her blond curls with a pink bow. "Don't you look divine." I kissed her soft damp forehead, her curls tickling my lips.

My love for her suddenly struck deeper inside of me than anything I'd ever felt for any man.

"I weared my white dress. Just like you and Aunt Jordan." She giggled, and I clung to her. Regret ratcheted its way from my stomach to my chest to my throat, bitter and hot. "Where's Daddy?" Pammy asked now, like she could sense everything that was wrong about this moment. She pulled away from my arms and stared uneasily at both Nick and Jay.

"He's gone in the other room for a moment . . ." I said.

Her eyes roamed slowly across Jay's face. He smiled at her, and she frowned. And the way her face turned in that moment, it hit me that she would someday grow to be a woman. I wanted more for her than to be a fool. I never wanted men to treat Pammy the way they treated me. I wanted her to be brave and bold, and fearless and independent. I kissed her head again and felt tears welling up in my eyes.

"I'm a mother," I announced to the whole room, like it was news. But then I looked Jay square in the eye. "I'm this little girl's mother."

Jay frowned, like he didn't understand. But here I was, weeks later, answering that silly question he'd asked me at Nick's. *Why couldn't we just erase the last three years?* That was why. She was why.

Nick looked at me, thoughtful. "She's a little you, isn't she, Daisy?" he said.

His words burned my face, my heart. Pammy had to be better. I wanted so much better for her. I had to make sure she was better.

A FEW HOURS later, after a long and tense lunch where I drank not one but two gin rickeys, we all ended up in the city, a suite at the Plaza Hotel with a few bottles of whiskey. I'd had too much to drink by then, and I could barely remember why we came here, or whose idea it was. Tom had made some big to-do about switching cars back in East Egg, and he'd driven Jay's yellow Rolls-Royce into the city with Nick and Jordan, forcing me in the coupe with Jay. I'd closed my eyes and pretended to sleep, until I actually had fallen asleep. I didn't understand what sort of game Tom thought he was playing, but all it served was to make him even crankier by the time we were all together again at the Plaza. And my uneasy nap had me feeling much the same.

It was so sweltering hot in our suite now, and Tom had trouble getting the windows open. I huffed, still drunk and annoyed—it seemed like someone as strapping as him should be able to open a goddamned window. The gin floated in my stomach, a hot swollen hatred for him. For Jay, too.

A bottle of whiskey opened, and the two of them drank and started going at each other. I heard them bickering, but their voices sounded very far away, and I could barely make sense of what they were saying. I felt groggy and it was too hot to argue. Didn't they know?

There was a party in the ballroom down below us, and suddenly the sounds of the wedding march floated up through the floor.

"Remember when you got married," Jordan exclaimed. I couldn't tell if she was trying to change the subject or to inflame the men even more. "It was a heat like this, wasn't it, Daise?"

Tom and Jay stopped going at each other for a moment. "Someone fainted," Tom said. Maybe I should faint right now? Would it put an end to this dreadful day? "Biloxi. Blocks Biloxi, and he made boxes, wasn't that right, Daisy?"

I remembered a man fainting straight out in the middle of the church, but I couldn't remember much else about him. Only that

Jordan had come to the rescue, carried him away. Jordan was always saving me. She was trying to save me now. "Is that right, Jordie? Blocks the box salesman?" I turned to look at her, and her face had gone a strange putrid shade of gray.

She nodded. "We carried him into my house because we lived just two doors from the church. And he stayed three weeks until Daddy told him he had to get out." She paused and cast her eyes into her whiskey. "The day after he left, Daddy died." She downed her drink, then added quickly, "There wasn't any connection."

I never knew the details around when her daddy died, only that he had while we were on our honeymoon. When I was still blissful and stupid in the South Seas.

"He gave me an aluminum putter," Jordan added. "I still use it to this day."

Tom didn't seem to notice Jordan was still talking, or her sad, scrunched-up face. He was telling Nick about Biloxi, and then he started going back at Jay, something about Oxford.

I stood and walked to the couch where Jordan was already sitting. I sat down next to her and smothered her with a hot, full-bodied hug. "I'm sorry," I whispered into her neck. "I'm sorry, I'm sorry. The last days you had with your daddy you were picking up the pieces of some stupid box salesman from my stupid wedding. And I never even knew until now."

"You're drunk, Daise." Her words tumbled hot into my hair.

"I know I'm not as popular as you," Tom was shouting, *shouting*, at Jay now.

"Why don't you calm down, old sport. There's something I need to tell you," Jay said.

"Tom's so jealous, isn't he?" Jordan whispered, sounding annoyed.

I looked at him again, and his face was red, bursting with anger and a sense of entitlement, a sense of possession. He looked like Pammy when you took away her favorite toy. Jay was angry now, too, his pupils flaring from the whiskey, his voice rising. The two of them, they both looked like a pair of drunken goddamned fools.

"I always thought it was us women who were the fools," I whispered. "But I was wrong, it's been the men all along, hasn't it?"

Jordan giggled a little and clung to me, planting a sloppy, drunken kiss on my cheek. "Fools rush in where angels fear to tread. My daddy always used to say that."

"Maybe we should all go back home," Mr. Agreeable Nick interjected from across the room. He was eyeing me and Jordan with trepidation, while trying to calm the other two men down.

Tom glared at Nick. "I want to hear what Mr. Gatsby has to tell me," Tom flamed, daring Jay, his voice even more agitated.

"Daisy never loved you!" Jay shouted at him.

I heard my name, and I leaned back against Jordan and closed my eyes. She wrapped her arms around me and held on tight. Sometimes, I felt like a prop in my own life. Like a marionette who everyone assumed didn't know how to move without a man pulling her strings. That wasn't true. That wasn't right. Only I didn't have the strength to make them believe it. Didn't they know it was too hot?

"She's never loved you," Jay was saying now. "She loves me."

"You must be crazy!" Tom shouted back.

"She only married you because I was poor and she was tired of waiting for me. It was a terrible mistake."

They shouted, on and on. I knew they were yelling about me, and I heard them saying something about Jordan, too. But their voices, their nonsensical ramblings about love, hovered somewhere above me in the thick, hot, drunken air. Their words were stupid, meaningless. Foolish. Untrue.

I opened my eyes again. And their anger was so palpable I could almost feel it burning up my skin, almost see the heat of the late afternoon and their voices rising in the air in visible swirling waves. I had the sensation that my life was exploding all around me, and I couldn't stop it. But maybe I didn't want to stop it? Maybe I wanted my life to explode.

I looked at Tom, his face even redder. "Once in a while I go off on a little spree, but I always love Daisy. In my heart I love her all the time," Tom insisted to Jay.

He loves me, in his heart?

I thought of Rebecca Buckley's plump pink child cheeks. Her small breasts illuminated in the midnight lamplight in the stables. Was he loving me in his heart then?

"You're revolting," I said to Tom, suddenly finding my voice. It was surprisingly loud and strangely sober. Nick looked at me, his mouth wide open. "Do you know why we left Chicago, Nick?" I said to him. "I'm surprised Tom didn't treat you to the story of that *little spree.*"

Jay walked over and stood next to me. "Daisy," he said softly. "None of that matters now." Yes, it did. It mattered to me. "Just tell him that truth—that you never loved him." Who was Jay to think he knew the truth about me?

"She loves me!" Tom spat at Jay, indignant.

"How could I possibly love you?" I snapped back at Tom. My words practically sizzled in the air, but they felt like the truest words I'd spoken in some time.

Jay smirked, satisfied by my outburst. But I didn't love him, either. I'd felt something for him, once, years ago. Maybe it was love or maybe it was the stupidity of a youthful flirtation. Now, I felt nothing. And that was the truth, the hard, hot truth. I felt nothing. I loved no one. Except my daughter.

"You never loved Tom," Jay was saying now. "Tell him, Daisy."

Tom's eyes met my eyes, and they were suddenly soft and vulnerable and a little hurt. It felt like the most honest look we'd given each other since the South Seas. "Not even in Kapiolani?" he said softly.

Kapiolani. I remembered that morning, the intoxicating scent of the Pacific and the morning dew on the grass that soaked through my dress to my knees. I remembered the inebriating power I'd felt, giving Tom pleasure, just like that, so fearlessly, out in the open. And the truth was maybe I had loved him then. Before he'd ruined it only weeks later, in Santa Barbara. Before he'd ruined me, years later in Lake Forest. And again here, this summer, in New York.

Tom and Jay went on arguing, but I couldn't listen anymore. I just couldn't bear it. Jordan had lain back against the couch and closed her eyes, draping her arm against her face—she was done too. I was hot and tired and I hated everything about this day, this suite, this burning useless moment in my life.

"I want to go home," I said, suddenly. And it wasn't East Egg I meant. It was Louisville and my normal-sized house and my childhood bed and the old snow goose trilling my name up the stairs. No one heard me—they were still arguing—so I said it again, louder. "I want to go home. . . . *Please,* Tom! I can't stand this anymore."

He suddenly turned from Jay to look at me, his face red with heat and anger, and something burned up in his eyes that looked strangely like desire. This fight, this stupid reckless fight made him want me again, and it felt like such a cruelty to only be wanted by your husband when he believed another man wanted you more. If that was Tom's idea of *love*, then maybe he'd never truly loved anyone or anything in his entire life.

"You two start on home, Daisy." Tom's voice softened, and I thought he meant me and Jordan. But then his face curled into a wicked grin and he nodded toward Jay. "In Mr. Gatsby's car," he added.

A smile erupted across Jay's face, like maybe he thought he'd won, and I wanted to tell him I was not some prize at the county fair, not some object to be tossed around and desired and gambled away.

But it was so hot in this room, and I could barely breathe, much less think. I didn't want to argue anymore; I didn't want to be in this suffocating room any longer. All I wanted to do was go home.

OUTSIDE ON THE street I walked two steps ahead of Jay. The air wasn't any cooler out here even though the city had fallen into the gloaming while we were all drinking and arguing up in the suite. Dusk hovered over us like a blanket, and as much as I wanted to race ahead of Jay, farther, faster, I felt weighed down by the hot air and too much gin.

"Daisy," Jay called out, running to catch up. "Wait."

"I'll get a taxicab," I said.

"Don't be silly." He dangled his keys at arm's length so I could hear the jingling close enough to my ear. "I'll let you drive. Come on, just get in the car, and we can talk."

I stopped walking and spun around. "I don't want to talk," I spat at him. "Don't you see I've grown quite tired of talking." The real truth sat still unspoken though. I was just . . . tired. So very, very tired.

He grabbed my hand and unfurled my fist, placing the car keys in my palm. "Then we'll drive to East Egg in silence."

The truth was, I'd never get a taxicab in this awful heat. I took the keys, my eyes caught on the bright yellow light of his Rolls-Royce, and I stomped toward it. I got into the driver's seat and started the ignition.

And it occurred to me as I drove down Fifth Avenue that this was exactly like that first time we met, in that sweltering August heat, Jay and I together, riding in a car. Only Rose was gone. And now I was the one driving.

That was the beginning; this would be the ending.

Myrtle

August 1922
QUEENS, NY

THE YELLOW CAR CAME RIDING THROUGH THE ASHY SWELTERING afternoon, beautiful and too fast, like a burst of sunshine.

I saw it from my upstairs window, watched it slow down, then stop out front for gas. Tom got out of the car. Tom!

I'm coming, I mouthed from my bedroom window, my prison, but Tom didn't look up.

I understood then that Cath must've gone out to East Egg, spoken to Tom just like I'd asked. He must've borrowed his friend's car, so I would know now it was time for us to head west, the bright yellow like a signal, a beacon of hope.

All I had to do was break out of my bedroom, where George had kept me locked in since last week, and run down the stairs.

But before I could move, George walked out of the garage and started talking to Tom. My heart flooded my chest, watching them. Only minutes later, Tom shook his head, then got back in the car and sped off, toward the city. But I knew. I just had to bide my time; Tom would come back again, when he thought it was safe.

I spent the rest of the afternoon getting the bedroom door lock undone with a bobby pin, the same way Cath and I used to do as girls when Father got mad and locked us in our room without sup-per. We'd undo the lock after we knew he was asleep, and then I'd sneak out in the dark and bring Cath back some bread so she wouldn't have to go to sleep hungry. As I did it again this after-noon, I suddenly remembered what it was like to feel young, to feel powerful. I'd feel that way all the time, as soon as I was with Tom. We'd have a sprawling, gorgeous estate by the Pacific Ocean, and I'd never be imprisoned again.

This beautiful thought made me hum a little as I dressed in my nicest red dress, put the diamond pins from Tom in my hair. And then I sat by the window, tapping my fingers against the ledge. I watched. And waited.

And I listened anxiously for George to come up the stairs, praying Tom would come back for me first.

LAST WEEK, I'D come back to Queens after seeing Cath in the city, and George had been waiting up for me when I'd tried to sneak in at half past midnight.

He'd sat at the kitchen table then with a bottle of moonshine, holding a gun in his hands, like he was waiting for an intruder. But he'd been waiting for me.

"Where were you, Myrtle?" he'd slurred.

I'd eyed the gun, put my suitcase down behind me, and hoped he was too drunk to notice it. "I just went to the city to visit with Cath. What are you doing up?" I'd asked.

"You think I can sleep while my wife is out running around?"

"Running around?" My laugh came out too high. "Hardly. I was helping fix Cath some soup. She's under the weather."

He'd frowned and massaged the gun with his drunken fingers.

Every fiber of my being had told me to grab my suitcase then, to run, to go back to the city. Maybe Cath's couch wouldn't be so bad? But George would only follow me there. And I'd told Cath I'd trust her, wait it out here. Wait for Tom to come and take me westward like he'd promised. Anyway, if I turned and ran, I was pretty sure George would shoot me.

I'd forced myself to smile, to walk toward him. It took every ounce of strength I had to lean in and rub his shoulders. "Darling, it's so late. Let's go to bed."

He'd stared up at me, his eyes glassy, desperate. But he'd let go of the gun, and he'd stood, wrapped his hands around my neck. At first he'd moved his fingers gently, massaging my collarbone with his thumbs. But I knew what was coming and a shiver erupted through my body. His hands began to squeeze. Tighter and tighter.

"George . . . I . . . I can't . . . breathe." I'd gasped for air, and he'd squeezed tighter still. I saw colors in flashes: purple and blue and yellow. Everything was bright and yellow.

And I'd thought: the yellow car had erupted into my colorless ashy life like a sliver of sunshine, once, leading me to Tom. All it had to do was come back, save me.

AND THEN, THERE it was again.

Just after dusk on the hottest night of the year. Darting forth from the twilight. A lightning bolt. A flutter of hope. My savior. My escape.

I ran toward it.

Daisy

JAY KEPT HIS PROMISE AND DIDN'T SAY A WORD AS I DROVE OUT of the city. I focused on the road, and it calmed me, sobered me. I rehashed all the night's arguing in my head, and suddenly it all felt so silly. So childish and stupid. Tom and Jay blind with rage and jealous and fighting, *over me*. I wanted neither one of them.

"Daisy," Jay said softly, as we approached the ash dump, "if you left him, I could give you everything you ever wanted. And I'd never hurt you the way he hurts you."

I thought about him forcing his hand up my dress by the pool, his girl, *Catherine*, running blindly down the steps of his veranda, mad as hell. "Wouldn't you, though?" I said softly. Every man, every wealthy man, was surrounded by temptation and need and burning with some sort of unquenchable desire. It occurred to me I might've wanted to love Jay again now if he were still poor, if I'd known there was a purity to his feelings like there had been back in Louisville. But he and Tom were cut of the same cloth. I wanted nothing to do with either one of them.

"What can I do to prove to you how much I love you?" he said, sounding desperate. "Tell me, Daisy. Tell me what to do and I'll do it."

I shook my head. "Jay," I said. "You have to stop."

"I'll never stop, Daisy."

His words felt like a punch, a god-awful truth settling in my stomach. And it hit me—East Egg was not going to be my permanent home. Jay would never stop gazing at my green light, across the sound. He'd never stop following me, chasing me. Tom would love it until he would hate it. He would desire me until he forgot about me. The realization overwhelmed me, and I lowered my eyes from the road for just a moment. Only a moment.

When I looked back up, we were approaching Wilson's garage, and there was a flash, a red streak of a woman, running out from the garage and waving her arms. That voluptuous body, plump cheeks, swirl of red hair. I knew her. I'd never met her before, but here she was, running toward me. "That's Tom's woman," I gasped.

She ran toward the car, like she had a death wish. And I thought, *everything Tom touches wants to die.*

And then what happened next seemed to happen both in slow motion, but also so fast I could barely see straight enough to try and stop it. Jay jumped across the seat, pushed my hands out of the way, and grabbed the wheel.

The car hit her with a horrifying thump, and I watched her catapult through the air, screaming, bleeding, clutching her breast.

Jordan

BLOCKS BILOXI.

His name was still rattling around in my head.

I'd fallen half asleep on the hotel suite's couch while the men got into their little row, and Blocks came to me in a semilucid dream. He reached for me, I screamed, grabbed the aluminum putter. And Daddy's face. Oh dear, sweet Daddy's face. And then Blocks had morphed into Jay Gatsby saying, *Jordan, I'm going to tell everyone your secret.* Had I dreamed that, too, or had he actually said that out loud inside the suite?

"Jordan." Tom woke me with his brutish, drunken voice, and I jumped up. "Let's go."

I looked around. Daisy was gone. Jay was gone.

"What happened to Daise?" I didn't dare ask Tom because I could tell just by the way he'd said my name he was still inflamed. But I whispered the question to Nick as we walked back out to the street. It was twilight now and the air had finally cooled the smallest bit. I took a deep breath, but my lungs still burned.

"She left with Gatsby, about a half an hour ago," he said, frowning.

And, yes, that was the obvious answer, but I supposed the real question was *why?* "Did Jay say something to her, about me?" I asked. My voice faltered a little. I was still a little sleepy and a little drunk and altogether unsteady on my feet.

Nick frowned, impatient. "I told you she loved him, didn't I?" There was something surprising in his tone, almost a little snide, a little *I told ya so.* I didn't know Nick had it in him to be vindictive.

I sighed and lay down in the back seat of Tom's coupe and closed my eyes again. Blocks, Jay, Tom, Mr. Hennessey. Even Nick. They were all the same, weren't they? They all wanted nothing more than to ruin me. It was utterly exhausting to be a woman.

I WOKE UP again when the car came to a sudden stop.

I sat up, expecting the bright lights of Daisy's East Egg mansion, but instead everything around me was smoky and gray and up ahead I saw the flashing lights of a police wagon. Tom got out of the car and walked toward the trouble, and Nick leaned his head out of the car, expectantly.

"Where are we?" I asked Nick.

"In the valley of ashes," Nick said. I frowned. "Corona," he clarified. "There's been some kind of a wreck." He paused. "Tom's woman lives here," he said thoughtfully, pointing to Wilson's garage off to my right.

Tom's woman? Here? We'd stopped for gas at Wilson's earlier on the way into town, but Nick hadn't said a word then. I'd always pictured the woman on the other end of the telephone as wealthy and refined, like Daisy. Somehow it made it worse to know that she was sad and poor, restless, wanting. I felt certain Tom had made her a thousand promises he would never keep. And taking her west had to be one of them.

Nick got out of the car, too, and walked up ahead to the crowd, where Tom was standing. But I lay back against the seat, closed my eyes again. The afternoon ran through my memory, hot and horrible and drunken. Bits and pieces of conversation and yelling tumbled around in my head and it was hard to tell if it was real or a dream. Blocks Biloxi and Jay and Tom. And Daisy. Why had Daisy left me there like that? What *had* Jay said to her?

After a little while the men got back in the car, rigid and silent. "What happened?" I asked. Neither one of them spoke for a moment.

"She was killed," Nick finally said, softly. "Myrtle Wilson was killed."

Myrtle. Tom's woman?

"He didn't even stop the car," Tom cried out. "He didn't even stop the goddamned car."

I shook my head, confused.

"Gatsby," Nick turned and whispered to me. "He hit Tom's woman with his car and didn't even stop."

I DID NOT sleep at all that night, and by six A.M. when the morning light had just begun to erupt above the sound outside my window, I had made myself sick with worry. For myself. For this woman I'd never met who Jay had run over and killed with his car. If he'd done that to her, what would he do to me when he learned I hadn't really been trying to help him this summer at all? The worry rose up, acidic in my throat, and I had to run to the toilet to vomit.

When we'd finally made it back to East Egg last night, I'd walked inside the house, and Daisy had been sitting at the kitchen table, crying into a bowl of fried chicken. I'd run to her, but she'd pushed me away then, saying "Jordan, I can't. I just . . . can't." Her words had stung like a slap, and then Tom ordered me to leave them alone. I'd gone up to my bedroom—what other choice did I have? But I'd lain awake all night, restless.

Now, hours later, I lay on the bathroom floor and leaned my head against the cool porcelain, my stomach lurching even once it was empty. There was nothing left. I had nothing left.

I suddenly heard Daisy calling my name. I stood quickly and splashed water on my face and ran back to my bed.

"Jordie." Daisy walked into my room, breathless. My stomach roiled again, and I held my breath, waiting for her to snap at me like she had last night, but instead, she climbed up on the bed and wrapped me in a hug. I held her tightly, fiercely. "Last night was just . . ." She pulled back, shook her head, and bit her lip, unable to finish her sentence.

I pulled her back for another hug, buried my face in her hair, and somehow it still felt as soft as corn silk and it still smelled a little bit like gin but like lemons, too. It soothed me and my stomach finally calmed.

She sat back and offered me a wan, tear-streaked smile. "I've come to say good-bye."

"Good-bye?" I whispered.

"I'm leaving Tom, Jordie." I shook my head, not understanding. "It was last night . . . It was the final straw. Jay and I were driving and then that woman . . . Tom's woman . . ." She buried her face in her hands, like she had been picturing the gruesome scene all night and she couldn't picture it yet again. Not another time. "And after I got home, I kept hearing Rosie's voice in my head, telling me to be good. How can I be good with Tom? I can't, Jordie. I just can't. I never will."

She leaned across the bed and kissed me softly on the cheek.

Her lips were warm, and they felt like sunshine and my childhood in Louisville, and I wanted Daisy to stay right here with me, forever.

"I'm going to go fix myself up now and go see Jay," she said. *Jay.* His name felt so abrasive, so awful, that the rest of her words rushed through my ears, thick and blurry and nonsensical. ". . . And then we're going to get ready to go," she was still talking. "But I'll write you as soon as we get settled, all right? You'll come visit us when you get a break from the tour, won't you, Jordie?"

Jay? Us. The words spun around in my head, making me dizzy, and I closed my eyes to try and understand what was happening. She wasn't just leaving Tom. She was leaving Tom for Jay. But Jay had just killed a woman last night. She wouldn't be safe with Jay. She would never be safe again. No matter what Jay would try to do to ruin me for it, I had to stop her now.

"Daise, wait!" I called after her.

But when I opened my eyes, it was too late. She was already gone.

Catherine

"A MORGUE IS NO PLACE FOR A LADY," THE PORTLY MUSTACHED coroner insisted as I demanded to be let inside.

"I'm not taking no for an answer," I spat back, my voice shaking through my tears.

I'd been in a deep and gin-soaked sleep when the telephone had rung at six o'clock this morning. Helen had answered it, shaken me awake. "Cath." Her brown eyes had loomed above me, wide-eyed with fear. "A detective's on the line for you."

I'd sat up in bed all at once, the startling revelation that my deepest fear had come to fruition. Had George finally hurt Myrtle so badly that she was in the hospital?

Two hours later, I was at the morgue in Flushing, and Detective Charles was asking me to sit down before he would tell me what was going on. "I don't want to sit down," I'd flared at him. "Just tell me what happened. Where's Myrtle?"

The words *dead, car, didn't stop* reverberated senselessly in my head. Mr. Wilson had been too shaken up to call me, he said, and that's where the detective had stepped in. His words were unexpected. Certainly untrue. "Let me see her," I'd demanded. "I have to see her."

And then Detective Charles had led me down the stairs, to the cool, dark basement morgue. The smell of formaldehyde and death turned my stomach, and I'd turned away from him and suddenly started gasping for air, trying not to wretch.

"Here." The detective kindly handed me a bucket, and I turned away from him to vomit into it. And that's when the coroner walked out, insisted that I not be allowed inside.

"I'm fine now," I said firmly. "I'm not taking no for an answer. I have to see my sister."

Detective Charles looked at me. He was tall, with brown hair peppered with gray. But his face still looked young, and I suspected the gray hairs were more a consequence of his job than his age.

"I haven't been in myself yet, but I think they got her cleaned up," Detective Charles was saying now. His voice was calm, even. Perhaps death no longer shocked him, he'd seen it too many times. "But it still won't be pretty, Miss McCoy."

I crossed my arms in front of my chest and stepped in front of the door to the morgue, resolute. I wasn't going anywhere until they let me see Myrtle.

The coroner finally sighed and stepped aside. The thing of it was, I didn't quite believe that she'd been hit by a car, that she was here, inside this cold, dark horrible place. Perhaps it was all a giant mistake, a ruse. Tom had come to take Myrtle westward after all and she'd faked her death to get George off their trail. And now the true accident was that they'd told me she was dead, brought me down here.

Even as Detective Charles held on gently to my elbow to lead me inside, pointed to the cold metal table in front of me, and I saw a red-haired woman's body, all but her head covered by a sheet. Even then, I did not believe it. I shook my head. "No," I said. "It can't be her. It's not her."

Detective Charles let go of my elbow. "I'll give you some privacy," he said gently. "But I'll be just outside if you need anything."

I nodded and stepped forward, trying to hold my breath. The smell of death hit me so strongly now, I was worried I'd vomit again. And I'd left my bucket outside.

The woman on the table resembled my sister, only a little. Her similarly colored red hair was matted with blood. When I stepped even closer, I saw a part of her left cheek was missing. I shuddered a little, closed my eyes for a moment. Then opened them and leaned in closer still. The dead woman's nose was slightly crooked and blue; her eyes were sealed shut.

I put my hand on her right cheek, still pristine, intact. But unbearably cold and rigid. I slightly turned her face with my hand, trying to get a good look at her. She resembled Myrtle in the most terrible, distant way. But she couldn't be Myrtle. I did not believe she was Myrtle.

Then my eye suddenly caught a sparkle underneath her matted, bloodied hair. A glint against the harsh overhead light. I gently brushed aside her hair, and there, trapped underneath the blood, the raw mottle skin, was a diamond hairpin. I pulled it out, held it in my palm, and let it catch the light.

Those hairpins are real pretty, Myrtle.

You'd better believe they're diamonds. Tom only buys me the best, Cath . . . Borrow them anytime you'd like.

I ran my fingers across the cool, perfect diamonds now, and then clenched the pin in my palm. I couldn't help myself, I let out a loud, keening cry. *No, no, no!* It couldn't be her. It couldn't be.

But it was. Myrtle was gone. Myrtle was dead.

My cry must've startled the men outside because Detective Charles and the coroner burst in. "Miss McCoy, are you all right?"

the detective asked. I was still sobbing, and I shook my head. I wasn't all right. I'd never be all right again.

Detective Charles took my elbow, led me out, up the stairs, outside where the morning was already hot, steam rising out of the subway grates. "Take a deep breath," he said gently. "Get some fresh air in your lungs."

I tried, but breaths still escaped my chest ragged, uneven. Hot air filled my throat and all I wanted to do was scream. "How did this happen?" I yelled at the detective. "Who did this?"

"We're trying to figure that out," he said. He lit a cigarette and blew out a ring of smoke. "Did your sister know anyone who owns a yellow Rolls-Royce?"

A yellow Rolls-Royce?

Jay. That last night he'd come to me, he'd driven up to the alley behind my apartment. *A Rolls-Royce. She's beautiful, isn't she, Cath?* he'd said of his new yellow car parked in the street.

It made no sense, but I knew it, deep down. It was him. It had to be. How many yellow Rolls-Royces could there be driving between the city and West Egg? I felt like I was about to vomit again.

"Witnesses said that was the car, and we've been working on tracing it this morning," Detective Charles continued.

I shook my head, and clenched my fists, feeling the diamonds from the hairpin dig into my palm. If Jay did this, if Jay killed Myrtle, then I would go out to West Egg right now and kill him myself.

"I have to go," I said brusquely to the detective, slipping the pin inside the pocket of my dress.

He nodded. "I'll get an officer to drive you back to your apartment."

"No, I'd rather walk and . . . take the train," I lied.

"Are you sure?" I nodded, and he pulled a card out of his jacket pocket. "I'll be in touch," he said. "But in the meantime if you think of anything, give me a call."

I took his card, gave him a clipped smile, slipped it in my pocket along with Myrtle's pin. And I walked away.

"Miss McCoy," he called after me, like he realized he'd forgotten to ask me something, but I pretended I didn't hear. I started walking faster.

Once I was out of his sight, I ran for the train. It was only a matter of time before the detective figured out who the yellow Rolls-Royce belonged to. And Jay and all his money now, he'd probably figure out a way to lie to the policemen or pay himself out of this. And he had to pay for what he'd done. I needed to get to him first.

IT WAS A little bit of a gamble, going to George's garage. But I imagined George would be flattened with grief, and he might not notice if I took one of his cars to drive out to West Egg. And even if he were present, I lied to myself on the train, it was possible he might let me borrow a car. That he might, for once, be kind or gentle.

I got lucky, though. The garage was empty when I arrived, the door strangely ajar so that it almost appeared abandoned now. My eyes wandered to the window upstairs, Myrtle's bedroom window, and hot, fresh tears ran down my cheeks. But then I went inside George's garage, rummaged through his work drawer. It was filled with keys, and two pistols. That was George in a nutshell: cars and guns. I'd worried for so long about how he'd use either one to hurt Myrtle.

I bit back the tears now, rummaged through the keys until I found a set that started a brown Ford truck. But before I drove away, I ran back, grabbed one of the pistols, and put it in my purse.

Just in case, I told myself. But that was a lie. I knew exactly what it was for.

My hands shook, and I put the truck in gear and pressed the gas so hard, the tires squealed as I drove off.

It had been years since I'd driven, not since the farm. But I sped down the road toward West Egg, my hands trembling against the steering wheel, my heart trembling against my rib cage. I could no longer feel the heat or think about where I was going, what I intended to do. I didn't have a plan.

If anyone were to ask me later—when Detective Charles would ask me later—I would swear it was never my intention to kill Jay. And maybe it was, or maybe it wasn't.

All I knew was that I ached for some sort of justice for my sister, some sort of way to ease this pain in my belly, this empty space that was already beginning to eat away at my insides.

All I knew was, Myrtle was gone. Myrtle was dead. And Jay Gatsby had to be stopped.

Daisy

I TOOK A BATH BEFORE LEAVING FOR JAY'S, TRYING TO WASH AWAY all the filth and horror of the night before. I lingered, scrubbing every last bit of my skin. And then, instead of the pretty white dresses I'd been lounging around in all summer, I pulled a short black dress out of the very back of my wardrobe.

This dress had been a gift from Mother for my twenty-first birthday, shipped to Lake Forest from her favorite tailor in Louis-ville, and supposedly quite fashionable for the kinds of parties she imagined we were attending in Chicago. It was above the knee, as had been the fashion only a year ago, unlike this summer when long hemlines were in style again. But I didn't care about that. The black dress reminded me of death. Of Daddy's and Rose's funeral, and I hadn't been able to bring myself to wear it. Until now.

I hadn't slept in almost twenty-four hours, but I felt too jittery to be exhausted. And every time I tried to close my eyes, even in the tub, all I could see was Tom's woman flying through the air. The shocked expression on her face, like she couldn't believe we'd hit her, she couldn't believe that she was about to die.

"We have to stop," I'd yelled at Jay after she hit the car last night, my foot going for the brake. But he'd shoved me out of the way and hit the gas with his own foot, his body covering mine, pressing against mine. I was no longer in control. (Was I ever really in control?) He was driving, on top of me. Smothering me. But he had to stop. He had to be stopped.

"Daisy," he'd said, and his voice was so soft I could barely hear it over the roar of the engine and the roar of the hot night and the roar of death in my ears. "There's nothing we can do, even if we do stop. And I won't let you go to jail."

Jail? But I hadn't done anything. Jay had grabbed the wheel.

What can I do to prove my love for you? he'd said, just before she ran out into the road. Did he not realize there would just be another city, another woman? They were disposable to Tom. We all were.

"I didn't hit her," I'd shouted at Jay, my voice trembling as I'd finally stopped the car, in East Egg, in front of my house. "You did."

"Oh Daisy." Jay shook his head. "You were driving."

"But you grabbed the wheel. It was . . . out of my control." Everything was, wasn't it. My marriage, my whole entire life. Even this car when I was supposedly in the driver's seat.

"I was trying to help you swerve, to miss her. But it was too late." Jay spoke so intently, that for a moment I wondered if he was telling the truth.

But then I shook my head. That wasn't what had happened. I'd been the one trying to swerve; I'd tried to stop. Jay had pushed me out of the way. Jay had forced the car to hit her.

"You were drinking, Daisy," he said softly. "Everything is blurry."

"No," I said. "That's not what happened." I would never hurt anyone intentionally, not even her. Would I?

Be good, Daise.

I was suddenly gasping for breath, unsure what was true and what wasn't. I'd pushed the car door open and run out of the car.

"Daisy, wait!" Jay cried after me. I'd ignored him, and I ran up the drive toward the house. "Daisy, I'll sit out here all night if I have to. I'll never leave you," he yelled.

I'd run into the house and sat in the kitchen and sobbed. And by the time Tom and Jordan got back, nearly an hour later, Jay and his car were gone.

BY MORNING, I knew what I needed to do.

I'd spent half the night arguing with Tom, going back and forth over who was to blame and for what. *Myrtle didn't deserve that*, Tom kept on saying. *She didn't deserve that*.

What did I deserve? That didn't seem to concern Tom as much.

I'd watched the sun rise over the garden, and a new clarity had suddenly washed over me. Jay had grabbed the wheel from me in the car, and Tom was constantly grabbing the wheel from me in our life. Enough. I wanted to be in control. I wanted to drive my whole entire life, all on my very own.

"I'm leaving you," I'd said to Tom all of a sudden, as dawn broke.

He'd laughed a little, like he didn't believe me.

"I'm done," I said. And I was.

Tom stared at me, his mouth a gaping hole.

But the thought of it, the delicious thought of it. Being free. Being in control. It burgeoned up inside of me like the yellow roses in the garden that had suddenly opened their faces to the sun last week. I could just get up, and I could leave. I could catch a train later this afternoon to Louisville with Pammy, and I could stop being Tom's wife. Just like that. I could be Daisy Fay from Louisville again and Pammy's mother. Away from Tom, I could make sure

Pammy wouldn't make the mistakes I'd made, that she would never marry anyone like Tom, or date anyone like Jay. That she could grow up strong and fearless. Nobody's fool.

"You're not going anywhere, Daisy." Tom laughed again.

"I mean it, Tom. I'm really and truly done," I'd insisted, petulantly.

We'd locked eyes and I'd refused to look away. And perhaps he'd finally believed me, because then he'd gotten up, stormed out of the house angry as a hornet, leaving to go god knows where.

But it didn't matter anymore. His absence already freed me.

I drank a cup of coffee to wake myself up, and I'd hatched a plan in my mind. First, I would go to West Egg, talk to Jay. Tell him once and for all to leave me alone. Tell him that I never wanted to see him again, that I was leaving, and he'd better not follow me. Then I'd pack up Pammy's things, and we'd get on the train to Louisville later today.

It was a fine plan, and I'd felt lighter than I had in years as I'd floated up the stairs to tell Jordan.

AFTER MY BATH, dressed in my funeral black, I finally made it out to the garage. Tom's blue coupe was gone. So was Jordan's car. I hoped she wasn't too disappointed in me. She had frowned when I'd told her of my plan earlier, and I hoped she would still love me once I was a disgraced woman. A divorced woman. But it couldn't be helped. This was what I had to do.

"Beautiful morning, isn't it, Mrs. Buchanan? But it's going to be another hot one," Ferdie said, pausing from his work polishing the white coupe. "Can I drive you somewhere?"

"No, Ferdie. I'm driving myself today," I insisted, even though the thought of driving again made my hands shake a little. It didn't matter that it was bright outside now, that I was completely sober. I could not forget the sound of her body as it hit the windshield, the look on her face. Oh, that god-awful look. But I was driving myself from now on, no matter what.

"Are you sure, Mrs. Buchanan?" Ferdie asked. "You look a little tired."

"Get me the keys," I insisted, obstinately. "I am perfectly well."

Ferdie complied, and I got into the white coupe and turned the key. I took a deep breath and gripped the wheel too tightly, but then I drove down the long drive slowly.

I stopped before turning out onto the main drag and lit a cigarette to calm myself. I took a few puffs and hung my left arm out the side.

And then, altogether calmer, I drove toward West Egg, the warm morning air swirling against my face.

Catherine

I SPUN THE FORD INTO JAY'S DRIVE, STILL BREATHING HARD AND crying, so that his house was blurry in front of me. It had only been a few days since the last time I was here, when Jay told me he'd never cared about me at all, but now it felt like a lifetime. I'd been hurt and angry when I left then, both at him and at myself for ever believing anything good about him. But I never would've thought that he was evil, that murder bubbled up inside his veins, that just a few days later he would *kill* Myrtle with his car and that he wouldn't even stop.

Myrtle was dead. Myrtle was really dead. I put my head down on the steering wheel and wept uncontrollably, unable to stop myself. Until I heard the sound of tires on gravel behind me, and I suddenly sat up.

I glanced in the mirror, a white coupe had pulled into Jay's drive, and unmistakably there she was in the driver's seat, pale and dewy and red-lipped: goddamned Daisy Buchanan.

I wiped at my tear-streaked face, grabbed my purse, and jumped out of the truck. "What are you doing here?" I shouted at her.

She got out of her car slowly, dropped her cigarette on the

ground, and crushed it under her black patent leather heel. "I could ask the same of you?" she said, shaking her hair back behind her shoulders.

"Jay Gatsby killed my sister," I spat at her. "He ran over her with his car. That's the man you love. A cold-blooded murderer."

The color drained from her face, and she was all at once a ghost with bright red lips. "Your . . . your . . . sister?"

Before I could respond, suddenly an explosion and a deep scream crackled the air.

"Gunshot," Daisy gasped softly. It had been years since I'd heard the sound of a gun go off, and it took me a second to realize she was right, and that the scream had been a feral cry, hard to tell if it was a man's or woman's or an animal's.

Daisy looked at me wide-eyed for a second, and then she started running away from the sound of the gun, toward the woods next to Jay's house. Out of instinct I followed after her. I was running, sweating, crying, breathing hard. What had I been thinking, coming here alone? I knew now that Jay was a murderer, and I hoped to God whatever shot had just rung out from behind his house hadn't led to him killing anyone else.

But the sound of that feral scream already echoed in my head, haunting me.

DAISY STOPPED RUNNING once we were loosely sheltered in the woods, the trees some flimsy protection. She was breathing hard, too, and she held her head down to catch her breath. "My cousin Nick lives just down that way," she said, her voice trembling, as she pointed back toward the direction of Jay's house. "If we could get back past Jay's house, we could run to Nick's and telephone the police."

I thought about Detective Charles, standing out in the street in Flushing, smoking his cigarette. What would he think if he found me here now with a gun in my purse, after I'd told him I had no idea about the yellow car?

"You're not going anywhere," a familiar man's voice slurred from behind me before I could answer Daisy. I turned, and there was George. Broken, forlorn, horrible, drunken George, with his shirt loosely untucked from his overalls and his hair all askew.

I almost felt a little sorry for him for a brief second, until he raised his arm, and he was holding one of his beloved pistols, aiming it right at Daisy Buchanan's head.

Jordan

DADDY ALWAYS USED TO SAY THAT JUSTICE WAS AN ARC. THAT IT started somewhere dark and awful and spun up and around until it ended rightly with him, just on the other side of a hill, up there on his judge's bench.

But there was no justice for a woman like me. Or for a woman like Myrtle. Was there?

And I couldn't think about Daddy, about justice, now. He was gone. Mary Margaret was getting married, and in spite of all my lies, I was no longer a golfer. All I had left was Daisy, and if I lost her, too, I didn't know what I would do. I couldn't let her leave with Jay this afternoon, not after what he did yesterday to Myrtle, running over the poor woman with his car, leaving her dead in the road. What would he do to Daisy, when in a matter of days or weeks or months, he'd realize she didn't love him, that she would never love him?

So I hatched a plan. I heard Daisy running a bath down the hall and I decided I'd go to West Egg myself, scare Jay off, threaten him. He'd been threatening me all summer and now it was my turn.

I snuck into Tom's study, stole his gun from the top drawer where I'd seen Daisy put it back weeks ago, and then I hopped into my car and raced over to West Egg, knowing only one thing for sure: I needed to get there before Daisy did.

I'd confront Jay, tell him to leave Daisy alone and to stop threatening me, too. I'd wave the gun around, show him that I really and truly meant business. I just wanted to scare him, just wanted him to know I was serious.

I didn't plan to hurt him. I never really planned to hurt him.

OR MAYBE I did?

I'd been lying to everyone all summer, and it was almost hard to remember how it felt to tell the truth anymore. Even to myself.

I parked my car at Nick's house—he didn't appear to be home. I already had it in my head that I didn't want anyone to see my car at Jay's. And then I jogged down the path toward Jay's property, but I didn't go up the drive, didn't ring the doorbell. Instead I walked around back and stood in the bushes behind the pool, branches tangling in my hair.

I could see Jay, inside his house, in his kitchen, walking around, finishing breakfast. And then the back door opened, and he walked out onto the veranda, stood at the edge and inhaled deeply, glancing at the great blue sky with a smile, as if he hadn't a care in the world, as if he hadn't just killed a woman the night before.

And God, I hated him so much in that moment, I suddenly understood that I was capable of anything.

Jay walked down the steps of the veranda, toward the pool. My heart pulsed in my chest, and I realized how crazy, how foolish this was. I should run away before Jay noticed me.

"Hello, Jordan," he said. *Too late.* He stared at my face, not seeming to notice the gun in my hand. "I suppose Daisy's talked to you?" His voice sounded calm, self-assured.

"Daisy's not going anywhere with you," I said. And then, that red-hot fire coursed through my veins, the same way it had in Atlanta when I'd ruined everything. And in Cannes when I'd been so mad at Tom I could barely see straight and I'd slapped him across the face. And in my bedroom in Louisville, when I'd swung my aluminum putter at Blocks Biloxi's head.

"All I want is to love her," Jay said. "To take care of her."

"I want you to leave Daisy alone." The fire burned up inside of me, and my words came out searing and angry.

He laughed. "I think you're forgetting everything I know, Jordan. About you. And about Daisy."

I stared at him, the gun so heavy in my hand now that my wrist began to ache. What did he know about Daisy? I shook my head.

"She didn't tell you? She was driving last night," he said. "She killed Myrtle."

Daisy was driving? Daisy killed Myrtle?

"And that's my secret now," Jay went on. "Mine and Daisy's." He paused for a second, smiled another little smug smile. "It'll keep her close to me forever."

It'll keep her close to me forever. Was Jay blackmailing her to run away with him, the same way he'd tried to blackmail me all summer? "No," I said. "I won't let you."

"Oh, Jordan." My name swelled with such arrogance in his mouth now. The heat in my veins turned to rage. "I'm the one with all the power here, not you."

And that's what it was, the thing that burned up inside of me most of all. That he believed I had no power. That everyone believed I had no power.

I had a lot of goddamned power right now.

I stepped out of the bushes, raised my arm up higher, pointed the gun straight at his chest. His face twisted, as he finally noticed what was in my hand. "What are you doing, Jordan? Put the gun down." He spoke softly, slowly, the way he might speak to a child. He smiled with an easy sort of confidence, certain that I'd never pull the trigger.

I suddenly felt calm, the way I did standing on the green, judging the distance to the hole. I closed one eye, judged the distance now, aimed, squeezed. The bullet was faster, louder, hotter than any golf ball. Its noise startled and deafened me, and I screamed.

Water suddenly splashed up from the pool as Jay fell back. And then the water calmed into beautiful ripples. It was only when the water began to turn red that I truly understood what I had done.

WHAT HAD I done?

What had I done?

I could barely see the trees in front of me as I ran on the path toward Nick's, because all I could see was Jay's blood oozing into the pool.

I have all the power, he'd said, his voice curling.

I know your secret, Jordan.

I know Daisy's secret, Jordan.

I'll tell everyone, Jordan.

No, no, no. *I* was the one with the power. *I* had the power.

But then why was my entire body shaking? Why was it so hard to breathe? I stopped running halfway down the path to vomit, and I hung my head between my knees, gasping for breath.

I had to get out of here, had to keep moving. Except then I realized I still had the gun. I held it in my hands, my fingers numb with the weight of it.

When I finally caught my breath, I turned around, back toward the woods on the other side of Jay's house. I'd bury the gun somewhere there, deep in the woods where no one could ever find it.

Halfway into the woods, I heard the sound of another gunshot, erupting into the air. And it was so close, so deafening again, that I thought, at first, I had done it myself, by accident.

But then I heard another sound, an unmistakable, horrible sound: my dear sweet Daisy screaming.

Daisy

August 1922

WEST EGG

I DIDN'T RECOGNIZE THE MAN, AIMING HIS GUN STRAIGHT AT MY head. But from the terrified look on her face, Catherine did.

"You," he said to me. "You did this." His voice was gravelly and drunken, and it was really just my terrible luck that I'd run into an unhinged vagabond in the woods, on the one morning in my life that I'd finally, finally figured everything out.

"George Wilson, put the gun down," Catherine said, a feeble attempt to sound commanding. Her voice trembled, betraying her. *George Wilson.* She did know him.

George shook his head. "She killed Myrtle and now it's her turn." *Myrtle. Wilson's garage. George Wilson.*

I inhaled sharply and put my hand to my mouth. This man was not a vagabond. He was Myrtle's husband. This was the man she betrayed with Tom? What a sad, terrible life she must've led.

"Jay Gatsby killed Myrtle," Catherine insisted sharply. She stood up straighter, tucked a strand of fire-colored hair behind her ear, and looked altogether instantly more composed than I felt.

"No." George shook his head. "They both did."

Catherine shot me a penetrating look and I bit my lip. What

could I say to her that wouldn't cause George to shoot me dead right here, in these woods? Well, yes, I was in the driver's seat but Jay had grabbed the wheel. *You were drinking, Daisy,* Jay had said. *Everything was blurry.*

It would be an awful way to die, to be shot and bleed out like a deer, hunted and filleted, underneath these oak trees. And what would happen to Pammy? I let out a little cry.

"George," Catherine was saying now. "Why don't you go up to the house. Jay Gatsby's up there. He's the one you're angry at. He's the one who did this. Yellow Rolls-Royce. The detective told me. That's his car."

George shook his head and waved his gun in the air. "He's dead," George said flatly. "Someone else got to him first. Maybe it was you, Cath." He laughed, almost sounding maniacal. "But you don't have the guts to shoot a man."

He was dead? *Jay was dead?* I knew I should feel something, but all I felt was cold and empty and desperate to get out of these woods, to get back in my car, and speed across the village to the bright open safety of East Egg.

George stopped waving the gun, raised his arm, pointed at my forehead. If I turned and ran, I'd never reach my car. He'd shoot me in the back. "I have a daughter," I said, my voice stretched and desperate. "A little girl. Pammy."

"George, come on," Catherine pleaded. "Put the gun down."

"It was Gatsby's car, but you were driving it," George said.

"Daisy wasn't driving, were you, Daisy?" Catherine turned to me when she spoke.

Jay was dead. Only the two of us were in the car; only the two of us knew exactly what had happened. He'd grabbed the wheel. *You* were drinking, Daisy. I won't let you go to jail. I shook my head. "It was Jay," I said. "Of course. It was all Jay."

"You killed her," George yelled at me, sounding delirious now. But he knew what he saw. I could lie to Catherine all I liked, but George had seen me, *me* in the driver's seat as the yellow Rolls-Royce had sped through Queens. "She was mine, and you took her from me." George was half yelling, half crying.

But he was wrong. She wasn't his, and she wasn't Tom's, either. She was just a woman, just a poor, stupid fool of a woman. Just like me.

His finger reached for the trigger, and I squeezed my eyes tightly shut, waiting for it: the sound of the explosion and the burst of pain that would soon rise in my chest. I heard Rose's voice so clearly in my head. *Be good, Daise.*

I tried, Rosie. I really tried. I wanted to. I was going to be. After today I was going to be.

The sound of a gunshot crackled in the air and I screamed. I waited for pain, for blood. But a moment passed, and I felt nothing at all.

I opened my eyes, and Catherine stood a few feet away from me, a gun smoking in her trembling hand. George was on the ground, the top part of his head in pieces. A sight so gruesome and revolting that I turned away and gagged.

"I killed him," Catherine said, her voice stretched in disbelief. "All those times he hurt Myrtle, and now . . . I killed him."

George had been wrong. She *did* have the guts to shoot a man, and thank goodness for that or I'd be dead. "You had to do it," I said softly. "You had to do it."

"Daise!" Jordan's voice shot out of the woods, somewhere just behind us. Catherine and I were still standing there, eyes locked, unmoving. Somewhere in the background a siren wailed, and then another.

Jordan ran out from the trees, saw me. "Oh my god, Daise, I heard the gun, and I heard you scream."

"I'm okay," I said. "I'm really okay." But my voice trembled so much my words came out more like gibberish.

Her eyes suddenly caught on George's bloody, broken head.

"He was going to kill me," I said. The sirens swirled closer. "Myrtle's husband . . . he thought I was responsible for her death and . . . he wanted to kill me."

"I had to do it," Catherine echoed my words back, her voice sounding far away, raspy.

Jordan looked at me and then at Catherine. She opened her mouth, closed it again, and then took a breath and walked toward George. It was only then that I noticed she was holding a gun too. Why was Jordan here? Why did she have a gun?

Jay Gatsby's dead. Someone else got to him first.

"Jordie," I murmured her name. "Oh, Jordie. What have you done?"

She wiped her gun with the skirt of her dress, wiping away any trace of her. Then she positioned it in George's hand, raising his limp arm to his head.

She stood, brushed off her hands, looked at me, then at Catherine again. "I didn't do anything," she said. "None of us *did* anything." She swallowed hard and met my eyes. "Jay Gatsby drove over Myrtle. And then this poor bereaved man. He came here and killed Jay to avenge his wife's death. Then he went out into the woods and he shot himself with the very same gun."

"He shot himself," Catherine repeated, stunned. "With the very same gun."

"We're gonna turn and walk out of these woods one by one, and then we'll never talk about this ever again," Jordan said firmly, looking hard at both of us. "Promise."

"I promise," I said.

"I promise," Catherine echoed.

WHEN I GOT back to East Egg, I was numb and exhausted and still shaking. I'd run to my car in Jay's drive as the sirens had approached, and then I'd sped all the way back through the Eggs to my estate. Now I wanted to speed away, farther, faster. Put the whole entire summer, the whole entire awful ordeal, behind us. Jay was right about one thing: I could not go to jail. I would never survive there.

We'll never talk about this ever again, Jordan had said, just an hour ago in the woods. And all three of us strangers or friends or *murderers*, we had agreed on that. Wherever Jordan had driven away to when she left the woods, it hadn't been here. I wasn't sure if or when I'd ever see her again, and that thought sank inside of me, a weighty, terrible sadness.

Tom was at the house, though, waiting for me in the dining room, with a bouquet of yellow roses on the table in front of him. Their stems were unevenly cut, and I guessed he'd gone out to the garden and trimmed them himself. "I'm so sorry, Daisy," he said, looking up, when I walked in. "Forgive me."

So many times, and so many promises, and never had I wanted to believe him more than I did right now. All those thoughts I'd had earlier about being in control. But it would be so much easier to cling to Tom now, to cling to the power that came with the Buchanan money and the Buchanan name. Nothing could touch me with that, with him. He would never let me go to jail.

"Oh, Tom." I carefully picked up a rose and held it to my nose.

The sweet floral scent washed away those other horrible ones: gunpowder and burning flesh and the overwhelming metallic odor of blood. "Would you hate me if I told you I had a little spree of my own, and that we had to move away from here? Immediately." I spoke softly, urgently.

Tom frowned. I imagined he pictured my *little spree* was with Jay Gatsby. Soon enough Tom would learn of Jay's death and take a strange sort of sadistic delight in it. But in that moment, I didn't correct him.

When he finally spoke, his voice was thick and earnest: "I could never hate you, Daisy."

He came to me and wrapped me in a hug, his arms powerful and tight. They were sometimes suffocating, but now they felt strangely freeing, too. Nothing could touch me when I was with him. He wouldn't let it.

He kissed the top of my head. "How do you feel about Minnesota?" he asked.

Catherine

I WASN'T BORN TO BE A FARM GIRL. AND I WAS NEVER GOING TO BE a farm wife.

As much as Father begged me to stay in Rockvale after we buried Myrtle next to Mother, to reconsider Harold Bloom and his dairy farm, city life called to me. No matter how much Father fretted about the dangers, about Myrtle's fate becoming my fate, I couldn't stand the thought of being isolated on a farm, or, becoming anyone's wife. My years in New York, the men I'd known there—Jay and Tom and even George, *especially George*, made me understand the only thing I wanted out of life was to never tether myself to any man at all.

Myrtle had become a victim of her own terrible circumstances. We women still had fewer rights, less control than men. And what would the rest of my life be if I stayed in Rockvale? If I did not keep on trying to fight for women like Myrtle. For women like me, I told Father.

"But Harold Bloom could give you such a safe and steady life," Father protested.

"I don't want a safe life," I told him, much to his chagrin. "I want a good life. I want a meaningful life."

I kissed him good-bye, promised him I'd be careful and that I would come back soon and often to visit. Then, in the beginning of November, Duke and I got on the train headed for Chicago.

CHICAGO WAS ALMOST as expensive as New York, and after all my years living in that god-awful shoebox with Helen, I wanted more space to call my own.

Our first day in this new city, Duke and I left our temporary rooming house and took a pink taxicab to the South Side, the grayest, dirtiest street I'd seen since I'd been to visit Myrtle in Queens. As I got out of the cab, I held Duke tightly under my arm for some sort of illusion of protection. But the truth was, he'd never hurt a fly—Duke was just like Myrtle, all bark and no bite.

I stood out on the sidewalk for a moment, staring up at the tattered gray awning above the storefront. I'd picked this place out of the directory on its name alone: *Wilson's Pawnshop: Goods Bought and Sold.* That had seemed a compelling enough reason to justify the taxi fare here, though now that I was actually on the gray, run-down street I did wonder if it might've been smarter to find a broker in a better neighborhood. But I was here nonetheless. I took a deep breath and walked inside.

A bell clanged against the glass, and the man behind the counter looked up. He was older, skinny, with graying hair and a wrinkled face. He eyed Duke, then me, then cast me a smile, revealing one severely unattractive front gold tooth. I wasn't sure what I'd been expecting when I'd caught on the name *Wilson's* in the book. That maybe going here would be some sort of final penance? But now I was relieved to see he reminded me nothing at all of George.

"Don't see too many pretty ladies like you around here," this

Wilson said, his eyes roaming uncomfortably down my face, to my chest.

I wanted to get in and out of here as fast as possible. I pulled the diamond hairpin out of my coat pocket and placed it on the counter. "How much can you give me for this? Diamonds are real," I said resolutely. "Don't lowball me or I'll walk out that door." There'd been plenty of other pawnshops in the book, and if Wilson didn't want to give me what I deserved, I truly would walk out.

He picked the hairpin up in his wrinkled, graying fingers, pulled out a magnifying glass from underneath the counter, and stared at the diamonds.

Ever since Detective Charles had come to see me with Myrtle's matching hairpin last fall, I knew I needed to get rid of this pin. I shivered now, thinking about what Detective Charles might do, what pieces of George's and Jay's deaths he might question if he ever found out about Myrtle's affair with Tom and my connection to Jay, or even that I still had and lied about this hairpin. After that, I knew I had to get this out of my possession as soon as I could.

Still, I'd sobbed a little this morning staring at the pin in my room, questioning my decision to come here. I'd cried, thinking, for a moment, that this hairpin was the last piece I had left of my sister. But then I'd wiped my tears and realized, the hairpin wasn't a piece of Myrtle at all. It was a gift to her from Tom, and I remembered that drunken afternoon at their apartment when he'd broken her nose. This hairpin was a symbol of everything that had ruined her. I despised it.

"Two thousand dollars," Wilson said now, putting his magnifying glass down.

"Don't insult me," I said, trying not to reveal the excitement I actually felt in my voice. Though the pin was likely worth more, two thousand dollars was a lot of money. It would pay the rent on a decent apartment and my living expenses for at least the year, probably two.

"Twenty-five hundred," he said. "That's my final offer."

"Three thousand," I demanded, resolute.

He examined the diamonds one more time with the magnifying glass, and then with a little nod of his head, we had a deal.

NOW, A NEW year dawned. Nineteen twenty-three shimmered before me and filled me with an unexpected sort of hope.

I had a new life in Chicago, a new apartment with a nice view of the frozen lake in the distance. A new job working for the Women's Trade Union League. It barely paid any money, but I had enough put away now to cover my expenses for a while. And we were working to open up a shelter for women who were unsafe in their homes. It would help women like Myrtle. And be the first of its kind in Chicago!

Sometimes I thought if I helped just one other woman the way I never was able to help my sister, then everything I'd done, every lie I'd told, it would all be worth it in the end. It would all mean something. My life would mean something. And maybe that was the last and biggest lie of all. That what I would do next with my life would be good enough to make up for what I had done.

Even in this new life of mine in Chicago, I dreamed of last summer sometimes still—the smell of the smoking gun and burning flesh, Daisy Buchanan's scream and Jordan Baker's ultimate cool head and practicality.

I'd seen both women in passing last summer when we'd all gone into the precinct, but since then I'd kept up with Daisy Buchanan in the society pages and Jordan Baker on the sports pages.

A promise was a promise was a promise. But I hoped that I would never speak to either one of these women again. Or that Detective Charles would never make his way to Chicago to visit me.

ONE AFTERNOON LATE in January, I saw Tom Buchanan.

I'd left work to go home, and he was suddenly just right there, walking ahead of me on Michigan Avenue. I recognized his unmistakable, arrogant swagger, even dressed in his overcoat, with the collar turned up against the cold. I slowed down, so I wouldn't catch up, but he seemed to sense me there, and he turned around.

His eyes caught mine, and that brutish hulking face was exactly and awfully the same as it was six months ago. I remembered the way he'd looked when he'd punched Myrtle in the nose, the way her blood had felt on my hands then and later in the morgue.

"Catherine," Tom said now. "Is that you?" He held out his arms to give me a hug, but I took a large step back. "You object to giving me a hug?"

"Yes," I said. "You must know what I think of you." I glared at him. Jay might have been driving the car, but it was Tom and George who'd driven Myrtle to such depths of desperation that she'd run out of her apartment that night, chasing what she must've believed was her last escape.

Tom opened his mouth, then closed it again. "You know I loved her," he said. "I went to clean out the apartment before we left the city, and I sat there among her things and the dog biscuits and I cried like a baby."

I stared at him for another moment, picturing Myrtle's blood on those very same hands he'd just used to reach for me. "You don't love anyone but yourself," I said. "And furthermore"—my voice rose in pitch, so I was almost yelling at him now—"if you ever see me walking again on the street, just pretend you never saw me at all. Keep walking by. You disgust me, Tom Buchanan," I said. One final, fleeting shot to the heart.

Then I spun on my heel and turned and started walking the long way home. Maybe Tom watched me walk away, surprised or hurt or angry. Or maybe he just kept on walking that arrogant walk, toward wherever it was he was going.

Either way, Tom Buchanan was behind me now. And I didn't look back.

Jordan

"MISS BAKER!"

I heard his voice as I walked off the green and I stopped walking, my breath catching in my chest. He'd followed me, all the way here, all the way to California?

I turned and faced him, forced a smile. "Hello, Detective."

Detective Frank Charles stood on the edge of the course, sweating in his three-piece suit. He tipped his hat, and I looked down, averting eye contact.

It was hot today, exceptional for a January day in Santa Barbara. Eighty degrees! And I had spent it tangled in a delightful day of golf and sweat and sunshine. I was in second place after round one—finally making my way back to the top after losing ground in my game for months and months.

Aunt Sigourney had passed away last September, and with the loss of my last family member came control of my entire inheritance—Daddy's money and hers, and the old bird had built up quite a nest egg over the years. After making a more than exorbitant donation to Mr. Hennessey, lo and behold, I was invited back on the tour, and I was quickly rising up the ranks again.

Jerralyn still hated me, and it was almost refreshing, the familiarity in the daily glares I received from her over breakfast.

Daisy moved to Minnesota only a week after that hot death-filled morning in West Egg, and we had written each other only the occasional letter since, filled with only the most mundane details about the weather. I missed her desperately, but I knew I had to stay away from her now to save her. To save myself, too.

I looked back up and Detective Charles was still staring at my face, like he could see right through me, like all my innermost thoughts were visible to him on an X-ray. It was disconcerting, to say the least.

"My, you're a far way from Flushing, Detective, aren't you?" I finally said, laughing a little, nervousness catching in my throat. This was the second time he'd come to find me in the past few months, and that was after he'd questioned me relentlessly in the days after Jay Gatsby's death. They felt like a haze now, those days, and who could even remember what I said then.

Every paper had reported that Jay Gatsby had been murdered by a grieving George Wilson, who'd then taken his own life. The case was officially closed. This detective's continued morbid, pesky fascination with it, and me, made no sense. But I couldn't help swallowing back the fear rising in my chest at his presence, nonetheless.

"I needed to talk to you again." Detective Charles pulled a cigarette from his pocket and lit it. He offered one to me, but I shook my head. We weren't friends; I wasn't about to share anything with him.

"Well, I'm very busy," I said flatly. "In the middle of a tournament, as you can well see."

"Let me buy you something to eat," Detective Charles said. "I found a good little diner around the corner. Nothing fancy. We can talk."

"Why, Detective, are you asking me on a date?" I said flippantly.

He held out his left hand, showing his thick gold wedding band. "I'm a happily married man, Miss Baker. It'll be twenty years this summer."

I SAT IN a shiny red booth across from the detective and tried to be patient as he deliberated over the menu and finally ordered only a piece of cherry pie. "Miss Baker?" he said.

"Nothing for me," I told the waitress. What I really needed was a G&T. But I couldn't order one here. Anyway, I hadn't touched the stuff since the summer, and I wasn't going to start again now, in the middle of a tournament. Now that I'd clawed my way back, I wouldn't let anything stop me. I'd gotten sidetracked the past few years by love and friendship and gin. And my true love, my true life, was golf.

"She'll take a piece of the pie, too," Detective Charles said.

"How do you know I even like pie?" I asked when the waitress walked away.

"Everyone likes pie, Miss Baker."

I put my hands on the table and sighed. "All right, I suppose I'll eat the goddamned pie. Now, the suspense is killing me. Why are we here?"

He reached into his jacket pocket, put the diamond hairpin he'd bothered me about last fall back on the table. I closed my eyes for a second. It had been in my hair that morning when I'd gotten tangled up in the bushes by Jay's pool. I'd gotten rid of the gun, staged everything perfectly, and then there was one little detail I hadn't thought about. It wasn't until hours later, when I went in for a much-needed bath at Aunt Sigourney's, that I'd realized the diamond pin was gone.

Here I was months and thousands of miles away from West Egg, and sometimes still, even now, I awoke in a sweaty tangle of sheets in the middle of the night, caught up in a never-ending nightmare filled with gunshots and Jay Gatsby's threats. Maybe it would all haunt me for the rest of my life. Detective Charles, too.

"I already told you," I finally said, "that's not mine."

"Half-truths have served you pretty well this past year, haven't they, Miss Baker?"

"I'm the most honest woman I know." I managed to say this with a straight face. The waitress plunked our pie slices down on the table and I dug into mine aggressively with my fork.

"Here's what I think," Detective Charles said. "I've done a little digging, spoken extensively with Mr. Carraway. Even telephoned down to Nashville, talked to your old roommate from the golf tour."

"Mary Margaret." Her name escaped my lips in a whisper. I hadn't said it out loud in so long, it didn't even feel real. She didn't even feel real. I dropped my fork and held my hands together to keep them from shaking. She was a married woman now, and there wasn't any way she'd told the detective what had really happened between us.

"I learned some interesting things. For one thing, you weren't on the golf tour at all last summer even though you told everyone you were. You didn't play in any matches. They'd asked you to leave. I guess you really did cheat, huh?"

I shook my head. "I simply took a little break," I snapped. "I'm back now, aren't I?"

"And for another thing, this may be Daisy's hairpin, but she gave it to you to wear. Nick Carraway said you had it in your hair all last summer."

I laughed a little. "Nick Carraway? You trust that man's eye to notice how I wore my hair?"

"And then I thought a lot about our conversation in South Jersey. You remember that, Miss Baker?"

"Sure." I nodded curtly. "You seem to have a penchant for harassing me in the middle of a tournament, Detective."

"I asked you about this hairpin then, and you suggested Daisy might've dropped it at Gatsby's." I shrugged, not quite remembering what I'd said to him that afternoon, only that my mind had been back in the game, *at long last*, and I'd wanted so badly for him to leave me alone so I could focus on golf. "But the thing is," he said now, "I never told you *where* I'd found the hairpin."

His words felt like a sudden punch in my gut, and for a moment everything in the diner seemed to stop moving. The entire world got silent and still and blood rushed through my ears until all I could hear was my own pulsing heartbeat. "Well, wasn't it obvious?" I finally said. He raised his eyebrows. "Why else would you have asked me about the hairpin?"

"So here's what I think happened," Detective Charles continued. "I think Mr. Gatsby found out you were lying about the golf tour and threatened to tell your friend Daisy. Maybe he even blackmailed you. He wasn't the nicest guy." I frowned, remembering that last gin-soaked afternoon at the Plaza, the way Tom and Jay were going at each other, the way the Saturday before he'd threatened to destroy me. "I think Mr. Gatsby threatened to tell Daisy your secret, and you shot him."

I closed my eyes. Inhaled. Exhaled. It was uncanny how close he was, and how far away, too. How much he didn't understand. And how I knew that I could **never make him understand. Never** tell him the truth. I *promised*. We all did. If my lie unraveled, Catherine's and Daisy's would come with it. I would never let that happen, no matter how many times the detective came to talk to me.

I opened my eyes and stared at him, unflinching. "You have quite the imagination, Detective. That sounds like some kind of a crazy made-up story to me." I pushed my pie away. "And even if it were true, you'd never prove it."

There it was, the only truth I'd ever tell the man, clear as day. He could think what he wanted, but he'd never prove anything unless I confessed. And that would never happen. Even with the hairpin. Daisy or a hundred other women really could've dropped it at a party last summer.

I flashed him my best Jordan Baker tournament smile, the one I put on up on the podium when I was proud and hot and tired and longing for a past I knew I'd never have again. And then I stood, and I walked out of the diner, just like that.

On the sidewalk, it was still hot, but it was almost dusk. The orange-pink sun fell and skimmed below the sparkling Pacific Ocean in the distance. I inhaled the delicious smell of the sea air, and I walked on, toward my hotel.

Detective Frank Charles

YOU'LL NEVER PROVE IT.

Certain things had come to haunt Frank over the long and winding course of his career, and he knew that last thing Jordan Baker would ever say to him would be among them.

He'd watched her walk out of the Santa Barbara diner, walk away into the warm January sunset, and dammit, he'd suddenly understood that she was right. Three women, three suspects. All of them lying to him, all of them tangled up tightly in those mangled threads of deceit. He'd never truly unravel them without a confession.

He knew it, deep in his gut, that his theory was right. He'd pictured the scene again and again in his mind: Jordan Baker standing there in the bushes by Gatsby's pool, holding the gun the way a certain kind of careless man held his glass of whiskey. It was illegal, illicit, but consequences be damned. He could see it all so clearly; Jordan had pulled the trigger, killed Jay Gatsby. Daisy and Catherine were covering for her. And yet, if none of them were going to talk, he never would prove it.

But what Jordan didn't know was, he didn't necessarily *need* to prove it. As far as the Long Island precinct was concerned, the case was closed and had been for months. Two not-so up-and-up men dead by each other's hands. No detectives were losing any sleep over it, except for him. He'd never arrest Jordan, charge her, bring her to trial—those were the things you needed proof for. No, all he needed to do was take what he'd found, what he *knew* in his gut, to Meyer Wolfsheim and collect his fifteen grand.

He had, in fact, intended to do that very thing in February, a few weeks after getting back from Santa Barbara. He'd scheduled a lunch with Wolfsheim, and they met at an underground place of Wolfsheim's, down by the docks. The booze was freely flowing and Wolfsheim didn't even bother to tell him to look the other way. Wolfsheim notoriously operated by his own rules, always had. "Whiskey?" he'd simply offered Frank instead.

And why the hell not? Frank had felt nervous and broke his rule about drinking on the job. (He wasn't *technically* on the job.) Then the two of them had shared a lobster lunch—the best goddamned lobster he'd ever eaten in his life and nursed a bottle of whiskey.

"So?" Wolfsheim finally said, wiping around his graying beard with his napkin. "Tell me the truth, Charles. Who did it?"

He'd left Santa Barbara with every intention of telling Wolfsheim what he'd learned about Jordan, what he knew for sure in that detective gut of his, even if he couldn't *prove* it. Until last week, when something else had gone down: a handless dead man, pulled from the East River, and word was he'd worked for Wolfsheim and had betrayed him. *We'll never get enough evidence to make an arrest,* Detective Lawrence, who was new to the precinct but had seen this kind of thing from Wolfsheim before in Brooklyn, had said. *But that's justice in Wolfsheim's world.*

What's that? Frank had asked, suddenly feeling nausea swelling in his chest.

Murder. Lawrence had shrugged.

And in that moment, when Lawrence had said *murder*, all Frank could think about was Lizzie.

"Well?" Wolfsheim urged Frank now. "Give me the full report."

Jordan Baker's name sat loosely on the tip of Frank's tongue, and part of him really wanted to say it. But then the other part of him knew what he would be unleashing if he did. No woman deserved that. And he knew he'd never be able to forgive himself if Jordan Baker turned up dead later.

"I'm sorry to tell you, Mr. Wolfsheim," Frank finally said, clearing his throat, trying not to let his voice betray his nervousness. "But I investigated this thoroughly and it was George Wilson all along."

Wolfsheim took a sip of his whiskey. "You're absolutely sure, old sport? No doubt?"

"Absolutely sure," he lied through his teeth. Wolfsheim had promised to pay him no matter what the result and he held his breath, waiting for him to take that promise back.

Wolfsheim nodded. "You know, Jay Gatsby was like a son to me. I don't trust the police, no offense, Detective."

"None taken," he said. Though, really, how was he supposed to take that?

"And I just wanted to make sure Gatsby got what he deserved. Justice. Whatever that means these days."

Frank thought about the handless man in the East River and felt the lobster rising up in his chest. He shouldn't have eaten so much. "I don't know," Frank spoke softly. "I tend to think justice finds a way of working itself out. We all get what's coming to us eventually."

Wolfsheim chuckled a little and shook his head. Then he motioned at a waiter, who walked to the table a minute later with a briefcase. "Here's your money, Detective, as promised."

It all felt so illicit, Frank wasn't sure whether to thank him or arrest him. But he knew he should take the money and get the hell out of there, before Wolfsheim changed his mind. He stood and grabbed the briefcase.

"Hey, Detective," Wolfsheim called after him. "Stay out of trouble."

Frank laughed a little in spite of himself. "You, too, Wolfsheim," he called as he walked out of the speakeasy. "You too."

"FRANK! THIS HOUSE! It's too much," Dolores exclaimed now as he led her inside their summer rental. Out in East Egg, just like she'd always dreamed. It wasn't as fancy or as large as the Buchanans'— and besides, that one was already rented for the summer by another couple—but he'd snagged a smaller one, on the same street. The house itself may have been less extravagant, but they had better access to the water.

"You deserve this house," he said. "We deserve this summer." And wasn't that true, after all they'd been through the past few years. Dolores's eyes already shone a little brighter, her cheeks a little pinker out here than they had been in Brooklyn.

"Still, I hate to think of how we only got here because of that awful man." She shuddered a little, and it wasn't clear whether she meant Wolfsheim or Gatsby. Dolores knew every last detail of his interviews and investigation and gut feelings, right down to Jordan's insistence he'd never prove anything over cherry pie in Santa Barbara and the lie he'd told Meyer Wolfsheim over lobster.

He didn't quite regret the choice he'd made with Wolfsheim, but something still sat unsettled in his gut about the whole thing. It was the thought of Miss Baker out on the golf course, and Mrs. Buchanan in that vast mansion in Minnesota, and Miss McCoy he'd heard had settled in Chicago. They'd all moved past what had happened last summer, onward with their lives. While Myrtle Wilson and Jay Gatsby would never get that chance. But maybe he did believe what he'd told Wolfsheim, too: we all get what's coming to us. Eventually.

Dolores reached up and grabbed his face with her hands. "You know what," she said softly. "Let's forget about who brought us here. We're here, aren't we? And you, Frank Charles, are one of the good ones." She stood up on her toes and kissed him softly on the lips.

Maybe he was one of the good ones, and maybe he wasn't. But Dolores looked so happy, and when all was said and done, she was the only woman whose future he truly cared about. He kissed her back, and then grabbed her hand. "Watch the sunset with me out on the veranda," he said.

She laughed. "We have a veranda!"

She clung to him and followed him outside, and suddenly they were twenty years old again, and everything was right with the world. There wasn't a thought of death or gloom or illness or anything bad at all.

"Look at that," Dolores said, pointing across the water, to West Egg. "They're having quite a party. Maybe we can get invited to the next one."

He looked to where she pointed, and he recognized the house immediately. He'd been there before, staring into the blood-red pool, rummaging in the bushes and discovering a diamond hairpin. It had been quiet then, hallowed by death. But almost a year had passed. It was a new summer, a new man's home.

There, across the sound, Gatsby's former house beat on: lit up, glittering, alive.

Daisy

AFTER A YEAR, I REMEMBER ONLY THE SMALLEST DETAILS OF OUR last days in New York: the bright yellow light of Jay's Rolls-Royce parked in front of the Plaza at dusk as he handed me the keys, the sound of a gunshot interrupting the wooded air in West Egg the next morning, the pounding of my own heart when I opened my eyes and realized I was still alive. Still breathing.

It's all far away from me now, a bad dream, a wayward memory. It never happened, or it happened to another Daisy, a woman who still had the smallest bit of hope, deep down. A woman who thought there could be such a thing as a *permanent home* for her and Tom. Maybe not New York, but Minnesota.

Except the year in Minnesota was long and frozen, and by summer I wondered if my blood had turned to icicles in my veins. Because I didn't feel any longer. Not pain, not pleasure, not fear. Not even when the detective came to our door unannounced last fall, nor when Tom began slipping away from me at night again through the never-ending winter and I'd awake to a cold and empty bed. Not even when Jordan wrote me in February and told me not to worry, she was fine, she was *certain* we would all be fine. But even that—worry, relief, Jordie—didn't penetrate my iciness.

The thing that finally did it was the sudden ring of the telephone on a cool summer evening in late July, just after supper, that voice on the other end of the line. Tom was off god knows where, and I'd fired Pammy's nurse in June because I hadn't at all liked the way Tom was looking at her.

Do you know how hard it is to find a good nurse? Tom had chastised me then, his voice tinged with disgust. But I had simply shrugged and told him I would be taking over all of Pammy's care myself, for the time being.

The phone jangled just as Pammy and I had been walking toward the stairs to get her ready for bed, and I grabbed her little hand and we ran to get it. "Daisy Fay." Mother's voice sounded small and very far away. "I'm not feeling so good."

And suddenly, I could feel something again, too: my body turned hot and my heart pounded restless in my chest. "We'll get the next train," I told her, breathless, clutching Pammy's hand.

"Oh . . . no. I don't want you to fuss or trouble Tom. I just wanted to hear your voice, that's all. I'm feeling better already."

I didn't explain to her how it would not trouble Tom at all, that I was unsure how long it would even take him to notice if Pammy and I left. "Mother, stop," I'd said instead. "We're overdue for a visit anyway. Pammy's so big, you'll barely recognize her."

The snow goose made a muffled noise, and maybe it was a protest or maybe it was a little cry of joy, but either way I told her I'd see her soon.

After I hung up, I faced the backyard, and suddenly there were a thousand bursts of gold and green light. Fireflies lit up the sky like sparks. It was Pammy's bedtime, but maybe it wasn't just yet. I pulled her toward the porch, then out onto the dew-covered grass. "Do you know," I told her, "my younger sister and I used to chase these lights and then I'd collect fireflies in glass jars."

"Mama," Pammy intoned quite seriously. "I don't know if that was very kind to them."

"No, no, my precious. I always let them go. I just wanted to watch their light, for a little while. They made me happy. I didn't ever harm them."

She'd frowned, unconvinced, and my god, for a second, I saw Rose in her eyes.

Be good, Daise.

Now, our train rolls through the familiar green of Clarksville and Jeffersonville, across the porous blue of the Ohio River, where Rose and I swam and chased those fireflies as girls along the banks. Maybe Pammy was right, that it wasn't very kind to trap them that way. Maybe their beauty is simply in the way they brighten the night, yellow and green and sparkling, free and unfettered.

As we near the station in Louisville, I can feel the heat already penetrating my skin, that gloriously, awful August heat. It was much too cold in Minnesota. Maybe that was my problem this past year. The heat made me do such terrible things before, but it kept me alive and feeling my whole entire life, too.

The train slows, and I clutch my handbag tightly to keep it on my lap. I think about my sweltering wedding day, the way the extravagant pink pearls had been so hot, so heavy around my neck. But now a small flutter of joy erupts in my chest, feeling their weight shift inside my handbag. Three hundred and fifty thousand dollars is a lot of money.

Pammy had fallen asleep somewhere outside of Kentucky, and only as the train comes to a complete and final stop does her head bounce up from my shoulder. She rubs her eyes and stands and looks out the window. Somewhere out there are the streets that led me to Jay, and then to Tom. But it is easy enough to push those memories away. I also treaded those same streets with Rose, with Jordie. Somewhere out there are the footprints of my beautiful, carefree girlhood.

"Where are we, Mama?" Pammy asks, gazing out the window, her eyes wide with wonder.

I think about it for a moment, and then I hold her tight to me, kiss the top of her head, and answer: "Home."

Acknowledgments

A HUGE THANK-YOU FIRST AND FOREMOST TO MY WONDERFUL editor, Sarah Stein, and the entire team at Harper Perennial, who, when I came to them with this idea, immediately shared my excitement and enthusiasm for the women of *Gatsby*, and who have helped shape this book and make it shine. I couldn't ask for a better team to usher this book into the world! Special thanks also to Hayley Salmon, Lisa Erickson, Jackie Kim, Heather Drucker, Kristin Cipolla, Stacey Fischkelta, Laurie McGee, Doug Jones, and Amy Baker.

Thank you to my amazing agent, Jessica Regel at Helm Literary, who is always unwavering in both her editorial and her emotional support, as well as her enthusiasm for my work, but especially for this book, which came to be in the midst of a pandemic. Thank you also to Lucy Stille and Jenny Meyer and the team at the Jenny Meyer Literary Agency for championing this book.

Thank you to my writing friends who first encouraged me to tell this story and then read early drafts and gave feedback: Eileen Connell, Maureen Leurck, T. Greenwood, and Brenda Janowitz; thank you all also for the text/email/phone emotional support on a daily basis. And thank you to Andrea Katz, an amazing friend and champion of all my books!

Thank you to my husband and sons, who were trapped in the house with me for months while I wrote this book, and who also

ACKNOWLEDGMENTS

listened to me talk endlessly about Daisy Buchanan and Jordan Baker every night at dinner and helped brainstorm plot points.

Thank you to all the wonderful booksellers, librarians, and readers who have continued to support my books and spread the word over the years.

And last but not least, thank you to F. Scott Fitzgerald, who created these women, this world, and *The Great Gatsby* itself, which has long inspired me as a writer.

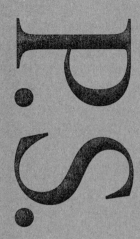

About the author

About the book

Read on

Insights,
Interviews
& More . . .

Meet Jillian Cantor

JILLIAN CANTOR IS a *USA Today* bestselling author of eleven novels, including *Half Life*, *In Another Time*, and *The Lost Letter*. Her books have been translated into thirteen languages and have been chosen for LibraryReads, Indie Next, and Amazon Best of the Month picks. Born and raised in a suburb of Philadelphia, Cantor lives in Arizona with her husband and two sons.

More with Jillian Cantor: An Essay

ONE OF THE earliest books that made me want to become a writer was *The Great Gatsby*. I read it (and fell in love) for the first time in a high school English class, then again a few years later during a college class for my English major. I kept my college copy and moved it across the country with me for graduate school, where I reread it a third time for inspiration in the midst of struggling to write my own first novel in a writing seminar. In the twenty years since then, that copy has become well-worn, as it has become one of a handful of novels I find myself returning to read over and over.

What I've always loved about *The Great Gatsby* is the beautiful prose, the way the book is both literary and sizzling with the drama of affairs, murder, and the recklessness of the Roaring Twenties. I love that it's glamorous and atmospheric, dark and eccentric all at once. I love that the characters are often unsympathetic, but there's still a part of me that wants so much to like them. And most of all, I'm intrigued by the point of view, that Fitzgerald chose the outsider, Nick Carraway, to tell this particular story.

Point of view has always interested me most as a writer, and maybe that's why I've found myself coming back to *Gatsby* as a reader, again and again. The way different stories unfold differently depending on who tells them is something I've considered often in my own work. What happens when we see familiar stories in new ways, from different perspectives? I've explored this ▶

question in my novels, while also thinking and writing about women's lives and their unique perspectives, so much so that when I returned again to reread *The Great Gatsby* a few years ago, I found myself thinking about just one question. What are the women in the novel thinking and feeling?

Everything we know about the women in *The Great Gatsby* is filtered through the eyes of the narrator, Nick Carraway, heavily influenced by his own often glowing perception of the enigmatic Jay Gatsby. But what if it wasn't? I wondered about Daisy's and Jordan's stories, and not just during that sultry summer on Long Island, but also in the years leading up to it. And what about the tragic Myrtle and her briefly mentioned sister, Catherine? How different would everything look from these women's points of view? How would they see Jay Gatsby—and that summer—differently than Nick does?

In early January 2020, I mentioned my curiosity about the women of *Gatsby*'s world to a few writer friends. One made me promise that I *had* to write a novel from Daisy's point of view. Another sent me a message about how her favorite line from *The Great Gatsby* is the one Daisy says when her daughter is born: "I hope she'll be a fool, that's the best thing a girl can be in this world, a beautiful little fool." A third sent me a news article she'd seen that same morning about how the copyright for *The Great Gatsby* was set to expire in January 2021. Suddenly I felt like the universe (and my writer friends) were telling me that this was something I needed to write at this very moment. And I already had a title: *Beautiful Little Fools.*

I did yet another reread of *The Great Gatsby*, only this time I highlighted every line and every detail and every mention of Daisy, Jordan, Catherine, and Myrtle. I constructed a timeline of their lives from 1917 to 1922, spanning Louisville to France to Chicago to East Egg, spanning Daisy's first meeting with Jay Gatsby as a teenager to her disastrous marriage to Tom in the years that followed, as well as Jordan's career and scandal as a golfer, Catherine's life as a single woman in Manhattan, and Myrtle's life in Queens above Wilson's garage. My own imaginings of these women grew from these small mentions (and the timeline set out) in the original novel. I also decided that my novel would be not just a female take on *The Great Gatsby*, but also a mystery, in the spirit of *Big Little Lies*. What if all these women had their own secrets, and they all came to a head that summer of 1922? And what if there was more to Jay Gatsby's death than Nick Carraway ever would've known?

By March, I had excitedly written the first fifty pages and a detailed outline. I had a plan to leisurely spend the next few months delving into the fictional world of these women. Little did I know that the real world was about to shut down, my kids were about to be at home twenty-four/seven, and I was going to be worrying about buying toilet paper. I took a break from writing for two weeks. (Remember those days when we thought we would only need two weeks to flatten the curve?) But by April, it was clear we were in a worldwide pandemic that wasn't ending anytime soon, and I had ▶

An Essay *(continued)*

Daisy, Jordan, Catherine, and Myrtle paused and waiting for me.

And so there was the stress and worry and homeschooling and figuring out how to use Instacart and curbside pickup, but there was also the glamour and terrible recklessness of Daisy and Tom Buchanan's marriage, Jordan pushing boundaries as a female golfer, Myrtle being trapped in a loveless marriage, and Catherine pushing forward as a suffragette. There were drunken parties in the midst of Prohibition, and sober mistakes in a world so unforgiving to women. There was friendship and motherhood, affairs and murder, darkness and eccentricity. Secrets and lies to unravel and reveal.

The week in the beginning of June when my husband and I had planned (in prepandemic times) to go to Hawaii to celebrate twenty years of marriage, I finished my earliest draft. Instead of the beach in Maui, I was on my back patio, well-worn college copy of *The Great Gatsby* in my hands, rereading yet again, highlighting details I might have missed that would make it into my revision. A few weeks later when a wildfire broke out in the mountains behind our home and we had to pack up to be prepared to evacuate, my tattered copy of *The Great Gatsby* went into a box with my most treasured photo albums.

The fire finally burned out, the pandemic raged on. By August I was living in the world's Covid hotspot, my kids' school year began remotely, and I dove back in to revise *Beautiful Little Fools*, debating over the perfect ending. I reread

The Great Gatsby one more time and also, at this point, watched every movie adaptation ever made (including my new favorite, a lesser-known version with Paul Rudd as Nick Carraway). I found it fascinating to see how each filmmaker in every era reimagined the world and the women of *Gatsby* just a little bit differently. They were originally Fitzgerald's fictional women, but then they were shaped and shifted by the points of view of the filmmakers. While it isn't a plot point in *Gatsby*, the hedonistic 1920s were born from the tragedy of the 1918 flu pandemic—the women I was writing about had sprung from such a similar time to the one I was inhabiting. I considered how they had been shaped by my point of view, too, writing them against the backdrop of this century's pandemic. And I wondered if my joy in bringing them to life, as fully drawn, complex people who are shaped by the time they lived in, was itself a way for me to rescue this time of my life, to create something beautiful.

Writing fiction has always felt like an escape from the real world for me, but also a way to process my own feelings about whatever is going on in my real life at the time. It's why I'm drawn to women, mothers, daughters, sisters, wives. I love taking on the roles of my female characters in my head, embodying their voices with my words on the page, but writing about themes that impact my own life too.

In my search for the perfect ending in the final stages of my revision, I realized the story I ultimately wanted to tell was one of women helping women in their ▶

An Essay *(continued)*

darkest moments, of self-preservation, of a fight for survival, and of the importance of home—all things I'd thought about many times in my real life in those long pandemic months. As much as I gave Daisy, Jordan, Catherine, and Myrtle a voice, maybe they gave me one too. ❧

Reading Group Guide

1. Is *Beautiful Little Fools* a reimagining of *The Great Gatsby*, or a murder mystery in its own right, or both? Whose story is this: Daisy's, Jordan's, Catherine's, or the *great* Jay Gatsby's?

2. Discuss the role point of view plays in the novel. How do Daisy, Jordan, and Catherine each narrate their story differently? What insights does each woman give to the plot and the reader? The original *Gatsby* is told through only Nick Carraway's point of view. What is his role in this novel?

3. Daisy begins with this thought: "Sometimes I think if I'd met Jay Gatsby later, say, after Daddy and Rose's accident, I wouldn't have even noticed him at all. I think how everything, how the whole entire course of my life, and his, might have turned out differently." Do you agree or disagree? How does timing play a role in Jay and Daisy's relationship, in Daisy's life, and ultimately in Jay's death?

4. Sister relationships play a big role in the novel. Compare and contrast Daisy and Rose's relationship with Catherine and Myrtle's. How does Rose influence Daisy's decisions? How does Myrtle influence Catherine's? How does the death of a sister impact both women in different and similar ways? ▶

5. Catherine and her roommate, Helen, are suffragettes, fighting for women's rights to vote, and in the end Catherine works to help abused women. Discuss Catherine's role as an early-1920s feminist. How do her ideas both reflect and conflict with those of Daisy, Jordan, and Myrtle?

6. Nick calls Jordan "an incurable liar." How does that description define her character? Is Nick right about Jordan? What do you see as Jordan's defining characteristic?

7. Mary Margaret tells Jordan that grief is "an endless, winding river," a refrain that comes back throughout the novel. Discuss how this applies not only to Jordan and Mary Margaret's relationship but also to the other characters in the novel. How does grief work as a recurring theme?

8. Is this novel a love story? If so, whose love story is it? Compare and contrast the romantic relationships in the novel. Consider Daisy and Jay, Daisy and Tom, Jordan and Nick, Jordan and Mary Margaret, Catherine and Jay, and Tom and Myrtle.

9. The title of the novel comes from the quote Daisy says in *The Great Gatsby* when her daughter is born: "I hope she'll be a fool—that's the best thing a girl can be in this world, a beautiful

little fool." Why is it fitting for the title of this particular book? Are any of the women in the novel *beautiful little fools*?

10. Detective Frank Charles was not a character in *The Great Gatsby*. Discuss the role he plays in *Beautiful Little Fools*. What do his chapters add to the novel? Compare and contrast his relationship with Dolores to the other romantic relationships in the novel.

11. *Beautiful Little Fools* revolves around unraveling who killed Jay Gatsby. But, in the end, there is more than one killer. Who would you consider guilty in the novel and why? Do you believe any of the characters are ultimately justified in their actions?

12. Reread *The Great Gatsby* and see how many references from the original you can spot in *Beautiful Little Fools*! Pay particular attention to the Plaza scene near the end of the book. How does the dialogue take on a different meaning in *Beautiful Little Fools* than in the original novel? ∾